I0748578

Book Three of the
Nordri Series

THE LEIKR TRIALS

JO VISURI

Pohjola Press

For my family and readers,
you are the reason The Nordri Series
continues to grow and flourish.

Also by Jo Visuri

The Nordri Series:

The Undiscovered Descendants

The Gray Fortress

The Leikr Trials

This is a work of fiction. Names, characters, business, events and incidents are the products of the author's imagination. Any resemblance to actual persons, living or dead, or actual events is purely coincidental.

Pohjola Press
Solana Beach, CA
For information on bulk orders, contact info@pohjolapress.com.

ISBN 978-1-7377639-7-0 [ebook]
978-1-7377639-8-7 [hardcover]
978-1-7377639-9-4 [paperback]

First edition 2025 printed in the United States

Illustrations by P. J. Visuri

Contents

Recap xi

Maps 1

Prologue 7

1. The Chase 9
2. The Team 31
3. The Requisition 45
4. The Surprise 51
5. The Sixth Member 64
6. The Course 69
7. The Plan 81
8. The Hall 90
9. The Escape 107
10. The Attempt 122
11. The Alley 133
12. The Aftermath 144
13. The First Day 159
14. The Lounge 178
15. The Second Day 191
16. The Naglfar 212
17. The Archives 229
18. The Two Plans 248
19. The Strategy 261
20. The Partner 274
21. The Semi-Final 280
22. The Party 301
23. The Confirmation 318
24. The Risk 331
25. The Broken Vow 350
26. The Stadium 374
27. The Reckoning 393
28. The Burn 405

29. The Return 419
Epilogue 434

Extras

Translation Dictionary 440

Thanks for reading! 443
Acknowledgments 449
About the Author 451

Recap

BOOK 2: THE GRAY FORTRESS

Elin's Recap

Okay, so... turns out surviving a Clan library break-in, awakening superpowers—or *megin* as the Clans call it—and watching your maybe-kind-of-crush get kidnapped isn't the end of the story. It's just the beginning.

After Aedan was taken by Tristan and his Aunt Adis, who are part of the *Stór-menni*—aka the worst people in the entire hidden supernatural world—I thought I'd lose my mind. And honestly? I almost did. Between evading Clan Hunters, planning Aedan's rescue with the Gradys and the Resistance, trying to control my visions (which, let's be real, have a terrible sense of timing), and basically lying to everyone in my normal life, things got *messy*.

Especially when I saw Aedan in a vision. For real. Like, present-time real. Apparently, my unique ability—Temporal Visions—decided to go next-level and start showing me things actually happening, not just random future flashes. Sounds cool, right? Except for the part where I don't understand how to control it—or the part where the *Chairman started seeing me back.*

And let's just say that created a serious problem in our rescue plans for Aedan.

I'd been staying with my family on Auor, protected by a Shield Wall. But even that didn't keep the nightmares away—or the Hunters. After a terrifying raid at the Gradys', we escaped through a tunnel beneath their house and regrouped at mine. Anders—my brother—finally learned the truth, and yeah, he didn't take it well. Who would? One minute you're studying astrophysics, and the next your sister is part of a secret, magical Clan.

To keep all of us safe and help me gain control over my abilities, we decided I needed a medallion—my own, not just Aedan's. So under the guise of a school trip to Paris, we left Auor and headed north. The Gradys, along with Gabriel, Bae, and Mr. Tibadeau, went toward Ginnungagap to rescue Aedan, and Mia, Joel, and I headed to the hidden village of Skogly. That's where I met Sigrid, another Dormant and legendary Forger, and Nodin—a Vestri with the calmest eyes and a *Ljós* I can still feel brushing the air when he walks past. He's... complicated. Everything got complicated in Skogly.

There, I learned about *Ljós*—a light only Dormants carry—and how dangerous it is to let it shine too brightly. With Sigrid's help, I took part in my Medal Forging Ceremony—a seriously intense experience involving shimmering herbs, ancient runes, and my own hidden light, my *Ljós*. The whole wild journey brought Mia, Joel, and me closer than ever, even as we all realized this war was bigger than any of us thought.

Meanwhile, the Resistance team—including the Gradys and Gabriel—kept moving toward Ginnungagap to rescue Aedan (no, I didn't go—and yes, I was seriously not okay with that). Gabriel, with his technopath abilities—he can literally talk to tech—became vital to the mission. But more than that, he is a good friend, kind, and quietly brilliant. The kind of person who made you feel like maybe, just maybe, things were going to be okay.

Even though I couldn't be there with them, I wasn't useless. I had my own way to help. Through my visions, I connected with Aedan—

and realized he wasn't in the fortress at all. He was in Falinvik, inside the Chairman's tower. And worse... the Chairman *felt* me watching. His presence slid into the vision like icy claws scraping across my mind. I barely made it out.

But what I had already seen will haunt me.

Aedan looked... drained. Like they were *taking* something from him. His eyes—normally fierce and stubborn—were dull. Empty. And that's when I knew: if we didn't reach him soon, we'd lose him. For good.

Now the Gradys and Resistance are chasing the wrong lead, and I can't let that happen. I'm the only one who saw the truth. The only one with visions strong enough to find Aedan or them. So I'm going to Falinvik. With Sigrid. And Nodin.

Because if we wait too long, there might not be anyone left to save.

~

Aedan's Recap

Let's just say this year hasn't exactly gone according to plan.

It started with me trying to help Elin uncover the truth about her Dormant heritage and ended with me locked in a stone cell in the Chairman's fortress, my wrist shackled by a *Hepta Baugr*—a *megin* dampner and tracking device—and my mind getting picked apart by someone I later found out was the Chairman himself. So... yeah. Not great.

My capture wasn't exactly heroic either. I was drugged, dragged off by Tristan and his lovely Aunt Adis Haugen (read: sarcastic), and dumped into a cell in a place called Ginnungagap. Sounds ominous, right? It was. But it wasn't all bad. In the middle of that circle of misery, I met Reo Itō—a former Austri emissary, a brilliant thinker, and someone who reminded me of what it meant to hold onto your mind, even when everything else is taken. We talked through the walls using string phones like we were in some kind of kid spy movie. And through those conversations, I learned things. Big things. Like the fact that the Chairman's been hiding the existence of the other Clans, and my family's records are missing from the Clan system entirely. Yeah... I have questions.

Then one day, I was gone—transferred to Falinvik. New city, new cell, same control. The Chairman didn't just want to interrogate me. He wanted to reprogram me. Reintroduce me to "Clan life" with his niece, Thyra, as my guide-slash-handler. She was tasked with training me for the *Leikr*—a brutal competition where Clan warriors fight for honor, or in my case, for the amusement of a dictator. The guy even put me on his team. His *team.* Like I'm going to wave his flag.

Things got weird after that. I started seeing Elin—not hallucinations, *real* visions. She found a way into my mind. For a second, it felt like I wasn't alone anymore. She told me my family had come for me. I told her I wasn't in Ginnungagap anymore, which meant they were trying to rescue me from the wrong place. And then... she was gone.

I held onto that vision, though. Because it meant Elin was alive. And trying. And that maybe—just maybe—there was a way out of all this.

In the last few days, I've been forced to play along—training, smiling, pretending I was just another competitor shopping on Baldur Street for the right blade or shield. But when Elin appeared—*actually* appeared—I nearly lost it. We had seconds, but I told her what I could. That I was in the Chairman's tower. That the *Hepta Baugr* had to come off before I could escape.

She promised she'd come back for me. And I believed her.

Because if there's one thing I've learned, it's that Elin doesn't break promises. And neither do I.

Tristan's Recap

I thought this would be my moment.

My first solo mission ended with the capture of the Unregistered Clan member (aka Aedan Grady), whom I promptly delivered to Ginnungagap. I expected recognition, maybe even promotion. Instead, I was forced to answer to Thyra Bjorndóttir—my rival, *now* my captain—and shipped off to Auor with a team that felt more like a circus act than an elite unit. Fenja, Magnus, a pair of twitchy techs... and me. We were there to raid the Unregistered's home and capture Elin.

We almost did.

I saw her again—Elin. In the snow, panicked and clever as ever. She led me away from the others, bought them time. I should have caught her. But someone—one of her crew—tackled me before I could. I woke up alone in the snow with nothing to show for it.

Then came the mission to Ginnungagap.

Thyra handed me control of the trap meant for the Unregistered's rescuers. I designed it myself. Every corridor covered, heat-signature cameras installed, guards positioned. I watched the screens as the intruders—six of them—slipped deeper into the fortress. And still, somehow... they got in and got out.

Worse, they released Reo Itō. I watched it happen in real time—a reunion caught on camera, a smile through a cell window, then a door popping open without explanation. And just like that, they vanished. A taunting message blinked on the surveillance screen. The fortress systems went black. All prison doors opened. And chaos ensued. I couldn't do anything but scream orders no one could follow.

During the disaster, I found myself in the Chairman's office. The system rebooted, and his screens fluttered to life. One of them held a classified personnel file—someone in a Commander's uniform, face redacted, labeled with a blinking DNA match alert. I don't know who it was. But it shook me. Why would the Chairman be looking at *that*?

I never got a chance to ask.

When I returned to Falinvik, Thyra met me with a *Láta* order. Stripped of rank. Reassigned to Internal Affairs. A death blow for a Clan Hunter's career—but better than being sent to Ginnungagap.

I said nothing.

Because I saw something she didn't. The Chairman may think the Gradys are gone. That Elin is cornered. But I know better.

They're headed here. And I've just been assigned to track all irregular activity in Falinvik.

So no... this story isn't over yet.

Maps

Nordri
Vestri
Austri
Sudri
The Dancing Dragons
Sigrid's Forge and Home
Lyngen
Thordalr
Skogly
Ginnungagap
Falinvik
Chairman's Tower
Thorne home
Litenhavn
Skjoldur
Nordri Fjord
Lejker Arena
Baldur Street

Norðri
Vestri
Austri
Suðri
Ginnungagap
Falinvik
Chairman's Tower
Thorne home
Skjoldur
Nordri Fjord
Baldur Street
Lejker Arena

Prologue

TRISTAN

The red alert incessantly flashed on the screen in front of me. Its intermittent squeal was impossible to ignore.

But all I could do was stare at it.

I was the only one left in the office. A few moments earlier, the room had been a hive of activity with Clan Internal Affairs personnel rushing in and out like their lives depended on it—which, given everything, it probably did. The scene had been a finely tuned orchestra with each crime scene technician playing their part with efficiency and productivity.

Once they finished their diligent forensic work, I, as the lead investigator, remained to comb through possible clues on the Chairman's holo-screens.

But I never foresaw the situation I now faced.

My knuckles were white from balling my fists so tightly, and my temple throbbed as anger coursed through my veins. Behind the alert, the holo-screen still showed the last document I had pulled up. The information contained within it was undoubtedly true. This was, after all, the Chairman's console.

The red alert was now pulsing faster, informing me that I only had ten seconds to make the biggest decision of my life.

Tapping "yes" would make me an instant hero to the *Stór-menni*, giving me my old life back and the promotion I had always hoped for. It was what I'd spent my days, nights, blood, and sweat working toward.

Tapping "no" would make me an instant outlaw, and I would be lucky to escape with my life. But the "no" might also be my only way to learn more about what I had uncovered moments earlier. And it would be a small but very satisfying act of retribution.

The red banner now read: **Five seconds**.

My fingers hovered in mid-air as I made my choice.

ONE

The Chase

ELIN

The hovercraft suddenly veered to the right. I clutched Nodin's waist tighter, my fingers numb from the cold—a jolt of sudden awareness threading through me. His body was tense and solid under my frozen hands, a quiet reminder that I wasn't doing this alone.

I squeezed my thighs against the bench to keep from sliding off. My gangly legs, uncooperative at the best of times, didn't help much as the hovercraft bounced and skidded through the air. Sigrid zigzagged in front of us, narrowly avoiding the stationary vehicles parked in mid-air.

I risked a glance behind us. The icy wind seared my amber eyes, its gusts whipping strands of loose auburn hair against the gray hood cinched around my head. The newer, faster *Stór-menni* hovercrafts managed the death-defying turn with unnatural ease.

This wasn't the plan. Our morning was supposed to be a quick reconnaissance mission. Quiet. In and out. Find the weak spot in Falinvik's power infrastructure and slip away before anyone noticed. Step one of Aedan's rescue: disable the grid, kill the *megin* dampener and tracking device known as a *Hepta Baugr* strapped to his wrist, and finally give him a chance to escape. It would've also dealt a serious blow to the *Stór-menni's* hold on the city—exactly what the Resistance needed to advance their campaign for a larger-scale disruption. But that had now all gone to dust.

"Nodin, they're still on us!" I yelled over the whine of our hovercraft's engine.

He didn't answer. His jaw clenched, eyes fixed on Sigrid, trying to keep up with her craft.

The falling snow stung my cold-kissed cheeks as we raced through the air. Our two-seater, motorcycle-style hovercraft—what I kindly called a rust bucket—was barely holding together. The Resistance typically used it as an "unremarkable" vehicle in its operations inside Falinvik. In no scenario was it intended for high-speed chases. Dented, rusting, and torn, it still ran, but how well was now the crucial question.

Falinvik had once been one of several Clan capitals, each tied to one of the legendary Clans: Nordri, Austri, Sudri, and Vestri. The Clans used to trade, argue, marry, celebrate—and exist together. And the others were still out there, but you'd never know it living inside Falinvik's Shield Wall. The *Stór-menni* believed they were the last. Chairman Arild had made sure of that.

"Duck!" Nodin yelled as he steered the half-dead, rickety machine into a tight dip under an aerial walkway.

I managed to lower my head just in time to avoid a collision with the bridge's icy underside. As we emerged on the other side, Nodin pulled the hovercraft into a steep climb, using the bridge as a temporary cover to shake our pursuers.

The engine let out a horrible screech as it strained to keep up with Nodin's commands, the sound ricocheting off the glass and steel buildings around us. We were in the modern quarter of Falinvik, where art-deco high-rises lined the streets, their mirrored facades catching the pale winter light—a gleaming testament to the Chairman's vision of a modern Clan city.

Up ahead, Sigrid appeared like a guiding flame, her arm cutting through the air as she furiously signaled us toward an alley on the right. She moved with the kind of precision that came from both skill and instinct. Tall and slender, with golden-brown hair streaked liberally with silver and white, she exuded a quiet authority. Her hair was neatly tucked into her cloak's hood, leaving her sharp, focused eyes unobstructed as she piloted the hovercraft with ease. Over the last few days, I had learned that she wasn't just a leader; she was a force to be reckoned with.

Having forged my medal and mastered her *Ljós* far beyond anything I could yet imagine, Sigrid was the most powerful Dormant Descendant I'd met. And since Skogly, she'd become something I hadn't even known I was missing: a mentor, an anchor in the stormy seas of everything I was still trying to understand. When the world tilted, she steadied it.

Watching her now, steering her hovercraft with fearless rigor, I felt a flicker of hope. But as the two *Stór-menni* guards closed in from behind, their engines roaring like angry beasts, doubt began to creep in. *Could she outmaneuver them?*

"Does she want us to hide while she takes on *two Stór-menni* by herself?" That seemed like a terrible idea. She'd never manage to shake them both.

As if answering my question, Sigrid gunned the engine of her hovercraft and sped straight down the snowy avenue, leaving a swirling flurry in her wake.

"She knows we don't stand a chance on this thing." Nodin pulled the rust bucket's handlebars into a hard right turn toward the alley. Spotting two snow-covered dumpsters on the ground and a protruding overhang from the building, he lowered the machine between the trash receptacles, backing under the overhang as much as possible. He carefully angled the hovercraft toward the entrance in case we needed to make a break for it.

"Quick, change your cloak to white," Nodin said as he fumbled for the small button on his cloak.

I mirrored his motion, my hands trembling slightly. The cold, the silence, the closeness—it all brought me back to the first time I saw him.

Nodin was part of the Vestri Clan and entirely too handsome for his own good. His light-brown, high-cheekboned face was framed by black-as-night hair that had been neatly braided into a single plait that poked out from under his hood. A narrow, still-healing scar ran from his left brow to his cheekbone.

We had met not too long ago in a Thordalr tavern when Mia, Joel, and I had been on our way to Sigrid's hidden refugee community of Skogly. But if I was being honest, I'd sensed him even earlier than that—back at the train station in Litenhavn. He was a Dormant Descendant like me—capable of extraordinary things beyond the typical Clan member's abilities. And that was saying something given that Clan members were superhuman: stronger, faster, and had better night vision than any normal human, or *Mannlegur* as they called us...I mean *them*. I was still adjusting to being a Clan member.

I'd only recently awakened my *megin*, and it had been just days since I received my medallion after a harrowing forging ceremony. Every Clan member had one to help channel their unique ability. Mine guided my temporal visions—fleeting glimpses of the past, present, and future. I was still learning to control my gift, and without another Temporal Visionary in the Resistance to guide me, I was on my own.

With my gloved hand, I finally managed to find the tiny camouflage button in my cloak. I held it until I saw the ripple of scales turn my cloak white. I looked up as I heard the roar of the *Stórmenni* hovercraft's engines. Both guards raced by the alley one after another in a blur of black and silver.

"I don't think they saw us," I said, letting out my breath.

"Yeah, they didn't, but they sure saw Sigrid," Nodin replied half-heartedly. "Hope she can shake them."

"You don't think she'll get caught, do you?"

"I hope not...but we'd better not wait here to find out. The guards will figure out pretty quick that they are only chasing one hovercraft and not two." With that, Nodin tried to restart the rust bucket's engine. It spluttered and coughed, trying to come back to life.

"Come on, come on!" Nodin let go of the start button and then pressed it again. The engine made a half-hearted *vroom* sound similar to that of my brother Ander's truck when its battery was drained. "No, no, this can't be happening *now*! Come on, you piece of—" Nodin kicked the left side of the hovercraft with his foot while forcefully pressing the start button.

VROOM! The engine roared, rising back to life.

Nodin didn't hesitate. He pushed the handlebars forward, directing the hovercraft out of the alley.

As we came out onto the avenue, for some reason, Nodin kept us low to the ground instead of easing the machine into the air. Inside Falinvik, the Clan did not use ground vehicles, so a thick layer of fluffy white snow blanketed the old roadways and lanes. The whir of the hovercraft's engine kicked up a snow flurry around us, creating a snow globe effect. A dead giveaway to our location.

"Why aren't we going up?" I yelled over the sputtering of the engine.

Gritting his teeth, Nodin yelled back, "Call it being practical! Would you rather plummet dramatically or glide to a slightly less humiliating crash when the engine quits?"

He dodged an overhang, jaw tight.

"Oh, so you do think we're about to crash?" I shot back.

"Not if I can help it." He glanced back at me, something flickered in his eyes, something not entirely about this rust bucket. A memory, maybe.

"What?" I demanded.

He grunted, swerving around a thick icicle hanging from a street sign. "Let's just say I've learned my lesson about aerial crashes and shield defenses."

The snow whipped around us in a frenzy. "Speaking of lessons, do you actually have a plan? Or are we winging it, Nodin-style?"

"Oh, there's a plan," Nodin smirked. "Step one: don't crash. Step two: don't freeze. Step three: hope Sigrid buys us enough time to—"

A distant boom echoed through the streets, followed by the faint sound of roaring engines.

I whipped my head toward the sound. "Was that—?"

Nodin grimaced, "Yeah, pretty sure that was Sigrid. Probably doing something both brilliant and reckless."

"We should go back."

Nodin shook his head, leaning lower to dodge a bridge overhang. "Not unless you feel like outrunning an entire *Stór-menni* battalion on foot. She's buying us a shot at an escape. We don't waste it."

"Some escape. Half-dead hovercraft, half-baked plan, and fully-frozen fingers," I muttered.

Steering the craft sharply down a side street, Nodin responded with a sly grin, "Admit it—you'd miss the thrill."

I clung tighter to Nodin as the hovercraft skidded over an icy patch. "Right now, the only thing I'm missing is a warm blanket and a working heater."

Nodin laughed as the craft shuddered but kept going. "Well, stay on board, and you might just live to see both. Assuming this thing doesn't explode first."

"Comforting. Really comforting."

The snow flurry around us began to settle, and for a fleeting second, I thought we were in the clear. But then a low, menacing hum cut through the air, sharp and unmistakable.

Nodin's head whipped around. "Oh, come on!"

I turned to see another *Stór-menni* patrol craft appear from the shadowed mouth of a side street, its polished silver and black exterior gleaming against the snow. Unlike our barely functioning contraption, this hovercraft was sleek, aerodynamic, and worst of all —fully operational.

The pilot spotted us immediately. The patrol craft let out a sharp, mechanical whistle as it surged forward, closing the distance.

"They've seen us!" I shouted, gripping the side of the bench.

Nodin's expression tightened. "Yeah, no kidding. Hold on!"

He yanked the handlebars hard to the right, sending our craft skimming along the snowy avenue. The engine sputtered angrily but complied, kicking up another flurry as we veered into a narrow lane flanked by abandoned buildings.

The *Stór-menni* patrol was faster, sleeker, and gaining on us by the second. A sudden burst of energy from its thrusters sent a gust of hot air against my back as the patrol closed the gap.

"Any brilliant ideas?" I yelled over the roar of the wind.

"Only one. Don't fall off!"

The patrol fired a warning shot, a blinding burst of light that scorched the snow a few meters to our left. The heat from the blast melted the edges of a nearby dumpster, causing its contents to spill onto the ground from the gaping wound.

"Okay, they're not playing around!" I said, panic creeping into my voice.

Nodin shouted back, "Neither am I!"

He jerked the handlebars left, guiding our hovercraft toward a decrepit overpass. We were reaching the outskirts of the modern city. The patrol hesitated for a split second, slowing as they calculated the risk of following us into the tight, debris-filled space.

"You're not seriously going under there, are you?" I asked, eyes wide.

Nodin grinned. "Watch me."

We dove under the overpass, the hovercraft skimming dangerously close to the snow-covered ground. Metal beams and chunks of ice loomed overhead, and the hovercraft's frame groaned in protest as we zigzagged through the narrow corridor.

The patrol craft followed, its streamlined body navigating the obstacles with terrifying precision.

"They're still on us!" I called out, glancing over my shoulder.

Nodin's jaw clenched. "Not for long."

Ahead, a massive support column loomed, its base surrounded by a jagged heap of collapsed concrete. Instead of swerving around it, Nodin accelerated.

"What are you doing?!" I yelled, bracing myself against the frame.

Nodin shouted back, "Trust me!"

At the last possible second, he yanked the handlebars up. The hovercraft heaved and sputtered but managed to lift just high enough to clear the debris. Sparks flew as the bottom scraped against the rubble, but we made it through.

The patrol wasn't so lucky. Their craft clipped the edge of the concrete, spinning out of control. The sleek machine skidded across the icy ground, slamming into the support column with a deafening crash.

Nodin let out a triumphant whoop as we shot out from under the overpass and back into the open avenue.

"I can't believe that worked!" I said, my heart still racing.

Nodin smirked, glancing back over his shoulder. "Told you. Never doubt my brilliance."

Before I could respond, another sharp hum cut through the air. I looked up to see two more *Stór-menni* patrols emerging from the haze of snow behind us.

"Brilliant, huh?" I said, narrowing my eyes.

Nodin's grin faltered. "Okay, maybe we should start working on step two."

"Which is?"

He hit the accelerator, sending us rocketing forward. "Run faster."

The roar of the pursuing hovercrafts grew louder, their engines a menacing symphony against the backdrop of the icy cityscape. My chest tightened as I looked over my shoulder—the *Stór-menni* patrols were closing in, and these weren't making rookie mistakes. They moved like predators, their hovercrafts weaving in tandem to box us in.

We were going to get caught.

I had to do something. I could feel my *megin's* steady beat as it thumped against my medallion. I didn't like using it—not when the stakes were this high, and especially not when I wasn't sure I could control it. But we were running out of options.

I closed my eyes, forcing myself to focus as the cold wind whipped against my face. The noise around me—the sputtering engine, the hum of the patrol crafts, even Nodin's muttered curses—faded into the background.

Breathe.

I took a deep breath in and focused my mind on the two patrols. I felt the familiar thump of my *megin* underneath my medallion. A buzzing began in my mind. It spread like a wire being pulled taut, and I let myself lean into it. The familiar white, thankfully painless, cloud flooded my mind for a few seconds before dispersing. Then I was hovering above the patrol crafts. They were splitting up, one angling left to cut us off while the other prepared to fire—

The vision blurred and fractured, a wave of static crashing through my mind. Pain spiked behind my eyes, and I gasped, clutching my head.

"Elli?" he called out, glancing back. "You okay?"

I sucked in a breath, blinking hard. "Trying to see," I muttered, pressing a hand to my medallion. "Just... hold them off."

His eyes narrowed, understanding flickering there. "Whatever you're doing, make it quick. They're gaining!"

I bit my lip, ignoring the throbbing in my skull. *Again. I had to try again.*

I took another deep breath, trying to calm my mind like Mrs. Grady had taught, despite the chaos surrounding me. The buzzing surged as I pushed harder, forcing my mind forward. This time, I dropped into the vision, and it sharpened—a glimpse of the patrols weaving through the snow, their crafts banking to force us toward a dead end. One of them fired, the shot missed us, but drove us into a narrow alley. A trap.

I quickly pulled my vision ripcord and opened my eyes. "Left!" I shouted, grabbing Nodin's arm.

"What?"

"Turn left *now*, or we're done!"

He didn't argue. With a sharp yank of the handlebars, he veered left, the hovercraft skimming dangerously close to the ground. Behind us, the patrol crafts hesitated, their pilots adjusting to our sudden shift.

The alley we shot into was narrow, lined with crumbling walls and dumpsters. Nodin's knuckles whitened as he kept the craft steady, the engine protesting with every sharp turn.

"This isn't exactly a brilliant escape route!" he shouted.

"It will be!" I said, glancing ahead. My head throbbed as I searched the flickering fragments of my vision. "Just keep going. There's a turn up ahead. Take it, and then..."

I tried to remember what exactly the vision had shown. There it was—a snowbank, partially collapsed, with just enough room for us to squeeze through.

"There!" I pointed, barely able to keep my voice steady. "That snowbank on the right! Go through it!"

"Are you insane?" Nodin snapped.

"Probably!" I shot back. "Just trust me!"

Muttering under his breath, he aimed the hovercraft at the snowbank. The patrol crafts roared behind us, their engines closing in. One of them fired, the shot skimming past us and sending up a plume of snow, which gave us enough cover for my plan.

Nodin punched the throttle. The hovercraft lurched forward, barreling into the snowbank. For a heart-stopping moment, I thought we'd miscalculated—but then the craft burst through, snow spraying in every direction.

On the other side was a collapsed warehouse, its rusted skeleton half-buried in ice and snow. Nodin guided the hovercraft into the shadows, cutting the engine as we slid to a stop.

We sat in silence, our breaths misting in the frigid air. The patrol crafts roared past, their pilots oblivious to where we'd vanished.

"That," Nodin said, turning to me with a raised eyebrow, "was either the dumbest or the luckiest move I've ever seen."

I leaned back, my head pounding as I tried to catch my breath. "Neither," I said, managing a weak smile. "Just...a little foresight."

"Foresight, huh?" He smirked. "You could've mentioned that earlier."

I shrugged, closing my eyes as exhaustion washed over me. "I wasn't sure I could do it. Plus, would you have believed me?"

He snorted, shaking his head. "Probably not, given how your training has been going."

Outside, the patrol crafts' hum faded into the distance. For now, we were safe—but I knew it wouldn't last.

"Do you think Sigrid made it?" I asked, the thought curling in my chest like a shadow that wouldn't leave.

"I guess we'll find out back at base." Nodin looked at his wrist and whispered something to the device strapped to it.

The device was something the Clan called a Communicator. It allowed individuals to discreetly talk to each other using the bones in their bodies to vibrate sound up to their ears, which came in handy when quiet was imperative.

The Resistance had made some modifications to the device. It now included a map projection feature, among other upgrades. And before it would even respond to a user, the Communicator required voice recognition with a passphrase.

Nodin held his wrist in the air as bright green lines of a map generated in front of him. A single blinking dot showed our location. The map, however, did not reveal the location of the Resistance base in Falinvik—another security measure. The wearers of the Communicators had been taught where the entrances to the underground Resistance base were. Nodin had earned the right to wear a Communicator while I had been determined to be too high-value of a target to get the honor.

"We aren't too far," he said, surveying the map. "I think this rust bucket will make it." He gave a swift kick to the engine, helping it whir back to life.

~

After about ten more minutes of playing hide and seek with *Stór-menni* patrols, we made it to the entrance of a long-forgotten metro system. I whispered a silent *thank you* to the universe as I was pretty sure I was frozen to the hovercraft seat by then.

The ancient metro system was a perfect covert operating base inside Falinvik for the Resistance. After the Nordri Clan had invented hovercrafts and aerial trains, they abandoned the subway system. The underground labyrinth was now mainly used for geothermal water pipes that ran underneath the city. The naturally occurring geothermal water not only supplied energy for the city, but it also helped heat buildings, and the warm pipes kept the few sidewalks and hovercraft-landing platforms clear of ice and snow. Or at least that's what one of the Resistance's engineers had explained to me and Nodin when we'd gotten a tour of the base.

But what lay beneath the city wasn't just old tunnels and forgotten technology.

It was a foundation—both literal and symbolic—of everything the Nordri once were. And just as he had buried their infrastructure, Chairman Arild had buried their identity. He hadn't just seized power; he'd reshaped it. To isolate the Nordri completely, he'd first severed communication with the outside world, blaming the Clan wars. Then he imprisoned emissaries and barred any visitors, silencing anyone who might speak the truth. And finally, he twisted language itself. The Nordri became the *Stór-menni*—"great men," the last of the Clans, rightful rulers of what remained. Everyone else? *Smá-menn*. Lesser.

As Sigrid had once told me, *if you make people believe they're alone, they'll fight to stay that way.* Even Aedan's family, who should've known better, had believed the lie.

That was the Chairman's power—convincing an entire Clan to forget who they were. To isolate, divide, erase.

Now, as we were about to descend into the bones of the old city, I could almost feel the weight of that forgetting.

The metro entrance was hidden beneath a deteriorating stairwell, its rusted metal gate camouflaged by snow and decades of grime. Nodin dismounted the hovercraft first, wincing and groaning like an old man as his legs straightened. I followed, almost toppling over as my frozen muscles protested the movement. The hovercraft groaned behind us, its engine wheezing like it was on its last legs. At least we weren't the only ones falling apart.

"Remind me never to sit that long in sub-zero temperatures again," I muttered, rubbing my hands together to coax some warmth back into them. The Clan clothing I was wearing was a godsend in the freezing temperatures, but even it had its limits—especially on long outdoor missions.

The gifted clothing had been given during our journey to the Falinvik Fjord, a quiet reminder of how it all began: Tristan's betrayal, Aedan's kidnapping, and my awakening. It was like a domino effect, each event crashing into the next with no chance to catch our breath. Sometimes, I wondered how I'd ended up here at all.

A few weeks ago, I was just Elin, starting junior year at my completely ordinary high school, missing my best friends.

Now? I had powers I barely understood, a medallion forged through fire and *Ljós*, and a place inside a hidden Resistance trying to piece back what the Chairman had shattered.

We were searching for Aedan's family—the Gradys—who vanished during their failed attempt to rescue him from Ginnungagap. And we were planning another mission, one that might actually get Aedan out.

Meanwhile, the Chairman had Aedan training for the *Leikr*—

the brutal, deadly Clan games that tested the limits of the strongest Clan warriors. Aedan might have been gifted, but even his abilities didn't make him invincible. The thought of him out there, surrounded by enemies, bled into my nights and chased me through my dreams.

As for his family... after Ginnungagap, we'd tried everything. Every trail turned to ash. Every search, a dead end. Even my ability, or my novice skill at wielding it, failed to find them.

How was I supposed to look Aedan in the eye and tell him that we'd failed him again? The guilt was a constant weight, pressing down harder with each passing day. It didn't matter that I'd tried my best; all that mattered was that it hadn't been enough.

And now I was here—buried beneath the frozen city of Falinvik, clawing at answers in the dark. Every step forward felt like sinking. And the more time passed, the more certain I became: we were running out of it. For Aedan. For his family. For all of us.

Lost in thought, I barely registered Nodin shooting me a smirk as he used the Communicator to tap against the side of the gate. A faint beep echoed in the cold air, followed by the metallic groan of the gate sliding open. Warm, humid air wafted out, carrying with it the weak scent of minerals and oil.

"Welcome back to paradise," Nodin said, stepping aside with a dramatic sweep of his arm.

I rolled my eyes but stepped through, feeling the welcome warmth seep into my frozen skin. Together, we pushed the rust bucket through the gate, leaving it hidden inside a niche on the right. The gate closed behind us with a heavy clang, plunging us into the dim, cavernous space of the old subway system.

As we walked, Nodin lifted his wrist and whispered something to his Communicator.

I raised an eyebrow. "Checking in with the Resistance?"

"Yeah. Something like that."

I frowned. He wasn't lying, exactly—but there was something in his voice, a weight he wasn't acknowledging.

He caught my look and flashed me one of his disarming grins. "Don't look so suspicious, Elli. You'll give people the wrong idea."

"Uh-huh. Because you are the picture of honesty."

"Absolutely." His smirk widened, but his fingers flexed slightly over the device before he lowered his hand.

I wasn't sure why, but I had the sudden feeling that whatever he had just checked wasn't just about our mission. The flicker of tension in his jaw was gone in an instant, replaced by his usual easy confidence, but the doubt lingered in the back of my mind.

I let it go—for now.

I trusted Nodin. After everything we had been through—escaping from the Thordalr tavern, teaching me about Dormants, and the dozen missions we'd run for the Resistance—he had proven himself over and over. He had been a crucial part of my medal-forging ceremony, steadying me through a trial I barely understood at the time. Even tapping into his own *Ljós* to support mine during it.

Ljós was something Dormants like us had, but the rest of the Clans didn't:

Nodin had explained it best. "*Ljós* is the electric light inside each Dormant," he'd said once. "Think of it as a companion to *megin*. It's what makes us different. But it also connects us. That's why Dormants can sense—or in rare cases like yours—even see each other when we're near."

Before we left Skogly, Brigitta—Sigrid's partner and the village herbalist—had given me a special tea she brewed herself, using herbs that grew near the geothermal vents in the forest. She said it would help me "*stay hidden*," that the tea would dim the glow of my *Ljós* so other Dormants couldn't sense me nearby. I hadn't understood how serious that was until Sigrid told me that in a place like Falinvik, with the Chairman's keen interest in Dormants, secrecy was survival.

Sometimes I wondered if the tea did more than hide it—if it dulled my chance to understand it at all. Still, I drank it. Every day. Because I had to. Because if anyone saw the glimmer—if the Chairman ever discovered who I really was—

That kind of truth could get me killed. Or worse, get everyone around me killed.

It was a constant pressure—always watching what I said, what I felt, what I let show. Some days it felt like I was holding my breath and didn't know how to let it out again.

And yet, despite all that—or maybe because of it—Nodin and I had fought side by side. Watching each other's backs in ways that went beyond instinct.

But trust didn't mean I had all the answers.

As we stepped deeper into the tunnels, the air grew warmer, carrying a stronger scent of minerals and oil. The main passage stretched out before us, its walls reinforced with steel beams long since tarnished by time. Overhead, a dim shine from strung-together lights pulsed in rhythm with the steady hum of machinery. The distant murmur of voices drifted through the cavernous space, weaving into the low mechanical thrum that filled the underground stronghold.

This wasn't just a hideout—it breathed.

After walking for another fifteen minutes in the dark and dank tunnel, we started to pass through a series of old metro platforms and alcoves that the Resistance had repurposed. Each one served a distinct purpose, its function dictated by the needs of the Resistance.

The first platform we encountered was a mechanical wonderland known as the Workshop. Shelves crammed with spare parts, tools, and blueprints lined the walls. Resistance engineers worked tirelessly, welding scraps of metal and calibrating stolen hovercraft components, and on other, more mysterious, innovative projects. A few paused to nod at us before returning to their tasks, the radiance of their torches casting flickering shadows on the walls.

Further down, a larger alcove had been converted into an underground greenhouse. Warm, humid air from the geothermal pipes created the perfect environment for growing food. Rows of plants thrived under artificial lights, their vibrant green a stark contrast to the gray and brown of the surrounding tunnels. Someone looked up at us from inside—most likely a Clan member blessed with the gift of a green thumb. I gave a quick wave to acknowledge them.

Across from the greenhouse, a heavily guarded recess was stacked high with weaponry and supplies—one of the many armories that the Resistance had spread out through the tunnel network. Resistance fighters stood watch, their eyes scanning the tunnel for any sign of threat. Inside, racks of ultra-modern weapons, crates holding unknown items, and shelves stocked with various orb-looking devices filled the space.

As we progressed down the tunnel, a quieter platform came into view. It housed the medical bay. Hovering beds made from salvaged materials lined one wall, while the other was cluttered with medical equipment and supplies. The soft murmur of voices carried from inside, along with the occasional groan of someone being patched up.

As we moved deeper, the tunnels widened into a massive cavern —the heart of the Resistance. This space had been the metro's central hub, and it still held traces of its original purpose: faded signs in Nordri script pointed toward forgotten train lines, and rusting tracks crisscrossed the floor.

The cavern was bustling with activity. People moved about with purpose, their faces a mix of determination and exhaustion. Makeshift meeting tables occupied the center, scattered with various-looking devices and diagrams. Screens salvaged from the surface displayed real-time feeds of *Stór-menni* patrols, their locations marked with glowing red dots.

Above, geothermal pipes snaked along the ceiling, their insulated surfaces pulsing with the warmth that kept the base habitable. Steam hissed from occasional leaks, adding to the damp, subterranean atmosphere.

"Looks like they're planning something," I said, nodding toward a group huddled by a particular screen, the content of which was only visible towards them.

"Always are," Nodin replied, his tone tinged with admiration. He nudged me toward a side tunnel. "Come on, let's report in and see if

Sigrid is back. We've got a lot to tell them—and a hovercraft that needs some serious repairs."

As we walked, I couldn't help but marvel at the ingenuity around us. The Resistance wasn't just surviving down here—they were thriving, adapting the forgotten remnants of the old world into tools for their fight.

One of the strangest innovations I had learned about upon entering Falinvik was that time worked completely differently here. It was an enigma shaped by the Nordri Clan's mastery of technology and their unyielding need for secrecy. Outside the city's Shield Wall, the flow of time was familiar—one day followed the next, governed by the steady rhythm of the sun and moon. But inside the shimmering, cloaking barrier that encased the city, time had been stretched, manipulated, and molded into something uniquely Nordri.

It wasn't immediately noticeable to newcomers. The sky still cycled from pale, wintry gray to the dark, star-speckled black of night. The sun still rose and set. But the shifts were deceptive, slower than what we were used to. It was as if someone had taken the natural progression of a day and unraveled it, pulling it taut across seven times its normal length.

"So technically, we arrived two days ago," I said, my voice echoing faintly off the cavern walls as we walked. "But in Falinvik time, that's... what, two weeks?"

Nodin nodded. "Yeah. Seven days here equals one day out there —what they call a '*vika*.' It's all thanks to the Clan's shield tech."

"How does it even work? The shield, I mean."

"You really want the long version?" he asked, smirking at me.

I deadpanned. "Well, considering I apparently have more time on my hands than I thought..."

He laughed, the sound a rare and welcome reprieve from the tension of the past few hours. "Fair enough. Okay, so the shield isn't just a physical barrier—it's a temporal one. It bends time within its boundaries, speeding it up relative to the outside world. The Nordri Clan developed it centuries ago to give themselves an advantage in warfare and innovation. One week in here means they've got seven times as long to prepare, plan, and produce as anyone outside."

Something about that gnawed at me. I slowed my steps. "Seven times the time, seven times the resources, seven times the training... Why would the Chairman need that kind of advantage?"

Nodin exhaled, his expression shifting. "They always claim it's about protecting the city." Then, after a beat, he added, "But you don't prepare this much unless you're expecting a war."

A chill ran down my spine, and for once, it had nothing to do with the cold.

I wrapped my arms around myself, trying to shake the unease crawling up my back. "But doesn't the time differences... mess with people? Their bodies, their minds?"

Nodin's gaze darkened. "It does with *Mannlegurs*. It's why Mia and Joel couldn't come with us. *Mannlegurs*, like them—get hit the hardest. Their bodies try to hold onto the rhythm of the outside world, but they can't. Sleep schedules, hunger, even aging—it all has to adjust. Our *megin* helps our body sync up to the city's time, adjusting seamlessly to the new rhythm, but for them...it would have made them have the temporal bends."

I glanced down at my hands, the callouses on my palms a reminder of the days—weeks—we'd spent navigating the Resistance's plans, training for the fight to come, and trying to figure out how to rescue Aedan. It had been several weeks, even in *Mannlegur* time, since Aedan had been kidnapped and held hostage by the *Stórmenni*. We'd almost succeeded in getting him out on our very first day in Falinvik, inadvertently bumping into him at the Baldur Street market when Sigrid, Nodin, and I were trying to locate Sigrid's Resistance contact. But our effort had been thwarted by the *Hepta Baugr* on his wrist, which effectively tracked his every move and was impossible to remove without the correct Clan medal and authority.

Our current failed scouting mission had been to gather information on the power station that controlled Falinvik's grid. Thanks to my visions and the ingenuity of Aedan's family, we knew that turning off the energy grid had worked in Ginnungagap, releasing the prisoners from their *Hepta Baugrs* and letting them escape. That had been about three weeks ago in Falinvik time—or three days ago in the outside world.

"And the Nordri? They're just...used to the 'extended' time?"

Nodin nodded. "Yeah. It's all they've ever known. To them, the rest of the world is the weird one, moving too fast for its own good."

The implications of the time distortion were staggering. Inside Falinvik, a year passed in just under two months of *Mannlegur* time. The Nordri could accomplish in a week what it took others nearly two months to do.

"No wonder they're so advanced," I murmured.

Nodin smirked. "Yeah, but it's not all perks. The shield isn't perfect. Maintaining it takes a massive amount of energy—they have that thanks to the geothermal—but if someone found a way to disrupt the shield, time would snap back to normal, and they'd lose their biggest advantage."

We both stopped talking as we reached the Resistance Commander's alcove. The space was a functional but stark room deep within the base, its walls fashioned from salvaged metal panels and insulated pipes. A single table dominated the space, cluttered with maps, diagrams, and a few flickering screens showing patrol movements around Falinvik.

Commander Yrsa stood at one end, her solid, no-nonsense presence radiating quiet authority. She was sturdily built, with the posture of someone who'd spent a lifetime earning respect rather than demanding it. Her ash-blonde hair, streaked with silver, was twisted into a low braid at the nape of her neck. A deep green cloak hung over fitted layers of practical wool and leather, softened by age but clean and well-kept. Her face was weathered yet striking, with high cheekbones, clear gray eyes, and a calm, commanding expression that made people listen the first time she spoke.

Beside her, Mr. McHaill leaned slightly on the table, his salt-and-pepper whiskers catching the dim light. His dark blue cloak draped over his thin frame, giving him the air of a patient scholar rather than a secretive rebel leader. His sharp eyes landed on us as we stepped into the room, carrying the weight of the mission we'd just returned from. Mr. McHaill had originally journeyed with me, Mia, Joel, and Aedan's family from Auor Island to the mouth of the Falinvik fjord, where we separated. The only thing we had been told about him was that he was from the Central Resistance Command, and he was there to liaise—whatever that meant.

"You're back," Yrsa said, a flicker of relief breaking through her usual steel. "And in one piece, I see. That's a good start."

"Barely," Nodin replied, approaching the table. "The *Stór-menni* patrols are tighter than we thought. We couldn't get close to the power station without getting spotted."

I stepped forward, brushing stray snow from my cloak. "Their hovercrafts were everywhere. We barely made it out. Sigrid took off to draw them away so we could escape on that rust bucket..." I hesitated, the words catching in my throat. "Is she back yet?"

"Not yet," McHaill answered, scrutinizing us.

Yrsa leaned over the table. "You mean you lost Sigrid?"

"She led two patrols away from us," Nodin cut in. "They were too fast—we couldn't outrun them. After we split up, the city was crawling with units. We couldn't regroup. I've never seen so many before."

"The *Stór-menni* might be onto us," Yrsa muttered. "Or at least, they suspect we've been poking around—especially after Ginnungagap. They wouldn't have taken that lightly." She tapped a command into her Communicator. "We'll send out a search patrol."

I let out a breath I hadn't realized I was holding, tension loosening slightly in my shoulders. At least now, someone was looking. At least now she wasn't just... gone.

Nodin shifted, voice low but steady. "We'll head back out tomorrow. Rework the route. There's a way in—we just haven't found it yet."

Yrsa glanced at him, the corner of her mouth tugging upward in the faintest of smiles. "I appreciate your enthusiasm, Nodin, but let's not go charging into a minefield just yet. We'll regroup, reassess, and come up with a plan that doesn't rely on sheer luck."

Before anyone could respond, the door burst open with a sudden clang, and Sigrid strode in, her boots crunching against the grit-covered floor. Snow clung to her hair and the edges of her cloak, which she discarded with a quick motion. Her cheeks were flushed from the cold, but her eyes sparked with something sharper—urgency, maybe even excitement.

"Sigrid, you made it!" I said. A rush of relief surged through me.

Sigrid raised a hand, cutting off any further greeting. Her breath was visible in the dim light, and her words came steady but charged with excitement. "My unplanned detour brought me a surprise."

The room went still. Yrsa's brow furrowed, and McHaill tilted his head slightly, his gaze sharp.

"A *surprise*?" Yrsa prompted.

Sigrid nodded, glancing at each of us in turn. "Yes, a good one."

The tension in the room thickened, a current of anticipation buzzing between us. I caught Nodin's eye—whatever Sigrid had found, it wasn't small.

TWO

The Team

AEDAN

As we entered the training arena and made our way to the weapons rack, Thyra turned to me without a word. I extended my arm automatically, and with the same practiced motion as always, she unfastened the *Hepta Baugr* from my wrist. By now, the whole process felt like second nature—a quiet ritual neither of us needed to think about.

I rubbed the pale imprint the device had left on my skin, the soreness matching the ache in my muscles after days of relentless training. Catching my reflection in one of the mirrored panels by the rack, I barely recognized myself. My black wavy hair was disheveled, and my normally sharp sea blue eyes were dulled with fatigue. The feeble stubble on my jawline was thicker than I liked, a reminder of how little time I'd had to care for myself since arriving in Falinvik. Lean but muscular, I'd always had the build of someone more reliant on agility than brute strength, and it was becoming increasingly clear that it wasn't an advantage here.

My clothes hung a little more loosely than they had when I arrived, evidence of the grueling last few months. I looked more like a scrappy survivor than a fighter—something I needed to change if I had any hope of surviving the *Leikr*.

The training arena was a marvel of old-world tradition meeting cutting-edge technology. The space was vast, the size of a football field, its perimeter lined with stone pillars etched in intricate runes that gleamed in the dim light. The runes, I'd been told, were a remnant of the Nordri Clan's earliest ancestors, who had built arenas like this for their *Leikr* trials long before the invention of modern weaponry. Above, a domed ceiling of glass and steel reflected the flickering flames of massive torches mounted on the walls, casting an otherworldly glow across the arena floor.

The arena floor itself was a blend of elements. Smooth flagstones carved from granite rock formed pathways interwoven with soft, synthetic turf patches that absorbed impact during combat. In the center stood a towering wooden structure that resembled a Viking ship's prow, its surface embedded with holographic panels that flickered to life during specific drills, projecting various training scenarios. Around the edges, a series of obstacles—walls to scale, pits to leap over, and narrow bridges suspended over yawning voids—hinted at the grueling physical trials that lay ahead.

"So, we've been training for three weeks for the *Leikr*—"

"*Vika*, not weeks," Thyra interrupted. "You should use the Nordri word to avoid confusion. You know time works differently here—in the rest of the world, it's only been three days."

"Okay, fine '*vika*'...that doesn't change the fact that I still don't know what the trials are actually about," I said, annoyed. "Every time I ask the others, I get the same useless answers: 'You'll see' or 'You'll learn soon enough.' Makes me wonder what everyone's trying to hide."

Thyra leaned casually against the weapons rack, her sharp, slate-blue eyes sizing me up. "There's a reason no one's telling you much about the *Leikr*. The less you know going in, the harder it is to get in your head about it—overthinking gets people eliminated."

I crossed my arms. "Great. That's *super* reassuring. It's certainly hard to overthink when all I've got are the scraps you told me before the Orbpods."

Thyra raised an eyebrow, unbothered. "And that's all you really need to know...sixteen teams compete. Early rounds are solo challenges. Later rounds are obstacle courses in the tunnels with paired team players. You rack up points for speed and how many teammates finish. Lowest-scoring team gets cut each round. Ringing any bells?"

"Sure, but that still doesn't explain much," I shot back.

She leaned in slightly, her tone sharpening. "There's really only two things you need to understand if you want to survive the trials."

"Which are?"

"First, the challenges and obstacles change every year. So even if I wanted to, I couldn't tell you what they are. All I can say is that the Clan Creators and Engineers design them to push limits, and they don't give anyone advance notice. It could be anything—a maze of shifting tunnels, a field of molten lava, or something else. One year, they threw in a Draugr. That was... messy."

"A Draugr?" I repeated the word unfamiliar but ominous.

Thyra raised an eyebrow. "Let's just say you don't want to meet one unprepared. It's bad enough facing the obstacles, but that brings me to the second complication."

"Okay," I said, trying not to let my unease show. "What's the second thing?"

Thyra's gaze darkened. "It's the other teams. Once the games begin, it's all-out war. Sabotage, traps, ambushes—everything's fair game, as long as it doesn't outright kill anyone. And if you're unlucky enough to be on the Chairman's team—"

"We are the Chairman's team," I interrupted.

Thyra's lips thinned. "Exactly. Which means you'll have the biggest target on your backs. Beating the Chairman's team is the ultimate *Sigra*. It's not just about winning; it's about making a statement. His team is always stacked with the strongest players, so every other team will be gunning for you from the start."

"Wonderful. So not only do we have to survive these mystery challenges, but we also have to survive everyone else's attempts to crush us just for bragging rights."

"It's not just bragging rights," Thyra said sharply. "Winning the *Leikr*, especially against the Chairman's team, brings prestige, influence, and perks that can change your place in Clan society."

"How great for them," I said, my voice laced with bitterness. "But I didn't ask to be on his team or in the *Leikr* to begin with. How are we supposed to survive this when everyone already hates us just for existing?"

Thyra stepped closer, her tone quiet but firm. "You survive by being smarter, faster, and more prepared than everyone else. You didn't choose to be on the Chairman's team, but that doesn't change the fact that you are. So either rise to the challenge and train or get crushed under it. Your choice."

She turned on her heel and walked away before I could answer. I knew she wasn't any happier about the situation, but I couldn't help take my frustration out on her. Even though I had started to feel a begrudging respect for her, Thyra was still my de facto warden, a *Stór-menni*, the Chairman's niece, and part of his plan to keep me a hostage and something bigger that I had yet to discover.

Ever since Tristan and his aunt had captured me and brought me to Falinvik, the Chairman himself had been trying to break into my mind and learn who my family was. As an unregistered Clan member and without my help, there were only a few ways to determine who my family was, and those had failed the *Stór-menni*. Yet, the Chairman was fixated on my bloodline. *Why? What was it about my family that kept him pushing, kept him digging—like my existence was some sort of a missing piece?*

The digital trail of my existence, including my family's DNA, was missing from the *Stór-menni* database. What was equally surprising was that my family's last name wasn't found in their records either, which meant that it wasn't real—or that the Chairman had lied about it being missing.

I had plans to discover the truth. But these days the only alone time I seemed to have was when I dropped into bed exhausted from training. Our schedule was beyond rigorous from sunup to sundown. As team captain, Thyra wasn't leaving anything to chance.

During the last week, our training had been focused solely on close combat with the weapons that Thyra had purchased from the shops at Baldur Street. And I had a lot to learn.

The Clan weapons were completely foreign to me. What a shield and sword constituted in Falinvik was a far cry from what I had seen in the Mannlegur world.

Never mind the fact that I'd never fought with weapons before—only with my ability. Thankfully, my father had the foresight to train Edvin, Claire, and me in that from the time we were kids. Those practices had been fun games we played in the forest, and as we grew older, the scenarios and grappling had become more intense. But we'd always had to hold back our full powers since we couldn't expose ourselves to the *Mannlegurs* or leave a trail for the Clan Hunters to follow.

Here, everything was different. Weapons were a must, and holding back was a liability.

At the far end of the arena was a bigger weapon rack that gleamed in the firelight, holding everything from traditional axes and spears to the sleek, futuristic weapons favored by the Nordri Clan. My attention was drawn to the glowing shields and shimmering sword hilts that hung there, deceptively simple in their dormant state.

A few paces away, Thyra grabbed a shield from the rack and looped her thumb through the small device. She flicked her wrist upward, and a translucent barrier sprang to life around her, shimmering faintly with blue edges—nearly impenetrable.

Her light-brown hair was pulled into its usual tight braided bun, practical and controlled, just like her. She moved with fluid precision, her build trim and athletic, every motion honed from years of training. There was no doubt she was beautiful—but it was the kind of beauty sharpened by discipline, by authority. The kind that kept people at a distance.

I watched her swing the shield in a graceful, dance-like arc, defending against unseen enemies as if she'd rehearsed it a hundred times. Probably had. Admiring her skill came easily. Forgetting who she was—the Chairman's niece, my team captain, and part of whatever plan had landed me here—that was harder.

She was impressive. Dangerous. And I still wasn't sure which one mattered more.

Watching her, I couldn't shake the realization settling in. The more I trained with these weapons, the more I realized how advanced the *Stór-menni's* arsenal was. Shields that could deflect energy strikes, blades that responded like extensions of the user—this wasn't just for sport or honor. This was preparation. *But for what?*

Even the shield in my own hands felt like proof of that. It weighed nothing, and yet during my previous practices, it had absorbed the full force of a strike from a Nordri training blade without so much as a flicker. My movements were much more crude than Thyra's, but I had at least learned to protect myself with it—although not without gaining a few cuts and bruises along the way.

As for the sword, it was equally impressive. As Thyra finished her shield practice, she walked over and handed me one of the hilts. I gripped it cautiously.

"Quit dawdling and start practicing. I saw you earlier, and you're still holding back," Thyra said, watching me carefully as I adjusted my stance. With a single swing, the blade ignited—if that was the right word for it. It wasn't fire, but it seemed alive, the steel-like substance glimmering as if infused with light. In a strange way, it felt like the blade moved with me rather than requiring effort to wield.

"I'm trying to get used to it," I admitted, swiping the blade experimentally.

"You'll need to stop thinking of it as a tool," she said, stepping closer. "Here, weapons are an extension of yourself. You will need to learn how to wield not only the physical weapons but also your ability at the same time."

"And how exactly am I supposed to do that if both my hands are occupied with a shield and sword?"

"You need to balance when to use the sword and when to use your ability. It's about precision, speed, and adaptability. Never drop your shield. Given how unpracticed you are, that would be a death sentence."

She gestured to the training dummies near the far wall—simple wooden frames dressed in holographic armor that thrummed with blue energy.

"Try again," she instructed, crossing her arms. "Focus on the movement, not the weight."

I couldn't help but wonder what Elin would think of all this. She'd probably have one of her sharp insights or clever ways to cut through the mystery surrounding the trials, making it all seem so obvious. I wished I could see her, but I knew she couldn't "visit" me through her visions, not now—not after what she told me about the Chairman. The thought of him seeing her whenever she tried to use her power to come to me sent a chill down my spine. I hated that she had to bear that risk, hated even more that it meant I couldn't feel her presence, even fleetingly.

Still, I couldn't stop thinking about the last time I saw her—on Baldur Street. Seeing her in the crowded market had been like a burst of sunlight in the dark, and for a moment, I let myself believe everything would be okay. But that hope was short-lived. My stomach churned every time I thought about my family. *Were they okay? Had they made it out of Ginnungagap after the prison break they caused trying to rescue me?*

Between the gossipy guards and my other team members, I'd heard rumors about the chaos their escape had created—stories of a daring breakout and the confusion that followed. It gave me hope that they'd made it out alive. But until I knew for sure, the uncertainty gnawed at me. I wished I could talk to Elin, hear her voice, and let her reassure me in that way only she could. Even if it was just to tease me about how ridiculous I looked fumbling around with this sword.

I raised the sword again and took a deep breath, steadying myself. *I needed to do this. I needed to survive this training and the Leikr so I could get back to my family, Elin, and my life.* I flicked my wrist, and my shield sprang up. I raised it in front of me as I swung, the blade cut through the air with an almost musical hum, its edge stopping just shy of the dummy's core. The holographic armor flickered, registering the strike as a successful hit.

Thyra gave a small nod of approval. "Better. But in the trials, the dummies will fight back—and so will the other teams."

I couldn't help but glance at the towering obstacle course in the middle of the arena. If this was only the third week of training, I couldn't imagine what the real trials would look like.

"We'll get to the course soon enough," Thyra said, a small smirk playing on her lips. "Today, once the rest of the team gets here, we will focus on combat with abilities. It's time. We can't wait any longer."

I swallowed hard. With the exception of Thyra, I had seen the other team members practicing with their weapons and abilities. *This was not going to be pretty.* The one small advantage I had was that I had been taking note of what their special power were and coming up with counter moves in my head.

Our current team consisted of Fenja, Magnus, Thyra, Einar, and me. Fenja and Magnus were part of Thyra's normal Hunter squad, but Einar she had chosen for his unique ability. Our sixth player had yet to join us, although Thyra assured us the last member would join the training this week.

The arena doors creaked open, and Magnus, Fenja, and Einar strode in, their footsteps reverberating against the cold stone floor. The atmosphere thickened with a quiet, unspoken tension. Magnus's massive frame filled the entrance, exuding an unshakable confidence that felt almost oppressive. His black thermal shirt clung to his giant muscular chest and arms as his dark eyes flicked to me for a split second before surveying the arena.

"You'd think they could've just skipped to the part where we're not risking our necks just for a show," Magnus muttered, his deep voice rumbling like distant thunder. He flexed his hands, as if recalling how his Stonebound Resilience turned his skin into an unbreakable, rock-like armor. It wasn't just defense—his fists, when clad in stone, could send shockwaves through the ground, cracking the floor and knocking opponents off balance. "This whole 'team bonding through danger' thing? Not my idea of a good time."

Fenja followed close behind, her steps light and deliberate. Her long black hair was pulled back, revealing her sharp, slightly Asian features. There was a calm, analytical air about her, as if she were constantly solving puzzles no one else could see. The three small metal marbles in her hand clinked softly as she rolled them in her palm.

"Bonding isn't the goal," she said dryly, her voice cool. "Survival is. They'll weed out the weak, and those left standing get the glory—if they're lucky enough to keep their limbs intact."

Her Metalshaping ability gave her an edge unlike any other. She could twist those marbles into any form she needed—blades, spikes, shields—all in an instant. I'd once seen her create a jagged whip mid-strike, tearing through targets with surgical precision.

Magnus shot her a glance. "Glory's overrated when it comes with a side of broken bones."

Fenja's lips curved in the faintest smirk. "Then maybe you're in the wrong place, Magnus."

Einar trailed behind them, his lean, muscular frame moving with the quiet efficiency of a predator. His sharp, observant light-green eyes scanned the arena, as though calculating every crack in the floor and shift in the air. It was unsettling, the way he seemed to see more than anyone else.

"None of us want to be here," Einar finally said, his voice low but steady. "But pretending it's not happening won't help. The faster we figure out how to work together, the better our chances."

Einar's Spectral Perception was as unnerving as it was impressive. His enhanced eyesight allowed him to see the hidden energy patterns in his surroundings—the vibrations in walls, the heat signatures in the air, and the vulnerabilities in his opponents. And then there was his Ghost Walk, a skill that let him phase through walls or dodge attacks with an eerie, fluid motion, as if he were slipping out of sync with reality.

Magnus huffed, crossing his arms. "You're assuming we even make it to the end."

"Better odds if we stop wasting time whining about it," Einar replied, his tone cool but pointed.

Magnus scowled but said nothing, while Fenja raised an eyebrow, watching Einar with mild curiosity.

"Let's just get this over with," Fenja said, the three marbles in her hand twisting into a sharp-edged spike before collapsing back into their original shape. "The *Leikr* isn't waiting for us to make friends."

The three of them weren't exactly warm to each other, but there was an undeniable respect in the air, born of necessity rather than camaraderie. They didn't have to like one another to acknowledge that each brought something vital to the table—and in the *Leikr*, that might be the only thing that kept us alive.

As I watched the others, my thoughts wandered back to Elin. What would she say about this team? She'd probably have some funny remark about Magnus's brute strength or Fenja's mysterious airs. And me? She'd probably remind me that I'd always find a way to make it work and that I had the skills if I just focused. I missed that—the way she could cut through my doubts without even trying.

Thyra's voice cut through the silence, sharp and deliberate. "Don't get too comfortable. We're here to train, not chat." The shift in her demeanor was unmistakable. Moments earlier, she'd been more relaxed, almost approachable, her words carrying the tone of a coach offering guidance. But the arrival of the team transformed her entirely. The commanding captain emerged, her presence magnetic and unyielding. With the others around, she wasn't just leading—she was asserting her authority, every word and movement a reminder that she was in charge.

Magnus grunted, his jaw tight, and moved to stand at the edge of the sparring area where Thyra stood. Fenja, not one to waste a moment, flicked one of her marbles in the air. It shimmered as it morphed into a spear, gleaming in the dim light.

Thyra gave us a final look, her gaze sweeping over the group. "It's time to see how you handle each other under pressure."

Magnus gave a low rumble, his muscles flexing as he cracked his knuckles. He was already looking at me, sizing me up, ready for the challenge. I returned his gaze, swallowing hard. I wasn't sure I was quite prepared for the raw power he brought to the table, but I wasn't about to back down.

A familiar beat surfaced in my mind—Zeppelin's "Immigrant Song." That howl. That charge. It wasn't fear I felt. It was something closer to defiance.

Thyra turned to Fenja and Einar. "You two, pair up. Let's see how your abilities fare against each other."

Fenja didn't hesitate. She morphed her floating spear back into a marble and waited. Her fingers poised, ready to shape the metal into something more lethal. Einar, calm as ever, narrowed his eyes, tapping into his enhanced vision, sensing the faint energies around him as he prepared for whatever Fenja would throw at him.

With a fluid motion, Fenja's marble shifted into a sleek, gleaming blade, its sharp edges catching the light. She stepped toward Einar with a fierce grin, her body low and poised for the first move.

"Ready?" she asked, the challenge in her voice clear.

Einar barely nodded, his focus sharp, his frame coiled like a spring ready to release. He wasn't one for words, but his quiet confidence was all he needed.

Thyra's gaze flicked over to Magnus and me. "Aedan, you'll face Magnus. Let's see if you can handle his power."

I took a deep breath, squaring my shoulders. Magnus, already grinning, was eager for the fight. He was the most physically imposing person here, but raw strength wasn't invincible. I had my telekinesis—if I played it right, I was hoping I could outmaneuver him.

I focused on the familiar hum of my *megin* in my body. The medallion the Chairman had given me grew warm on my chest, centering my *megin*. The air seemed alive, charged with potential. Around the edge of the sparring area, rocks and pebbles lined the ground—perfect tools for shifting the odds in my favor.

Magnus and I took our positions, the space between us charged with anticipation. Fenja and Einar were already circling each other, their eyes locked, each preparing to strike.

Magnus wasted no time, lunging forward with his sword ignited, the blade shimmering with a pale blue hue in the arena's dim light. I darted back, raising my hand to telekinetically snap a nearby stone between us, forcing him to adjust his footing. But his recovery was fast—too fast. His bulk moved with alarming agility, and he swung his blade toward me in a heavy arc.

The shield loop on my thumb flared just in time. A translucent barrier flickered to life, absorbing the blow with a resonant hum that jolted up my arm. My knees buckled slightly, the force driving me back a step. I gritted my teeth and channeled my telekinesis to shove Magnus a few paces away.

He laughed, low and sharp, his grin full of unshaken confidence. "Nice trick. Let's see how long you can last."

Before I could reply, he surged forward again, his speed unnerving. I swung my blade low, hoping to trip him up, but he saw it coming. His skin turned to impermeable stone, catching the strike, and his sword flicked downward in a counterattack. I dodged, barely, raising my hand to pull a chunk of loose stone from the ground and hurl it at him.

Magnus didn't even flinch. His sword shattered the stone midair, fragments scattering harmlessly. "That all you've got?" he taunted, his voice brimming with a mix of amusement and challenge.

Frustration clawed at me as I scrambled to stay out of his reach. My mind flashed back to my father's grueling lessons. *"A blade is a tool,"* he'd said during one of our countless sparring sessions. *"But your mind is the real weapon. Control the fight, control the space—make them react to you."* He'd drilled it into me that my telekinesis was my greatest strength, the key to turning any situation in my favor. But here, against Magnus, it felt like trying to hold back a landslide with pebbles.

I shifted my stance, trying to channel that lesson. Using telekinesis, I sent a spray of smaller rocks from the arena's edge hurtling toward him. It wasn't meant to injure, just distract. Magnus flinched slightly, raising his shield to block the barrage. Seizing the moment, I feinted left and darted right, angling my blade for his side.

The tip grazed him, enough to sting but not enough to matter. Magnus spun away, his growl turning into another maddening grin. "Not bad," he said, his voice edged with mockery. "Did your old man teach you that?"

I didn't answer, focusing on catching my breath. He wasn't wrong—my father had prepared me for moments like this. But Magnus wasn't just strong; he was relentless. And I was running out of moves.

He lunged again, faster than I could react. His shield slammed into mine, the impact sending a shockwave up my arm and forcing me to stumble back. My telekinesis was struggling to keep up, my *megin* drained from repeated bursts of control. Magnus saw it, too, his grin widening. "You're slowing down," he said, circling me. "This ends soon."

I braced, trying to muster the strength for one last counter. But before either of us could move, a sharp whistle echoed across the arena, cutting through the tension like a blade.

Magnus froze mid-step, his grin fading. I lowered my shield and turned toward the sound, my chest heaving. A tall figure emerged from the shadows at the arena's edge, their steps measured and deliberate. A hood obscured their face, but their presence was undeniable—a quiet, commanding authority that silenced the entire room.

Thyra straightened, her voice ringing out, calm but firm. "Finally. Our sixth member has arrived."

Magnus glanced at me, his expression unreadable, then back to the newcomer. "Guess that's enough for now," he muttered, lowering his blade.

I didn't respond, too focused on the stranger. *Whoever they were, they'd just saved me from getting completely destroyed.* But as they stepped further into the light, I couldn't shake the sense that they weren't here to make things any easier.

THREE

The Requisition

TRISTAN

The woman's cries for her child were only outdone by the toddler's wails for his mother. The black cloaks of the Clan Internal Affairs troopers, or IA troopers, swirled around the rest of the small cottage, looking for other unregistered children.

"Please... *please*, sir. Don't take him. He's my only child—just a little boy," the mother sobbed on her knees, clutching at my leg.

"DON'T YOU TOUCH HIM!" The boy's father yelled, straining against the metal clasps of the *Naglar* that pinned him firmly against the wall by his wrists.

"You know the rules," the Sergeant chided. "All children must be evaluated and registered for mentorship by the age of four. And according to the RDS—" He held up the small electronic RDS, or Registration and Detection Scanner, in his hand, wagging it back and forth "—your son is several months past his fourth birthday...and has a warrior ability."

The Sergeant's statement flooded me with memories of my own requisition day. Waiting until the last possible moment, my parents had followed the Clan rules and brought me to the local registration office on my fourth birthday. After the counselors determined that I had a warrior ability, my parents were given a requisition date. The date they would have to give up their child to an unknown mentor with the same warrior *megin* for rearing and education.

Seared into my memory was the look of agony across my mother's face as she buried her head into my father's shoulder as the counselors led me away from our home's front porch. My father had stood stoically next to her, wrapping an arm around her shoulders. I still recalled the burning anger and fear that had flooded me in that moment. *Why weren't they fighting to keep me?* That question had haunted me to this day.

This child's father had fought. And after enduring, I-don't-know-how-many electric shocks from the *Naglar*, he was now fixed against his own home's wall, helpless to do anything.

In that moment, the boy's father kicked the shin of a passing IA trooper, who yelped out in pain. The boy's father's face showed a momentary look of satisfaction before another surge of electricity ignited from the *Naglar,* rendering him momentarily unconscious.

His wife cried out in protest, lunging toward her husband only to have the strong arm of a trooper push her back onto the floor.

"Ma'am, I suggest you remain calm. You and your husband have already garnered several deductions on your files today, given all of —" he gestured around the room "—this. And I'm sure the last thing you want is to end up on the Reformation List. A cell at Ginnungagap assures you'll never see your child again."

The woman buried her face in her hands as sobs racked her body anew. From the corner of my eye, I saw something flicker from the crying toddler's outstretched hand. Remembering my own childhood response, I rushed towards him, closing my hand around his.

On my requisition day, believing that my parents weren't fighting for me, my anger had burst forth from my palms. The flames had barely sparked when the registration counselor fixed me with a cold stare and said, "Tristan, you have a choice to make. Either you put that flame out, and we proceed to the hovercraft...or you throw it and doom your parents to Ginnungagap. The choice is yours." I had let the flame fizzle...even at that age, the stories of the dreaded gray fortress had reached my ears.

Looking at the toddler's face before me, turmoil swirled inside me like I was being requisitioned all over again. Without thinking, I scooped him up.

"Hush, now," I whispered in his ear. "That will not help them. It will only make things worse...so take a deep breath."

To both the Sergeant's and my own surprise, I strode out the door carrying the little boy to the waiting registration counselor in the automated hover vehicle, or AHV. I deposited the crying child in her arms and closed the door. Pausing for a moment, I rested my head against the top of the AHV before tapping the roof as a signal for it to leave.

This had been our third and last unregistered requisition of the day, and none of them had been any easier. I gave a sharp nod to the sergeant who stood framed in the doorway, his expression unreadable, then turned away as the mother's sobs carried into the icy air. The crunch of snow beneath my boots was the only sound I focused on as I walked away.

The cold bit at my face—sharp, unrelenting—but I welcomed it. It cleared my head better than the recycled air of the AHV ever could. I kept walking, past the line of troopers packing up their equipment and the dim glow of the hovercraft's lights, until I reached the slush-covered streets of Falinvik proper.

It wasn't long before the paved streets gave way to the uneven cobblestones of Baldur Street, where the buildings loomed like relics of an ancient time forced to coexist with the present. Their dark lumber facades were a chaotic blend of shadowy eaves and intricate carvings, dragons and serpents twisting into the sky like spectral sentinels. The decorative tops created unpredictable hazards for the AHVs zipping overhead, adding a layer of disorder to the street's already bustling atmosphere.

The shops lined the road in a perfect row, their façades melding into one another like puzzle pieces. Each doorway was recessed into an alcove, shrouded by a slanted overhang that ran the length of the street. Whether by design or accident, the structure provided a natural shield for the comings and goings of patrons—a fitting touch for a place where discretion was often as valuable as the IOUs that acted as Clan currency. Above it all, faint neon lights buzzed in sickly hues, casting an eerie shine on the slick stones below.

A cold wind cut through the street, tugging at my coat, and I ducked my head to brace against it. My boots scraped against the cobblestones exposed by the geothermal heating pipes that ran under the street, melting the snow and ice. As I trudged toward the tavern I now called home, the air smelled of machine oil, damp wood, and street food, a sharp contrast to the clean efficiency of the Clan Hunter headquarters. There, the scent of oiled leather and the hum of sleek technology had reinforced a sense of power and prestige. Here, every step reminded me of how far I had fallen.

The tavern came into view, its squat frame slouched between two larger buildings like it had given up on standing tall. Wooden beams carved with runes framed the entrance, relics of a time long past, while slightly glowing panels of blue light hummed in the windows, a nod to the Nordri's tech-savvy pride. It was the kind of place you'd expect to find cheap ale and cheaper company, not someone like me.

Not that I was anyone anymore.

I paused outside the door, glancing up at the building as if seeing it for the first time. When I arrived, the accommodations had felt like a slap in the face. *A room above a tavern in the Baldur district?* It was a far cry from the quarters I'd had as a Clan Hunter, where every detail—from the pristine floors to the state-of-the-art tech—had reminded me of my status. Now, the only reminder was how much I had lost, thanks to Elin.

The tavern door creaked as I pushed it open, and the smell of smoked meat and stale ale hit me like a wall. I paused at the threshold, catching my reflection in a faintly polished panel near the entrance. The face staring back at me was familiar yet foreign, framed by sandy brown hair that I kept neatly trimmed beneath the hood of my black Clan cloak. My pale green eyes, sharp and alert, had once been praised for their keen observation, though now they seemed burdened by the weight of what I'd seen—and what I hadn't accomplished.

My light olive skin looked slightly dull in the low light, the long days taking their toll. My features—delicate yet undeniably masculine—often earned compliments, though I'd always found them more a distraction than an asset. Tonight, my cloak hung slightly askew, a testament to the chaotic day I'd endured, but the black clothing underneath was immaculate, its crisp lines and tailored fit a stubborn holdover from my days as a Clan Hunter.

I straightened my cloak reflexively, the motion automatic, as if neatness could shield me from the disarray of my surroundings. The main hall was dimly lit, the kind of place where shadows lingered a little too long, and the hum of conversation never quite reached a roar. Locals huddled at worn wooden tables, some carved with crude runes of their own, and above them floated a Viking-style chandelier. The old mechanical motor that kept it aerial buzzed feebly, giving away its age.

I climbed the creaking staircase to the upper floor. The carved banister was rough beneath my fingertips, another detail that betrayed the building's age and the indifference of those who maintained it. My room was at the end of the hall—a box barely big enough to hold the essentials. The bed creaked under the slightest movement, the desk was scratched and weathered, and the holo-screen flickered like it was on the verge of dying. Functional, sure. Comfortable? Not in the slightest.

Inside, I dropped my bag on the desk and slumped into the chair. The weight of the day pressed down on me like a lead cloak. I pinched the bridge of my nose and forced myself to focus.

This was temporary. That's what I told myself every day. Clan Internal Affairs wasn't where I belonged. It was a means to an end, a pit stop on my way back to the life I'd earned. Keeping an eye on Falinvik, monitoring whispers for Elin or the unregistered's family—

that was my way out. Bringing one of them in would do more than redeem me; it would make the Clan Hunters beg to have me back.

I leaned back in the chair, letting the creak of the wood cut through my thoughts. If I could deliver Elin or even the Unregistered's family—my exile to IA would be over. The higher-ups would have no choice but to restore my rank. The image of that moment—of walking back into those pristine halls with my head held high—was enough to keep me going.

But even as I clung to that thought, the day's events gnawed at me. *Why had I stepped in with the child? Was it guilt? A misguided attempt to make peace with my past? Or was it something far more dangerous—something that felt too much like rebellion?*

And then there was the memory that refused to let go—the glimpse I'd caught of the Chairman's screens during the Ginnungagap fiasco. The power reboot had revealed a classified file that should have been buried behind layers of security, its details burned into my mind. A black-and-white photo of a man in a high-ranking uniform, his eyes obscured by a black bar, the words "DNA UPLOAD CONFIRMED" blinking ominously below. The resemblance to the Unregistered was undeniable, and the questions it raised were endless. *Who was he? Why hadn't his file been updated with the others into the current system? And why was the Chairman so interested in him?*

I couldn't shake the feeling that I'd stumbled onto something monumental. And if I could only figure out what it meant, it would be a useful bit of leverage.

Through the small window above the desk, the warm glow of Falinvik's city lights spilled across the streets below, a stark contrast to the cold uncertainty that gripped me. Somewhere in that sprawling city lay the answers—and my opportunity. I just had to be smart enough to find them before someone else did.

FOUR

The Surprise

ELIN

Sigrid's declaration of a surprise had left the room buzzing with anticipation, and when she stepped aside, all eyes turned to the hallway. Tension hung thick in the air as I held my breath, bracing for whoever—or whatever—might emerge.

From the shadows, a small figure stepped forward. My heart skipped a beat as I recognized the petite Korean woman. I'd met her on the journey to Falinvik Fjord. Her glossy black hair, neatly cut to frame her face, gleamed under the dim lights. Her sharp eyes scanned the room with quiet confidence, but it was the faint smile tugging at her lips that hit me the hardest—a warmth I hadn't realized how much I'd missed.

"Bae?" The name escaped my lips in a rush, disbelief and relief tangled in my voice.

Her gaze landed on me, and her familiar, warm laugh filled the room. "Elin! Still managing to find the thick of trouble, I see."

Before I could move, McHaill stepped forward, his sharp eyes narrowing as he studied her. "*Bae*, what in the Nine Realms are you doing in Falinvik? I thought you'd be back in Auor after *Ginnungagap*."

Bae's smile widened with a hint of amusement. "McHaill. Still the same, I see. Direct and to the point."

"You two know each other?" Yrsa asked, her tone tight with suspicion.

McHaill gave a curt nod, his attention still on Bae. "She's Resistance, from Auor Island. And yes, we've worked on many missions together."

My voice broke through before anyone could say more. "Bae, what happened? The last time I saw you, you were with Aedan's family. Did they—?"

Her expression softened, but a shadow passed over her features. "After I helped the Auor team complete their mission and used my portal to send them back to my garage," she said, referencing her unique ability to open a portal to her garage on Auor Island from anywhere. "I made my way to the rendezvous point outside *Ginnungagap*. The plan was to wait for the rescue team to emerge with Aedan."

She paused, her gaze distant, as if replaying the memory. "At first, everything seemed under control. But then it happened: the prison break. Prisoners poured out of *Ginnungagap* like a flood, their desperation fueling the chaos. The air was thick with smoke, shouting, alarms blaring, and the heavy stomp of *Stór-menni* guards rushing to contain the situation. It was like standing on the edge of a storm."

Bae drew a breath, her hands clenching briefly before she forced herself to relax. "I had to reposition several times to avoid getting spotted. The guards were everywhere, rounding up escapees or chasing down anyone who looked suspicious. I held out as long as I could, hoping to spot Aedan's family in the crowd or get a signal from them."

Her voice faltered slightly, the regret clear. "But at a certain point, it became clear—they weren't coming. Either they were caught, or... they'd found another way out. I had to make a choice: stay and risk getting caught myself, or retreat and try to figure out what had happened from a safer vantage point. By then, the *Stór-menni* were closing in, and staying wasn't an option."

The room was silent, her words hanging heavily in the air. My chest tightened at the thought of Aedan's family lost in that chaos, their fates unknown. "You don't know if they made it out?"

Bae shook her head slowly, her lips pressing into a thin line. "No. I've been trying to piece together anything I can since then. I've searched everywhere I could, but there was nothing concrete to follow. Every hint of lead brought me closer to Falinvik, so here I am."

Yrsa's brow furrowed, but her tone softened. "And you didn't think to send word ahead?"

Bae shrugged lightly, though her eyes glinted with quiet determination. "I had no one to contact and no working devices to communicate with," she explained. "After using my portal to send the rest of the Auor team back to the garage, I was on my own. No connections to the Falinvik Resistance, no way to get a message through. Honestly, it feels like pure luck that I spotted Sigrid at all."

Sigrid leaned against the table. "Luck, or maybe you were just in the right place at the right time. Though I wouldn't exactly call my situation back there lucky."

Bae chuckled softly. "When I saw you racing past on that hovercraft with two *Stór-menni* patrols on your tail, I figured anyone causing that much havoc had to be Resistance. The explosion was what really caught my attention, though. I assumed it was part of your plan."

"Plan might be a strong word," Sigrid interjected dryly, crossing her arms. "That explosion was more improvised. I needed to distract them, and sacrificing my hovercraft was the best option I had at the time. It worked, but they didn't make it easy."

Bae nodded. "I followed the sounds of the explosion, sticking to the shadows to stay out of sight. I watched the guards scramble to regroup, and when I saw you walking away from the chaos...alive and determined...I knew I had to take a chance and approach you."

"And you decided that the middle of a *Stór-menni* patrol zone was the perfect place to introduce yourself?" Sigrid raised an eyebrow.

"I waited for the right moment," Bae said with a grin. "You didn't exactly look like you wanted company, so I made sure it was clear before stepping out."

Sigrid sighed, though her expression softened slightly. "I'll admit, you caught me off guard. But you knew enough about the Resistance...and about Elin and Aedan...to convince me you weren't a threat. Lucky for you, I'm not the shoot-first type."

Yrsa's gaze flicked between them, her expression contemplative. "So, you've been on the run since *Ginnungagap*," she said, addressing Bae. "And now you're here, bringing us this story—and yourself."

"That's right," Bae said firmly. "I'm here to help. Whatever you need to find Aedan's family and rescue him, I'll do it. I owe them that much."

The room fell silent for a moment, the weight of Bae's words hanging in the air. I caught her eye, feeling a flicker of hope despite everything. I was beyond grateful she'd found us. Her arrival felt like the first step forward in a journey that had been stalled for far too long.

McHaill cleared his throat, breaking the silence. His sharp eyes flicked between Yrsa, Sigrid, and Bae before settling on the maps and plans spread across the table. "We need to regroup and figure out our next move. Given what we've just learned, there's a lot to consider. Yrsa, Sigrid, and I will start working on a plan of action."

He turned his gaze to me and Nodin. "Elin, Nodin, why don't you two show Bae around the base and help her get settled. Find her an empty bunk and introduce her to the layout. We'll call you back in once we've made some progress."

My stomach sank, and I exchanged a quick, disappointed glance with Nodin. Being sidelined from the planning wasn't exactly what I'd hoped for, but McHaill's tone left no room for argument.

"Yes, sir," Nodin muttered, his reluctance evident.

Nodin turned to me with a sly grin, his dark braid catching the dim light. "Looks like we've been given the most prestigious job in the Resistance. Tour guides to the stars."

I rolled my eyes, trying to suppress a smile, but something about the way his grin lingered made my heart skip. It was a harmless joke, but the warmth in his voice felt oddly personal. *Stop it, Elin.*

I turned to Bae. "Come on. Let's get you set up."

Bae's smile was warm and genuine, cutting through the tension. "Lead the way, oh prestigious guides."

Nodin held out an arm with a dramatic flourish. "After you, esteemed guest. Let us dazzle you with our subterranean splendor."

We stepped out of the command room and into the sprawling tunnel system that made up the Resistance base. The hum of activity echoed around us—distant voices, the clink of metal on metal, and the faded hiss of steam escaping from geothermal pipes above.

"This place is...impressive," Bae said, her eyes darting around the dimly lit tunnel as we walked. "A lot more organized than I expected for an underground operation."

"It's a mix of old and new," I explained, gesturing to the worn steel beams lining the walls and the flickering, salvaged lights overhead. "The tunnels were part of an old metro system that the Nordri abandoned years ago. The geothermal pipes make it perfect for a base...it's warm, hidden, and self-sustaining."

Nodin leaned closer to Bae, dropping his voice conspiratorially. "Don't let her undersell it. The real magic is in the questionable canteen cuisine and the charming company. Both are unforgettable experiences." His usual grin flickered for just a second, so fast I almost missed it—but there was something else beneath the humor. A shadow of another thought, another place he wasn't speaking about. Then, just as quickly, it was gone, replaced with his signature smirk.

Bae laughed, her eyes crinkling at the corners. "I'll keep that in mind."

As I spoke, the sight of Bae walking beside me stirred memories of the journey to Falinvik Fjord, when we'd been part of a small, determined group. My thoughts wandered to Mia and Joel, who had been with us. They and Brigitta were back in Skogly, Sigrid's hidden haven for Clan member refugees. Thankfully, they were safe but worlds away from this underground labyrinth and me. A pang of longing hit me as I thought about them—they were my connection to my normal life, or at least what it used to be, which was easy to lose in my new reality. Plus, their sharp wit and steady presence had carried me through so much. I wondered what they were doing now. *Were they helping Brigitta? Did they miss me as much as I missed them?*

And then, as always, my thoughts drifted to Aedan. The image of him pulled at me, unspoken feelings swirling in the pit of my stomach. *Was he okay? Was he holding up under the strain of Leikr training?* Knowing he was out there, isolated and under the Chairman's thumb, made me feel restless. I pushed the thoughts aside, but they lingered like a shadow.

Nodin's voice broke through my rumination. "First stop: the canteen, where you'll find the Resistance's finest gossip, grumbling, and... creative culinary experiments."

The canteen was alive with chatter and the clatter of trays and utensils. Metal tables, each with mismatched chairs, were scattered across the room. Resistance members in a variety of gear—some in full Clan tactical outfits, others in casual, worn clothing—sat in groups, laughing, arguing, or just scarfing down food like it might be their last meal. One table erupted in laughter as a man with a shock of red hair mimed an exaggerated sword fight, while another group huddled around a map, gesturing furiously as they debated strategy.

"Welcome to the social hub," I said with a flourish. "If you want to know what's going on or just hear the worst jokes—this is the place."

Bae's gaze swept the room, her lips twitching into a smile. "Looks like quite the crowd. I think I'll fit right in."

Nodin leaned closer to Bae, his tone a playful whisper. "Pro tip: steer clear of Red Beard over there. He fancies himself a comedian."

Bae chuckled, her smile widening. "Thanks for the warning. I'll tread carefully."

We moved on, the noise of the canteen fading behind us as we entered a quieter section of the base. The bunk rooms were small, ship-like cabins, each with two stacked beds along with a narrow locker for personal belongings and just enough space to turn around without bumping into something.

"This is your new palace," Nodin said, swinging the door open to an empty room. "It's not glamorous, but it's functional. And the beds creak just enough to keep you on edge."

Bae stepped inside, looking around with an amused smile. "It's cozy. I've had worse."

I leaned against the doorframe, watching her settle in. "Well, if you ever need anything, just holler. Or bang on the wall. These rooms aren't exactly soundproof."

"I'll keep that in mind," Bae replied with a laugh.

Our final stop was the training area, a space that seemed to hum with life and purpose. As we stepped inside, Bae's eyes widened, drawn to the seamless blend of old-world sparring equipment and cutting-edge tech. Fighters clashed in the sparring ring, their weapons humming with energy, while others practiced hand-to-hand combat with their abilities on padded mats. Overhead, holographic projectors flickered to life, casting shimmering opponents into existence for target practice, adding to the atmosphere of intense focus.

"Now this," Bae said, her voice filled with admiration, "is awesome."

"Right? It's like stepping into a Viking tech dream," I said, gesturing to the high-tech sparring dummies and racks of swords.

Nodin pointed to a nearby hologram, where a fighter narrowly dodged a glowing opponent's attack. "Just don't let it hit you. Trust me...it hurts."

Bae smirked. "Good to know. And what about sparring with real opponents? Any volunteers?"

Nodin's grin widened as he grabbed a wooden sword from the rack. "Oh, I'm always happy to demonstrate. But fair warning: as Elli knows, I make a pretty unforgettable first impression."

Bae raised an eyebrow, a mischievous glint in her eyes. "Oh, don't worry...so do I."

I stood to the side, arms crossed, as I watched. I'd seen Bae practicing during our boat trip to Falinvik Fjord, but only in a defensive capacity. Now, seeing her step confidently into the ring, I couldn't help but feel curious—and slightly apprehensive.

"Bae, just so you know," I called out, hoping my teasing would mask my nerves. "Nodin's wind tricks are all flash and no substance."

Nodin pivoted to shoot me a mock-offended look, one hand theatrically pressed to his chest. "Flash and no substance? Elli, you wound me. You'll regret underestimating my charms—and my skills."

Bae chuckled as she selected a slim training sword from the rack, testing its weight with an elegant flick of her wrist. "I don't know, Nodin. You've got a lot to prove after that introduction. Let's see if you live up to the hype."

Nodin's grin widened as he stepped into the ring. "Oh, I always deliver, Bae. Prepare to be impressed." With a dramatic flourish, he raised his sword, sending a playful gust of wind swirling around him. Loose strands of his dark hair lifted with the current, adding to the air of theatrical flair. But as I watched him move—quick, confident, always in control—a thought crept in that I couldn't shake. *How much of what he showed us was real? And how much was carefully chosen?*

"Shall we dance?"

Bae raised an eyebrow, her expression amused but focused. "By all means. Lead the way."

The match began with a sudden clash, Nodin making the first move. He swept forward with a sharp strike aimed at Bae's side, but she parried with ease, her movements precise and deliberate. As Nodin pressed the attack, she evaded his blows with a dancer's grace, her smaller frame making her quicker on her feet.

"Oh, come on," Nodin quipped, sending a burst of wind to unbalance her. "You're making this too easy."

Bae stumbled slightly but recovered quickly, her eyes narrowing. With a flick of her hand, a small, shimmering portal appeared beside her. She slipped her sword through, and it reappeared behind Nodin, stopping just short of his ribs.

Nodin froze mid-attack, then turned slowly, his expression a mix of surprise and begrudging admiration. "Okay, that's new. I didn't see that one coming."

I stared, my mouth slightly open. "You can do that? Why didn't you say anything? I thought you could just open portals to your garage."

Bae grinned, a touch of pride in her expression. "Big portals take more energy. Small ones are easier...and a lot more fun to play with. And they come in pretty handy."

Nodin raised his sword in mock surrender. "I'll give you that one. But don't get too comfortable...I'll be ready next time."

Bae smirked. "We'll see about that." She glanced at me, her tone light but firm. "All right, Elin. Your turn."

My stomach tightened. "Me?" I asked, taking a step back. "I don't think—"

"Yes, you," Bae said, her tone encouraging but firm. "This is what training is for, remember?"

Nodin tossed me a wooden sword, and I fumbled to catch it. The weight was awkward in my hands, and I gripped it tightly, as if squeezing harder might make me a better fighter. My heart thumped in my chest as I stepped into the sparring ring, acutely aware of every set of eyes on me.

"I'm not sure I'm ready for this," I admitted, trying to keep the tremor out of my voice.

My stomach tightened, the weight of the wooden sword unfamiliar and heavy. It wasn't just about swinging a blade; it was about being good enough to make a difference, to matter in a way I wasn't sure I could. The thought of failing wasn't just scary. It was paralyzing. *What if I froze when it mattered most? What if I let Aedan down again?*

"Come on, Elli," Nodin said, leaning casually against the ring's edge. "Don't leave me as the only one embarrassed today. You'll be fine. Besides, what's the worst that could happen? It's just practice. Plus," he added with a wink, "you've got me here to cheer you on."

"Easy for you to say," I muttered, shooting him a look, my heart pounding as I stepped reluctantly into the ring. Every doubt I had about my ability screamed louder with each step.

She gave me a warm smile. "Don't worry, Elin. I'll go easy on you. Just focus on staying calm and using what you've learned."

Nodin added with a grin, "And if you mess up, at least you'll look good doing it. I mean, not as good as me, but still."

I couldn't help but laugh, shaking my head. "You're impossible."

The match began slowly, Bae circling me with fluid steps, testing my movements. Her first strike came low, and I barely managed to block it, my arms shuddering from the impact.

"Good," she said encouragingly. "Now keep your stance steady."

I adjusted my footing, trying to mimic the balance Sigrid had drilled into me during our endless hours of training. Bae struck again, faster this time, and I parried clumsily. My breathing was shallow, my muscles tense.

"You've got this!" Nodin called from the edge of the ring, his grin infuriatingly charming. "Just imagine it's me you're swinging at. That should motivate you."

I rolled my eyes but couldn't stop the flicker of a smile. My stomach twisted with something I couldn't quite name: annoyance, amusement, and something else. I glanced down at the wooden sword in my hand, trying to focus. *Aedan wouldn't be here teasing me like this. Aedan would—no.* I shook my head, trying to clear my thoughts. *Now wasn't the time for comparisons.*

Focus, Elin. Focus. I tried to steady myself, reaching for the buzzing pulse of my *megin.* The sensation flickered to life, faint and unsteady against my medallion, and I closed my eyes for the briefest moment, willing my temporal vision to kick in. When I opened them, a flash of the future flickered—a glimpse of Bae's next move.

She lunged toward me, aiming for my left side. Reacting instinctively, I raised my sword to block, the wooden blades connecting with a satisfying thwack.

"I did it!" The words burst from me before I could stop them, and a flicker of pride warmed my chest.

"Don't celebrate too soon," Bae warned, a mischievous glint in her eyes. She spun away, her hand brushing the air as a small portal opened beside her. Before I could fully process what was happening, she reached through and repositioned her weapon for another strike.

Panic flared as I scrambled to keep up, but my temporal vision faltered, leaving me blind to her next move. The flat of her wooden sword tapped lightly against my shoulder.

"Hit," she said gently, stepping back with a knowing smile.

I groaned, the sting of defeat mingling with reluctant admiration. "That was sneaky."

"That was strategy," Bae corrected, lowering her weapon. "You just need more practice with your ability. When it works, it's brilliant."

Nodin stepped forward, a playful swirl of wind circling him. "All right, ladies, let's not wear Elli out. We need her in one piece for the next round of charm practice."

I shot him a glare, but my smile lingered. Despite the nerves and the missteps, I felt a flicker of hope reignite.

"You're doing better than you think," Bae said, her voice sincere. "Your ability could be a game-changer, Elin. Don't doubt it." She smiled at me as she stepped away to place her sword on the rack.

Nodin moved closer, his grin softening into something warmer. "She's right, you know. You just need to believe in yourself more. You're stronger than you realize."

His words hit harder than they should have, and for a second, I couldn't meet his gaze. He wasn't just teasing now. There was something sincere in his tone that made my chest tighten—not just with guilt, but something else. *Something I wasn't ready to name.* Aedan's face flashed in my mind, and I turned away quickly, mumbling, "Thanks."

As I stepped back, I thought I caught a flicker of something in Nodin's expression, something fleeting, unreadable. Like he understood *exactly* what I was feeling. But before I could figure it out, he turned away, his usual smirk slipping back into place as if nothing had happened.

I let out a slow breath, my grip tightening around the wooden sword in my hand. Its surface was worn smooth from countless practice sessions, a silent testament to the effort it took to grow stronger. My thoughts drifted to Aedan. *Was he training right now? Was he exhausted, just like I was? Or was he facing something far worse under the Chairman's watchful eye?*

The Chairman always had his reasons for doing things, but what he was putting Aedan through. It felt personal. *Why?*

Whatever the reason, we were going to get Aedan back. And if I was going to play any part in rescuing him, I needed to grow stronger —not just in skill, but in determination. Setting the sword back on the rack, I resolved silently: *I wouldn't give up. For him, for all of us, I would keep pushing forward.*

As I turned away from the rack, the familiar weight of my medallion brushed against my chest. My hand found it instinctively, fingers grazing the cool metal. Beneath it, I felt the smallest flicker— the delicate rhythm of my *Ljós*, like sparks just under the surface of my skin.

It was always there, hidden but alive. If I focused, I could sense it —the tiny lights drifting in my chest like fireflies. Gentle. Mysterious. But if I focused too long or if I reached too deep, they began to swirl. They became unpredictable: bright and erratic, like a storm barely held at bay.

If I were being honest, it scared me. I didn't know what would happen if I let them spin too far out of control.

Falling into step behind Nodin and Bae, I tried to shake it off. But the storm lingered in my thoughts, churning just beneath the surface.

Nodin had this way of breaking through it all—the silence, the tension, and the fear—with a joke or a glance that saw a little too much. And sometimes, when I least expected it, I found myself wanting to lean into that lightness. To breathe, just for a second.

But that wasn't fair.

Not to Aedan.

He was the one I needed to save. The one who mattered most.

So why did Nodin's voice still echo in the back of my mind? And why did it feel—just for a heartbeat—like he understood something I hadn't admitted even to myself?

Trying to push it aside, I caught up to Bae, who was chatting animatedly about the base's training facilities. Her presence was like a breath of fresh air, easing some of the weight on my shoulders. Seeing her reminded me of home, of the people who had kept me steady through everything. I could almost hear Joel's sarcastic commentary about the bunk rooms or Mia's steady encouragement for my practice. And see my brother, ever-protective Anders, waiting just outside the training room door, arms crossed and eyes soft, ready to make sure I was really okay.

Bae's arrival had brought something vital to the surface: no matter how dark or uncertain the path ahead, we weren't alone. We had people worth fighting for—and people who would stand and fight with us.

FIVE

The Sixth Member

AEDAN

The sixth member strode into the arena, their steps unhurried but deliberate, as if the weight of their presence was enough to command the room. Their hood was pushed back, revealing a man with strikingly sharp features, pale skin, and raven-black hair swept neatly away from his angular face. His icy blue eyes swept over us, lingering just long enough to convey that he wasn't impressed. His posture radiated arrogance, as though he believed the room already belonged to him—and the rest of us were just clutter.

"Eirik," Thyra said, her tone clipped, though her expression betrayed a flicker of something unreadable. "You're late."

Eirik smirked, a hint of mockery curling at the corner of his lips. "And yet, here I am, precisely when I meant to arrive."

Magnus let out a low grunt, his jaw tightening. "Great. Another charmer."

Eirik ignored the comment, his gaze cutting to the rest of us. "So, this is the team I've been picked for. How quaint." His voice was smooth, almost velvety, but a venomous undertone made my skin prickle.

Thyra crossed her arms, her expression hardening. "You weren't picked. The Chairman assigned you here."

Eirik's smirk grew, his eyes locking on Thyra with a cold familiarity that made me wonder just how well they knew each other. "Details, Thyra. I'm here now. That's what matters."

"Who's this?" Magnus asked, gesturing toward Eirik with a dismissive wave. "Another recruit to keep us all in line?"

Thyra's tone was curt, brooking no argument. "He's your new teammate. Eirik."

Eirik's smirk deepened, and before anyone could respond, he raised a hand. The shadows around his feet twisted unnaturally, stretching and coiling as if alive. They slithered across the floor, dark tendrils weaving toward the center of the arena with a sinuous, deliberate grace.

Without warning, the shadows snapped forward, curling around Magnus's feet and yanking him off balance. Magnus hit the ground with a heavy thud, his stunned expression quickly morphing into a deep scowl.

"What the—" Magnus started, pushing himself up, but Eirik cut him off with a mocking laugh.

"Relax, big guy," Eirik said smoothly, retracting the shadows in one fluid motion. They pooled harmlessly at his feet once more. "Just thought I'd show you what I bring to the table."

"Not impressed," Magnus growled, pushing himself up and brushing off his pants.

Fenja watched Eirik with narrowed eyes, her hand hovering over the marbles in her palm. "Flashy," she said coolly. "But control means nothing if it's all for show."

Eirik's smile didn't waver. "Oh, I assure you, it's not just for show." He turned his gaze to Einar, his icy eyes narrowing slightly. "And you? I've heard about your Spectral Perception. Tell me, does it let you see what's coming next?"

Einar's expression remained impassive, though his shoulders

stiffened. "Sometimes," he said, his voice measured. "But you're predictable enough."

The tension in the room spiked. Eirik chuckled softly, his gaze shifting back to Thyra. "Charming group you've assembled. Truly."

"They're skilled," Thyra said evenly. "And they've earned their place here."

Eirik arched an eyebrow. "Have they? Or is this just another of your little projects, hoping to shape the unshapable?"

The jab hit Thyra harder than I expected, and I caught a flicker of irritation in her eyes before she masked it with her usual composure. "You're here to train, not to critique. If you think you're above this, feel free to take it up with the Chairman."

Eirik's smirk faltered, if only for a split second. "Oh, I wouldn't dream of it," he said smoothly. "I'm here to play my part. Shall we begin?"

Thyra didn't answer immediately. Her gaze swept over the rest of us, then landed on me. "Aedan," she said, her tone brisk, "you'll spar with Eirik. Let's see how well you handle yourself against someone with a little flair."

My heart dropped.

Of course, it was me.

Eirik scoffed, his arms crossing as his shadows curled lazily around his boots. "Spar? With him?" His tone dripped with disdain, as if the suggestion alone was an insult. "I didn't realize we were lowering the bar so much."

Thyra's jaw tightened, her sharp gaze narrowing. "Like I said before, we are here to train as a team, Eirik, not critique them."

"Training is precisely why I'm suggesting we skip the sparring," Eirik countered smoothly, tilting his head. "If you're trying to prepare us for the *Leikr*, then let's do something worthwhile. The obstacle course. It's a real test of our abilities."

Thyra hesitated, her eyes flicking briefly to me. I could see the calculation behind her gaze, the unspoken question of whether I was ready for something like that. My stomach twisted. She wasn't wrong to doubt me; I wasn't sure I was ready either.

"I'm not sure that's the best idea," she said finally, her voice measured. "The team's not fully cohesive yet. Some members—" Her eyes lingered on me. "—might need more time."

Eirik's smirk deepened, his arrogance radiating off him in waves. "Time? In case you've forgotten, Thyra, the *Leikr* doesn't wait for anyone to be ready. If they can't handle the obstacle course, they'll be a liability in the real thing. Better to find out now, don't you think?"

I resisted the urge to mutter, *welcome to the jungle,* under my breath. It would've been too on-the-nose—Guns N' Roses sarcasm didn't exactly match the vibe. But the chaos brewing in the room? That felt right on cue.

The shadows at Eirik's feet rippled again, as if mirroring his determination. Magnus scowled, crossing his arms but saying nothing. Fenja's eyes darted between Eirik and Thyra, her face impassive, though the tension in her posture was clear. Einar stood still, watching, his expression unreadable.

Thyra's lips pressed into a thin line. For a moment, it looked like she might push back, but then her shoulders stiffened, and she nodded once. "Fine. The obstacle course it is, but we do it as a team, not pairs."

Eirik's smile was victorious, and the way his gaze flicked toward me felt like a challenge. "Excellent. Let's see what this team is made of."

Magnus let out a low growl, his tone dripping with sarcasm. "Great. This should be fun."

Thyra stepped forward, her commanding presence slicing through the tension. "You all know the drill," she said, her tone firm. "The course is designed to push you to your limits. Teamwork is essential. No one gets left behind."

Her eyes locked on Eirik, her voice sharpening. "That includes you. You're part of this team now, whether you like it or not."

Eirik gave a mock bow, his smirk never wavering. "Understood, captain."

Thyra didn't dignify him with a response. Instead, she motioned for us to follow her. The atmosphere was heavy as we moved through the arena and into the adjoining chamber where the practice obstacle courses waited. My heart pounded in my chest, the mix of anticipation and dread making it hard to breathe.

SIX

The Course

AEDAN

As we stepped into the vast training arena, the air grew colder, sharper—like the space itself had been designed to intimidate. The high ceiling stretched so far into the darkness above us that it felt like a storm could gather up there without anyone noticing.

Thyra headed towards a black platform that served as the nexus for the different course paths. I could see the obstacles looming ahead, a sprawling nightmare of jagged walls, swinging pendulums, narrow ledges, and shifting platforms. Flames shot up from random sections, while sharp mechanical blades moved in unpredictable patterns in another. Overhead, rope bridges swayed precariously, leading to platforms shrouded in mist. It was chaos incarnate.

"Remember," Thyra said, her voice cutting through the sound of grinding gears and hissing steam, "this isn't just about individual strength. In the *Leikr*, you will be paired with a teammate to run the course. You'll need to rely on each other."

Eirik let out a derisive chuckle. "Or not."

Thyra's glare was sharp enough to cut steel. "Everyone plays their part, Eirik. That's an order."

He shrugged, his shadows curling upward like lazy serpents. "Fine, fine. Let's get this over with."

"We are only running the Niflheim simulation today and practicing as a group," Thyra instructed, as she tapped something into the screen attached to the podium on her left. Her fingers hesitated briefly over the control panel—just long enough for me to notice—before she tapped the final command.

Niflheim? I racked my brain to remember the old Norse bedtime stories my mother used to tell me. I was pretty sure Niflheim was one of the Nine Realms. If I recalled correctly, it was a frozen wasteland. I swallowed hard. *That did not sound promising for a first course experience.*

As we lined up at the starting point, the others exchanged glances, their determination evident despite the tension. I tried to steady my breathing, but the sight of the shifting platforms and spinning blades made my pulse pound. This was beyond anything I'd trained for.

Eirik stepped beside me, his cold, amused gaze flicking over my trembling hands. "Try to keep up," he said smoothly, his voice barely above a whisper. Then, without waiting for Thyra's signal, he surged forward, his shadows propelling him over the first obstacle with effortless grace.

I caught the spark of irritation that crossed Magnus's face. He muttered something under his breath, eyes narrowing on Eirik's back. The platform where the rest of us stood turned green, indicating that the obstacle course was now active. A red timer, hovering near the ceiling, lit up and started to log the time.

The first obstacle stretched out before us, a chasm so wide it seemed to swallow the air around it. The mist below writhed with unnatural movement, and the floating stones leading across hovered unevenly. Some spun slowly, others tilted like cruel teases in the wind, daring you to try.

"Of course," I muttered, my voice tight. "Why wouldn't the first test involve falling to my death?"

Magnus grunted, already sizing up the leap. "Sadistic," he muttered, louder than necessary. "That's what this is." His shoulders were tense, jaw tight—like this wasn't just about the course, but something deeper pressing at him.

Thyra's piercing voice snapped me out of my spiraling thoughts. "Move. *Now*. Work together!" Her gaze softened slightly as she turned to me. "Stick close."

I nodded stiffly, my heart pounding. Heights had never been my thing—more like my personal nightmare. Even as a kid, climbing a tree higher than the first branch was enough to send my pulse racing. *And now?* This was a whole new level of terror.

Fenja stepped forward, her fingers deftly spinning the marbles in her palm. With a flick, they expanded into gleaming metal platforms, anchoring to the unsteady stones.

"One at a time," she said. "These won't hold more than a person."

Magnus went first, his massive frame making the platforms groan, but he leapt across with ease. Einar followed, his steps eerily precise, as if he could see the exact angle of every stone. Watching them didn't help. The stones seemed to mock me, tilting and shifting, the vapor below writhing as though eager for me to fall.

I forced myself forward, every muscle screaming at me to stop. The first leap wasn't far, but my legs felt like lead. As I landed, the platform tilted sharply, and my arms flailed for balance.

My legs locked, the fear rising in my throat. I could almost hear my mother's voice, calm and firm: '*Breathe, Aedan. Just breathe. The only way out is through.*' But hearing it and believing it were two different things.

The platform wobbled again— panic clawed at my chest. Then a sudden rush of air steadied me, and I froze in surprise.

"Focus. Use your ability," Thyra called, her voice steady but laced with something I couldn't place—tightness, maybe, or fatigue. Her hand raised slightly, the slightest trace of air swirling around her.

Was she controlling the air? My mind reeled as the realization hit me. I hadn't seen her use her ability before—she'd never mentioned it or even hinted at the power she held just beneath her carefully controlled demeanor. But it was clear. The subtle shift in the air, the way the currents wrapped around me with precision—she was helping me.

Below, the fog writhed restlessly, as though daring me to slip. Gritting my teeth, I forced my focus inward, reaching for the hum of my *megin*. The medallion around my neck grew warm against my chest as the familiar sensation of my telekinesis flared to life. Back home, I'd practiced my telekinesis with soda cans and chess pieces—never vertical cliffs and life-or-death leaps.

The glowing stones ahead blurred slightly as I concentrated, the strain building behind my eyes. With a mental push, I anchored the next platform in place.

I leapt, the air rushing past me like a scream. My breath caught mid-leap, then jolted back as I landed hard and barely stayed upright.

"One step at a time," I muttered through clenched teeth, my voice barely audible over the howling wind. The fog seethed, hungry for a misstep, but I forced the fear down. I couldn't look back. I wouldn't let it win.

Halfway across, one of the stones spun wildly just as I prepared to jump. Dread coiled its way up my ribs. I stretched out a hand, telekinetically locking the platform in place before jumping. The strain made my head throb, but I landed—barely.

The final leap was the worst, the gap larger than the others. My legs felt like jelly, my breath shallow. "You've got this," I whispered to myself.

Telekinesis surged through me as I pushed against the platform, giving myself an extra burst of momentum. The leap felt like it lasted forever, the fog pressing against my senses with a relentless, suffocating presence. I hit the rock ledge hard, stumbling forward, and Magnus grabbed my arm to brace me.

"Not bad, kid," he muttered. Coming from him, it felt almost like a compliment.

I gave him a quick nod, drawing in a shaky breath as the adrenaline ebbed.

The team moved on to the second obstacle, which lay beyond a short tunnel. I groaned when I saw it. Of course, it had to be climbing an ice wall—an impossibly tall, glistening monstrosity of frost and shimmering danger. It stretched upward like a cruel joke. It was like I was living my personal heights nightmare with this course. Embedded in the wall's surface were glowing runes that pulsed with a strange energy.

Magnus, ever the one to act first, reached out to touch one. A flash of icy blue light shot through his arm, and he recoiled with a growl, shaking his hand. "What the—"

"Don't touch the runes," Fenja snapped, stepping closer to inspect the wall. Her dark eyes scanned the frost-covered surface with precision. "They're traps. No one touches them."

Eirik was already halfway up the wall, his shadows carving grips and footholds into the ice with unnatural ease. His movements were smooth, arrogant, and unhurried as if the obstacle didn't deserve his full attention. He never glanced back, never offered advice. Just a silent, looming figure climbing toward the top.

Magnus growled, glaring at Eirik's back. "Figures he wouldn't bother to warn us."

Fenja ignored him, her marbles shifting and stretching into sharp metal spikes. With a flick of her wrist, she embedded one into the wall. But as Fenja approached the wall, she seemed to inspect the remains of Eirik's shadows lingering in the ice. Though faint and beginning to fade, they had left behind grooves and divots.

"These'll hold if we're quick," Fenja said, placing her foot on one of the grooves left by Eirik's shadows. She tested it, and it held firm. "Guess even arrogance can be useful."

Driving a spike next to a groove, she announced, "I'll also leave my spikes as extra handholds in difficult spots. Use them, but don't put too much weight on any single one. They should hold, but they're not invincible."

She started her ascent with practiced precision, her spikes clicking against the ice as she scaled the wall. Her movements were deliberate, each one calculated to avoid the pulsing runes. Occasionally, she paused, shaping another spike and hammering it into the ice for the next person to use when Eirik's grooves didn't seem sufficient.

Einar followed, his movements eerily efficient. He paused for a moment, his head tilting as his Spectral Perception allowed him to map out the safest route. "The runes have a pattern," he said, his voice calm. "Avoid the clusters—they're more likely to trigger."

Phasing in and out of the wall like a ghost, Einar climbed without hesitation, bypassing danger with unnerving grace. He reached the top in what felt like minutes, standing there with an air of calm triumph.

Stepping up to the wall, Magnus shook his head, jaw tight, muttering something under his breath. "Guess it's my turn," he said, but there was a heat behind his words that hadn't been there before.

He slammed his stone-covered fists into the ice, carving out deep grooves to grip, ignoring Eirik's prior ones. Every movement felt like more than just climbing—it was frustration, barely contained. The wall shuddered slightly under the force, but he kept going, brute strength driving him upward. He miscalculated once, his foot slipping dangerously close to a rune, but he caught himself, growling in frustration.

I stood at the base, staring up at the shimmering surface. My chest tightened. After the previous obstacle, I should've been more numb to the height—but it still clawed at me, that gnawing fear of falling. My palms were slick, and my heart drummed in my ears.

"You'll be fine," Thyra said, stepping beside me. Her voice was softer than I expected, almost encouraging. "Just focus on the next move, not the whole wall."

Her air currents swirled indistinctly, tugging at my clothes as if to reassure me she'd help if needed. I nodded, taking a deep breath. This wasn't about fear—it was about survival.

I reached for the first of Fenja's spikes and placed my foot into Eirik's grooves as I started to climb. Ice tore at my skin with every gust, but I kept going. One spike, one breath. The cold numbed everything but the voice in my head and the steady burn of my *megin*, bracing the spikes as I shifted my weight. Each step was deliberate, my focus locked on the next move.

"Don't look down," I muttered to myself, recalling Elin's advice when we rappelled the cliffs on Auor Island. She wasn't here to support me with her ropes this time, but her instructions were still valuable. "One move at a time."

Halfway up, the wall seemed to stretch endlessly, its icy surface glittering like a cruel challenge. My fingers had become numbed against the ice, and *then it happened*—I forgot to stabilize the spike I was using. As I pulled myself up, it came loose.

Without mercy, gravity yanked me downward.

The drop felt infinite, my breath catching in my throat as panic surged like a cold wave. I could feel Thyra's air current slowing my momentum like invisible hands, but they weren't enough to stop it. I slid down the ice wall, my boots scraping ice chunks loose as I went. Desperately, I clawed the ice with the spike still in my hand. Finally, using my telekinesis, I hammered the spike into the ice, and my descent stopped. My breath came out in rushed puffs as I dangled precariously, the memory of my childhood fall surging back with paralyzing clarity. Below, the world spun into a dizzying blur.

I scanned frantically for a foothold. The only one within reach gleamed faintly—a cluster of runes surrounding it. Too close, too dangerous. If I misjudged by even an inch, the entire thing would trigger, and enchantment would numb my leg, leaving me as good as lost. My arms trembled with the effort of holding my weight, fingers screaming against the strain.

Think, Aedan. My thoughts were a jumble of desperation. My *megin* stirred within me—a survival call. I closed my eyes, focusing past the frenzied beat of my heart. A flicker of control sparked, then grew.

Before I could test my grip, a strong air current rushed around me. It wasn't random—it was precise, purposeful, and steadied me. *Thyra.* Her currents embraced me, pushing my body back toward the wall with measured strength.

My brain, unhelpfully, queued up The Beatles' "With a Little Help from My Friends." A touch sentimental for nearly plummeting to my death, but I wasn't about to complain.

With a surge of telekinetic force, I pushed against the air currents and heaved myself upward, narrowly avoiding another rune's lethal flare. My fingers fumbled before catching a groove just above. The rough ice bit into my skin as I clung to it. My pulse thumped like a war drum, adrenaline surging as I found a safe foothold.

"Don't stop," Thyra called, her voice cut through the roar of the wind, firm but calm. "You're almost there."

A rush of exhilaration and terror coursed through me as I locked eyes with her below, her outstretched hand still guiding her currents. I wasn't safe yet, but Thyra's unwavering focus ignited something fierce within me.

The wind rose, shrill and taunting, like it knew how close I'd come to falling. I clenched my jaw and reached for the next groove. Using my telekinesis, I stabilized the spike as I hauled myself up, my arms trembling from the effort.

I pushed forward, Eirik's grooves and Fenja's spikes guiding me. I was careful to avoid the glowing runes, each one a reminder of the danger. My muscles burned, my breaths tight and shallow, but I kept climbing. When I finally reached the top, I collapsed onto the platform, my breath heaving.

"Nice work," Magnus said grudgingly, offering me a hand.

Fenja nodded, her expression unreadable. "Not bad," she said.

Thyra reached the top moments later, her air currents carrying her effortlessly over the final ledge. She didn't look at me, but her slight nod was enough.

Sometimes I wondered what she was really thinking behind that perfect composure. There was a crack there—I could feel it—but she never let it show for long.

Thankfully, the next obstacle didn't involve heights or climbing—something I was deeply grateful for. But it was no less daunting. A series of massive ice pendulums swung in chaotic patterns, their heavy blocks adorned with shining runic designs that seemed to hum with malicious intent. They moved faster than seemed possible, their icy surfaces gleaming with sharp edges.

Eirik, of course, was the first to step forward, his shadows coiling around him like obedient pets. With casual ease, he used them to shove the pendulums aside, clearing a path for himself without a second thought for the rest of us. He glanced back with an insufferable smirk and then disappeared to the other side.

Magnus hadn't said much since the wall, but something was clearly boiling under the surface. Not just irritation—something deeper. His fist tightened with every step, like he was holding back more than words. Maybe it was the course, maybe Eirik, or maybe something else entirely. Either way, he looked like he was done playing by the rules.

He stepped up, and for a moment, he just stared at the pendulums. His massive frame bristled with tension, and his fists curled into stone. He stood like a dam holding back a flood—silent, until the crack finally split down the middle.

"I'm done with this nonsense," Magnus growled. Before any of us could react, he charged forward, his stone fists crashing into the first pendulum with a deafening crack. The massive ice block shattered into shards, scattering across the arena floor.

"Magnus, what are you—" Thyra started, but he didn't stop. He swung at the next pendulum with even more force, reducing it to rubble in one blow. Each strike sent tremors through the floor, his growls echoing with every swing.

"I didn't ask for this," Magnus snarled, smashing another pendulum into tiny pieces. "This stupid course, this stupid *Leikr*. You want me to play their game? Fine. But I'm doing it my way."

One by one, the pendulums fell, his relentless strength turning them into harmless chunks of ice. The final block shattered with an earth-shaking boom, leaving the path completely clear.

Magnus turned back to us, his chest heaving, ice dust clinging to his hair and clothes. "There, how's that for teamwork?" he asked gruffly. "Now it's easy."

For a moment, none of us moved, stunned by the sheer force of his frustration. Then Fenja broke the silence with a dry chuckle. "Effective," she said, her lips twitching in the faintest smirk. "Though not exactly subtle."

Magnus shot her a glare but said nothing, stepping aside to let the rest of us pass.

I followed cautiously, stepping over the shattered remains of the pendulums. The path was clear, but the weight of Magnus's outburst lingered in the air. Even Thyra seemed momentarily thrown off, her gaze lingering on him with a glimmer of something more than irritation—something quieter. Not just concern, but understanding. Like she knew exactly what it felt like to reach a breaking point.

By the time we all made it to the other side, Magnus had crossed his arms and was leaning against the wall, his expression unreadable. "Let's keep moving," he said shortly, as though he hadn't just reduced the obstacle to rubble.

I glanced at Thyra, half-expecting her to reprimand him, but she simply nodded, her face composed. Whatever she was thinking, she kept it to herself.

The final obstacle loomed ahead as a large open area surrounded by ice cliffs. The arena lights dimmed, and a guttural roar shook the air. A massive troll shimmered into existence, towering like a nightmare plucked straight from Norse legend.

Its grotesque face was dominated by a bulbous, pockmarked nose and glinting, cunning eyes that radiated malice. Shaggy, matted hair hung like a wild mane around its head and shoulders, framing its twisted expression. The troll's overalls, stitched together from mismatched patches of leather and burlap, barely clung to its enormous frame, with one strap perpetually slipping off its broad shoulder.

The troll's hands ended in thick, clawed fingers, one gripping a crudely carved wooden club nearly the size of Magnus. The club, adorned with faintly glowing runes, struck the ground with a thunderous crack, sending jagged fissures racing through the ice. As it moved, its heavy, flat feet stomped with deliberate menace, each step vibrating through the arena. The creature let out another earth-shaking roar, its misty breath reeking of damp earth and decay, making it clear this was no ordinary hologram—it was a projection designed to terrify and destroy.

"Spread out," Thyra ordered, her tone cutting. "It's too big to take head-on."

Magnus charged first, his fists turning to stone as he struck the troll's leg. The hologram flickered but didn't falter. Fenja flanked it, her metal shaping into long, sharp spikes that she hurled at its chest.

Einar darted behind it, deliberately sliding on the ice and phasing through a sweeping strike from its club. "It's vulnerable at the back!" he called, his sharp vision picking up the glint of a weak spot.

Eirik stood back, his shadows surging forward to tangle the troll's legs, slowing its movements. "You're welcome," he said coolly, as if deigning to help was a favor.

I watched, my mind racing. The troll roared again, rearing back to swing its club. Fenja and Magnus dodged, but the others were too close. I focused, reaching for my telekinesis, and yanked a pile of loose stones into the air. With a shout, I hurled them at the troll's arm, the impact disrupting its swing just enough to throw it off balance.

"Now!" Thyra called.

Magnus struck again, his stone fists slamming into the troll's knees. Fenja sent another wave of spikes into its chest, and Einar lunged at its back, his blade slicing through the weak spot. The troll staggered, flickering violently.

I saw my chance. Summoning the last of my *megin's* strength, I pulled a massive ice boulder from the edge of the arena and hurled it at the troll's head. The impact shattered the hologram, the troll dissolving into particles of light.

The silence that followed was deafening.

Thyra's gaze swept over us, lingering on me.

"Good for a first run," she said, though her tone was measured. "But not good enough. In the *Leikr,* you'll be facing all these obstacles as just a pair. Plus, there will be another team competing against you who will try to make it even more impossible. Finishing the course in the shortest possible time is everything—this was way too slow."

But even as she delivered the verdict, I couldn't shake the flicker I'd seen in her—during the fall, during the climb. Something more than duty. Something personal.

Eirik chuckled, his shadows curling lazily. "Told you we needed better standards."

I bit back my retort, frustration and exhaustion seething in my chest. As much as I hated to admit it, Eirik was right about one thing: if I couldn't handle this, I didn't belong here.

The obstacles were brutal, and in the *Leikr*, I'd be facing solo challenges I couldn't even begin to imagine. And as for the obstacle courses? Who knew who I'd end up paired with—if we even made it that far in the trials. The problem for me was—I didn't have a choice in being there. For me, the only way out of the *Leikr* was through it.

SEVEN

The Plan

TRISTAN

In the black evening sky, the IA building loomed ahead, its angular structure a patchwork of sleek metal and dark glass, reflecting the muted glow of Falinvik's lights. Snow crunched underfoot as I approached, the cold biting through my gloves. Winter had tightened its grip on the fjord, glazing the streets in ice and fresh snow. Despite the city's technological advancements, it couldn't completely escape the season's icy grasp.

I adjusted my collar against the chill, grateful that my workday was finally over—at least the part anyone cared to track. My shift had been another grueling exercise in futility, chasing petty offenses and assigning meaningless penalties.

Under orders from my direct supervisor, Watch Commander Kolve, I spent the day sifting through reports of Clan members accusing their neighbors or coworkers of being "unpatriotic." Most of the accusations were trivial, little more than thinly disguised attempts at revenge or social one-upmanship. My task was to visit both parties involved, verify the validity of the claims, and, if warranted, issue formal warnings along with deductions to their Clan files. It was tedious work, devoid of any real significance.

At least today hadn't been another set of Unregistered requisitions. My stomach turned at the thought of the last one—the four-year-old child forcibly removed from his parents for failing to enroll him in the Clan Mentorship Program on time. The mother's pleading had lingered in my mind longer than I liked. I'd reminded myself that the law didn't make exceptions for negligence, but the image of the boy's wide, tear-filled eyes still gnawed at me.

Tasks like that made me question how far I'd fallen. This wasn't what I'd trained for. Not what I'd built my career on. My demotion was a humiliation I couldn't let stand.

And it was *her* fault.

Elin. Her name alone made my jaw tighten. She was the reason I was here, reduced to working in the shadows instead of standing at the forefront of the Chairman's forces. She'd made me look like a fool, slipping through my fingers when I'd been so close to catching her. That one failure had derailed everything.

I stopped just outside the IA building, staring up at its sleek façade. The design hinted at *Stór-menni* sophistication, with luminescent energy conduits lining the exterior and Security Aerial Surveillance Units, or SASUs, patrolling the roof. Yet it lacked the imposing grandeur of the Clan Hunters' headquarters or the sharp efficiency of the Chairman's tower. This building, like the job inside, felt like a pale imitation of the greatness I once commanded.

I swiped my new IA medal at the entrance, having had to forfeit my Clan Hunter medallion to Thyra upon my demotion. The disc was smaller and duller than the medallion I'd given up—iron-gray with the IA's symbolic twin ravens etched in pale silver, their wings knotted together in endless lines. Like Odin's ever-watchful messengers, they seemed less an emblem of wisdom than of scrutiny. My runes circled the rim, sharp and utilitarian, now more code than ornament. It felt lighter too, as if the medal itself carried less weight—less honor. A badge of surveillance, not command.

The scanner's faint hum blended with the distant whir of aerial patrols overhead. The doors slid open with a soft hiss, releasing a wave of warm air that stung my frozen cheeks.

Inside, the building buzzed with quiet activity. Holographic screens hovered above desks, data streams hummed in quiet rhythm, and security droids patrolled the halls, their sensors scanning for anomalies. Agents moved with purpose, their voices low as they exchanged reports. The space was modern, sure, but it lacked the productivity and cutting-edge precision I'd come to expect from the Clan Hunters.

This was where I'd ended up. It was better than a cell at Ginnungagap, but not by much.

Every wasted day here only deepened my resolve to claw my way back. I hadn't been born to deal with the complaints of minor officials or issue meaningless fines. I was better than this. I would prove it. And I had a plan.

The warmth of the interior did little to thaw my mood as I made my way through the main floor, my boots leaving feeble tracks of melting snow. The tasks of the day had drained me, but this moment—my unofficial search—was what kept me going. No one had assigned me to find the Unregistered's family or Elin. But if I could bring them in, it would all be worth it.

My medal gave me access to most of the building, and no one questioned me as I navigated toward the quieter sections. Despite the IA's technological advancements, the department operated on a smaller budget than the elite Clan Hunter division. Its systems were efficient but lacked the elite-level accuracy I'd grown accustomed to. Even the staff here seemed less sharp, their focus scattered by the endless churn of petty infractions.

Toward the back of the building, I found a narrow alcove tucked behind a row of filing cabinets. It was quiet enough, away from prying eyes. I slid into a chair at a terminal, its holographic display springing to life with a faint shimmer. My medal gave me access to the basics, but what I needed wasn't in the official files. Fortunately, I'd come prepared.

I pulled a small, sleek tablet from my pocket, its Clan Hunter tech advanced enough to bypass and outpace the IA's security protocols. It was one of the things I had quietly taken with me as I had cleared out of my Clan Hunter quarters. With a soft click, I connected it to the terminal. The holo-display flickered, unlocking folders I had no right to access.

My pulse quickened as I searched for anything linked to the Unregistered's family or Elin. My hands moved in sharp, practiced motions. Rows of encrypted files floated in the air, shimmering slightly as I expanded, sorted, and flicked them into layered columns with a sweep of my fingers. I dragged my hand across the interface, filtering for references to them. Nothing. I rotated the data field, swiping aside duplicate logs, zooming in on metadata tags.

My eyes caught on a folder called "SASU Recon Logs." The Security Aerial Surveillance Units, or SASUs, were *Stór-menni* drones that patrolled Falinvik and surrounding areas. High-tech, precise, and ruthless. I tapped my index and middle fingers together, and the folder expanded into a grid of floating thumbnails, each labeled with timestamps and coordinates—recordings from recent patrols.

At first, the footage was underwhelming—endless city blocks, patrols capturing nothing more than pedestrians and mundane infractions. I flicked through the logs, frustration building. If the Unregistered's family and Elin were hiding, they wouldn't be in the heart of Falinvik. I needed to think broader.

On a whim, I pinched the air and dragged the map outward, shifting the focus toward the city's outer rings. It was the area where the Clan Council and those in the Chairman's inner circle made their residence. Rows of snow-covered houses scrolled past—grand estates nestled in the affluent edges of the city. It felt like a long shot, but the Unregistered's rescue party had proven resourceful. If they had allies, they could be anywhere.

One file stood out: "Restricted Footage—Northern Patrol." A curious pang stirred in my chest. The timestamp matched the days after the rescue attempt at Ginnungagap. Something about it didn't sit right—why restrict footage in such a secure, quiet area?

I slid the file forward with a flick, rotating it into view, and opened it with a double-tap. The recording started to play with sweeping views of pristine estates. Snow blanketed manicured lawns, and automated plows carved perfect paths from AHV landing platforms to front doors. Then I saw it—a sprawling mansion at the end of a street, its high-tech defenses glowing faintly. My stomach tightened.

I twisted my hand to zoom in, flicking through angles like puzzle pieces. One of the drones' recordings revealed movement in the backyard. A small group of people trudged through the snow, their heavy winter gear making them hard to identify.

That was odd. No one went for a walk in the snow and freezing cold—especially in that neighborhood.

I pinched my fingers to zoom in further. A cold knot formed in my gut as I recognized one of them—a muscular man in his twenties in heavy winter gear, his broad shoulders unmistakable. He'd been part of Elin's group at the boat dock in Auor. I recognized him from the image Thyra had shared with me during our unsuccessful night raid on Auor.

I leaned closer, the holographic interface pulsing slightly as it reacted to my proximity. It wasn't definitive, but it was enough. The Unregistered family and perhaps even Elin had to be there.

Property records confirmed the house belonged to Commander Jorik Thorne, a high-ranking member of the Clan Hunters. That explained the mansion's defenses. The Unregistered's rescue party wasn't hiding in some forgotten corner—they were here, protected by someone in the Chairman's inner circle. Thorne's name alone was enough to keep most investigators at bay. But not me.

And what a coup that would be if I discovered his involvement in aiding them.

Before I could dig further, an alarm blared—a high-pitched beeping that sent my pulse racing. I yanked the bypass tablet free, cursing under my breath. The holographic display flickered, then snapped to red—its soft shine replaced by a pulsing warning sigil.

"Unauthorized Access Detected."

Footsteps rang out—sharp, deliberate, approaching fast.

My pulse spiked. With a flick of my wrist, I collapsed the holo-interface, its light folding in on itself like burning paper. I slipped from the alcove in one smooth motion, posture relaxed, every step measured.

As I rounded the corner, I almost walked straight into Watch Commander Kolve, his imposing figure blocking the narrow hallway. His IA uniform strained against his girth, the buttons looking as though they were waging a losing battle. Startled by the sudden encounter, his gray hair fell forward, and with a quick swipe, he brushed it back into place. His sharp brown eyes locked onto mine.

"Tristan?" he said, his voice edged with suspicion. "What are you still doing here? Most of the team's already gone for the night."

"Late report," I replied, forcing an air of nonchalance. "Needed to tie up some loose ends before tomorrow."

Kolve's gaze lingered, his frown deepening. "You look like you've been at this for hours. Don't overdo it."

I nodded, offering a tight smile. "Of course."

He stepped aside, letting me pass, but the tension in his posture told me he wasn't entirely convinced. I moved briskly toward the exit, my every step measured to avoid drawing attention.

As I reached the main doors, a security drone hovered into view. Its sensors scanned me, its mechanical hum unnerving. For a split second, I thought it would stop me, but the device whirred away, its interest elsewhere.

I stepped outside, the icy wind biting at my face, but I didn't relax until I was inside my AHV. I breathed in deeply and then purposefully let out the breath slowly. That had been close. Too close.

I started the vehicle and asked it to take me to the tavern on Baldur Street. While it navigated the Falinvik's aerial traffic, I replayed the footage on my tablet, pausing at key frames. The glow of the screen cast shadows across my face. The estate loomed like a fortress, its gates lined with Valkyrie statues dusted in snow.

This was it. The Unregistered's family had to be here, protected by one of the most influential commanders in the Clan Hunters. It wasn't just a lead—it was proof.

This was my chance to make things right. To show the Chairman that I still had value.

But the blaring alarm and Kolve's suspicion weren't lost on me. I'd come close to being caught. And if I was going to pull this off, I'd have to be smarter. The stakes had never been higher, and failure wasn't an option. I had to have the Unregistered's family and Elin actually in hand this time before giving away my secret.

With the shadows of the estate lingering on the screen, one thought nagged at me: *How would I capture them without help?*

This wasn't just about sneaking around anymore. I needed a plan that wouldn't just get me access—it had to give me control. And it had to be bulletproof.

The Unregistered's family and Elin had to be my arrest. I wasn't about to let some IA squad stumble upon them or let someone else claim the victory. It was mine.

But how could I lead the raid without raising suspicions? Thorne was untouchable to most. The IA didn't move on a commander's home without undeniable evidence. I'd need something irrefutable. Something the IA couldn't ignore.

I stared at the footage, replaying the brief glimpse of Thorne's estate. Absentmindedly, I tapped my fingers on the seat's armrest. A thought began to form.

Thorne's high-tech defenses weren't just overkill—they were suspicious. If I planted the right evidence, something that made it seem like those defenses were protecting illegal weapons or contraband, the IA wouldn't hesitate to act. They would need someone experienced to lead the charge, and that someone *would* be me.

I'd spin the narrative just right. Thorne's mansion was a hub for smuggling weapons under the IA's nose. The *Stór-menni* Clan Council had strict regulations on armaments, even for those in high positions.

Kolve would have to agree. Granted, he was already suspicious, but if I tied my expertise to the success of the mission, he'd have no choice but to let me lead. After all, my experience with Clan Hunter defenses made me uniquely qualified. *Who better to breach Thorne's fortress than someone who had trained with and operated against the very technology embedded in its walls?*

I smiled to myself as the AHV reached the rundown tavern. For the first time in weeks, a flicker of satisfaction stirred in my chest.

The next day, I drafted the anonymous tip, sending it through a carefully masked channel. Within hours, whispers began circulating through the IA. Thorne's name was being mentioned in the context of unregistered weapons, and I could see the wheels turning. By evening, an operation was being discussed.

But Kolve was watching me. I could feel it. His questions from the night before lingered, his sharp gaze cutting through the casual façade I tried to maintain. And then there was the lingering tension of the alarm I'd triggered. The IA's systems hadn't fully cleared the breach. If anyone traced it back to me, everything would unravel.

That evening, as I finalized the raid's preparations, Kolve appeared at my desk, his arms crossed, his presence heavy with authority. "You've been *awfully* busy, Tristan," he said, his tone deceptively light. "Care to share what you've been working on?"

I forced a smile. "Just following up on yesterday's reports. Nothing exciting."

His eyes narrowed slightly, the weight of his suspicion palpable. "Funny. I heard there was some unusual activity in the system last night. Something about unauthorized access to restricted files."

My stomach twisted, but I kept my expression neutral. "Sounds like a glitch. The system's been acting up all week."

Kolve leaned forward slightly, his voice dropping a notch. "Glitches don't usually coincide with personnel being in places they don't belong. You wouldn't know anything about that, would you?"

My pulse quickened, but I held my ground. "Of course not. I'm just doing my job."

He didn't look convinced, but after a moment of silence, he straightened. "Well, it seems you've been selected for this Thorne operation." His tone dripped with reluctance. "And as much as I hate to admit it, you're the most qualified for the job. Your Clan Hunter experience makes you the logical choice to lead the team."

I bit back my triumphant grin and instead feigned surprise. "You're putting me in charge?"

Kolve's jaw tightened, his displeasure clear. "Don't make me regret it. This raid needs to be precise, efficient, and above all, legal. We're not giving Thorne any excuse to drag us through the mud."

I nodded, fighting to keep the satisfaction out of my voice. "Understood. I'll make sure everything is by the book."

"You'd better," he said, his gaze hard. "And, Tristan? If I find out you're playing games, it won't end well for you."

"Of course," I replied smoothly, my voice steady despite the tension coiled in my chest.

Kolve lingered for a moment, as if waiting for me to slip up. When I didn't, he turned on his heel and walked away, leaving me alone at my desk. I exhaled slowly, my grip on the edge of the desk relaxing.

He was onto me, but it didn't matter. By the time he figured out what I was really doing, it would be too late. I'd have the Unregistered's family and Elin—and the victory I needed to reclaim my place.

With the shadows of Thorne's estate burned into my mind, I reviewed my plan one last time. Tomorrow, I'd set it all in motion.

EIGHT

The Hall

ELIN

The clang of wooden swords echoed through the underground chamber, punctuated by Sigrid's sharp commands. Sweat dripped down my temple, and my fingers tightened on the hilt of the training weapon. Across from me, Sigrid moved with a grace and ferocity that felt untouchable. Her strikes were precise, her movements fluid, and her eyes sharp as a blade.

Who knew she could fight this way? From the moment I met her, Sigrid had exuded authority and strength; her skill in forging medals —especially Dormant ones—was nothing short of remarkable. But seeing her fight was something else entirely: every movement honed, every strike as swift and sure as a blade.

I'd sparred with Nodin before, and while Sigrid's technique was razor-sharp, refined through years of visible discipline, Nodin fought with a different kind of mastery. His movements weren't polished in the same way, but they flowed too naturally to be untrained. It made me wonder how much Nodin had trained before coming to Falinvik, and why he rarely talked about it.

"Focus, Elli!" she barked, her voice cutting through the haze of my exhaustion. "You're too slow. If you keep hesitating, you won't survive your next encounter with the *Stór-menni*."

I shifted my stance, my legs trembling slightly from the constant motion. "I'm trying."

"Trying isn't enough." She lunged, her weapon arcing toward me with deadly accuracy. I barely managed to block, the impact jarring my arms. "You have an advantage no one else has," she continued, her tone as relentless as her attacks. "Your ability can show you your opponent's moves before they make them. *But you have to use it*."

I nodded, gritting my teeth as I stepped back, narrowly avoiding another strike. Sigrid had insisted we train this way—combining combat with the use of my temporal vision. She believed that if I could master seeing quick bursts of the future while under pressure, it would become my greatest weapon. But so far, all it felt like was a constant battle against my own mind.

"Again," Sigrid commanded, stepping back to give me room to reset.

I closed my eyes for a brief moment, centering myself. The faint pressure of my medallion against my chest was a steady reminder of my *megin*. The world around me shifted as I reached for my temporal vision, threads of possible futures flickering at the edges of my mind.

Sigrid moved. I saw it—the arc of her blade, the shift of her weight. I adjusted, raising my sword to block before she even started the motion. The wooden swords collided with a resounding crack, and a flicker of triumph surged in my chest.

Sigrid smiled, "Well done! I may not say it often, but you've come a long way in a short time."

I let out a breath and lowered my sword. The praise caught me off guard, and didn't do much to settle the swirl of questions still pressing at the edge of my mind.

"Sigrid," I said, hesitating as she turned away. "Can I ask you something?"

She paused, waiting.

The others had filtered out already, but I still lowered my voice.

"It's about *Ljós*. I know it needs to stay hidden. I drink Brigitta's tea every morning to keep the glow down. I don't say a word about it to anyone who doesn't already know. I've done everything I'm supposed to. But when it pulses, or spikes, or does something I wasn't expecting...what then?"

Sigrid slowly straightened, then turned to face me. Her expression was unreadable. "You're already doing more than most could in your position."

"That's not the point," I said. "You and Nodin—you're the only others like me that I know. If I'm not supposed to use *Ljós*, then fine. But if I *am*...if I might *need* to...shouldn't I be learning how? Because right now, it feels like I'm flying blind."

"It's not that simple," she said gently. "Training *Ljós* isn't like practicing with a sword or with your *megin*. It takes time. Discipline. A stillness you don't get from short bursts between missions."

"I'm not asking to become an expert overnight. I just... I need to understand what I'm carrying around."

Sigrid stepped closer. "You're carrying something powerful. And constant. *Ljós* doesn't answer to the moon gods. You've noticed that, haven't you? Your abilities don't waver—even when the moon does."

I nodded slowly. "Yeah. I thought it meant something was wrong with me."

"It doesn't. It means you're Dormant. We don't fade. Not with the moon, not with time. But that steadiness also makes us volatile if we're not ready."

I looked down at my hands, suddenly aware of the pulse humming beneath my skin.

"That's why you haven't trained me?" I asked. "Because I'm not ready?"

"Because it's not safe," she said. "For you. For the others. For the Resistance. If we were somewhere else...if we had months, not moments...I'd train you every day."

"And here?"

Sigrid's eyes held mine. "Here, you do what you've been doing.

Stay quiet. Stay steady. And when the time comes...we *will* train you."

Her words echoed in the silence that followed, and for a moment, I let them settle. *Stay steady. Wait for the right time.*

It reminded me just how quickly everything had changed. It had only been a few days in *Mannlegur* time since I'd journeyed to Skogly.

Going to Sigrid had been Aedan's sister Claire's idea. I could still hear her voice, calm and steady, urging me to go. *"Go to Skogly, Elin. You'll be safe there. Find Sigrid. She can forge you the medal you need to gain control and block the Chairman from your visions. And stay there, no matter what happens."* Claire had always been like that—a pillar of strength, unshakable and pragmatic, even when the world seemed to crumble around her.

Would she ever have imagined me here, in Falinvik, training with Sigrid instead of hiding in Skogly as she'd urged? I doubted it. Claire had believed I'd be out of harm's way, tucked far from the dangers of the Chairman and the *Stór-menni*. But fate, or my own stubbornness, had pulled me straight into the heart of the storm.

The thought of Claire sent my mind spinning. *Where was she now? Where were the Gradys? Were they still safe, still hidden? Or had the Stór-menni already found them?* My heart twisted as a wave of uncertainty crashed over me.

The question lingered, pressing against the edges of my consciousness, and before I could pull back, a vision surged forward in a blur of white, dragging me into its relentless grip.

I was no longer in the training chamber. The air turned colder, crisper, and the weak scent of polished wood and burning birch filled my senses. I found myself hovering above a grand room with vaulted ceilings supported by beams of dark oak. The walls were adorned with intricate carvings of runes and mythological scenes, each panel a testament to the wealth and power of the home's owner.

A fire crackled in the stone hearth, its flickering warmth unable to dispel the sharp tension between the two figures in the room. One of them, a middle-aged man with an imposing presence, stood near the flames. His thick black cloak, trimmed with silver fur, bore the Chairman's insignia on its front, a symbol of his power and influence. The Clan Hunter medallion resting proudly on his chest further marked him as a figure of high rank and authority.

As part of my training, the Resistance had drilled me on the ranks, medals, and uniforms that defined the hierarchy of Falinvik, and this man embodied the upper echelon. His pale blue eyes, cold and calculating, locked intently on the person standing opposite him.

Tristan.

He was dressed in the black uniform of Clan Internal Affairs, the cloak's hood pushed back to reveal his sandy brown hair and pale green eyes. His features were set in an expression of controlled authority, but there was a sharpness in his gaze that made it clear he wasn't here to make small talk.

"I don't appreciate the insinuation, Investigator," the man said, his voice low and even, though the threat in it was unmistakable. "You come into my home, accuse me of smuggling weapons and harboring fugitives, and expect me to simply roll over?"

Tristan didn't flinch. "I don't expect anything, Commander Thorne. But the fact remains—fugitives have been traced to this area, and your house is the only logical place they could hide."

Thorne's lips twitched in something that might have been amusement or disdain. "Logical, perhaps, but unfounded. If you think I would jeopardize my position by aiding fugitive Clan members, you're sorely mistaken."

My gaze drifted past the two men, drawn to the far corner of the room. A backpack sat partially hidden behind a large chair, its faded fabric and patched straps unmistakable. My heart raced as I recognized it. It was Claire's. The Gradys *were* there.

So many questions buzzed in my brain. *Why were they at this Clan Hunter's home? Had he captured them? Why wasn't he given them up to Tristan?*

Tristan's voice interrupted my thoughts. "You'll forgive me if I don't take your word for it," he said, his tone cool but edged with steel. "We both know the Chairman doesn't tolerate traitors, no matter how high their rank."

Thorne stepped closer, his towering presence casting a shadow over Tristan. "And we both know that the Chairman values results over theatrics. Considering your recent...missteps, I have little patience for more of your dramatics—wasn't the fiasco at Ginnungagap enough for you? But fine. If you're so certain of your accusations, search the house. But when you find nothing, you'll owe me more than an apology."

The air between them was electric, charged with the weight of unspoken threats. Tristan didn't move, his pale green eyes locked on Thorne's, as if trying to read the man's thoughts. Then, without a word, he turned and left the room, his cloak billowing behind him.

The vision shifted slightly, and I saw the hallway beyond. Tristan's expression darkened as he pulled a small device from his pocket—a scanner of some kind. He glanced over his shoulder before activating it, the device emitting a faint hum as it swept the area. He was searching for something, anything, to confirm his suspicions.

My focus returned to the room just as Thorne moved toward the chair. He bent down, his hand brushing against the backpack, but before he could do anything else, I yanked the ripcord of my vision.

The training chamber snapped back into focus. The wooden sword was an inch from my face, and Sigrid's voice cut through the haze.

"Elin!" she barked, her frustration palpable. "What are you doing?"

I stumbled back, my breath coming in short, sharp gasps. The weight of the vision still pressed against my mind, but Sigrid's glare demanded my attention.

"You can't stay in your visions for that long," she continued, lowering her weapon. "Do you have any idea how dangerous that is? If this were a real fight, you'd be dead—or worse."

"I'm sorry," I managed, the words tumbling out in a rush. "I—I saw something."

Sigrid's eyes narrowed. "You're supposed to see my movements, not wander off into some other time."

"No, this was different." I stepped closer, my voice urgent. "I saw Tristan. He's going to raid Commander Thorne's house. And the Gradys...they're there. I'm sure of it."

Her expression shifted, the frustration giving way to something sharper, more focused. "You're sure?"

I nodded, the image of the backpack burned into my mind. "They're hiding there. But Tristan's close. If we don't move fast..."

Sigrid didn't wait for me to finish. She turned toward the door, her voice clipped and commanding. "We need to act now. Get your gear. If you're wrong, we'll deal with it. But if you're right..."

She didn't need to say the rest. We both knew what was at stake.

The freezing wind whipped with falling snow into a frenzy, stinging my face as we crouched behind a cluster of dense pines overlooking Commander Thorne's estate. Snow and ice crunched faintly underfoot as Sigrid signaled for us to move closer. Her hand gestures were precise, her steely eyes scanning the estate for any signs of movement. I tightened the strap on my cloak, trying to ignore the tension knotting in my stomach.

My breath puffed in the cold air, each exhale clouding my line of sight for a moment before fading into the dark. The familiar weight of the medallion under my cloak grounded me, but it wasn't quite enough to settle the nerves twisting in my gut.

My fingers fumbled inside my cloak, seeking the small flask Brigitta had given me for my *Ljós* tea. The tea sloshed faintly as I pulled it out, its herbal scent and warmth a brief reprieve from the biting cold. I took a quick swig to dull the edge of my *Ljós* light—it wouldn't do for any other Dormants to notice me now. Especially since, according to Nodin, the brightness of my *Ljós* was a little hard to ignore. Frequent sips of the tea were crucial for me in Falinvik, and weirdly, it had become a comfort. Even so, my thoughts were scattered, racing between the vision and the fear that we were already too late.

Nodin leaned closer, his breath visible in the frigid air. "See anything yet?" he whispered. His voice was steady, but there was a flicker of something else in his tone—something heavier, as if he was hoping for an answer to a question he wasn't asking aloud.

I shook my head, gripping the edge of my cloak tighter. "Not yet."

The tea might have masked my *Ljós*, but it did nothing to ease the sinking feeling that time wasn't on our side. The vision had seemed so clear, so urgent. But now, as we crept toward the sprawling, rune-etched mansion, doubt gnawed at me. *What if we were too late? What if my vision hadn't been of the future?*

The wind picked up, cutting through my cloak like a blade. I shivered, pulling it tighter around me. Nodin noticed, stepping closer until our shoulders brushed.

"You'll freeze at this rate," he murmured, draping his own cloak over both of us.

I stiffened at the unexpected closeness. My heart raced, not just from the cold, but from the way his presence seemed to fill the space around me. His warmth seeped through the layers, but something about the gesture felt weighted, like he wasn't just shielding me from the temperature. I glanced up at him, but his gaze was distant, locked onto the estate ahead. For a brief moment, I wondered if there was something—or someone—he was thinking about that he hadn't spoken of.

"Thanks," I said, my voice barely audible over the wind. He didn't reply, but his silence held an unspoken depth.

The house was eerily quiet, its high-tech walls glowing faintly with embedded runes. The front gates were slightly ajar, and faint trails of bootprints marred the pristine snow leading away from the back of the house.

Sigrid held up her hand, signaling for us to stop. "We're too late," she whispered, her voice low and grim.

My heart sank as we crept closer, staying within the cover of the trees. From our vantage point, we could see IA troopers methodically packing up equipment into their sleek black hovercrafts. The scene was one of precision, the troopers moving with practiced efficiency. A group of people was being led from the house, their forms blurred by the distance and the falling snow.

I strained my eyes, hoping to catch a glimpse of familiar faces, but they were too far away. The swirling snow obscured everything beyond the outlines of cloaks and the faint shimmer of weapons held by the IA troopers.

"They've got them," I whispered, a lump forming in my throat. "The Gradys—they've been captured."

Sigrid's jaw tightened. "There is nothing more we can do here." She motioned for us to pull back, her sharp gaze lingering on the scene for a moment longer before she turned and led us away.

The Resistance transport had dropped us well short of Thorne's to keep us off the patrols' radar. It made sense—until we were the ones left slogging through the snow to reach the pick-up point. Even with the Clan's weather-resistant cloaks and boots, the best there was, the cold still found the cracks. It crept into our muscles, numbed our fingers, and turned every step into a fight against exhaustion. We'd stopped talking a while ago, saving what little energy we had.

Then, through the blur of falling snow, a warm glimmer emerged —soft at first, then brighter, like it had been waiting for us. A sign swayed lazily in the wind, casting golden light across the drifts like a promise. *Odin's Horn.* It looked less like a mead hall and more like a rescue. I could've kissed it.

Without a word, Sigrid led us toward the hall. My boots

crunched through the snow, the cold biting at my cheeks, and settling deep in my bones. Each step felt heavier than the last, dragged down by the image of the Gradys being led away—helpless, outnumbered, lost. The lights ahead pulled my focus, sharp and steady, a reminder that the world kept spinning no matter who it left behind.

When we finally reached the door, the mead hall's warmth hit us like a shock—laughter and firelight spilling into the night, as if nothing outside had changed. A jarring contrast to the icy disappointment that clung to all of us like frost.

As we slipped further inside, the shift from the biting cold to the smoky, crowded heat was almost dizzying. Snow steamed off our cloaks and boots, puddling at our feet as we peeled back hoods and shrugged off layers stiff with frost. I flexed my numb fingers, feeling them sting as the blood rushed back in.

Around us, the faint hum of aerial droids buzzed through the air, weaving between the long wooden tables like oversized bees in a hive. They ferried trays of food and drink through the raucous crowd, their small engines whirring above the clink of horns and bursts of laughter.

One zoomed dangerously close to Nodin, who ducked with a scowl.

"Wonderful," he muttered. "As if we weren't already low enough, now the machines are mocking us."

Bae smirked, nodding toward a droid zipping past with its tray. "Careful, Nodin. You'll hurt its feelings, and then it might 'accidentally' spill boiling soup in your lap."

Nodin threw her a look of mock indignation. "Great. Droids with a grudge. That's exactly what we need."

Sigrid didn't even glance back, her focus already on the crowded hall. With a sharp, decisive motion, she claimed an open spot at one of the long wooden tables that stretched the length of the room. Dropping onto the bench with a heavy sigh, she scanned the bustling crowd, her sharp eyes taking everything in, even as she motioned for the rest of us to sit.

"Well, that was a bust," Nodin muttered, slumping onto the bench beside me. He ran a hand down his damp, dark braid, frustration etched into his handsome features.

"We didn't have enough time for a good plan," Bae said bluntly, taking a seat across from him. Her angular features were still set in a scowl, strands of her short, black hair sticking to her damp forehead.

Her words lingered in the air, but they didn't feel like the whole picture. My mind turned back to the scene at Thorne's estate, replaying the tension between him and Tristan, the way he'd deflected every accusation with unnerving ease. There was something I couldn't shake, something that didn't add up. "Why would someone like Thorne—a Clan Hunter commander—help the Gradys?" I asked, breaking the silence. "It doesn't make any sense."

Nodin raised an eyebrow, tearing into a piece of bread that had just been delivered by a droid. "It doesn't, unless there's something we don't know about him."

Bae leaned forward, her sharp features illuminated by the radiance of the central fire pit. "Or something we don't know about the Gradys," she added, her tone contemplative.

Sigrid's expression didn't change, but there was a flicker of something in her eyes—a knowing glint that passed too quickly to catch. She took a deliberate sip of mead from the horn she grabbed from a passing droid before answering, her voice measured. "There are layers to every allegiance in Falinvik. People are rarely what they seem on the surface."

"That's a cryptic non-answer if I've ever heard one," Nodin muttered, earning a warning glance from Sigrid.

I frowned, my fingers fidgeting with the edge of my cloak. "But you know something, don't you?" I pressed, my eyes searching Sigrid's face. "About Thorne. About why he'd risk everything to protect them."

Sigrid met my gaze evenly, but her lips thinned into a tight line. "I know enough to say this—what Thorne did is bigger than we can unpack here. But right now, it doesn't matter why. What matters is finding the Gradys before it's too late."

Her words hung in the air, heavy with unspoken implications. My chest tightened, the weight of our failure pressing down even harder. But I nodded, recognizing that Sigrid wasn't going to reveal more—at least not yet.

My thoughts kept churning. "The Gradys *were* there. I saw their things. That backpack—"

"And now they're not," Sigrid interrupted, her tone cutting but not unkind. She leaned her elbows on the table, her cloak pooling around her. "We've lost the advantage. But we'll regroup and decide on our next move."

A droid zipped past, its flat tray laden with plates of roasted meat and bread. Bae reached out, snatching a plate and a horn of mead with practiced ease. "Regroup," she muttered, tearing a chunk of bread off with her teeth. "That's code for figuring out how to fix this mess."

"We don't have a choice," Sigrid said, her voice firm. "The Gradys are still out there. Wherever the IA is taking them, we'll find them. We're not done."

Nodin let out a bitter laugh, slouching against the back of the bench. "Sure, because tailing a fully armed IA convoy sounds like a breeze. What's next? Asking them politely to hand the Gradys over?" His words were laced with frustration, but there was something else there too—something almost... resigned. Like he wasn't just frustrated about the Gradys, but about something deeper. The thought gnawed at me, but before I could press, he smirked, lifting his horn of mead. "To regrouping, then. And to making sure the next plan actually works."

"Enough," Sigrid snapped, her glare silencing him. "You think this is hard? It's nothing compared to what's at stake. If the IA figures out who the Gradys are—who Liam is—we'll have more than just a failed mission to answer for."

Her words hung heavy in the air, and for a moment, none of us spoke. What did she mean '*who Liam is*'? Who *was* Mr. Grady? I knew he'd been part of Clan Protective Services before the Gradys escaped from Falinvik—that much had been shared. But the way Sigrid spoke, it felt like there was more to the story, something deeper and far more dangerous. I glanced at her, hoping for some clarification, but her sharp gaze made it clear she wasn't offering any more answers.

Around us, the hall reverberated with life, the sounds of camaraderie and indulgence starkly at odds with the tension at our table. I forced myself to take in the scene, trying to distract from the knot tightening in my chest. The mead hall was enormous, its vaulted ceiling supported by dark wooden beams carved with runes that seemed to glow faintly in the firelight. A long central fire pit crackled, its flames licking upward and casting dancing shadows on the stone walls. The iron chandeliers hovering near the ceiling hummed softly, their warm light illuminating the packed tables below.

A droid bard stood in one corner, its polished bronze and wood form strumming a lyre. Its face, a smooth runic panel, shimmered slightly as it sang an old Nordri ballad in a hauntingly perfect tone. The patrons didn't seem to mind its artificial presence, raising their horns and clapping in time to the music.

Aerial droids zipped between the tables, balancing trays of food and drink with uncanny precision. One swooped low, depositing a plate of spiced potatoes and a horn of mead in front of Nodin. He didn't bother thanking it, muttering instead, "Finally. At least the drones know how to do their job."

Bae snorted, picking at her plate. "They're efficient because they're programmed to be. We, on the other hand, are very much human."

"And failing spectacularly," Nodin shot back, his tone bitter.

I shifted uncomfortably, staring down at the bread on my plate. "It's not over yet," I said softly, my voice faltering. "The Gradys are still somewhere out there."

As the others debated the mission's failure, I felt Nodin's eyes on me. When I finally glanced his way, he leaned in slightly, his voice low enough for only me to hear. "You're harder on yourself than anyone else here. You know that, right?"

I swallowed, unable to hold his gaze for long. "Maybe I deserve to be," I said, staring down at the untouched bread on my plate.

"You don't," he said firmly, his tone softer now. There was something in his expression that made my chest ache—like he wanted to say more but couldn't. Before I could respond, he leaned back, the moment slipping away as easily as it had come.

"The IA is still a step ahead of us," Sigrid said. "But that doesn't mean we stop. This is what the Resistance does. We adapt. We find a way."

Her words resonated, pushing through the haze of doubt. I clenched my fists under the table. I couldn't change what had happened, but I could make sure it didn't end here.

Bae raised her horn, her expression grim. "To adapting."

Nodin raised his own horn with a smirk. "And to the free food. At least the *Stór-menni* give us that much."

"Generous of them," Bae said dryly, taking a sip. "Two plates and three horns per visit. Just enough to keep everyone thinking life here isn't completely rigged."

I'd learned that it was a standard ration at a Clan tavern provided by the *Stór-menni's* system. The policy was supposed to ensure no one went hungry, a shining example of the Clan's commitment to equality. But as I'd already learned, equality was a relative term in Falinvik.

"It's generous, sure," Nodin muttered, gesturing toward the droids delivering food and drink. "But let's not forget, there's a reason the higher-ups have estates like Thorne's while we're sitting here hoping a hovering tin can doesn't spill mead on us."

"It's all part of the *Stór-menni's* illusion of fairness," Sigrid said, her voice sharp but not loud enough to carry beyond the table. "They give just enough to keep most people content. Food, housing, healthcare, transportation—all provided, but the quality and comfort aren't uniform. The more you bow down to the Chairman, the higher your rank, the higher your rank, the better the perks. And the rest of us are left fighting over scraps."

"Well," Nodin said with a wry grin, "at least the scraps are served with a generous helping of false hope. Pairs nicely with disappointment, don't you think?"

Their banter brought a faint smile to my lips, but it didn't erase the weight in my chest. I stared at the horn of mead in front of me, my fingers tracing absent patterns in the condensation. The weight in my chest wasn't just the mission's failure—it was the gnawing guilt that twisted tighter with every passing second. I hadn't touched my food or drink, and the others had started to notice.

"This is my fault," I said finally, breaking the silence that had settled over the table like a thick fog. My voice was low, strained. "If I had realized the vision was happening in the present and not the future—if I'd been faster, clearer—we could've done something. We might have stopped them from taking the Gradys."

Sigrid's sharp gaze pinned me, her expression unreadable. For a moment, I thought she might agree, and the thought made my stomach churn.

"Elli," she said firmly, her voice cutting through my spiraling thoughts. "Stop. You're not to blame for this."

Bae leaned forward, her dark brown eyes steady as she met my gaze. "She's right. Without your vision, we wouldn't have even known where to start. We'd still be stumbling around, chasing dead ends."

"But we were too late," I said, my voice cracking. "What's the point of seeing if I can't act in time? What good am I to any of you if my power just—just shows me things I can't fix?"

Nodin reached across the table, his hand brushing against mine. His dark braid hung loose over one shoulder, and his expression softened in a way that almost surprised me. "Elli, listen to me. You're not a machine. You can't just flip a switch and know exactly what's happening when. Your visions—they're complicated. No one here expects you to have all the answers."

His words were reassuring, but for the briefest moment, something flickered in his eyes—like he wasn't just talking about me. Like he knew exactly what it was like to carry the weight of something bigger than himself, something he couldn't always control. Before I could ask, he leaned back, the moment slipping away as quickly as it had come.

"And no one blames you for what happened today," Sigrid added, her tone softer than usual. "The IA moved faster than any of us anticipated. That's on them, not you."

Bae gestured toward the droid bard in the corner, her lips quirking into a faint, wry smile. "If anyone's to blame, it's probably that guy for singing about heroes while we're sitting here with empty hands."

The attempt at humor coaxed a reluctant smile from me, though it was fleeting. "It just... feels like I should have known. Like I should have done better."

Sigrid leaned forward, her presence commanding but not overwhelming. "Do you know what I see when I look at you?" she asked, her piercing gaze holding mine. "I see someone who's been through more in a matter of weeks than most people endure in a lifetime. Someone who's learning to wield a power that's rare and unpredictable, all while trying to save people who mean everything to her. And despite all of that, you're still here. Still fighting."

Her words hit me harder than I expected. I swallowed the lump rising in my throat and nodded faintly, though I didn't entirely believe her yet.

"She's right, you know," Nodin said, his smirk returning. "Without you, we'd just be sitting around, probably arguing over which tavern to visit next and pretending we know what we're doing."

"And drinking bad mead," Bae added dryly. "This place is at least tolerable."

The corners of my mouth twitched, and I finally reached for the horn of mead, taking a small sip. It was warm, sweet, and slightly spiced, the taste grounding me in the moment.

"Thanks," I murmured, my voice barely audible over the din of the hall. "All of you."

Sigrid's nod was curt but approving, and she leaned back, her gaze shifting to the fire pit at the center of the room. "We'll figure this out," she said, her voice steady. "This is a setback, not the end."

As the aerial droids zipped by, carrying plates of food and drink to the rowdy patrons, I let the warmth of the fire seep into my bones. The failure still lingered, but it didn't feel quite as suffocating. For now, I had a moment to breathe, to regroup, and to prepare for whatever came next. Because Sigrid was right—this wasn't the end.

NINE

The Escape

ELIN

The hiss of steam from the geothermal pipes at the Resistance base seemed louder than usual as I slid into my narrow bunk, the echoes filling the cramped space like an unwelcome reminder of everything we'd lost. The mead hall's warmth and noise had faded, leaving only the bitter taste of failure clinging to the edges of my mind. The tight quarters, with their creaking metal beds and faint scent of damp stone, had once been a strange sort of comfort—an anchor in the chaos of Falinvik. But tonight, even that familiarity couldn't calm the restless energy thrumming through me. Not after seeing the Gradys taken. Not after realizing how close we'd come... and how far away they still were.

I dug around my Clan backpack and found my phone. I turned it on. The screen illuminated, showing that, miraculously, I had one bar, just enough service to get a message through to Anders. Daily updates had been part of the deal when I told him I was leaving Skogly, where I was going, and why. Technically, given the Falinvik's weird time flow, it meant Anders was getting about seven messages a day—but I don't think he minded. For me, it was a comforting link to home, a small piece of my normal life to hold onto.

I typed a quick message:

> Hi Andee - Back at base. Mission = . IA snatched the Gradys before we could get to them. You're probably now spiraling but relax—I'm fine. Tired and annoyed, but FINE.
>
> Sigrid already on it with a new plan.
>
> Love you . Don't stress too much (just enough so I know I'm your favorite sibling).

With a ding, Andee's reply popped through:

> Hi Elli — getting the Gradys is bad. Really bad. Glad Sigrid's got a plan, but don't take unnecessary risks. Promise me you'll be careful. You're more important than any mission.
>
> And you know you are my fav… even if you are a pain. Keep me updated. Always.

I sent a quick reply.

> Promise.

I turned the phone off to conserve its battery and tucked it back into my bag. I pressed my hand against the medallion on my chest, the cool surface grounding me as I closed my eyes. My focus drifted toward the Gradys, their faces swimming through a sea of guilt and uncertainty that plagued me. They had to be somewhere, and I needed to find them.

Taking a deep breath, I reached for my *megin*, letting its faint warmth build in my chest. I focused on the Gradys, willing my vision to show me something—anything. The air around me seemed to thicken as I pushed harder, the pressure in my head building with every passing second.

But no matter how hard I tried, the same vision came rushing back in a blur of white, unbidden: Tristan and Thorne. The tension between them crackled like a live wire, and Claire's backpack sat in the corner, screaming at me to take action. *Why did this vision come so easily when what I needed lay just out of reach?*

I clenched my fists, my nails biting into my palms. "Not them," I whispered through gritted teeth. "The Gradys. Show me the Gradys."

I tried again and again, but eventually, exhaustion overpowered my will. My eyes grew heavy, and a fitful dream overtook me.

I FOUND MYSELF STANDING IN A STRANGE, EVER-SHIFTING place. Claire, Edvin, and Mrs. Grady were huddled together, their faces tense with worry. The space around them refused to stay still. One moment, they were in a dimly lit tavern, the scent of ale and woodsmoke heavy in the air. The next, they stood in a sunlit garden, flowers blooming in impossible hues. Then, a bedroom with a quilted bedspread, the walls lined with bookshelves. The scenes blurred together, overlapping and twisting, as though I was looking through a kaleidoscope.

"Where are you?" I breathed, trying to steady myself against the dizzying shift of surroundings.

Claire turned to me, her expression urgent. Her lips moved, forming words I couldn't make out as the dream started to slip away. She pointed behind me, her gestures frantic. Before I could turn to see what she was indicating, a sound woke me, leaving me gasping in the cold of my bunk room.

I sat up, clutching the edge of the bed. My breath came in shallow gasps, my heart racing as the dream fragments swirled in my mind. *Was that a vision or just a dream? What did it mean? Why had the setting been so disjointed, so surreal?*

Before I could unravel the puzzle, muffled voices sounded from Sigrid's cabin next door. I strained to make out the words, but the metal walls distorted them. Wrapping my cloak around me to ward off the chill, I slipped out of bed and padded toward the door.

The hallway was dimly lit, the faint hum of machinery vibrating through the subway walls. I followed the sound of the voices to Sigrid's cabin, its door ajar. Peering inside, I saw McHaill standing near her small desk, his blue cloak catching the light. Sigrid was leaning against her hovering bed, her arms crossed, her face unreadable.

"...confirmed," McHaill was saying in his low, measured tone. "The convoy stopped at Skjoldur before dawn. It matches the spotter reports."

Sigrid's eyes narrowed. "And you're sure? We can't afford a wild chase."

"I wouldn't bring it to you if I wasn't," McHaill replied. "This is our best lead."

"Skjoldur," I murmured, stepping into the room. Both heads snapped toward me, Sigrid's brows lifting in mild surprise.

"Elli?" she asked. "What are you doing up?"

"I heard you," I admitted, glancing between them. "Skjoldur?"

McHaill exchanged a glance with Sigrid before answering. "The IA took last night's detainees there."

My stomach twisted. The Gradys. "Do we have a plan?"

"Not yet," Sigrid admitted, crossing her arms. "We need blueprints of the detention center before we can move. It's too dangerous to go in blind."

"And do we have them?" I asked, though the answer was already clear from Sigrid's tense expression.

"Not yet," Sigrid said. "But I know someone who might be able to help."

Her words hung in the air, and I didn't miss the flicker of unease that crossed her face. Whoever this contact was, they came with complications.

Before I could press further, a door creaked open down the hall. I turned to see Nodin striding toward us, fully dressed and startlingly awake. His hair was neatly combed back into his braid, his boots laced, as though he'd never gone to bed at all. He looked irritatingly good—composed, that is. *How could someone look so put together after the day we'd had?* My stomach twisted as I glanced away, frustrated with myself for noticing. *Not the time, Elin.*

"What's all the noise?" Nodin asked, his tone casual, but his sharp eyes betrayed his alertness. He didn't look the least bit groggy, unlike Bae, who appeared in the hallway moments later, stifling a yawn.

"Nodin, you're—" I started, but he cut me off with a small grin.

"Early riser," he said simply, but there was something in his voice, something evasive.

Bae crossed her arms, her watchful eyes scanning the room. "If this is about the Gradys, we're in."

Sigrid sighed, pinching the bridge of her nose. "It's not that simple. The contact is in Baldur Street."

"That's all the more reason not to go alone," I said firmly. "You'll need backup, and we're coming with you."

Nodin nodded. "Elli's right. If this contact can help, then we're better off going as a team. Besides," he added with a smirk, "we've already been to Baldur Street once."

Sigrid's lips pressed into a thin line, but before she could argue, she relented. "Fine," she said, her tone heavy with resignation. "But keep a low profile. We can't afford to draw attention. So, Elli, take a *few* sips of Brigitta's tea."

I gave a quick nod in reply and headed back to my room before Sigrid could change her mind. As we geared up, I couldn't shake the feeling that Nodin was keeping something from us. But there was no time to dwell on it—not when the Gradys needed us.

~

The streets of Baldur were a contrast of old-world charm and shadowy allure. The cobblestones glistened under the faint neon lights buzzing overhead, casting an eerie brightness over the carved wooden facades of the tightly packed buildings. Baldur Street, as it turned out, was more of a large neighborhood than one street. A labyrinth of twisting alleys and hidden entrances, where whispers carried secrets as easily as the wind carried the smell of fried street food. It was the sort of place where you kept a firm grip on your wallet—and weapon if you had one.

Sigrid led the way with purpose, her Clan cloak drawn firmly around her shoulders, while Bae and Nodin followed closely. I stayed just behind them, my eyes wide as I took in the sights of the infamous district.

Carved serpents and dragons intertwined on every wooden beam, their glowing eyes seeming to follow us as we passed. The dark timber buildings were crowded together, their eaves jutting like teeth. It made me think of Mia's architectural word for it—Dragestil. She would have loved this. A sudden ache for my friends and family formed in my chest. At least they were safe in Skogly and Auor.

Between the buildings, signs flickered and pulsed, promising fighting pits and high-stakes games. A distraction for the desperate—Sigrid called it, the *Stór-menni's* moral blind spot. As long as people had their vices, no one noticed the cracks.

We'd been on Baldur's market street once before, our first day in Falinvik. The day we'd almost rescued Aedan. But we'd never waded this far into the shadowy world.

"Do people actually live here?" I whispered, leaning toward Nodin.

He smirked, but it didn't quite reach his eyes. "Live, survive, thrive—depends on your perspective. It has a kind of charm if you know where to look." There was something in his tone, a familiarity I couldn't place. Had he spent time in places like this before?

"Yeah, charming like a snake pit," Bae muttered, keeping her sharp eyes scanning the alleys.

Sigrid stopped in front of an unassuming door nestled between a pawnshop and what appeared to be an abandoned antiquities store. Above the door, a wooden sign read *Saga's Oasis* in elegant script, with a smaller holographic marquee beneath it flashing *Explore Any World You Can Imagine!* in bright gold letters.

"This is it," Sigrid said, her voice low. She pushed open the door, and we stepped into a dimly lit lobby filled with an odd mix of smells —incense, metallic oil, and something faintly citrusy.

The atmosphere was a blend of old Norse aesthetics and cutting-edge technology. The main room was dimly lit, with wooden beams carved in serpentine dragons and swords arching overhead. At the center of the room was a long bar made of polished dark wood, inlaid with luminescent screens that scrolled through drink options. Behind the bar, several machines with blinking lights offered a variety of cocktails. High above them were shelves lined with bottles of traditional *Mannlegur* spirits, unusual for Falinvik.

The seating area consisted of low, carved tables surrounded by plush, mismatched sofas. In one corner, a towering statue of Fenrir, the legendary Norse wolf, watched. Its green eyes flickered—probably hiding lenses underneath, scanning the patrons who milled about, laughing, drinking, or whispering in hushed tones. To the left was a row of doors marked with incandescent numbers—my guess, private holo rooms. Through half-open doors, I caught glimpses of surreal scenes—a jungle here, a gambling table at a saloon there.

"Cozy," Nodin quipped, glancing around. "Definitely screams 'trustworthy establishment.'"

"I think it's amazing," I said, marveling at the seamless blend of ancient and futuristic. "It's like stepping into a dream."

"Or a nightmare," Bae muttered, eyeing a shifty figure who slipped out of one of the holo rooms.

Sigrid didn't comment. She strode up to the bar and rapped her knuckles against the wood. Then she tilted her head toward the back. The bartender, a man whose rolled-up sleeves revealed heavily tattooed arms in runic patterns, nodded and disappeared through a hidden panel behind the bar. Moments later, a woman emerged from the back—a striking figure with short, jagged silver hair, sharp features, and piercing green eyes that matched the wolf statue.

"Well, well," the woman said, her voice smooth and laced with amusement. "Sigrid. To what do I owe the pleasure?"

"Saga," Sigrid said curtly. "We need to talk. Privately."

Saga's gaze flicked to the rest of us, her smile widening. "And you've brought friends. Charming ones, too." Her eyes lingered on Nodin, who gave her a cheeky grin and a mock bow.

"We don't have time for games," Sigrid said firmly. "It's urgent."

Saga's smile didn't falter, but her eyes hardened. "Urgency doesn't make me more inclined to help, you know. Why don't you tell me what this is about?"

Leaning closer to Saga to make sure no other patron overheard, Sigrid whispered bluntly, "We need the blueprints to the Skjoldur detention center."

Saga raised an eyebrow and let out a low whistle. "That's a tall order. Skjoldur's tech isn't exactly easy to bypass, even for me."

"You can do it," Sigrid said, her tone brooking no argument.

Saga leaned against the bar, crossing her arms. "Oh, I can. The question is, why should I? Sticking my neck out this far is risky."

"You owe me," Sigrid said, her voice like steel.

Saga hesitated, her confident veneer faltering for a split second. "That was a long time ago," she said softly. "Things are different now."

"Not different enough to erase what I did for you," Sigrid countered. "This isn't just about me, Saga. Lives are at stake."

Saga's green eyes flicked between us, and for a moment, the only sound was the faint hum of the holo rooms and the muffled laughter of patrons. Finally, she sighed and straightened up. "Fine. Follow me."

Saga led us to one of the holo rooms at the end of the hall. Inside, the space was stark and empty, save for a single chair in the center of the room and a control panel on the wall. She moved to the panel and began tapping away, her fingers flying over the holographic keys with inhuman speed.

"You're a Code Weaver," Bae said, watching her in awe.

Saga smirked without looking up. "That's one name for it. Technopath is another. Doesn't make cracking Skjoldur's security any less of a headache."

Sigrid's gaze was sharp, her tone laced with something I couldn't quite place. "How you've managed to stay out of the Chairman's clutches with an ability like yours is nothing short of a miracle."

Saga chuckled, a sly grin spreading across her face. "Miracles? Please, Sigrid. You should know by now it's all about who you know. And with this—" she raised her hand, making a circular motion "— place? Let's just say I've got more connections than most."

After several minutes, the room around us shimmered, the blank walls morphing into a three-dimensional map of the detention center. It was intricate and detailed, every corridor and cell block rendered in vibrant lines of light. Saga manipulated the map effortlessly, zooming in and out, highlighting key points.

"There you go," she said finally, stepping back. "Skjoldur detention center, in all its glory. I've marked the weakest entry points, but I'd move fast. Their security updates daily." Studying the map intently, Sigrid pulled out a small device from her cloak's pocket and began scanning the map. "This will do. Thank you."

Saga waved a hand dismissively. "Don't thank me yet. If this goes south, you were never here, and you don't know me. Plus, I think this makes us even."

"Not even close... but understood on the rest," Sigrid said, finishing the scan and pocketing her device. "In any event, appreciate the help. Take care of yourself, Saga."

As we turned to leave the room, Saga called out, "Sigrid?"

She paused, glancing back.

"Be careful," Saga said, her voice uncharacteristically soft. "Skjoldur isn't the kind of place you walk out of easily."

Sigrid nodded, her expression unreadable.

The door to the holo room slid open, and we stepped into the dimly lit hallway of the lounge. The faint hum of the holo equipment was quickly replaced by the distant sounds of raised voices—angry, sharp, and escalating.

I glanced at Nodin, whose brow furrowed in alarm. "What's going on?" he muttered, already tensing like a spring.

Before anyone could answer, Saga appeared behind us, her movements swift and deliberate. Her usual sly confidence was replaced with a sharp edge of urgency. "IA troopers. It's a raid," she hissed, her eyes narrowing. "Follow me. Now."

The air seemed to grow heavier at her words, tension crackling through the corridor. Shouts from the front grew louder, punctuated by the sound of chairs scraping against the floor and glass shattering. People began pouring out of the private holo rooms, their faces a mix of panic and determination as they pushed and jostled to escape. The once-shadowy lounge erupted into chaos.

Saga moved quickly, her boots clicking against the polished floor. She led us down the corridor, her head swiveling to check behind her. "Keep your heads down," she said sharply. "And don't stop for anything."

I nodded, clutching my cloak closer around me. The sudden rush of bodies spilling into the hall made it difficult to keep our group together. The patrons, desperate to avoid a run-in with IA, shoved past us, their fear palpable.

Through the melee, I caught a fleeting glimpse of black uniforms and the gleam of weapons at the far end of the lounge. My heart clenched. They were here, closing in.

And then I saw him.

Tristan.

How was he here? He moved with calculated precision, his pale green eyes scanning the chaos like a hawk searching for prey. My breath caught in my throat as he passed through a patch of flickering light, his black IA cloak swaying with his purposeful stride. Then, for a heartbeat, his gaze faltered—turning in my direction. My pulse thundered in my neck as our eyes locked. Recognition seemed to flicker across his face, and his sharp gaze narrowed as if he was about to step toward me. My blood turned to ice.

"ELIN, come on!" Sigrid's urgent voice shattered the moment. My body jolted, and I tore my gaze away, my mind whirling. Without looking back, I pushed through the crowd like a salmon swimming upstream to catch up with the rest of our group. It felt like the air had been sucked out of the room, leaving me weightless and reeling.

With a purposeful stride, Saga led us to an inconspicuous doorway at the end of the corridor. With a quick flick of her wrist, a panel slid open to reveal a narrow staircase leading down into the depths below. She waved us through. "Move it. Hurry down!"

She didn't have to ask me twice. Seeing Tristan in Falinvik was like stumbling into a predator's lair—his turf, his rules. Every nerve in my body screamed to run. *But why was he in an AI uniform and not a Clan Hunter one?* A question for another day—escape was the only thing that mattered now.

We scrambled down the stairs, the sound of the chaos above echoing faintly. Before the door slid shut behind us, Saga's voice called down, laced with a hint of mischief, "This is where I leave you. I've got some guests to greet. Just follow the tunnel to the back alley exit, and good luck!"

The air grew cooler and damp as we descended, the space lit by dim, flickering lights embedded in the stone walls. My breathing was ragged, and my mind raced with questions, but the urgency of our escape left no room for answers.

A few steps down, my foot slipped on the slick stone step, and for a heart-stopping second, I thought I'd fall. A hand shot out, gripping my arm firmly and pulling me upright.

"Careful," Nodin murmured, his voice low but steady. For a moment, I couldn't move. My pulse was already racing from the escape, but now it pounded for an entirely different reason. His touch, his presence—it was reassuring, solid in the chaos. The briefest flicker of calm settled over me, like I could lean on him and not crumble under the weight of everything.

But that flicker turned sour almost as quickly as it came. *What was I doing? Letting myself feel safe, even for a second?* Aedan's face flashed in my mind—his smile, his steady determination. He was the one out there alone, the one I had to save. And here I was, distracted by Nodin's steadying hand, his quiet strength.

I pulled away, shaking off the moment like water from my cloak. "Thanks," I mumbled, keeping my eyes on the uneven steps ahead of me. But the warmth of his hand lingered on my arm even as we pressed forward.

As we reached the bottom of the stairs, I nearly collided with someone standing at the next corner. A jolt shot through me as recognition hit like a thunderbolt.

"Claire?" I whispered, my voice trembling.

She turned, her light-green eyes wide, framed by wavy black hair damp with sweat and snow. "Elin!" In a heartbeat, she crossed the distance between us—slender, graceful, and fast as ever—gripping my arms before pulling me into a fierce hug. Her presence hit me like a beacon in the dark, overwhelming and anchoring all at once.

Relief surged through me, followed by a ripple of guilt. For the briefest moment, I wondered if Claire—or the Gradys—had noticed the way I'd hesitated with Nodin on the steps, a fleeting distraction that now felt all too selfish.

Behind her, Aedan's brother Edvin stood with his parents, Liam and Dara Grady. Edvin towered over them, tall and broad-shouldered, his wavy black hair flattened by the damp, his normally playful face drawn with tension. Beside him, Mr. Grady's rugged build was unmistakable—strong and solid, a pillar of calm under pressure. Mrs. Grady, slim and graceful, clutched his arm; her sea-green eyes shimmered with warmth shadowed by deep sadness, a quiet strength bracing her slight frame.

Gabriel Tibadeau hovered near them, his lean frame taut with alertness. His ebony skin caught the low light as his keen gaze scanned the shadows, always calculating, always a step ahead. My French teacher, Mr. Tibadeau, stood at his nephew's side, taller, broader, his deep-set gaze steady and protective, his own weathered hands clutching a battered Clan backpack to his chest like a shield. Both of them had been instrumental in helping with Gradys' attempt to rescue their son from Ginnungagap.

A fifth man lingered slightly apart, calm even in the chaos. Older, with silver threading his black hair, he moved with a quiet dignity. His features were unmistakably Asian, and something about the serene set of his expression—wary but unflinching—told me immediately he was not someone to underestimate.

"Bae! Sigrid!" Claire's voice was filled with relief as she witnessed them descend the final step. "You're here! What are you—"

Her words were cut short as Sigrid stepped into view. "Dara? Liam?" Sigrid's voice caught, betraying a rare hint of emotion. "By Freya's grace, it's good to see you."

Bae stepped closer, her expression oscillating between disbelief and joy as she took in the familiar faces. "You're alive," she said, her voice barely above a whisper. "We thought you were—" She stopped herself, the words hanging heavy in the air.

Gabriel's guarded expression melted into a rare smile as he extended a hand toward Bae. *"Incroyable! C'est trés bon de vous voir* —It's *so* good to see you all," he said, his native French slipping through as his deep voice brimmed with warmth.

"We need to keep moving. Don't mistake my urgency for lack of joy at this reunion," Sigrid interjected, her tone brisk but her eyes lingering on the Gradys. "But we have a small window to escape."

Mrs. Grady clasped her hands tightly, her voice quivering. "Are they after us?"

"IA raid," Sigrid confirmed, her jaw taut. "And they're not the understanding type."

As the sound of boots scuffling above grew louder, Bae whispered, her gaze darting back toward the stairs. "We need to go *now*."

Gabriel didn't wait for further discussion. He pushed past us, his hand brushing the wall as he activated another hidden panel. A narrow passageway opened, revealing another tunnel stretching into darkness. "*Suivez-moi!* This way," he commanded, urging us to follow him.

Before anyone could step forward, Mr. Tibadeau's lighter French accent broke through. "And who's he?" He gestured at Nodin, his tone cautious.

Nodin, who had been quiet until now, flashed a roguish grin. "Name's Nodin. Not my usual way of making new friends, but hey, nothing brings people together like running from the law, right?"

"Nodin's with us. And who's your friend?" Sigrid asked, nodding toward the Asian man.

Mr. Grady stepped forward. "This is Reo Itō, a trusted friend. We found him at Ginnungagap."

"A pleasure to make your acquaintance," Reo said with a small, polite bow.

Sigrid gave him an appraising look, her nod curt but respectful. "The pleasure's mutual. I'm sure there's a story worth hearing—" Her tone turned sharper as she started ushering everyone toward the passage "—but right now, deeper introductions will have to wait."

Edvin, his sharp eyes scanning Nodin briefly, nodded and grabbed a bag from the ground. "Fine by me. Let's move."

We moved as one, a strange, hastily assembled group driven by the same desperate goal. The air in the tunnel was damp and cold, the walls slick with moisture and faintly glowing with algae-like runes that provided just enough light to guide our way. The faint echoes of boots above us were a chilling reminder of how close the IA troopers were.

"I can't believe we found you," I murmured to Claire as we walked. "We thought you—"

"Later," Claire interrupted gently, her hand briefly squeezing mine. "We'll catch up later. Just stay close."

Ahead, Sigrid's voice rang out, sharp and steady. "Quickly, everyone. Pray they haven't found the back alley exit."

Her words hung in the air as we pressed further into the tunnel, the weight of the pursuit bearing down on us like a storm. Despite the fear coursing through me, the presence of the Gradys was a flicker of hope—a light in the darkness. But joy would have to wait. Right now, escape was all that mattered.

TEN

The Attempt

AEDAN

The endless days of *Leikr* training had pushed me to the brink. Every muscle in my body ached, and my *megin*—my telekinetic ability—was growing more unreliable with each session. The exhaustion from sparring matches and harrowing obstacle courses we ran every day was taking its toll. It wasn't just physical fatigue, though; it felt deeper like my power itself was struggling to surface.

Today, the cracks in my focus were impossible to ignore. During a sparring match, I felt the flow of my *megin* falter just as I tried to deflect an incoming strike with my telekinesis. We were nowhere near a new moon, so my *megin* should've been fine. But, instead of redirecting the energy, it misfired, sending Einar's blade careening unpredictably across the room. The force spun me off balance, and I hit the ground hard, gasping in frustration.

"Stop!" Thyra's voice cut through the tension like a knife. She stepped forward, her gaze sharp but concerned. "You're done for the day, Aedan. No arguments."

I opened my mouth to protest, but her hand shot up, silencing me. "Your telekinesis is too unpredictable...and now apparently a hazard. You and your *megin* are running on fumes. Rest. Now. And take the day off tomorrow. We'll need you performing your best for the actual *Leikr*."

The order landed with the dull finality of a closing chord—like the end of a Springsteen ballad where the hero doesn't win, just survives another round.

Her air currents stirred faintly, brushing against my skin in a silent, supportive manner, like she was reminding me that she had my back. It was an odd thing—her constant help. *Why bother? What was in it for her?* I'd been puzzling over those questions since I met her. The only answer that made sense was the Chairman. He had entrusted her with me—and for some reason that I had yet to figure out, I was his golden prize.

I gritted my teeth and nodded. My end goal remained the same—survive and escape. If I had to play along and trust Thyra's judgment to do that, then so be it.

The next day, I was confined to my luxurious but locked room, a far cry from my sparse cell at Ginnungagap. The oversized bed, warm fireplace, and sweeping views from the glass walls were distractions I couldn't afford. Thyra had ordered me to rest, and while I had spent most of the day lying around, I knew that tonight, I had my chance to gain some answers. There were too many questions gnawing at me, too many pieces of the puzzle left unsolved.

As I stared at the horizon where the last glimmers of red and orange burst forth from the sunset, my thoughts drifted back to Ginnungagap and Reo Itō, the Austri emissary who had been locked in the cell next to mine. I hoped he was ok. There had been no time for goodbyes when the *Stór-menni* guards had dragged me away in the middle of the night.

Reo had been more than a comforting voice during my bleakest hours in Ginnungagap—he was also a treasure trove of knowledge about the four Clans and Falinvik's history. One story in particular had stayed with me: the Chairman's wife, who had once held the prestigious role of *Goði*—a representative of her Clan in the now-defunct Four Clan Assembly. It was an incredible honor, yet beyond that title, Reo hadn't been able to uncover anything else about her. It was like she'd been erased from history— a missing mystery. And it haunted me.

I couldn't shake the feeling that she was the key to understanding the Chairman's ultimate goal. And then there was the matter of my family—the missing DNA, our last name that wasn't our last name. *Had my parents been hiding something all along? Or was the Chairman feeding me lies, trying to rattle me into submission?* Whatever the case, I was determined to find out the truth.

It was time to take advantage of the opportunity that I saw every day while being escorted by the guards to training. A placard near the AHV landing pad listed the floors of the building—and the 26th floor was marked as the Chairman's office. The discovery had sparked an idea that had only grown since I first spotted the placard: his office had to hold the answers I needed. If I could just get inside, maybe I could finally piece together the connection between my family and his plans.

The guards wouldn't make it easy, but they had one critical weakness: they underestimated me. They thought locking me in this room was enough to keep me out of trouble. They didn't know about the silent calculations I'd been making—the subtle observations I'd stored away during my time here.

Tonight was my chance. Yesterday, I'd overheard one of the guards say that the Chairman was out for an inspection tonight, which meant he wasn't in his office. It was the opportunity I'd been waiting for—and thanks to Thyra, I was well-rested for it.

I paced the room, formulating my plan.

I was on the 25th floor of the Chairman's high-rise. My *Hepta Baugr* was tied to this building when I wasn't with another person, so its distant alarm shouldn't be a problem—given that I was staying in the building. I knew the high-speed elevators, which were more like vertical bullet trains on the building's outside, were guarded. *And the stairs?* A brief memory surfaced of the last time I'd been escorted through the building—the guards had been just as thick there, their bulky forms stationed at every landing. Clearly, neither of those was an option.

If I couldn't use the obvious paths, I needed another way.

I turned to the expansive windows of my room, which offered a sweeping view of the city. On the AHV rides to and from the training arena, I'd seen that the building's exterior wasn't entirely smooth. Thick architectural beams crisscrossed the structure like ribs, and inset maintenance platforms were visible at intervals. A risky option, but one I couldn't ignore.

I approached the glass wall, pressing my palm against its cool surface. The height made my stomach churn, but I pushed the fear aside. *At least, that was one good thing about the obstacle course training.* It had forced me to face my fear of heights and find a way to push through it. I'd never have had the nerve—or the skill—to attempt what I was about to do when I first arrived in this room.

I slid open the small window panel I'd found earlier, grateful that whoever designed this luxury prison had prioritized ventilation over total security. The cold night air rushed in, biting at my skin as I stepped onto the narrow ledge outside. Below, the city lights glittered like distant stars, and the hum of the metropolis reverberated dimly in my ears.

I leaned out carefully, gripping the frame as I surveyed the beams running across the building. They were wide enough to walk on but slick with frost. Thanks to the *Leikr* training, I knew my telekinesis could steady me—if it didn't betray me again. I hoped I—and it—had rested enough.

I took a deep breath and stepped onto the beam, the icy surface threatening to send me plummeting to the city below. My *megin* flared, steadying my footing just enough to keep me balanced. *One step at a time,* I told myself, moving cautiously toward the adjoining platform. The icy wind howled around me, tugging at my clothes and numbing my fingers.

For a split second, I imagined what Elin would say if she saw me now—probably something exasperated about how reckless this was. Then again, she might just smirk, tell me to stop overthinking, and keep moving forward. That thought steadied me more than my *megin* did.

After what felt like an eternity, I reached a maintenance hatch set into the building's outer wall. The edges were crusted with frost, but I focused my telekinesis, gently easing the latch open. The hatch creaked slightly as I slipped inside, dropping into a dimly lit maintenance corridor.

The whir of machinery filled the narrow space, and the faint scent of oil and dust hung in the air. I crept forward, my senses on high alert. The Chairman's office was still a floor above me, but this route bypassed the guards. If I could find a way up through these maintenance shafts, I might still have a chance.

I moved quickly but quietly, scanning the walls for anything that resembled an access ladder or another hatch leading upward.

Eventually, I found what I was looking for: a narrow ladder leading to the next level. The climb was grueling, the rungs cold and slick under my fingers. I pushed past the ache in my arms and the burning in my lungs, my determination propelling me upward. My *megin* hummed faintly against my medallion, ready to catch me if I slipped.

At the top, another hatch led to a dim corridor on the 26th floor. I eased it open, slipping through as silently as I could.

The hallway beyond was eerily quiet, the polished marble floors reflecting the soft shine of the overhead lights. I crept forward, my heart pounding as I approached what I believed to be the Chairman's lobby. The open door was a grand, imposing thing—dark wood inlaid with intricate runes that seemed to pulse dimly with energy.

The room beyond was breathtaking in its scope and detail, as though I'd stepped into a mythic memory rather than a physical space. It resembled a massive Viking gathering hall, but it was no crude replica. At the center, a circular hearth blazed, its flames commanding attention as they painted the room in vivid, shifting hues. The walls were crafted from rich, honeyed wood, each plank polished until it looked alive. Full-length Norse dragons were carved into the beams, their snarling heads jutting from the cornices, gemstone eyes glinting in hues of amber, sapphire, and garnet, tracking every movement. The air carried the scent of aged wood, leather, and a faint metallic tang.

Ancient shields and banners adorned the walls, punctuated by ceremonial seaxes gleaming in the fire's flickering light. Three massive iron chandeliers, suspended by intricately etched black chains, bathed the room in a golden light, their shadows flickering like ghosts. Opposite the fireplace stood a gleaming wooden desk, polished to perfection, an anchor of modern authority amid the relics of a bygone age. The space was oppressive and awe-inspiring, a seamless blend of ancient power and calculated intimidation.

As I stood in the doorway gawking at the grandeur, a voice froze me in place.

"Well, well," came the calm, measured tone. "I wasn't expecting a guest tonight."

I turned slowly, my breath catching as I saw him. The Chairman stood at the end of the hallway, his gray eyes gleaming with curiosity and something sharper—amusement.

For a moment, neither of us spoke. The silence pressed heavily between us, broken only by the faint crackle of flames from the central hearth. Then the Chairman took a step closer, his presence somehow filling the corridor.

"Tell me, Aedan," he said, his tone almost conversational. "What brings you to this floor? I thought your quarters were more than sufficient."

My mind raced, searching for an explanation, a way out, but all I could do was meet his gaze and hope he couldn't see through the facade of calm I was desperately trying to maintain. "I need to stretch my legs a bit," I replied as casually as possible, even though we both knew it was a lie.

I immediately prepared a song in my head, ready to start singing in case he tried penetrating my mind. I reached for Jim Croce's "I Got a Name"—defiance wrapped in melody. It wasn't armor, but it was mine. I'd learned during my time at Ginnungagap that the Chairman was a powerful Mind Interventionist.

"Oh, *relax*, I won't try reading your mind," he said, waving his hand as if casting the ridiculous thought away. "I've no interest in hearing whatever song you've no doubt already selected. You've always been a worthy opponent on that front...thanks to your *father*, I'm sure." He emphasized the word in a way that made me question whether he now knew who that was. At Ginnungagap, he'd tried in every way possible to gain information about my family, whether through me or bullying the staff in mint-green tunics and white lab coats. But now that I thought about it, after my move to Falinvik, he hadn't tried once to penetrate my mind.

When I didn't respond, he continued, "Since you are here, Aedan, I would appreciate a moment of your time. Won't you join me in my office?" It wasn't a request but a command—and I had little choice. I followed his billowing gray robes through the ornate lobby to another set of double doors on the opposite side.

The Chairman's office was a jarring shift from the lobby—a sleek, minimalist expanse encased in glass, with the city sprawling below. A deliberate statement, I realized, as my gaze swept over the space. Its emptiness echoed a sense of control and precision. Every detail was curated, nothing extraneous, just cold efficiency.

On the right side sat a sleek, gray desk paired with a hovering chair that radiated quiet dominance. I noted the thin slit embedded in the desk—concealed holo-screens that only activated when needed, angled exclusively for the Chairman's eyes. Those screens held access to all of the *Stór-menni's* information—including the truths that I sought. *But how would I ever be able to get to it?* I was pretty sure there was a security layer just to make the screens appear.

As we stepped further in, the doors sealed behind us with a quiet finality. Moments later, and as if summoned by the Chairman's will, an armchair appeared, constructed from metallic beads bubbling forth from the floor in front of his desk.

"Please have a seat, Aedan," the Chairman said, indicating the armchair as he rounded the desk to sit on his hovering throne. I felt like refusing, but it seemed silly to remain standing in the cavernous space. "I heard that you are having some trouble with your *megin*...an overextension of use?" His voice sounded almost concerned.

There was no point in lying. There was no doubt that Thyra's training report had been thorough.

I gave a curt nod.

"Well, we certainly can't have that...not with the *Leikr* about to start," he replied as if I'd given a fulsome response. He waved his hand at the corner of his desk, muttering something I couldn't quite catch. A small slit opened in the tabletop. He placed his hand inside and drew out a small, delicate-looking device. "Give me your arm."

I hesitated. *What was that thing? And what was he going to do with it?*

"Come, now this won't hurt a bit...and you'll feel *so* much better after," he said as he held out his hand to take my arm. Again, there wasn't much choice. I could refuse, and he would simply call in the guards and force me. I was still his prisoner despite recent appearances. I held out my arm.

"No, the one with the *Hepta Baugr*... we'll need to remove that first. Oh, and just a friendly reminder—all my floors are equipped with instant *megin* dampeners, so let's keep any of your displays in check, shall we?" His tone was disturbingly cordial, like a host chatting with a guest, as if he wasn't the same man who had repeatedly tried to invade my mind and left me writhing in agony. It set my teeth on edge. I also didn't know what an 'instant *megin* dampener' was, but knowing the Chairman, I guessed that it wouldn't be pleasant.

The Chairman released the *Hepta Baugr* from my wrist and, in the same motion, brought the small device to my arm. He held the device close to my arm's underside.

Loath to say anything to the Chairman, I reluctantly asked, "What is that thing?"

"It's a device of my own invention... a source of energy. You'll understand soon enough." His voice was calm, almost too calm, as he pressed the button on the small device. A sharp sting followed as a needle pierced my skin, and then it began—*the glow*.

It crept up my arm, a steady, golden pulse that radiated warmth as it spread, inch by inch, consuming my body. The sensation was unsettling yet intoxicating, like a forbidden embrace. My *megin* roared to life, thundering in my veins, but the warmth didn't stop. It coiled around my power like an old friend returning, wrapping me in a heat that both soothed and conquered.

It felt amazing. My *megin* was begging me to use my abilities. I felt more powerful than I ever had. The Chairman's cold gray eyes watched me closely, a faint, knowing smile playing on his lips as if he could read every thought I was too shaken to say.

"Yes, you feel it, don't you?" The Chairman's voice was a mix of pride and craving, like he wanted to be one experiencing it.

I nodded cautiously, unable to form a coherent response. Every nerve in my body was alive with energy, my *megin* thrumming in a way I'd never experienced before. It was overwhelming—powerful, and frightening all at once.

"This is just the beginning," he murmured, his tone thoughtful, almost distant. "You've always had a way of adapting...it's in your nature, I suppose."

The words landed heavily, their meaning just out of reach. *What did he mean by my nature?* The question burned in my mind, but before I could ask, he continued, his voice taking on a casual air.

"It's curious, really, how much we inherit without ever realizing it." His gaze lingered on me for a moment, sharp and assessing, before he gestured toward the door. "Guards, please escort Aedan back to his room. He'll need to rest. The *Leikr* is fast approaching."

Then, almost like an afterthought, he added, "Oh, and one last thing, Aedan—do make sure you perform well in the *Leikr*. Your team's lives may very well depend on it. I'd hate to see them suffer for any... missteps on your part."

His meaning was unmistakable. Either I played my role doing my best, or the Chairman would make sure my teammates paid the price. For a fleeting moment, I wondered if that was a real threat—to me, personally. But then, images of Magnus, Fenja, Einar, and Thyra flickered through my mind.

They might have been on the wrong side, but from what I'd gathered over the past few days, they weren't exactly willing participants—not in the *Leikr*, maybe not even in the *Stór-menni* itself. And they certainly didn't deserve to suffer for any of my actions.

Eirik, on the other hand—

The appearance of two guards disrupted my thoughts. Their towering forms flanked the doorway. I was pretty sure the Chairman called them with his ability since his voice never rose beyond a conversational tone. I hesitated despite the Chairman's threat, my mind racing with questions that remained unanswered. For the first time, I felt reluctant to leave. Still, I turned and followed the guards, knowing no answers would be forthcoming tonight. My steps were heavy with unease despite the new power coursing through me.

Back in my room, I paced restlessly, my mind racing as the guards worked to seal off my escape route. The energy from the injection still surged through me, each movement crackling with power, each thought sharper than before.

I watched in silence as they welded the small window panel shut, erasing the path I had used. *Well, so much for a second time using that route*, I thought grimly, but my focus quickly shifted. My *megin* thrummed with a potency I couldn't fully comprehend, and I needed answers. The Chairman hadn't replaced the *Hepta Baugr* on my wrist—*a careless oversight, or a calculated move?* Either way, it was an opportunity.

I waited until the guards finished and left, the heavy door sliding shut behind them. Turning to my desk, I decided to start small. Normally, telekinetically lifting it would require a decent effort, but as I reached for my *megin*, feeling for it against my medallion, it responded instantly. The desk shot into the air with a fraction of the effort it would have taken before, hanging there as if weightless.

I lowered it gently, my breathing uneven. *It wasn't just easier—it was effortless.* Half the energy I usually needed, maybe less. My mind whirled with possibilities and questions. *What had the Chairman done to me? Why did it feel so good? And, most unsettling of all, what price would I have to pay for whatever this was?*

I wished I could talk to Elin. She had a way of looking at things from a different angle, of questioning what others might take at face value. I wasn't sure what she'd say about this—whether she'd see it as an opportunity or a trap—but I wanted to hear her thoughts.

I sank onto the edge of the bed, the pale shine of city lights spilling through the windows as I stared down at my hands. The power thrumming through me was intoxicating, but one thing was clear—*it wasn't mine.* And I couldn't shake the feeling that *it wasn't a gift—it was a leash.*

ELEVEN

The Alley

TRISTAN

The Holo Lounge was in complete turmoil. Screams cut through the pounding bass, the music now warped and crackling like a dying machine. Lights flickered in jagged bursts, casting fractured shadows over shattered glass and overturned furniture as panicked patrons fought to escape. But I wasn't focused on them. My eyes scanned the crowd, locking onto the retreating forms of Elin and the Unregistered's family.

It had been her. *Elin.*

I'd know her anywhere—the long strands of auburn hair, the fire in her amber eyes, the defiance etched into every step. She had slipped through my fingers too many times before. But not this time.

A twisted mix of disbelief and satisfaction curled in my chest. I finally found her after hunting her like a shadow through this city, through every dead lead and vanished trail. She was the ultimate prize.

The Chairman would be so pleased. I couldn't wait to bring both her and the Unregistered's family in. I was so close.

It was through sheer luck that the entire operation had turned in my favor. One of our Replicant spies had witnessed Elin's crew entering the Holo lounge, transforming my frustration over the failed raid at Thorne's estate into an unexpected advantage. It had flushed them out into the open, forcing them to make mistakes—leading them straight into our sights. And, thankfully, saved me from yet another uncomfortable conversation with Kolve.

The Replicant spy network was especially strong in Falinvik, and their abilities made them indispensable. Some found their talent unsettling—the ability to duplicate themselves into multiple versions, each sharing a mental link—but it was incredibly useful for spy work. The moment one of them witnessed something, the knowledge was instantly transmitted to all their copies—so what one knew, they all knew. I had made a point of taking one with me to Thorne's just in case.

"Secure the entrances and search the lounge," I barked to the IA troopers, keeping my tone controlled despite the adrenaline surging through me. "No one leaves. The Unregistered's family and the Dormant are here. Take them alive. That's a standing order from the Chairman."

The troopers snapped to action, their dark cloaks twirling amongst the uproar of the lounge. One trooper disappeared into a side hallway to seal the rear exit while the others spread out, herding the crowd away from the hall where I'd last seen Elin and her group vanish. The way Elin's team had moved—it had been hasty but *coordinated*—like they had a planned exit.

Of course! They weren't just running blindly. They were escaping. And most likely, they were heading outside.

Pressing my lips into a thin line, I activated my Communicator. "Sweep for hidden passages. But send no more than necessary—we need boots on the exterior now."

I tapped my foot impatiently. Waiting for the troopers to assemble would take too long. "You four, with me," I commanded. "They're heading for an exterior escape route. We need to cut them off before they disappear."

The five of us pushed through the tumult of the Holo Lounge

and out into the icy streets. The bitter wind bit at my skin, but I barely noticed. My mind was already racing ahead, analyzing.

We needed more help to track them. The Baldur district was a labyrinth, full of blind spots and hidden paths. It was the perfect place for fugitives to vanish. Without a second thought, I reached into the small bag strapped to my waist and tossed four small SASUs into the frigid night air.

The tiny drones flitted over alleyways, scanning heat signatures and tracking movement. Their data streamed directly into my Communicator's interface, painting a virtual map of the area. For a tense few moments, the feed revealed only scattered figures—civilians, stray animals, and residual heat from recent activity—but then, a cluster of signatures seemed to appear from nowhere. It confirmed my suspicions—Elin's group had taken an underground route and was emerging several blocks away.

"There," I muttered, eyes locking onto the signal. I increased my pace. "Move. Now."

We swiftly navigated the frostbitten streets, following the SASU's coordinates until we reached the small alleyway. At the far end, a cluster of figures huddled together, their breath misting in the freezing air. Their body language screamed urgency, poised to bolt. A few stragglers were still climbing out of a hole in the ground, their shoulders tense, movements hurried as if they knew how little time they had left.

The dark alley was narrow—an advantage for us. Elin's group wouldn't have room to spread out, limiting their movement. But the open exit at the far end posed a problem. We needed to seal it off.

I tapped my Communicator, issuing a command to the four SASUs. Instantly, their red lights blinked in acknowledgment, zipping into position. Within seconds, they formed a precise, shimmering square at the alley's exit, ready to engage and block any escape attempt.

My boots crunched against the ice as I stepped forward, flames already curling at my fingertips. My presence alone cast flickering shadows against the alley walls.

A broad-shouldered man with a hardened stance turned his head. His wary eyes locked onto mine. Recognition flared, followed by tension.

I smirked. "Going somewhere?"

The rest of Elin's group scrambled out, their breath coming in harsh puffs against the cold air. Elin was the last, her amber eyes flashing with defiance even as she realized the trap had already been sprung.

My lips curled into a grim smile. Elin's group would be no match for five highly trained troopers.

"Cut them off," I commanded the troopers at my side, gesturing for them to move in. "No one escapes."

"Move!" The tall, broad-shouldered man shouted, stepping in front of their group. He braced like a battering ram.

"*Edvin*, no!" a woman's voice called, but it was too late.

The man—Edvin—charged, his boots cracking against the frozen alley floor as he swung his fist with brutal efficiency. My trooper barely managed a flinch before he was airborne, colliding with the alley wall hard enough to send fractures splitting through the frost-covered stone. He collapsed with a strangled groan.

Super strength. Noted.

"Seize him!" I barked.

Two troopers surged forward in response, but before they could reach Edvin, a blur of motion shot past me. A flash of dark hair and sharp agility—suddenly, one of the troopers' weapons was gone, wrenched from his grip before he even had time to react. The female thief skidded to a stop beside Edvin, twirling the confiscated weapon with infuriating ease.

Beyond them, at the far end of the alley, I caught movement. Three figures were desperately trying to bring down the SASUs, but they were failing. The SASUs moved like a pack of mechanical predators, weaving through the air with razor-sharp precision. Their metal bodies reflected the neon signs above, their targeting sensors blinking an ominous red. Blue bolts shrieked as they fired in calculated bursts, carving glowing lines into the ice. The trio ducked and twisted, locked in a frenzied dance of survival, barely evading the relentless assault.

The wiry man, his Asian features partially hidden beneath the shadows of his hood, moved with eerie precision, trying to smash the machines with quick, deft motions from his long sword, but he kept having to dodge the barrage of projectiles. The brown and silver-haired woman thrust her hands outward, straining as if to exert her power over the flying orbs, but her focus wavered each time a streak of energy nearly singed her. The shortest of the three, an agile Asian woman, tried opening small portals to swat the drones, but she was barely keeping up, her movements growing sloppier with every failed attempt.

I barely spared them a second glance. Their efforts were a distraction at best.

"Claire, heads up!" Elin shouted.

The female thief—Claire—didn't hesitate. As the other trooper lunged at her, she twisted away in a blur of movement, flipping over his head with impossible speed before landing a precise kick to his knee. He crumpled sideways, off-balance. Claire used the momentum, pivoting on one foot and slamming the stolen weapon across his back. He hit the ground with a grunt, his weapon clattering to the side.

Super speed. That explained her ability to disarm and disable so cleanly. We needed to take her out—before she could disarm anyone else.

"GET HER!" I growled at my remaining troopers.

The rest of Elin's group moved with surprising coordination, working in sync despite their disorderly retreat. An older man near the back—his black and silver hair catching in the dim light—raised his hands, and the shadows around us twisted unnaturally. A second later, duplicates of their group flickered into existence, distorting the alley with a mirage of moving figures. One of my troopers, foolishly reacting without thinking, fired at them. The blue bolts passed through harmlessly, striking nothing.

An Illusionist. Clever. The trickster god Loki himself would have been proud.

"Stop wasting your *megin*!" I snapped, my irritation growing.

Beside the Illusionist, a woman stood calm and composed, her hands clenched at her sides. There was something eerily still about her, as though she wasn't afraid—not even in the face of overwhelming odds. Suddenly, I felt my *megin* pounding in my veins uncontrollably. I barely had time to process it before the flames in my hands blazed hotter, wilder—out of my control for a split second.

My pulse kicked up a notch. *What the—?*

An empath with power amplifier abilities—it had to be.

She wasn't just standing there. She was *amplifying* abilities—mine included. I clenched my fists, forcing my flames back into submission, but the momentary flare had taken its toll. I could feel my *megin* thrumming too strongly beneath my skin, pushing, ready to consume everything.

Then the wind shifted.

Not naturally—deliberately.

I barely had time to react before a sudden blast of air slammed into me, sending me skidding back several feet. The wind was cold, raw, and biting, like it had fangs, and my hands stung as I caught myself against the icy ground.

I cursed to myself, my flames flickering as I steadied my stance. My eyes locked onto a tall, fit man standing slightly apart from the others. His dark braid whipped around his face, his hazel eyes sharp with focus. He looked like a Skraeling, which was impossible. The remnants of the Vestri Clan's fierce warriors had died long ago. The way he moved with the wind—deliberate, controlled—wasn't normal.

Wind manipulation.

I exhaled sharply, irritation spiking. That explained the strange gusts earlier.

"Nodin! Keep it up!" Elin shouted.

So he had a name.

A new player, but a dangerous one.

I cursed under my breath. *This wasn't just a fleeing band of fugitives. This was a coordinated force.*

My eyes flicked to my Communicator. *Time to end this.*

"We need reinforcements. *Now.* Converge on my coordinates." My voice was sharp, clipped, cutting through the uproar.

"Elin!" I called, stepping forward, flames licking up my arms, casting flickering shadows across the alley walls. "Enough games. Surrender now, and maybe I won't incinerate your friends."

She hesitated, her wide eyes darting around as if calculating her chances. The glowing medallion on her chest caught my eye.

My stomach twisted. *When had she gotten that? And, more importantly—when and how had she awakened her powers? Dormants didn't just awaken their powers by themselves. Yet, she had a medallion, so she had to have powers.*

She wasn't attacking, but she wasn't yielding either. *What were her powers?*

I took another step forward.

The air rippled.

Before I could react, a golden barrier snapped into existence between us. My flames blazed forward, colliding with the shield and sputtering across its gleaming surface. Heat rippled outward, but the barrier held.

I turned my focus on its source—an older, well-built man with dark skin standing a few feet away, his hands raised in front of him. His face was tight with concentration, sweat beading along his brow as he maintained the shield against my fire.

"HURRY! Tibadeau can't hold it forever!" the older woman with brown and silver hair beside him shouted, trying to regroup Elin's team behind the shield.

At the same time, several new IA troopers arrived, flooding the alley with overwhelming force. I smiled as the realization dawned on

Elin's group. Their movements, once sharp and decisive, faltered for the first time. Eyes darted between the advancing soldiers and their companions, shoulders tensing. Even Edvin, the brute of the group, took a half-step back before bracing himself.

Claire shot a glance at Elin, and for a fleeting moment, hesitation flickered across her face. The older man, the Illusionist, exhaled sharply, his fingers twitching as if already knowing the illusions wouldn't hold against this kind of force for long.

They were outnumbered. Outmaneuvered. Their escape was slipping through their fingers.

I let the moment stretch, savoring the shift in their confidence. *Now, they understood.*

"You're boxed in," I said, my voice carrying a dangerous edge. "And outnumbered. It's time to end this."

To drive my point home, a trooper gifted with energy pulse abilities—thrust a hand forward, sending a ripple of unseen force through the alley. The Asian woman, still engaged with the SASUs in the back, didn't see it coming and was thrown backward, colliding against the alley wall with a sharp gasp.

She groaned, pressing a hand to her ribs as she tried to rise, leaning heavily against the wall. The fight was draining them. I could tell their *megin* was beginning to wear out. Claire, gripping her stolen weapon, flexed her fingers, her usual effortless agility now slowed—fatigue creeping into her limbs. Even Elin, whose defiant stance had never wavered, was now scanning the alley, clearly looking for any way out, her amber eyes flicking between the walls as she calculated their dwindling options.

The truth was—there were *none.*

"Elin! Move!" someone yelled.

A burst of mist clouded the alley—*no, not mist. Illusions.*

The older man was at it again, distorting the battlefield with deceptive flickers of movement. The trooper beside me cursed, trying to refocus, but the Illusionist had already scrambled the field.

"*ENOUGH!*" I snarled.

I threw my hands forward, sending a controlled blast of fire into the cloud of shifting illusions, forcing clarity back into the space. A yelp rang out—one of them had been too slow to move.

Then a large crack lit the alley like a lightning bolt.

Tibadeau's shield flickered—then collapsed.

The moment it shattered, a ripple of shock ran through Elin's group. Edvin's stance stiffened, his fists clenched tighter as if bracing for the inevitable. Claire cursed under her breath. Even the Illusionist, normally so composed, staggered a step back, his breathing heavier now, his hands trembling slightly at his sides.

Elin's gaze darted around wildly, her chest rising and falling with shallow breaths. They had been holding their ground, fighting back against impossible odds—but now, with Tibadeau's shield gone, the last of their defenses had crumbled.

And they clearly knew it.

A flicker of panic crossed her face before she shoved it down, jaw tightening. But I had seen it.

I smirked.

Before I could move to take advantage, the whine of an engine cut through the air.

A sleek Hover Transport Vehicle, or HTV, appeared above the alley, its engines kicking up a flurry of snow and ice from the rooftops while its lights blinded us as they swept across. The bitter wind lashed against the vehicle, and for a moment, I thought the sheer force of it might foil their rescue. But the Resistance pilot was skilled—she fought against the turbulence, lifting the HTV higher despite the Arctic winds clawing to pull it back down. As the vehicle stabilized, maintaining its altitude, a sharp hiss sounded. An unusual mechanism lowered from the transport's underbelly—a retractable platform of gleaming blue energy, broad and stable like a floating lift, designed to carry multiple people at once.

"GO, GO!" a voice called from above as the platform lowered. Two figures leaped down, Resistance fighters armed with rifles. The blue spark of their bolts flashed throughout the alley, making the IA troopers dive for cover.

"Get on!" one of the Resistance fighters shouted, gesturing frantically to Elin's crew.

Jets of blue light tore through the alley as IA troopers returned fire. With a flick of my thumb, my Clan shield burst in front of me, protecting me from the barge.

"Gabriel, come on!" Edvin yelled, turning toward the last member of their group—a quiet man who had been tinkering with a fallen weapon earlier.

I barely saw the movement before a trooper with electric abilities lunged, gripping Gabriel's wrist in an iron hold, electricity surging from his fingertips into the man's arm. Gabriel stiffened, his face contorting in pain. His free hand twitched toward the fallen weapon he'd been toying with before—but it was too late.

"NO!" Elin screamed, reaching down, her hand outstretched toward him.

But Gabriel had already gone rigid, his body convulsing under the surge of electricity. His face twisted, teeth gritted, but his eyes—those dark, intelligent eyes—remained focused. Calculating. Accepting.

Elin lurched forward. *"NO!"*

Gabriel's gaze flickered up to her, steady despite the pain. He met her eyes, the slightest twitch of his lips forming words barely heard over the chaos.

"Go."

"Elin, *no*!" Edvin grabbed her before she could jump off the platform. "We can't—"

"GABRIEL!" Mr. Tibadeau's anguished cry rang out as the HTV lurched upward, lifting them out of reach.

The platform disappeared above the rooftops, the Resistance fighters firing cover shots until the HTV was out of sight.

I turned back to the man still in our grasp. Gabriel breathed out harshly, his muscles tensing as another shock of electricity coursed through him. He didn't fight back with overt powers—no retaliation, no escape attempt. But the keen intelligence in his gaze told me one thing: he wasn't defeated.

"Well," I said, letting the fire in my hands dim as I stepped closer. "Looks like you're staying. And a good thing too, since we have a lot to talk about."

It was a small victory, given how close I'd gotten to capturing Elin, but one I would take. Whoever this man was, he held answers, and I wanted them.

TWELVE

The Aftermath

ELIN

The cabin of the modified Hover Transport Vehicle, or HTV, was silent except for the muffled sound of the engines. Snow still clung to our cloaks, but it was nothing compared to the ice gripping my chest. *Gabriel was gone.*

My hands wouldn't stop shaking. Every time I closed my eyes, I saw him—Gabriel's face in that final moment, his quiet acceptance as the IA trooper grabbed him.

He had risked everything to help us—to help Aedan. In the short time we'd known him, Gabriel had become part of our team, a steady presence through the chaos. Without him, the Gradys would never have made it out of Ginnungagap. We all owed him more than we could ever repay.

Someone had draped a thermal blanket over my shoulders, but the chill went deeper than skin. *We'd escaped. We'd found the Gradys. But at what cost?*

Claire's arms had wrapped around me the second we stumbled into the HTV, holding on like she wasn't sure I was real. I barely managed to return the embrace before Edvin pulled us both into a rough, wordless hug, his usual bravado stripped away.

Mrs. Grady pressed her hands to my face like she was memorizing me, whispering something too soft to hear. Mr. Grady's grip on my shoulder was firm, steady—something solid in the turmoil. Their warmth was a brief flicker of light against the dark. But only a flicker.

Because then reality set back in, and the silence that followed was heavy.

Mr. Grady exhaled a shuddering breath, his voice breaking through the quiet. "Thank you," he said, addressing the Resistance fighters, his usual warmth laced with exhaustion. "You got us out just in time. We owe you."

The pilot, a fierce-looking woman with short-cropped hair and the Resistance's symbol of a broken chain stitched onto her gray cloak, glanced at him in the rearview holo-display. Her hands never wavered on the controls as she guided us into the lower air lanes, weaving through the industrial underbelly of Falinvik.

"Commander Yrsa sent us," she said, her voice rough from the cold. "She figured you might run into some trouble when the IA movement popped up on our boards by the Holo Lounge."

One of the Resistance fighters—a tall man with a scar running along his jawline—grunted as he dropped onto the bench next to Reo. "If we'd been a minute later, you'd all be in IA custody." He didn't say 'or worse,' but we all heard it.

I swallowed hard, my hands clenching into fists. But we hadn't been fast enough for Gabriel.

Across from me, Mr. Tibadeau leaned against the cold metal wall of the HTV, his face twisted in pain. A burned mass of flesh marred his left forearm, a deep, ugly wound from Tristan's fire.

Sigrid knelt beside him, her usual confidence stripped away as she struggled to rip a piece of cloth from her sleeve. "We need med supplies!" she called toward the front.

One of the Resistance fighters quickly grabbed a first-aid kit from the panel beneath the seats and tossed it to her. Tibadeau gritted his teeth as Sigrid pressed a cooling gel pad against the raw wound, the pain sharpening the lines on his weathered face.

Near the back of the cabin, Bae slumped against the side wall, cradling her ribs. She had been thrown hard against the alley wall during the fight. I hadn't seen how bad it was in the chaos, but now, under the cabin's blue lights, I could see how she held herself stiffly, like every breath hurt.

"Bae?" I started, but she shook her head, forcing a smirk.

"I'm fine," she muttered, though the strain in her voice told me otherwise. "We got out, didn't we?"

The words hung in the air like a slap.

Not all of us.

My breath hitched. I stared at the metal floor beneath me, clenching my fists until my nails dug into my palms.

"Elin?" Claire's voice was softer than usual.

As I dragged my gaze from the floor, my eyes met Nodin's. His expression was unreadable, but something in his eyes made my throat tighten—an understanding that went beyond words. He knew what this felt like. Not just the loss, but the helplessness that came with it. I wasn't sure how I knew, only that I did. His knee brushed against mine where we sat, whether intentional or not, and its warmth seeped through the cold weight pressing down on me. For a fleeting second, I wanted to ask—*who had you lost?* But the words never left my lips. Instead, I let that small, steady warmth anchor me, a flicker of calm in a storm I couldn't control.

Claire sat across from me, her face drawn and pale. Her eyes held the same haunted look as mine. Edvin was silent, his broad shoulders hunched over and his head in his hands. No one knew what to say.

Because there was nothing to say.

Gabriel was in IA custody.

I forced myself to breathe, looking away from their gazes. There would be time to process everything later. Right now, we had to get back to the base and get Mr. Tibadeau and Bae medical attention.

The HTV descended into the metro tunnels, slipping beneath

the city like a ghost. The last remnants of old-world transit systems stretched out in the darkness—abandoned platforms, rusted tracks, and walls covered in decades of graffiti.

"End of the line," the pilot muttered as she maneuvered the transport toward a sealed tunnel entrance, its old warning lights still flashing a faint, dying red.

A coded transmission pinged from the HTV console, and after a tense moment, the tunnel doors rumbled open, revealing a massive underground hangar.

Inside, Engineers hurried between makeshift workstations, tending to half-assembled vehicles and scanning the security feeds flickering on the overhead displays.

As the HTV touched down on a reinforced platform, I could see that a medical team was already waiting for us. The pilot must have called ahead.

The moment the doors opened, the cold air rushed in again. Resistance medics climbed aboard, assessing injuries with swift precision.

"Help Tibadeau first," Sigrid called, waving them over. "He has a bad burn."

Two medics rushed to Tibadeau's side, carefully helping him out of the cabin. His face was tight with pain, but he didn't complain.

One of the Resistance fighters turned toward Bae. "You too. Come on, let's get those ribs checked out."

Bae grunted but didn't resist as they helped her down the ramp.

As soon as they were clear, the rest of us climbed out into the cavernous space, our boots echoing across the concrete floor. Nodin fell into step beside me. His arm brushed against mine, not quite a touch but close enough that I could feel the shift in the air between us. He didn't say anything, but when I hesitated—my mind still reeling from the fight, from Gabriel—his fingers grazed the small of my back, the briefest of reassurances before falling away.

It was a simple gesture, fleeting and natural, but it sent an unsteady ripple through me. Nodin always had that effect—his presence filling spaces I hadn't realized were empty. I told myself it was nothing. Just a teammate grounding another after a mission gone wrong. But deep down, a quiet voice whispered something else.

At the far end of the makeshift hangar, Commander Yrsa and McHaill stood waiting.

Yrsa's piercing brown eyes flicked over us, taking in the fact that our team had grown since we left the base.

"What happened?" Yrsa asked, her voice steady but firm.

My throat tightened. I forced myself to meet her gaze—I wouldn't break down.

"We were ambushed," Sigrid said, her voice raw. "IA hit the lounge just as we were leaving. We got out, but they cornered us. We fought, took some hits... your team showed up just in time, but not soon enough." She exhaled sharply, then added, "One of us—Gabriel —was captured."

Thankfully, Sigrid kept it brief. I wasn't ready to relive the whole thing just yet.

Yrsa's jaw tightened. McHaill muttered a low curse.

"I see," Yrsa said, her expression unreadable. "A definite complication. Who is Gabriel? And these others—who are they?" She nodded toward the newcomers. I'd forgotten that Yrsa had never met the Gradys.

Sigrid's lips pressed into a thin line before she answered. "Well, if there's any bright side to this debacle... we found them. These are the Gradys—Liam, Dara, Edvin, and Claire." Sigrid gestured toward the others. "This is Reo Itō. And Mr. Tibadeau—whom I've yet to properly meet—was taken to the medbay. Gabriel is his nephew, I believe."

Yrsa's sharp gaze swept over the newcomers, assessing them with quiet intensity. "I see. Good to meet you all." Her tone was measured but edged with a hint of suspicion. "And quite the coincidence... stumbling upon the Gradys at just the right time." She let the words hang for a beat, her expression unreadable, before she continued, "Lucky break, indeed."

McHaill grumbled. "You don't actually think they had anything to do with the IA ambush, do you? I've known Liam and Dara for years—they're above suspicion."

Mr. Grady stiffened but kept his voice measured. "I can assure you, my family wants nothing to do with any *Stór-menni*. Calling them in for an ambush? That would be the last thing we'd ever do."

Yrsa's gaze remained sharp. "Yes, well, I'm sure you understand why your ties to Commander Thorne—a *Stór-menni* and high-ranking Clan Hunter—raise some questions."

Mr. Grady exhaled, his expression tight. "I can see how it might look... and I'm happy to explain. Just not here." He gestured subtly toward the hangar, where workers lingered, pretending not to eavesdrop.

Mrs. Grady stepped beside him, her voice softer but firm. "We only want our son. We need to rescue him as soon as possible...the *Leikr* starts within days. Those games should have been abolished long ago—they're barbaric." She glanced briefly toward the hangar, then met Yrsa's gaze. "We have no intention of disrupting your operation or putting anyone here at risk. We're not your enemies—we just need to save our family."

Yrsa studied them for a moment before nodding. "Fine. We'll talk in my office."

"Wait!" I pushed forward, my pulse hammering. "What about Gabriel? We can't just leave him with IA and Tristan. We need to help him."

I lifted my chin, meeting Yrsa's gaze with determination.

Her expression didn't waver. "There's nothing we can do for him right now," she said flatly. "Standard IA procedure is to take him to their headquarters for processing before he's sent to a detention center. We don't have the manpower or capability to mount a rescue from their stronghold."

Then, without another word, Yrsa gave a curt nod and turned, motioning to the others to follow. She led the way through a side door that separated the hangar from the rest of the base's underground corridors.

The air smelled of cold stone and faint machine oil, and our footsteps echoed against the tunnel walls. Up ahead, the Gradys walked alongside McHaill, their low voices discussing things I couldn't quite make out.

Yrsa weaved through the tunnels, speaking briskly with a group of Resistance fighters and giving orders as they moved. That left the rest of us—me, Claire, Edvin, Nodin, and Reo—to trudge along behind them in heavy silence.

Leaving Gabriel behind hung over us like a thick and wet mop. The weight of it pressed on all of us.

"Alright, I can't take this," Edvin muttered, stretching his arms behind his head. "Somebody say something before we all collapse into another awkward silence."

"Don't want to strain your one brain cell trying to process emotions, huh?" Claire quipped, glancing at him. Only she could tease her twin brother like that and get away with it.

"Exactly," Edvin shot back without hesitation.

"Fine," Nodin interjected, rubbing his hands together as if to ward off the lingering cold. His hazel eyes flicked toward Reo, studying him thoughtfully. "Since we're stuck on this little march, let's do introductions properly. I'm Nodin, and yes, I control the wind. No, I don't do party tricks. And no, I won't cool your tea or chase your papers when you leave the window open."

Reo's refined features remained calm, his expression unreadable as he gave Nodin a polite nod. "I shall refrain from asking, then. Though, in my experience, abilities often become far more interesting when applied to unexpected situations." His soft voice carried a subtle lilt, a hint of his Japanese heritage woven into his words.

"Like parlor tricks?" Nodin asked, arching an eyebrow.

"Like battlefield strategy," Reo corrected smoothly.

Nodin tilted his head, intrigued. "So, what's your story, then? You're clearly not just some street fighter we picked up."

"Indeed, I am not," Reo said, clasping his hands behind his back as he walked. "Before all of this, I was an Austri emissary. Diplomacy was my trade."

"Diplomacy?" Edvin snorted. "Yeah, that's real helpful when you're dodging IA troopers and fireballs."

"You'd be surprised," Reo replied, unbothered by the remark. "The ability to read a situation, understand motivations, and predict movement is just as vital in battle as it is in politics."

"So... you talk people to death?" Edvin smirked, clearly fishing for a reaction.

"If done correctly, yes," Reo replied, completely serious. His calm demeanor made Edvin frown as if trying to figure out whether he was joking.

Nodin chuckled. "I think what he's saying is—he's good at reading people. Probably means he knows more about us than we know about him."

Reo inclined his head slightly. "Observation is a skill I have spent many years cultivating."

"Alright, then, Reo," Claire said, giving a wry smile. "What have you observed about us?"

Reo glanced at her, then Edvin, then Nodin, before finally settling his gaze on me.

"You," he said to me, his dark eyes scrutinizing me, "have considerable power, but you are uncertain. You hide it well, but not from everyone. You take much upon yourself... perhaps too much. Your heart drives you, but your mind holds you back. It is as if you are in constant debate with yourself, torn between what you can do and what you think you should."

I stiffened, caught between irritation and something harder to define.

Reo's gaze lingered on me a second longer as though he were studying a painting, a flicker of something unspoken in his dark eyes. His expression softened—curiosity giving way to realization. He tilted his head slightly, almost as if he were piecing together a memory. Then, with quiet certainty, he said, "You're her. The one Aedan spoke of—Elin."

I blinked, caught off guard. "What?"

"Aedan-kun," Reo clarified, his voice calm but steeped with something heavier. "He spoke of you often when we were imprisoned together at Ginnungagap. At first, I thought it was just an idle way to distract himself, but the more he described you...the more I understood how much you meant to him."

The air seemed to still, and I wasn't sure if it was my imagination or if Nodin's presence at my side had suddenly shifted.

"You were at Ginnungagap *with* Aedan. What did he say?" I asked, my voice barely above a whisper.

"He spoke of your strength," Reo said, his tone measured but sincere. "How you never gave up, no matter the odds. How you always fought for what you believed in, even when it seemed impossible. He admired that about you. You were what kept him going."

My chest tightened. The thought of Aedan, alone in that horrible place, holding onto the memory of me—it was both a comfort and a fresh wave of pain.

"He... *really* said that?"

"Often," Reo replied. "More than you might think. He believed you were capable of far more than you knew."

For a moment, the only sound was the echo of our footsteps in the corridor. I could feel the weight of Nodin's gaze, and when I glanced at him, there was something unreadable in his hazel eyes.

"Well, now," Nodin said, his tone light, though there was a subtle tension beneath it. "That's a lot to live up to, isn't it, Elli?"

I should have laughed. I should have rolled my eyes and shoved his shoulder like I usually did. But instead, I just felt... guilty.

"She'll manage," Claire cut in, her voice steady and confident. "She always does."

"Yeah, but no pressure," Edvin added, attempting to break the tension. "Just, you know, carrying the hopes and dreams of our fearless warriors on your shoulders. Totally normal stuff."

I gave him a weak smile, but my mind was elsewhere. Reo's words lingered like a weight I couldn't shake, and Nodin's presence beside me only made the confusion in my heart harder to untangle.

Aedan had spoken about me with admiration and hope. And yet, here I was, walking alongside Nodin, who, despite his teasing demeanor, had a way of anchoring me in a way I couldn't explain.

The emotions churned in my mind like a maelstrom, but I forced myself to keep walking. Whatever I felt for either of them didn't matter right now. We had bigger battles to fight.

"What about the rest of us? What have you observed about us?" Claire inquired, looking at Reo and subtly changing the subject.

"You," he continued, looking at Claire, "are sharp and deliberate. Calculated. You don't rush into things, and you see angles that others don't. But you hold back—whether from strategy or restraint, I'm not sure yet."

Claire's expression flickered, but she didn't deny it.

Reo's gaze shifted to Edvin. "You rely on strength, but you underestimate your own instincts. You pretend not to think too much, but it's an act. When things go wrong, you react quickly—and smartly. You just don't like people knowing it."

Edvin opened his mouth, paused, then frowned. "Alright, well... now I feel weirdly exposed. Thanks for that."

Reo only nodded, then turned to Nodin, his expression unreadable. "And you," he said after a moment, "are used to being underestimated. You use that to your advantage, even when it's inconvenient. But you're also holding back something. You test the waters, never fully committing to a path until you know exactly where it leads."

Nodin's lips quirked, his hazel eyes glinting with something amused—but wary. "Well, now," he said, voice slow. "Aren't you just a walking human lie detector?"

"I prefer 'keen observer,'" Reo said lightly.

For the first time since we'd met, Nodin didn't have a ready quip. He held Reo's gaze, the flicker of amusement in his eyes dimming for just a heartbeat. Then it was gone, replaced by his usual easy smirk. But I'd seen it—that hesitation, like Reo had hit something real beneath the surface. Something Nodin didn't want anyone to see.

"And what about you?" Claire cut in, folding her arms. "You seem to know a lot about us. What do we know about you?"

Reo's dark eyes flickered with amusement. "Only what I allow you to."

Edvin exhaled dramatically, throwing his hands in the air. "Fantastic. We've got a walking riddle dispenser. Next thing you know, he'll be talking in prophetic riddles about doom and destiny."

Claire smirked. "If you want, I can start keeping a tally of how often you panic over 'ominous vibes.'"

"I don't panic," Edvin shot back. "I strategize. Like, for example, I've already decided that if anyone here starts muttering warnings about 'the path ahead,' I'm turning around and walking the other way."

"If only you strategized as much in battle," Claire quipped, sighing for dramatic effect.

Edvin scoffed. "Hey, I land my punches just fine, thanks."

"Sure," Claire said smoothly. "Right up until you throw one at the wrong person and end up on your back."

Edvin crossed his arms, narrowing his eyes. "That happened *one* time."

Claire raised a brow. "One memorable time."

Nodin chuckled. "I don't know, Edvin. Sounds like you might need a backup plan."

"My backup plan is running faster than the problem."

Reo, who had been silently observing, finally spoke, his voice dry. "An excellent strategy—unless the problem runs faster than you."

Edvin blinked, then grimaced. "Alright, you know what? I liked it better when you were just being mysterious."

Nodin chuckled, and even I felt some of the weight in my chest lift slightly. It was a brief reprieve from everything—from Gabriel, from the fight, from the gnawing sense of failure—but I held onto it.

Because I had a feeling we'd need every small moment of levity we could get.

The moment we stepped inside Yrsa's office, Mr. Grady wasted no time starting to explain while the rest of us gathered around the large metal table in the center of the room.

"Thorne is an old family friend," he began, glancing at his wife, who nodded in agreement. "After Ginnungagap, we had no contacts in the Falinvik Resistance, no way to get a message to McHaill, and no idea where the base was these days. Thorne was our only option."

"And you're sure he didn't betray you?" Yrsa asked, arms crossed.

"Thorne would never," Mr. Grady said firmly. "Keeping us was a massive risk for him—one that may have cost him everything. His house, his standing, everything he built. No, I'm certain neither IA raid was because he gave us up. They found us another way."

Who was Thorne to the Gradys? They'd never mentioned him before, yet here was a man willing to sacrifice everything for their safety. What kind of bond could inspire that level of loyalty?

McHaill nodded. "IA has gotten more aggressive. They have Replicants tracking movements throughout the city now. I've seen them myself. The *Stór-menni* are sending them to the places the SASUs can't go—taverns, mead halls."

Yrsa sighed, pinching the bridge of her nose. "Alright. And what exactly was your plan?"

"Rescuing Aedan," Mr. Grady said, voice resolute. "We were working on a way to get him out, but we need Gabriel. Without him, the plan doesn't work."

I snapped to attention, my pulse quickening.

"Wait, you have a plan?" I asked, barely containing my hope.

Mr. Grady hesitated before nodding. "Yes. It's the only thing we've been working on since Ginnungagap. And Thorne was instrumental in helping us. You see, Gabriel figured out a way to disarm the *Hepta Baugrs*."

The room fell into stunned silence.

Yrsa's expression darkened instantly. "You mean to tell me Gabriel knows how to neutralize the most sophisticated power dampener the *Stór-menni* have?"

"Yes," Mr. Grady admitted, his hesitation evident. "But only he can do it. He's a very talented Technopath. After just a few days of tinkering with the *Hepta Baugrs* that Thorne supplied, Gabriel cracked it—figured out the vulnerabilities in the design and how he could 'talk' to them. But without him, we can't do it."

"If IA finds out what he can do, they won't just keep him locked up," McHaill muttered, running a hand through his beard. "They'll rip the knowledge from him and use it against us."

"Gabriel isn't just our best shot—he's our only shot at dismantling the *Hepta Baugrs*," Mr. Grady said, his jaw tightening. "And you're right, McHaill. If they break him, if they even suspect what he can do, the *Stór-menni* won't just hold him. They'll force him to improve the very thing we are trying to break."

Yrsa exhaled, rubbing her temples.

"I understand," she said. "I do. But we don't have the resources to launch a rescue mission for one person."

My stomach dropped.

"You're seriously saying no?" I demanded.

Yrsa shot me a sharp look. "Elin, this isn't about what I want—it's about what we can realistically do. Launching a full-scale rescue at IA headquarters is suicide. We don't have the numbers, the supplies, or the luxury of risking it all for one person. We're hanging on by a thread as it is." Her tone was cold, but the frustration beneath it was unmistakable.

"So what, we're just leaving him there?" I asked, my voice rising.

"I have to think about more than one person," Yrsa snapped back. "The Resistance isn't about saving one person or one family—it's about fighting for all of us. If we use up resources to rescue Gabriel, what happens to the others who need us?"

My fists clenched at my sides.

Gabriel was our friend.

Aedan was trapped.

And Yrsa was telling us to just—what? Move on?

I barely noticed the way my breathing had quickened, how my nails dug into my palms.

EEEEEHHH! EEEEEHHH!

A shrill warning siren echoed through the halls, breaking my thoughts. It was followed by a voice over the intercom: "Maintenance approaching Northwest entrance. Illusionists to stations. Illusionists to stations" EEEEEHHH! EEEEEHHH!

The sharp blare of the alarm jolted through the room like a physical force. Mrs. Grady clutched the doorframe, her eyes wide as she shouted over the noise. "What is happening?" she demanded, instinctively moving closer to her family.

Yrsa remained unshaken, her calm demeanor a stark contrast to the sounding alarm. "Nothing to be concerned about," she said evenly, as if the alarm were a mere inconvenience. "It is our monthly visit from the geothermal maintenance workers. The Illusionists will handle it, but we must maintain complete silence until they pass our sector."

Yrsa glanced at her watch. "We have a few minutes before they arrive. I suggest everyone get comfortable. You never know where they'll decide to conduct their work."

Sigrid, standing near the wall with arms crossed, gave Yrsa a disbelieving look. "Let me get this straight: every month, you have to stop everything—and I mean *everything*—remain completely silent, scramble your Illusionists to make this place look like an ordinary subway tunnel, and hope, *Odin forbid*, there's no emergency while they're here?"

Yrsa met Sigrid's pointed stare without flinching. "Precisely. It's a great inconvenience, I'll admit. But one of the many challenges we endure to maintain our presence in these tunnels. This location is our critical advantage in the fight. So yes, we put up with the maintenance workers or the occasional stray SASU—or worse—that finds its way down here. Because if we want any chance of success, what choice do we have?"

"Well," Sigrid replied with a sly edge to her voice, "that depends on how much help and resources you're willing to offer our friends here."

For a moment, I didn't understand what she was getting at. Then, it clicked: the Bubble Shield Wall—BSW—an ingenious invention her engineers at Skogly had developed.

In Skogly, the BSW could encase an intruder in an invisible, seamless sphere. To the person trapped inside, it would look as if they were surrounded by the same landscape—the forest, streams, and boulders they'd seen before entering the commune. The BSW would guide them through the area without them realizing they were being redirected. They could walk straight through the heart of Skogly without hearing or seeing a single home, person, or clue that an entire village was concealed within.

It was genius. A self-contained illusion requiring no constant effort, and far less manpower than Yrsa's approach.

Yrsa's calm façade faltered slightly as she caught the knowing glint in Sigrid's eye. She narrowed her gaze, clearly suspicious but intrigued.

I suppressed a smirk. Sigrid always had a way of delivering exactly what was needed—but on her terms.

THIRTEEN

The First Day

AEDAN

The towering *Leikr* Stadium loomed before us, its sleek, ultramodern architecture a stark contrast to the ancient Viking traditions the games were meant to honor. The smooth black metal exterior gleamed under the daylight, contributing to the shine of the arena's glass dome. From the outside, peeking through the transparent dome, I could see massive holo-screens encircling the stadium's upper ring, already displaying team introductions, aerial shots of the competitors filing in, and promotional reels of past *Leikr* champions.

As we walked toward the entrance, my breath came out in small puffs in the frigid air. I swallowed against the tension knotting in my stomach. Part of me wished I had my iPod and headphones—something familiar to ground me. Maybe Van Morrison's "Into the Mystic" or Croce's "Operator." Anything that could trick my brain into thinking this was just another day.

But it wasn't. It was the first day of the Leikr. I let my breath out slowly, rolling my shoulders as tension coiled through my muscles. I should have been exhausted from training, from the relentless drills that pushed us past our limits—but I wasn't. If anything, my body felt sharper, faster. Stronger.

Whatever the Chairman had injected into me was still making my *megin* strum with energy. Over the past two days, I'd tested it—carefully, subtly, when I was sure no one would notice. A faster reaction in a sparring match. Lifting more than I should have been able to. A small push of telekinesis here, a slight increase in speed there. Nothing obvious, nothing reckless. Just enough to see what it could do.

And it could do a lot. My abilities were sharper, more precise. The strain I usually felt after extended use had lessened, and my *megin* responded faster than ever before. *But it wasn't normal. It wasn't mine.*

That fact sat heavy in my chest, a gnawing unease that I couldn't shake. The Chairman never gave without taking. *So what did he want in return?*

My fingers flexed at my sides, and I pushed the thought away, shifting my focus back to the present.

The inner competition ring was vast, easily the size of several football fields. The ground was a strange black material that seemed to shift and ripple like water on a lake in the flickering flames of the giant torches mounted on the walls. The smoke from the torches was accented by a strange metallic tinge that left the air smelling like charred earth. Similar to our training facility, large stone columns with faintly glowing runes encircled the arena, a nod to the Nordri Clan's forefathers. It reminded me of the Colosseum in Rome—an ancient battleground—but here, history met innovation, blending Viking heritage with modern precision in a striking fusion of old and new. At the stadium's center was a massive *Leikr* insignia, luminous with electric-blue light.

"Impressive," I muttered, half to myself.

Thyra, walking beside me, smirked. "Looks even bigger from the inside, huh?"

I nodded, scanning the lightly filled audience seats. Though sparsely occupied now, I assumed the place would be packed in the later rounds when eliminations thinned the competition. Clan banners hung from the upper decks, swaying gently in the controlled artificial breeze. Here and there, small groups of spectators, likely sponsors, Clan officials, and elite warriors, watched as we entered.

I cast a glance at Thyra. She looked as sharp as ever, her movements fluid, her gaze assessing the competition even as we walked. No sign of strain, no hesitation. You'd never guess that she'd need to skip a day of training as well.

I wouldn't have even known if I hadn't overheard Eirik grumbling to Magnus about it. *"Thyra actually took a rest day. First time I've ever seen her sit one out."*

It had barely registered at the time, just another passing comment between teammates. But now, standing beside her in the *Leikr* Stadium, it hit differently. Thyra wasn't the type to take breaks. And the fact that she had, on the exact same day I was ordered to rest, struck me as odd. Maybe it meant something, maybe it didn't.

Either way, I had bigger problems to worry about right now. Like surviving the *Leikr*.

Near the entrance, a row of holo-terminals flickered to life, displaying teams, rules, and live footage of competitors. Before we could fully take it in, a booming voice echoed through the stadium, amplified by unseen speakers.

> *"Welcome to the Leikr! Over the next seven days, the finest warriors, strategists, and navigators will prove their mettle in a series of grueling challenges and obstacle courses."*

I tightened my grip on the straps of my gear bag, trying to focus as our team moved through the main entry into the arena. Fenja walked just ahead, her black hair catching the ambient light, her expression neutral but her hands flexing slightly at her sides—a subtle giveaway of her tension. Magnus strode beside her, calm as ever, with the solid, unshakable presence of someone who could lift a mountain if he had to. Behind me, Thyra had joined Einar and Eirik, their voices low as they murmured about strategy.

"Ladies and gentlemen, get ready for this year's epic showdown! Here's how it's going down: six challenges, one for each team member —so captains, strategize wisely! Over the next two days, teams will tackle three challenges per day, pushing their skills to the limit.

And let's not forget, folks—teams are allowed to defend their player from interference, but direct assistance in Challenges? That's a one-way ticket to disqualification! On the flip side, interference against rival teams is fair game, so expect plenty of sabotage, strategy, and high-stakes clashes as the competition heats up!

But that's just the beginning! For those who survive, the real test begins—five grueling days of obstacle courses, where teams will face off head-to-head. And here's the kicker: each course gets tougher, testing every ounce of strength, stamina, and grit. Remember, the team with the slowest times—or those who can't finish—will be eliminated. By week's end, only two teams will remain standing. Who will rise to glory in this year's finals?"

I exhaled slowly. Sixteen teams, reduced to two, in a week. No pressure.

I caught up to Magnus, who'd stopped walking to take in the arena, his expression unreadable. Fenja, meanwhile, had her gaze fixed on the competition ring. "Six challenges, five courses," she said softly. "They've really made sure there's no room for error."

The announcer's voice continued deep and commanding, every word reverberating through the massive space.

"And now, here's a twist to keep things interesting! This year's Leikr comes with a brand-new rule: obstacle course pairs will be decided by the officials. That's right—teams won't get to choose their lineup! So, adaptability and cohesion will be critical."

Walking up to us, Eirik cracked his knuckles. "So we don't get to pick our partners anymore."

"Just another way to keep us on edge," Einar muttered, arms crossed.

"It's a twist, but we've been training for it," Thyra said, rolling her shoulders.

As we stepped further inside, I felt the weight of dozens of eyes locking onto us. The other competing teams—warriors, seasoned Clan Hunters, and hardened fighters—stood clustered in their own groups, assessing the competition. It was a sea of color as most teams had already donned their *Leikr* uniforms. Each team had a designated color. Ours was the Chairman's color—a charcoal gray. It might as well have been a bullseye, given the intense scrutiny we were getting.

A nearby team in their black and crimson uniforms watched us with expressions ranging from mild curiosity to outright disdain. One of them, a towering brute with jagged scars lining his arms, sneered. "Fresh blood?"

Eirik's eyes narrowed, but before he could respond, Thyra simply smirked. "Why don't you worry about your own team? You'll need the head start."

The man scoffed but didn't push further, returning to his group.

I glanced at another team—a lean, ruthless-looking squad clad in Sapphire, their stances poised and calculating. One of them, an athletic man with sharp, almost predatory eyes, tilted his head slightly in our direction. He didn't look away.

"Friendly crowd," I muttered.

Magnus's low chuckle rumbled beside me. "You're not here to make friends, Aedan. Remember that."

Eirik grinned. "Plus, it wouldn't be fun otherwise."

The announcer's voice boomed again.

"All teams, please proceed to the assignment terminal to receive your first challenge. The Games begin in one hour. This year's Leikr

celebrates the resilience and power of the Nine Realms! Each challenge will honor the essence of these ancient worlds while testing the Clan virtues of strength, agility, stamina, combat, strategy, and navigation. Only the best will advance. Let the Leikr begin!"

Thyra gave us all a sharp look. "Alright. This is where it starts. No mistakes."

I nodded, my fingers flexing at my sides. No mistakes.

We were in it now.

And there was no turning back.

THE STADIUM'S HUM VIBRATED BENEATH MY BOOTS, A STEADY thrumming of technology and anticipation. The holo-screens above flickered, replacing the glowing *Leikr* insignia with a live feed of the Challenge. Magnus stood among fifteen other formidable contestants, each positioned within their own stone circle on the arena floor. The once-uniform black surface had seamlessly reshaped itself into the Challenge layout, shifting into place as if responding to an unseen command. In front of participants, three massive chains lay in succession—each one more formidable than the last, their sheer size and composition making it clear that brute strength alone wouldn't be enough to break them.

Thyra had chosen Magnus for the first challenge. Strength. The task was brutal, but if anyone could break Fenrir's chains, it was him.

The rest of each team was standing on its own designated high-rise platform, marked by their team's colors. Positioned for an unobstructed view of the field, these platforms circled the arena and provided a direct line of sight to their contestant and the competition. More than just vantage points, they were strategically designed battlegrounds—allowing teams to defend their own and sabotage their rivals in full view of both their opponents and the watching spectators. Every move, every interference, was meant to be seen.

As we stepped into our positions on our platform, Thyra unfastened the *Hepta Baugr* from my wrist with the same quiet efficiency she used during training. It was a familiar ritual by now—silent, practiced. Just enough freedom to help the team. Nothing more.

The announcer's voice boomed across the arena, setting the stage.

> *"The first challenge is inspired by the binding of Fenrir; you must shatter these chains through sheer might. But be warned—brute force alone will not see you through. The chains are enchanted, each one crafted to resist strength differently. Adapt, endure, and prove yourself."*

I felt eyes on us, scanning, measuring. The other teams weren't just watching—they were waiting. Wearing the Chairman's color meant that the second Magnus made progress, they would act. They wanted us out. If disrupting Magnus's challenge could weaken us early, they'd take the chance.

The challenge began. All sixteen towering contestants rushed forward to the first chain. A red timer appeared in the corner of the holo-screens.

Magnus stepped up, his hands curling around the chain—thick, brutal iron links that gleamed under the torchlight. He didn't hesitate. He braced, muscles tightening, and pulled.

The metal groaned, resisting. I could see the tension in his arms, the slow shift as the chain began to bend under his force. The sound of straining iron filled the stadium before—*snap*. The chain shattered, fragments clattering against the stone.

The holo-screens flared: "**Gray Team: First Chain - Complete**."

It noted the time and completion in the team scorecard, which was displayed on a second holo-screen.

A murmur rippled through the competing teams, but there was no awe—only calculation. On their platforms, opponents subtly shifted, adjusting their stances, their team members positioning themselves for a clearer line of sight to Magnus. It was obvious—they weren't just watching anymore. They were preparing to strike.

A sudden gust of wind cut across the arena, unnatural and focused on Magnus. The second chain lurched sideways, shifting out of Magnus's reach.

"Vargyr," Thyra muttered.

I followed her gaze to a competitor in black and crimson, their fingers splayed, manipulating the currents to throw Magnus off.

Eirik moved first.

A dark tendril snaked from his shadow, twisting through the air and latching onto the chain, anchoring it. The wind died in an instant.

"Nice try," Eirik called, his voice low, amused.

The wind user scowled but didn't push further. Not yet.

Magnus didn't even glance up—he grabbed the second chain.

This was different. The stone chain had no give, no weak points to exploit. Brute force wouldn't be enough.

Magnus shifted his stance, his fingers digging into the rough stone links. Instead of pulling, he applied pressure, seeking out the natural stress fractures.

For a moment, nothing happened. Then—*CRACK.*

A splintering sound echoed as hairline fissures spread like lightning across the stone.

Magnus gritted his teeth and pulled, this time absorbing the tremors from the chain into his own body, his stance solidifying as though he were part of the earth itself. His skin hardened, a faint stone-like sheen running along his arms and shoulders. He was using his ability.

With one final, earth-shaking pull, the chain ruptured.

The holo-screen flared: "**Gray Team: Second Chain - Complete.**"

I barely had time to breathe or celebrate before the ground beneath Magnus lurched. A competitor from the Green Team had slammed his palms to the ground and was now manipulating the earth—a Geomancer.

Magnus's circle buckled, the stone floor splitting open beneath his feet. He was about to be swallowed whole.

"Not today," Fenja muttered.

She flicked her fingers, and slivers of metal from the broken chain lifted into the air—a dozen, then more. They shot forward, stabbing into the trembling ground, forming a metallic scaffold that stabilized the terrain beneath Magnus.

Magnus shot her a quick nod of thanks and turned toward the final challenge.

The last chain wasn't solid—it shifted, flickering like candlelight. This was the true test. Magnus reached for it—and it dodged.

I cursed. *This wasn't going to be simple.*

The chain wasn't just enchanted; it was alive, resisting his grip. Then, to add insult to injury, a sudden flash of golden light flew across the field—an Illusionist's trick. This time, it was Team Sapphire. For an instant, the gleaming chain seemed to split into three, each duplicate vibrating at a different frequency. A feint. A distraction.

Magnus hesitated, his eyes flicking between the illusions, unsure which chain was real. Every second of hesitation was a victory for the teams working against us.

I clenched my fists. *I could let this happen—let Magnus fail, let the Gray Team be eliminated in the first round. It would let me walk away from the trials without having to compete.* And before the Chairman's warning, I'd entertained that thought more than once. But now, the consequences of that decision were wrapped around my throat like a tightening noose.

I stretched out with my *megin*, feeling for the energy flow in the correct chain. The illusions were clever, but the real chain had a rhythm, an energy flow that set it apart. If Magnus moved at the right moment, he could catch it before it shifted away. I knew I could help, and now I didn't have a choice. With a silent curse, I reached out my telekinesis, subtly slowing the correct chain's vibration and movements just enough for Magnus to seize it.

The second he touched it, the chain reacted violently.

A spurt of energy erupted outward, sending crackling arcs of blue lightning streaking up his arms. Magnus gritted his teeth, refusing to let go.

Suddenly, a sharp whistling cut through the air.

My stomach dropped.

An incoming projectile—one of the opposing teams had launched a steel spear straight for Magnus's ribs.

Before I could think another thought, Thyra reacted. Her air current slammed into the weapon mid-air, diverting it just inches away from Magnus's side. It struck the ground with a deafening *clang.*

Focused on the chain, Magnus barely winced at the sound. He pulled, the effort making his face contort in odd ways. The chain fought back, coiling around Magnus's arms like a python. Its energy surged, trying to force him to let go. But Magnus planted his feet, his muscles solidifying like stone, his resilience ability awakening fully.

The electricity rippled, but he absorbed it, channeling the raw force into his grip. His veins throbbed with power, his body adapting. The hue of his skin took on a gray stone-colored tone—he had become unbreakable.

The stadium held still.

Then—an explosion of light. The chain snapped.

The holo-screens erupted. "**Gray Team: Challenge Complete**."

A mix of cheers and murmurs rippled through the spectators in the stadium. But the opposing teams weren't cheering. They were watching. *Scheming.*

Pumping his fist in the air, Magnus turned to us, his gaze locking onto ours.

No words were needed.

Round one was ours. But the real battle was just beginning.

"Congratulations, Gray Team! First to complete the Strength round—an impressive display! As a reminder to all our spectators and contestants, the one-hour rest period between rounds begins now. Be sure to take advantage of the many refreshments available in the main hall before the next challenge commences!"

Eirik crossed his arms, his lips curling into a wicked smirk. "The other teams are still at it. Now's our chance for some payback." His gaze flicked toward a group struggling with the second chain, his fingers already twitching as shadows flickered at his heels.

"No, we defend only," Thyra snapped, stepping closer, her voice sharp with authority. Her gaze burned into him, unwavering. "We have a big enough target on our backs as it is. You want to make it worse? Go ahead and hand them a reason to come after us in the next round."

Eirik scoffed but didn't push further, though the tension in his shoulders didn't ease.

Fenja, who had been watching Magnus catch his breath, finally spoke up. "Besides, if you think a cheap shot now is worth whatever payback comes later, you're not thinking like a strategist." She tossed her braid over her shoulder, her black eyes glinting. "We'll get our revenge—when it actually counts."

Eirik rolled his eyes. "Okay, okay. *Fine*."

I turned to Einar, still unsettled. "I don't understand. Not all the teams have finished competing. How can the rest period start now?"

Einar, ever the practical one, simply shrugged. "It's triggered by the win," he said. "The winning team gets the most rest as a reward. The others will have to take whatever time they can get once their player finishes."

Fenja smirked. "Which means the longer they struggle, the worse off they are for the next round."

The *Leikr* was more brutal than I thought, which was saying something. It purposely punished the struggling teams without mercy.

Thyra sighed, shaking her head. "Let's not get cocky. This was only the first round."

I nodded, though I couldn't shake the unease. One victory down. Five more to go.

~

From the scraps Thyra managed to gather before the trials were officially announced, we learned that the next round paid tribute to Freyr and Gjallarbrú—names pulled straight from Norse myth, now twisted into tests of stamina and speed. After some debate, it was clear: Fenja's precision and Einar's spectral edge gave us the best chance. They would take them on.

I had to dig deep to recall my mother's stories about Freyr, the god of prosperity and battle, and Gjallarbrú, the mythical bridge spanning the river Gjöll, leading to Hel's realm. Neither sounded like something I wanted to experience as a Challenge.

The announcer's voice boomed in the arena as the rest period came to an end.

> *"For our next round, we honor the legacy of Freyr. And the Challenge demands agility, precision, and nerves of steel. Inspired by the legendary sword of Freyr—said to fight on its own—our competitors must navigate a lethal storm of enchanted blades. Captains, choose your contestants wisely, as this is a deadly round!"*

Above us, the holo-screens flickered, shifting to display the next event. The stadium floor rumbled beneath our boots, reconfiguring. A new arena formed—smaller, circular, its perimeter lined with floating blades that hovered, spinning in unpredictable patterns. A faint, metallic whirr filled the air, the sound of steel cutting through nothingness.

Fenja sighed, securing her long black braid into a bun. "Guess that's my cue."

"Good luck!" Thyra said, giving a meaningful nod to Fenja. "We have your back."

The Dancing Blades of Freyr was a test of precision and control, the kind of rhythm that made me think of fingerpicked guitars and layered harmonies—Croce, Simon, Lennon. Artists who made complexity look effortless. Fenja was like that—every move calibrated, every dodge a note in a song only she could hear.

The Black and Crimson team wasted no time making the challenge even harder. Other teams took their shots, but none were as relentless or devious. The moment Fenja stepped onto the circular stage, where spinning, enchanted blades weaved unpredictable patterns through the air, their team's Metalshaper began subtly altering the blades' trajectories, making them whip toward her at unnatural angles.

I saw Fenja adjust instantly, her own ability sending a faint ripple through the air as she magnetized certain blades, redirecting them just enough to slip through gaps with hair's breadth precision. But Black and Crimsons weren't done. The same wind manipulator who had plagued Magnus struck again—sending a violent gust at her stage, disrupting Fenja's control and forcing the blades into a frenzied spiral.

Just as Fenja adapted mid-dodge, another stronger gust slammed into her side at the worst possible moment—when she had no way to counterbalance. A spinning blade whirled past, slicing clean through her sleeve and leaving a thin trail of blood in its wake. Fenja barely managed to regain her footing, her jaw tightening against the pain. But every time she used her power, she risked triggering more blades. The moment she overcorrected, several new ones activated, closing off the remaining safe paths and turning an already brutal challenge into a lethal gauntlet.

I felt tension coil in my gut. *This was bad.*

Then, Thyra countered. With a subtle flick of her fingers, she sent an opposing air current, steadying Fenja's balance just enough for her to regain control. Fenja darted forward, twisting mid-air, sliding past a series of razor-thin blades, and in a final surge, snatched the glowing relic at the center of her stage. The moment she did, the blades froze, and the holo-screens flared: "**Gray Team: Challenge Complete**."

The Black and Crimson team looked on from their platform, their expressions unreadable. But I could feel the tension shift. *This was becoming personal.*

> *"And what a finish! The Gray Team secured second place in this round, just seconds behind the Mauve Team, who edged them out with a time advantage! That was a win for the ages—blink, and you might've missed it!"*

We also acknowledge the grueling elimination of the Yellow Team. The *Leikr* is no game for the faint-hearted, and we honor their captain's sacrifice. This arena tests the limits of strength, skill, and resilience—and sometimes, the cost is high."

Despite the raucous crowds cheering for the teams still competing, a heavy silence settled over our group as the holo-screens flashed the brutal confirmation—**Yellow Team eliminated**. I swallowed hard, the weight of it pressing into my chest. I hadn't even noticed them among the competitors, and now—just like that—they were gone. A team erased. A life lost. And yet, the game pressed on without hesitation.

"Did anyone even see them compete?" I asked, my voice lower than I intended.

Thyra's expression was grim as she shook her head. "Barely. They must've been struggling from the start."

Einar's breath snapped out, sharp as flint. "And now they're just... done. No second chances."

Eirik's jaw tightened. "This is *Leikr*. You don't make it through? You don't make it at all."

"Cold way to put it," Thyra murmured, though her tone held no real disagreement.

Magnus, who had been watching the screens with narrowed eyes, finally spoke. "It's a reminder." His fists clenched at his sides. "This isn't just about winning. It's about survival."

No one argued. Because we all knew he was right.

As we waited for the next challenge to be announced, Fenja climbed back up on our platform. She straightened to standing, wiping a thin streak of blood from her forearm, her sleeve still tattered from the blade that had come too close.

"You alright?" I asked, watching as the holo-screens above the stadium replayed highlights from the last challenge. Her near miss was shown in slow motion—Black and Crimson's wind manipulator knocking her off-course just enough for a blade to clip her.

"You mean the Challenge with the twirling death blades, or this?" She lifted her arm, showing her tattered sleeve. Before I could answer, she shook her head dismissively. "It's nothing. Though if I see that cowardly *Argr* from the Black and Crimson outside of the *Leikr*, I might put a metal spike through his foot."

"That's the spirit," Eirik smirked, stretching his arms like he hadn't just watched Fenja nearly get diced into pieces.

The others kept talking—Fenja muttering something about payback, Eirik tossing out another careless joke—but their voices faded into the background.

I kept my eyes on Fenja. The way she moved—shoulders squared, jaw tight, refusing to let anyone see how close she'd come to breaking. It reminded me of Elin.

I hadn't let myself think about her since the *Leikr* started—not really. But now, in this breath between battles, her face rose, uninvited and vivid.

Had she seen the competition? Was she watching?

The holo-screens around the stadium were broadcasting every Challenge to the entire city. The Chairman wanted a spectacle, and he was making sure everyone got one. If she was out there, somewhere beyond these walls, she would see exactly what I was being forced to do.

Would she understand? A fresh knot twisted in my gut. I was standing on the wrong side of the line, wearing the Chairman's colors for the whole world to see.

I balled my fists, forcing my thoughts back into the present. There was no room for distraction. Not here. Not now.

Magnus, who had been leaning against the railing near me, nodded toward the opposing platform. "They're still looking at us."

I followed his gaze. The Black and Crimson team wasn't focused on their next challenge. They were focused on us. Their captain stood at the center, arms crossed, saying something to his teammates. The wind manipulator who had sabotaged Fenja smirked at her across the distance, as if taunting her.

Just then, the stadium trembled, the smooth black arena floor shifting and reforming, unveiling the next challenge. A long, narrow bridge materialized across the competition ring, stretching into a mist-covered abyss. It was treacherous—sections already swayed precariously, parts disintegrating only to reform unpredictably. The air around it shimmered with heat in some places, while other sections looked slick with ice.

Einar stepped closer to the edge, staring at the shifting bridge with silent calculation. His fingers flexed at his sides, the subtle tension in his shoulders the only giveaway of his focus.

The announcer's voice boomed again throughout the stadium.

"Warriors, prepare for the next Challenge—a true test of stamina! Inspired by Gjallarbrú, the bridge to Hel's realm, this round will push competitors past their limits! A treacherous path of collapsing terrain, shifting obstacles, and scorching flames stands between them and victory! The race to Hel begins now! Competitors find your marks."

Running the Gjallarbrú should have been about endurance. But thanks to our number one rivals, it became a full-on death trap. The bridge stretched across the stadium like a twisting serpent. Einar started strong, his Spectral Perception allowing him to see the bridge's weaknesses before they collapsed, his footing precise even as sections crumbled away. Then the Black and Crimson team struck.

Their fire wielder hurled flames onto the bridge, making the planks smolder and warp, forcing Einar to adjust his footing mid-sprint. At the same time, their plant manipulator sent growing vines lashing across the bridge, slithering toward Einar's ankles to pull him off balance.

I swore under my breath—they weren't just interfering; they were hunting him.

Eirik acted first. Shadows coiled from his own form, clashing with the green tendrils in midair, cutting the vines into tiny pieces. Meanwhile, I reached out with my *megin*, using my telekinesis to counteract the tilting bridge, just enough to stabilize the worst of the shifting terrain. Einar, unfazed, charged ahead, dodging flames and collapsing planks, his expression locked in determination. With a final explosive push, he leapt across the last crumbling section, rolling onto solid ground just as the final segment collapsed behind him.

The holo-screens blared: "**Gray Team: Challenge Complete!**"

The Black and Crimson team didn't look pleased. If there had been any doubt before, there was none now. We weren't just another team to them in the *Leikr*. We were their problem.

The announcer came back on, echoing across the arena.

> *"And the Gray Team reclaims the top spot! An impressive finish from the Chairman's team—though, really, would we expect anything less? The day's eliminations will be announced once the final team completes or falls in this challenge. But don't forget, folks—tomorrow brings the final rounds of Leikr Challenges! You won't want to miss it! And before you leave, be sure to collect your exclusive holo-memorabilia card from today's events at the kiosks near the front gate. Until then, warriors and spectators alike, prepare for what's to come—because the Leikr waits for no one!"*

As the main holo-screen flickered back to the *Leikr* insignia, the teams who had completed the round began retreating to their respective platforms. The tension in the air was undeniable, but there was also a strange sort of relief—we had survived the first day.

But barely.

I let out my breath slowly, rolling my shoulders as we regrouped near the edge of our platform. Magnus was stretching his arms, shaking out the residual tension from the Challenges. Fenja was casually toying with a small metal fragment, likely a leftover piece of the broken chains, flipping it between her fingers like a coin. Eirik, predictably, looked like he was still itching for a fight.

"Well," Einar muttered as he stepped back onto the platform, wiping sweat and soot from his face. "The Black and Crimsons clearly have it out for us."

"No kidding," Fenja scoffed. "They weren't interfering—they were targeting us like prey."

"They were testing us," Magnus said, rolling his shoulders. "Next time, they'll go for real weaknesses."

"Yeah?" Eirik smirked. "Good luck finding any."

Thyra shot him a sharp look. "They don't need luck, Eirik. They're coordinated and strategic."

I glanced at the Black and Crimsons across the arena. They weren't celebrating. They were *still* watching *us*.

"They're planning their next move," I said, my voice low.

"Let them," Eirik said with a lazy stretch. "They'll just be disappointed when they fail."

Thyra rolled her eyes. "Arrogance gets people killed."

Eirik smirked. "Confidence wins wars."

Fenja snorted. "There's a difference between confidence and whatever that is."

Einar sighed. "Either way, we need to be ready. They learned something about us today. Next round, they'll use it."

Magnus cracked his knuckles. "Then we'll just defend harder."

I glanced at the scoreboard on the holo-screen. The final rankings flashed across them. The Yellow, Orange, and Aqua teams had been eliminated. The Crimson and Black team was in second place.

"We're not just any team to them," I said. "We're blocking their path to victory."

Eirik's grin widened. "Good. I like being an obstacle."

Thyra muttered something under her breath before shaking her head. "Come on. We need rest."

Eirik smirked. "Sure, grandma."

Thyra's glare could have shattered stone. "Say that again, and you won't be making it to the next round."

Fenja coughed to cover a laugh. Magnus just sighed.

I rubbed my temple, the pulse beneath my fingertips ticking like a warning. Tomorrow was going to be a long day—for a lot of reasons—but mostly because it was my turn. My first challenge. And after everything I'd seen today, I knew it wouldn't be just a test—it would be a gauntlet.

At times like this, I used to lean on music. Let a song carry the weight when everything felt too heavy. Now all I had was my *megin* pulsing through me and the knowledge that tomorrow, I'd have to face whatever came—alone and wide awake. And I had no idea which realm they'd throw at me, only that it would be brutal.

One thing was certain: every team in this stadium would be watching, waiting, sharpening their blades—ready to draw blood. Starting with mine.

And if I wasn't ready?

I wouldn't get another chance.

FOURTEEN

The Lounge

ELIN

The Resistance lounge was one of the few places in the underground base that didn't feel like a war zone. It wasn't much—just a carved-out section of the old subway tunnels, its walls lined with weathered brick and reinforced with metal beams darkened by time. The ever-present hum of geothermal pipes thrummed through the walls, radiating a steady warmth that kept the chill of the underground at bay. Steam occasionally hissed from unseen vents, carrying with it the faint, mineral-rich scent of heated rock and damp earth.

Worn rugs covered the cold concrete floors, their frayed edges curling slightly, muffling footsteps against the solid ground. The furniture—a mismatched collection of patched-up couches, pillows, and chairs—was scattered in a rough circle around the room's centerpiece: a massive holo-projector mounted to the ceiling. The device hummed softly, a low-pitched whirr blending into the ambient noise of the base.

Unlike the holo-screens scattered throughout the base, this projection wasn't bound to a single surface. It hung in the air, a three-dimensional image so sharp and immersive that it felt as if we were standing inside the stadium itself. The shifting glow of the holo cast flickering light onto the walls, illuminating the dust motes drifting through the warm air.

The lounge was a refuge—an illusion of comfort nestled within the bones of a forgotten world. But as the *Leikr's* center arena materialized in front of us, any sense of peace vanished.

I inhaled sharply.

This was it—my first time seeing the *Leikr*. For weeks, I had only heard vague mentions from the Resistance, and no matter how many times I questioned Sigrid, she refused to give me answers. She always deflected with the same, unsettling response: *"Let's hope it doesn't come to Aedan having to compete."*

But now, there was no more guessing. *No more unanswered questions.*

I was about to see the trials for myself.

Once we'd decided to watch the *Leikr*—given that the trials were projected into every home and venue in Falinvik—Mr. Grady had taken it upon himself to explain the structure and rules over breakfast, filling in some of the gaps. But no amount of explanation could have prepared me for this moment.

Because there—standing among his team—was Aedan. Dressed in the Chairman's gray colors.

The lounge fell into stunned silence.

Mr. Grady leaned forward, his expression tightening. "No." The word barely left his lips, more exhale than a sound.

Mrs. Grady's breath hitched. Her fingers dug into the armrest, gripping so tightly her knuckles turned white. A quiet tremor passed through her as her eyes locked onto the screen, brimming with a mother's worry and love. "Oh, Aedan..." she murmured, barely above a whisper, as if saying his name might somehow reach him across the distance.

"He's on *that* team?" Edvin muttered, his brows furrowed in disbelief.

Claire's lips parted slightly, eyes locked on the projection. "Why? Why would he—?"

No one had an answer.

I stared at Aedan, my stomach twisting.

I knew he hadn't joined the *Leikr* willingly. I knew he didn't *want* this. But seeing him in the Chairman's uniform, standing there like he belonged... it felt like a knife slipping between my ribs.

"That's bad, isn't it?" Nodin finally broke the silence, his voice quieter than usual. "I mean—worse than it already was?"

Mr. Grady rubbed a hand down his face, weariness breaking through his worry. "It means he's wearing a target on his back."

"Wouldn't he have a target *anyway*?" Nodin asked, still watching the holo-image.

"Not like this," Mr. Grady said, his expression grim. "The Chairman's team will have the best resources, the best training. But every other competitor will want to take them down first. And that means Aedan's not just fighting to survive the *Leikr*—he's fighting every other team who wants to prove a point."

Nodin's jaw tightened slightly as he watched the holo-projection, something flickering in his expression—an edge of something darker beneath his usual sarcasm. "People under the Chairman's watch don't come back the same," he muttered, almost to himself. "Even if they survive, there's always... something missing."

His words sent a chill down my spine. I wanted to argue, to say that Aedan wasn't like the others—that he'd never let the Chairman change him. But as I looked at the screen, at the way Aedan stood so still, so unreadable, doubt gnawed at the edges of my certainty.

The thought wrapped around my ribs like barbed wire.

The holo-image shifted, zooming in on the first competitor stepping onto the battlefield. The moment passed, but the weight of what we had just seen lingered.

Aedan was in the Chairman's colors.

And the entire world was watching.

The first challenge was a trial of pure strength. One of Aedan's teammates—a massive competitor with a build like a fortress—stepped into the ring. Chains, shining with ancient runes, coiled around him. The challenge was brutal, relentless, pushing every contestant past their limits as they tried to break through the enchanted bonds.

I had no idea who this man was, but he was powerful. He fought through the test with a measured, unshakable focus, breaking through the final chain with his ability and sheer force.

"Gray Team: Challenge Complete!"

A sliver of tension loosened its grip on my chest.

One challenge down.

The holo-projection expanded, showing the other competitors still struggling. A few teams were falling behind. Others were barely holding on.

The announcer's voice boomed.

"With the first challenge won, competitors will now have a one-hour break before the second round begins! Spectators, enjoy the entertainment, and competitors—recover while you can. The Leikr waits for no one."

Nodin leaned back into the couch, crossing his arms behind his head. "Well, that was fun. Anyone else feel like we've aged ten years in the last five minutes?"

Edvin snorted, shaking his head. "Just five? You're being generous."

A few strained chuckles rippled through the room, but the tension remained thick and unshakable. No one really felt like laughing.

The holo-projector flickered, shifting to replays of past *Leikr* highlights as the hour break stretched before us. The Resistance lounge, once taut with the weight of the competition, settled into a quieter hum of murmured voices and rustling movements.

Mrs. Grady's hand drifted to her temple, her brow furrowed with worry. "We should talk about Gabriel."

I forced my focus away from the screen, from the lingering image of Aedan's team securing their first victory, and back to the room.

Bae, still resting in a patched-up armchair with one hand gingerly pressed against her bandaged ribs, shifted slightly. "Sigrid got the Resistance on board, but only under the condition that we wait until he's transferred out of IA headquarters to the detention center."

"That's assuming the transfer actually happens," Mr. Tibadeau added gruffly, flexing his injured arm in its sling. The burn he'd suffered during our escape was healing, but slowly.

Mrs. Grady nodded grimly. "We have no way of knowing when it'll happen. It could be days. Weeks."

"Or tomorrow," Bae interjected, her voice dry.

The thought sent a shiver down my spine.

"We need a backup plan," I said. "We can't just sit here hoping we get lucky."

"Unless you've got a map of IA headquarters, breaking in before the transfer isn't an option," Mr. Grady said. His tone was matter-of-fact, but there was an edge of something else there.

Nodin let out a low whistle. "Well, technically—" He stopped, jaw tightening for a brief second before he forced a smirk. But I caught the flicker of something else in his expression—like he'd almost said too much.

Mr. Tibadeau shot him a sharp glare.

Nodin held up his hands. "Relax, I wasn't suggesting a full-blown 'Mission Impossible.' Just, you know, a well-thought-out, slightly illegal retrieval mission with a touch of recklessness."

Bae sighed. "He's not wrong."

Mr. Grady's jaw tightened. "Breaking into IA is suicide."

"And leaving Gabriel there isn't?" I shot back.

A silence settled over the room.

Mr. Grady finally sighed. "Let's see what information the

Resistance can pull before we get ahead of ourselves. If a window opens, we'll act."

The conversation lulled after that, tension hanging heavy in the air.

As the hour break stretched on, the discussion inevitably turned to the Gradys—where they had been after Ginnungagap, how they had survived, and, most pressingly, how they had escaped.

Mr. Grady's expression darkened. "The moment the system rebooted, all hell broke loose. We barely made it out before the whole place turned into a war zone."

I leaned forward. "What happened?"

Mrs. Grady clasped her hands together, her knuckles white. "Gabriel did exactly what he said he would. He hacked into their security system, triggered a full restart, and the next thing we knew, every cell door was open, and the *Hepta Baugrs* keeping the prisoners restrained were disengaged."

"The entire prison?" I asked, glancing between them.

"The entire prison," Mr. Grady confirmed.

He sat back, eyes wide. "Well... that's one way to make an exit."

"But it didn't go smoothly, did it?" I pressed.

Mrs. Grady shook her head. "No. The prisoners turned on each other. On the guards. On anyone in their path," she said grimly. "Some of them just ran, trying to escape. Others... they weren't looking to run. They wanted revenge."

I swallowed hard. "And then?"

"The guards retaliated," Mr. Grady continued. "Weapons and abilities were being discharged everywhere. Chaos. The whole place was coming apart. We had no choice but to fight our way out."

Bae shifted in the chair with a wince, one hand pressed to her ribs. "And you found Reo instead of Aedan."

Mr. Grady nodded. "We did. Pure luck, really. We had no way of knowing Aedan had already been transferred to Falinvik for the *Leikr*. If it weren't for Reo, we might have wasted precious time searching Ginnungagap for him."

Nodin tapped his fingers against his knee. “And you got out but lost Bae in the chaos.”

Mrs. Grady’s expression darkened. “The whole prison was in upheaval. We tried to reach our meeting point, but it was impossible —barricades, rioting prisoners, guards at every turn. We had to make a choice, and we hoped...” She exhaled. “We hoped you’d portal safely back to Falinvik when we didn’t show.”

She turned to Bae, her voice quieter. “We had no idea you stayed.”

Bae’s lips pressed into a thin line. “I wasn’t going to leave without knowing if you made it,” she said, her voice edged with concern. “You could have been trapped, injured, or worse. I had to be sure.”

Mrs. Grady’s expression softened, guilt flickering across her face. “We didn’t know that,” she murmured. “And without a way to communicate, we had nowhere to turn.”

“So you went to Thorne,” Sigrid said flatly, arms crossed.

I frowned. “Thorne—the Commander in the Clan Hunters.”

Nodin’s gaze flickered toward the holo-image, but he didn’t speak. For a fraction of a second, his expression shifted—thoughtful, calculating. Like Thorne’s name meant more to him than he was letting on.

“The same,” Mr. Grady confirmed.

I shook my head. “Why would he help you?”

Mr. Grady hesitated before finally saying, “Before all of this... before the Chairman started hunting us, before we had to run— Thorne and I were colleagues in Protective Services.”

That statement sank in slowly.

“Trusted colleagues,” Mrs. Grady added. “And when we had no one else left, he was the only person we could risk turning to.”

Sigrid’s expression was unreadable. “And he helped you escape?”

“He did,” Mr. Grady said simply.

There was no elaboration. No further details.

And something told me I wouldn’t get more than that.

Instead, Mrs. Grady changed the subject. "We had a plan to get Aedan before the *Leikr* even began."

I sat up straighter. "You did?"

Mr. Grady nodded. "Using his ability, Gabriel was going to get us inside the Chairman's tower when we knew Aedan would be there. We planned to strike when the Chairman was on one of his scheduled visits to Ginnungagap."

I blinked. "And you knew that... how?"

"Thorne," Mrs. Grady answered.

His name carried even more weight now.

"But then Gabriel was captured," Mr. Grady finished. "And the plan fell apart."

A heavy silence settled over the room.

They had tried. They had been ready to risk everything for Aedan. But now, Aedan was inside the *Leikr*, and Gabriel was imprisoned. And we were all scrambling for a way forward.

Before I could dwell on it further, the holo-projector flickered to life once again.

The hour was up.

The battlefield had transformed—this time into a deadly storm of floating, enchanted blades, spinning in unpredictable patterns.

> *"The next challenge tests agility, precision, and the ability to adapt! Inspired by Freyr's legendary sword—a weapon that fights on its own —competitors must navigate a relentless storm of steel!"*

From the competitors' platform, a woman stepped forward. Tall, dark-haired, with the same sharp presence I'd seen earlier beside Aedan. Another member of his team.

The moment she entered the arena, the blades came to life.

She was fast. Calculated. Slipping between the arcs of spinning steel like she could see their paths before they moved. Other competitors struggled—one barely avoided losing an arm, another was knocked back by the sheer force of the enchanted weapons. The other teams on the platforms tried to sabotage her, particularly the Black and Crimson, and just as it seemed as if their interference might finally pin her down, she adjusted. A calculated shift, a redirected blade, and suddenly she was sprinting toward the relic at the center of the battlefield.

A final dodge—a twist midair—her hand closed around the glowing artifact.

The holo-screens in the stadium flared: "**Gray Team: Challenge Complete!**"

Bae let out a low, impressed hum. "She's scary good."

"She's probably trained for years for this," Mr. Grady muttered, expression tight. "Aedan hasn't."

Before I could process his words, the holo-image shifted. It zoomed out again, displaying the remaining competitors still locked in battle. The Black and Crimsons were close behind, their contestant weaving through the chaos with equal ferocity. Another competitor in yellow struggled—barely able to keep up.

Then—

A sharp, slicing arc. A blade, too fast to dodge. A scream.

The lounge went still.

The holo-projection replayed the moment in slow motion. The captain of the Yellow Team had misstepped. The blade struck clean, slicing deep into his side, and he staggered. He tried to push forward, but another blade came, and then another—his footing gone, his strength failing. He collapsed.

And then—nothing.

The holo-image cut to the scoreboard. **"Yellow Team: Eliminated."**

The announcer's voice echoed, but the energy had shifted.

"And we have our first loss of the Leikr. The Yellow Team captain has fallen, a grim reminder that the Leikr does not offer second chances. We honor his sacrifice."

The holo-projector replayed the last few seconds again, as if that made it easier to process.

My pulse kicked beneath my skin.

Before this moment, the *Leikr* had been brutal. Unforgiving. But I hadn't yet *felt* the weight of it. The sheer finality.

But now?

Someone had just *died.* And it was only the second round. Mrs. Grady pressed a hand to her lips, her face pale.

Bae leaned forward, her voice a whisper, saying what we all were thinking. "That could have been Aedan."

No one responded.

We all knew the truth. *It still could be.* A cold weight anchored itself in my chest.

Even Nodin had nothing clever to say. His usual humor was absent as he ran a hand through his hair, his gaze locked on the screen.

After a long silence, Edvin's voice cracked through the stillness. "Okay, so... anyone else suddenly have the urge to punch something?" The room was silent.

Nodin glanced sideways at me, his voice quieter now. "Elli?"

I blinked, dragging myself out of the haze of horror. "What?"

His smirk was softer than usual. "Just checking if you're still breathing."

I huffed out a breath, trying to shake the icy weight in my chest. "Barely."

He nudged my knee with his. "Then we'll call that a win."

"They don't... stop it? The medics don't step in?" Bae asked.

"They don't intervene unless the body's removed from the battlefield," Mr. Grady said grimly. "That's how it's always been."

I swallowed against the rising nausea in my throat.

It wasn't just sport. It wasn't just spectacle. The *Leikr* demanded blood.

And Aedan was still in it.

I gritted my teeth, forcing myself to focus as the holo-projector panned to the remaining competitors. The match wasn't over yet. A handful of warriors were still struggling through the enchanted blades, though now, some hesitated—shaken by what had just happened.

"Gray Team: Challenge Complete!" the stadium holo-screen declared again, a stark reminder that Aedan's team had taken another victory.

But it didn't feel like a victory.

Not with the Yellow Team's captain lying motionless on the arena floor. The holo-projector flickered again, shifting to an overhead view of the stadium as the last few competitors fought through the storm of blades.

"This is just going to keep happening, isn't it?" Claire muttered, still pale. "Every round. More of them will—"

She didn't finish the sentence. She didn't have to.

I clenched my fists, my heart hammering against my ribs. The air in the lounge suddenly felt too heavy, too thick. I needed space.

Without a word, I pushed myself to my feet and slipped out of the lounge, barely noticing if anyone looked up. The sound of the *Leikr* still echoed behind me, but the farther I walked, the quieter it became.

I needed air. I needed to do something.

I ran a hand over my face, trying to force my mind back to what mattered. *Aedan. Focus on Aedan.* He was the one who needed me. The one trapped in the Chairman's game. The one I should have been thinking about.

And yet, Nodin's voice echoed in my head instead.

"Just checking if you're still breathing."

I shook my head. *Stupid. I didn't have time for this. For him.* For the warmth curling in my chest at the way he had nudged my knee, grounding me without a word.

Stop it, Elin.

But the truth settled like a weight I didn't know how to lift. The longer Aedan had been gone, the more Nodin had filled the spaces he left behind. His quips, his steady presence, the way he always had some sarcastic remark to cut through the worst of it—

I clenched my fists. *I didn't want that. I couldn't want that.*

Aedan was the one in danger. Aedan was the one I had to save. Not just from the *Leikr,* but from the Chairman's grasp. I had to pull him back before he became something unrecognizable.

And yet, standing in the dim corridor, *I wasn't sure if I was holding onto Aedan... or just trying to stop myself from slipping further toward Nodin.*

The thought unsettled me, creeping in at the edges of my mind like a shadow I couldn't shake. I dragged a hand through my hair, forcing myself to focus. *This wasn't about me.*

Aedan was still in the *Leikr*. Still fighting. And the last time I had tried to reach him—to use my *megin* to see him in real time—it had gone horribly wrong. The Chairman had sensed it, clawing into my vision with those sharp, piercing gray eyes.

But Aedan was at the stadium now. And there had been no sign of the Chairman there. *Surely the distance between them was too great for the Chairman to sense me.*

If I could just see Aedan—just for a moment—it might be enough.

I slipped down a quieter corridor of the base, pressing my back against the cool stone of the subway walls. My fingers found the medallion around my neck, gripping it tightly. I closed my eyes, grounding myself. And told my *megin* to find Aedan.

At first, there was nothing. Then—white light flared in my mind. Familiar, painless.

It was working.

The light faded, and I was hovering above the competitor platforms.

Aedan was there.

Standing tall, his face set in a neutral mask, his stormy sea-blue eyes locked onto the arena below. A pang shot through my chest. He looked *different.* Colder. Sharper. I wanted to call out to him, to say *something.*

Then—pressure.

A sharp pulse of energy slammed into me. My vision wrenched sideways, the scene dissolving into nothingness. A presence—cold, invasive—pushed against my mind.

No.

A pressure, suffocating and inescapable, pressed down. The same force from before. The same dark presence.

I tried to pull back, but it was too late.

The Chairman had found me.

"Curious, aren't we?" His voice slithered through my thoughts, dripping with amusement, slow and deliberate, like a predator toying with its prey. *"I thought I might see you again... though I must admit, I was hoping it would be in person."* A pause. A shadow of something darker curled beneath his tone. *"Soon enough, I think. Until then."*

A searing pain erupted through my skull. The pressure exploded behind my eyes, ripping me back into my own body. My knees buckled. I gasped, stumbling back against the wall as my vision blurred. Before I could fully steady myself, footsteps approached—fast, purposeful.

"Elli?" Nodin's voice cut through the ringing in my ears. His hands were on my arms, steadying me before I collapsed completely.

I forced my eyes open, meeting his worried gaze. His expression was tense, more serious than usual.

"You reached out, didn't you?" he said, his voice barely above a whisper. But there was something else in his tone—something that made my stomach twist. Not just worry.

Recognition.

FIFTEEN

The Second Day

AEDAN

The morning came too soon. The second day of the *Leikr* dawned cold and gray. The scent of metal and char lingered in the stadium's air from the previous night's challenges.

I stood at the edge of our platform, staring out over the shifting arena as the final day of *Leikr* Challenges began to take shape. My *megin* should have been running low after helping my team during yesterday's competition, but instead, I felt restless—too awake.

Whatever the Chairman had injected into me was still coursing through my veins, sharpening my senses in a way that didn't feel natural. My body reacted faster than it should, my stamina never seemed to wane, and my *megin* burned too hot, almost electric beneath my skin. I flexed my fingers, staring down at my palm. *What did he do to me?*

I tried to push it out of my head and focus on the very real, immediate challenge ahead, but the questions twisted in my thoughts like tangled roots. *What was this thing?* My parents might have known, might have understood the price of whatever was coursing through my veins—but they weren't here. And right now, I would have given anything to talk to them.

Not just about the Chairman. About all of it. *How to survive the Leikr. How to make it through this in one piece.* They must have seen these games before they escaped Falinvik, must have known how brutal they were.

But were they even safe now? Was Claire and Edvin? Had Elin found them?

The uncertainty twisted in my gut, knotting itself around the nerves already tightening my stomach. *So many unknowns, so many questions without answers.*

I tried to swallow back the unease. My mother would have had advice for this. She always did. I could almost hear her say, *"Trust yourself, Aedan. That's the one thing they can't take away from you."*

I needed to focus on today—on the *Leikr*. Everything else would have to wait. Survival came first.

I turned toward my teammates. Magnus sat on the platform's edge, adjusting his leather vambraces absently, while Thyra stood with arms crossed, deep in thought. Eirik paced, watching the other competitor platforms.

"We need to retaliate."

Thyra exhaled sharply. "No, we don't."

Eirik's sharp grin widened. "*Oh?* I think we do. They nearly got Fenja cut in half yesterday, tried to burn Einar off the bridge, and took their shot at Magnus when they thought no one was looking."

I caught Fenja's expression—cool, unreadable—but the way she tapped her fingers against her arm told me she agreed. She wasn't the type to let things slide.

Thyra shook her head. "Let them play their games. We focus on our team. On winning."

Eirik scoffed. "You're really going to let them walk all over us?"

"I'm saying we play smarter." Thyra's slate blue eyes flashed. "If we start fights in the Challenges, we're making enemies for every round—especially the obstacle course. We survive first. We win first. Then we take them down."

Eirik rolled his shoulders, unconvinced. "They're already our enemies—how much worse can it get?"

Fenja let out a quiet snort, but she didn't argue.

Thyra leveled him with a glare. "A lot worse. You think they've been a problem so far? Just wait until we give them another reason."

Eirik smirked but didn't respond. I didn't doubt that it could get a lot worse. The Black and Crimson team had already shown they were willing to go beyond simple interference. If we provoked them outright, who knew what they'd try next?

Still, part of me understood Eirik's frustration. It wasn't just about getting through the *Leikr* anymore. It was about proving we weren't just the Chairman's pawns, that we could fight back. But was that really the smartest move?

I clenched my jaw. My mother would have said *to choose your battles wisely*. My father would have told me *that sometimes the best way to win was not to fight at all—just to endure*. But I wasn't sure how much endurance I had left.

Thyra glanced at the holo-screens above the arena. "So from yesterday, we know what's coming for today—combat, strategy, and navigation."

Eirik grinned, cracking his knuckles. "And obviously, I'm taking combat. Finally, something worth my time."

Thyra gave him a dry look. "Try not to make a spectacle of yourself."

"Oh, I absolutely will."

Ignoring him, she continued, "I'll take strategy, and Aedan—you're on navigation."

I frowned slightly. "Because you think it'll be the easiest?"

Thyra met my gaze evenly. "Because I think it's the best use of your abilities."

Eirik snorted. "That's a nice way of saying 'yes.'"

Before I could respond, the announcer's voice boomed over the stadium, cutting through the morning tension.

"Warriors! Today, you face your final three Challenges before entering the true battle of the Leikr! Each Challenge tests a Clan virtue— combat, strategy, and the mind's ability to navigate the unknown! Will you rise to the legends, or will your name be forgotten? But before we begin, let's take a moment to honor a distinguished guest—please give a warm welcome to Chairman Arild!"

A deafening roar erupted through the stadium, amplified by the sound boosters embedded in the walls. The reaction was too perfect, too synchronized—artificial in a way that made my skin crawl. The Chairman had ensured his reception was as grand as the spectacle itself.

I scowled, barely resisting the urge to look away as the Chairman rose in his high box, flanked by other members of Clan Council. He offered the crowd an appreciative wave with his expression one of cool confidence, the easy charm of a man who knew he controlled every piece on the board.

My stomach twisted. *Of course, he was here. Of course, he wanted to be seen.* This wasn't just about the games—it was about reminding every single competitor, every spectator, and every Clan member where true power lay.

A hush fell over the arena as the Chairman stepped forward. He extended his arms, commanding silence with the ease of someone who had spent decades cultivating authority. His voice, deep and resonant, rolled through the stadium as if the very stones obeyed him.

"Warriors of the *Stór-menni*, sons and daughters of the Clans—hear me."

The sound boosters sent his words reverberating across the arena, making it impossible to ignore. I could feel the weight of them settling over us, pressing like an unseen force.

"For generations, we have stood as the last and greatest of Earth's defenders. While the weak have faded, while lesser men have surrendered to time and ruin, we have endured. We have not forgotten the truth—the fate woven into our very blood. We are the chosen. The last shield against the storm."

The crowd erupted in cheers, fists raised in salute. The Chairman waited, letting the adoration crest before he raised a single hand. Silence fell instantly.

"You know why we are here. The *Leikr* is not a mere contest. It is not sport. It is not entertainment. It is a proving ground. A forge that shapes the steel of our warriors, separating the iron from the dross. For when the end comes—when *Ragnarök* rises from the shadows of time—it will not be the weak who stand against it. It will be the strongest among us. The fiercest. The unyielding."

A shiver ghosted down my spine. Not from the speech itself—I had heard versions of this before, woven into the very fabric of *Stór-menni* ideology. It was the way he said it. The absolute conviction. The certainty that he was not speaking in metaphor or legend.

"*Ragnarök* is not a myth. It is not a story to frighten children or a warning whispered by the old. It is a certainty, a promise of fire and blood. It is coming. And when it does, the *Stór-menni* will stand alone against it. If we are not prepared, if we are not strong enough—then we are already dead."

He swept his gaze over the competitors, lingering just long enough to make each of us feel watched, weighed, measured.

"That is why the weak must fall. That is why only the best may rise. The *Leikr* does not reward mediocrity. It does not offer mercy. It demands excellence. It demands sacrifice. It demands champions. And it will find them."

Another explosion of cheers. The fevered, desperate kind. A chant rose in the stands—"For the *Stór-menni*! For the Last Battle!"—echoing, pounding, suffocating.

I flicked a glance at Thyra. If anyone should have been pleased by her uncle's presence, it was her. But instead of pride, I caught something else—a flicker of something sharp and fleeting, gone before it could settle. A grimace, barely there before her expression reset into cold neutrality.

Interesting.

Maybe I wasn't the only one who resented being paraded around like one of the Chairman's show ponies.

> *"To honor our esteemed guest and set the stage for today's rounds, we're giving you an exclusive sneak peek at today's Challenges! Competitors, keep your eyes sharp—this might be the only advantage you get!"*

The announcer's voice echoed through the stadium again.

The arena floor shifted, reshaping itself as the first battleground formed. The smooth black stone cracked and broke apart, forming jagged rock formations. Circular rings of stone rose from the ground, glowing with Nordic runes.

> *"First, we honor the Einherjar, the fallen warriors of Valhalla! In the Duel of Einherjar, you will battle a legend reborn—one whose strength and skill will test your worth as a warrior!"*

I glanced at Eirik just in time to see his grin stretch wide, like a kid who'd just been told he could punch someone and get rewarded for it.

Of course, he was excited. Meanwhile, I was still processing the fact that the *Leikr* had somehow managed to create an Einherjar—a warrior from Valhalla—and bring them into the ring.

I knew the stories. My mother used to tell them when I was younger, her voice dropping to a hushed, dramatic whisper. The Einherjar were the best of the best—the kind of warriors so good at fighting that even death couldn't make them stop. Instead of staying dead like normal people, they got to train, feast, and fight each other in endless battles until *Ragnarök*. Basically, a Viking Fight Club, but with immortality and better food.

And now Eirik was supposed to fight one?

I resisted the urge to rub my temples. "So, just to recap," I muttered, mostly to myself, "Eirik has to duel an undead war god."

Eirik rolled his shoulders, completely unfazed. "Relax. It'll be fun."

I gave him a flat look. "For you, maybe. I'm just hoping they don't have to scrape what's left of you off the arena floor."

Eirik just laughed, like the idea of being obliterated by an undead war machine was the highlight of his week.

Before the dust settled from the previous sneak preview, the arena changed again. The towering stones dissolved into liquid, reforming into twisting corridors, shifting walls, and towering obelisks wrapped in shining silver light.

"Next, we honor Loki, the trickster god! In Loki's Web, competitors will find themselves trapped in an ever-changing maze of deception, tricks, and illusions. Only those with sharp minds and sharper instincts will escape!"

Loki. *Of course, it had to be Loki.* Because nothing said great time like being trapped in a maze designed by the god of lies himself.

I barely resisted the urge to sigh. *Trickery, deception, and impossible illusions?* Thyra's hands clenched at her sides, her jaw tightening just enough to show her annoyance.

I couldn't blame her. It wasn't just a test of intelligence; it was a test of patience. And with Loki involved, the only guarantee was that it would be *infuriating.*

And then, the entire battlefield collapsed into nothing.

The ground beneath us darkened, shadows swallowing the arena whole until there was nothing but an endless abyss stretching in every direction. Faint, eerie lights flickered in the void like distant stars, but they weren't stars. They were something else—trails of pale, ghostly fire forming jagged paths that twisted and coiled like the skeletal remains of a ship's wreckage.

I went still.

This was my challenge.

"And finally, we honor Naglfar—the cursed ship of the dead, fated to sail at Ragnarök! In Naglfar's Passage, competitors must navigate the broken paths of the damned, crossing the void where lost souls drift and treacherous routes lead only to doom! Only those with a keen mind and steady resolve will reach the other side before the ship claims them as its own!"

Fantastic. My challenge was a cursed death voyage.

I tried to keep my expression neutral, but my stomach tightened.

I should have felt relieved—this wasn't a combat challenge, wasn't endurance or brute strength. But looking at the shifting paths below, my pulse kicked up. *What if I couldn't do it? What if I failed?*

I clenched my jaw.

There was no room for doubt. Not now.

I felt Thyra's gaze on me. She didn't say anything, but I saw the unspoken warning in her eyes.

Focus. Don't hesitate.

The announcer's voice boomed again.

"Competitors! Prepare for Round 4 of the Leikr!"

The arena exploded into movement.

And we were in it.

Eirik rolled his shoulders, his usual smirk firmly in place, completely at ease despite the fact that he was about to fight an Einherjar. The rest of us would be fighting to survive when our turns came. But Eirik?

Eirik was excited.

"This should be interesting," I muttered under my breath, more to myself than anyone else.

Eirik huffed a laugh, rolling his shoulders. "Please. Easiest round yet."

Fenja scoffed. "Big words."

"They're only big if I can't back them up."

Magnus gave him a measured look. "Just don't waste energy. The real fights start after this."

Eirik smirked, completely undeterred. "The only fight that matters is the one you win."

I pressed my lips together, biting back a retort. *His confidence was irritating, but what was worse? He wasn't wrong.*

The guy was arrogant, reckless, and generally unbearable. But his power? His power was terrifying.

I'd seen him fight in training, seen how effortlessly he manipulated the shadows around him—how they slithered, bent, and lashed out at his command like living things. Against an opponent that wasn't expecting it, it was devastating.

I wanted to believe he'd slip up—that his ego would be his downfall. But the truth was, Eirik was just as dangerous as he thought he was. *And he knew it.*

Thyra crossed her arms. "Just take the fight seriously. No showing off."

Eirik smirked. "I don't need to show off."

I rolled my eyes. "Could've fooled me."

The stadium trembled beneath us, cutting off whatever snarky comeback he was about to throw my way.

The announcer's voice rang through the air, booming with excitement.

> *"Duel of Einherjar competitors to the starting podiums! Spectators, keep your eyes sharp—this is a battle of legends reborn! The battlefield shifts, the warriors rise, and only the strongest will stand victorious! Face the test, or fall in defeat!"*

Eirik climbed down from our platform and strode forward to the starting podium, rolling his wrists, his shadow curling at his heels like an eager predator.

Circular arenas materialized at the stadium's center. The smooth black surface morphed into stone battlegrounds, cracked and uneven. Ancient Nordic runes flickered along their edges, pulsing with an eerie glow. Then, from the far end of each ring, golden projections flickered, materializing into different Einherjar warriors who stepped forward into each ring.

Eirik's Einherjar was massive—easily a foot taller than him—his ethereal armor shimmering like sunlight on water. A massive battle-axe materialized in his hands, the weight of it making the ground tremble beneath his stance.

Eirik, standing at the other end of the ring, cracked his knuckles. He grinned, eyes gleaming with anticipation.

The battle began with a deafening clang of steel. The Einherjar lunged, his axe carving through the air like a falling meteor. The first strike nearly took Eirik's head off. He barely ducked in time, his usual grin flickering—there and gone in an instant. He adjusted his stance, shifting weight between his feet, fingers flexing around his blade hilt. Thinking harder now.

The ghost-warrior stepped forward, slow and deliberate. Eirik feinted left—too obvious—and the Einherjar caught his blade mid-air, shoving him back. He stumbled, not much, but enough.

But the arena wasn't just a battleground—it was alive.

Pillars of stone erupted from the ground, shifting unpredictably to cut off movement and obscure visibility. One shot up between Eirik and the warrior's next swing, deflecting the axe just enough for Eirik to dart forward, using the stone as a launch pad and his shadows as leverage. He flipped over the Einherjar's head, slashing downward with his energy-infused sword mid-air.

The blade hissed as it ignited, the lighted blade colliding with the warrior's armor. Sparks flew. The Einherjar barely flinched.

The warrior retaliated, swinging his axe in a broad arc. Eirik ducked, rolling just before the axe split the stone where he had been standing a second before. The impact sent shockwaves through the ring, cracking the ground beneath him.

I gripped the railing, scanning for threats beyond the ring. I wasn't naïve enough to think the Black and Crimson team would just sit back and let this play out. And I was right.

Out of the corner of my eye, I caught a subtle movement on their platform. Their wind manipulator had his fingers splayed, subtly directing a gust of air toward Eirik's footing. It was meant to be unnoticeable, just enough to throw him off balance at a critical moment.

Before I could react, Thyra moved.

She flicked her fingers, barely noticeable to anyone but me. A sudden countercurrent of air slammed into the Black and Crimson manipulator's gust, neutralizing it before it could reach Eirik.

I shot her a glance, but she didn't look at me. Her eyes were locked on the battlefield, her expression cool and composed. No words, no acknowledgment—just silent, calculated defense.

Down in the arena, Eirik was still grinning. He had started using his shadows now to weave in and out of the Einherjar's vision, leaving behind afterimages that forced the warrior to react to attacks that weren't real.

But the Einherjar wasn't just some mindless brute. The runes along the battlefield flared brighter, spreading across the stone and nullifying Eirik's shadows within the ring.

Thyra tensed beside me. "They thought ahead. He can't use his abilities in there."

Eirik's posture shifted—leaner, sharper. He went for brute force.

He was relentless. Without the ability to use his shadow, he relied on speed and aggression, ducking inside the warrior's reach, using his energy shield to absorb impact, and countering with rapid, precise sword strikes. As much as I hated to admit it, Eirik was an impressive fighter even without his ability.

The Einherjar reeled under Eirik's rapid strikes but refused to go down. With a roar, the warrior slammed his axe into the stone, shaking the battlefield.

Eirik barely managed to stay on his feet. The Black and Crimson team saw their moment. Their illusionist flicked his wrist—and suddenly, there were two Einherjar.

I swore under my breath.

Eirik hesitated for half a second, his eyes flicking between the two warriors—*which one was real?*

I turned sharply to Einar. He didn't need prompting—his Spectral Perception was already active. His gaze flickered, tracking the flow of energy between the projections.

"There," he muttered, nodding toward the leftmost warrior. "That one's real. The other's a fake."

I didn't hesitate. I reached out with my *megin*, sending a subtle telekinetic nudge toward Eirik's left side.

He got the message instantly.

Eirik pivoted, blade igniting in a brilliant flash of light, and drove his sword straight through the true warrior's chest.

The runes along the blade pulsed, feeding into the strike, and the Einherjar reeled back, his spectral form cracking, golden light spilling from the wound. The runes around the ring dimmed a fraction.

But the warrior didn't go down easily. Even as his form fractured, he fought harder, his axe swings faster, more erratic. The battle stretched on—longer than Eirik likely expected. The crowd cheered as he continued to block, counter, and dodge, his breathing growing heavier, his movements slower. The endless onslaught was starting to wear on even him.

Then, with one final push, using the small shadow now at his feet, Eirik vaulted over the warrior's head, twisting mid-air, and drove a final, brutal sword swing to the back of the Einherjar's skull.

The spectral warrior shattered into golden mist.

The holo-screens flared: "**Gray Team: Challenge Complete.**"

The spectators roared. Eirik strode back toward our platform, his breathing heavy, sweat glistening on his skin. He rolled his shoulders and glanced at the remaining competitors still battling their Einherjar. We had come in second by a few minutes, losing to the Black and Crimson team, who were celebrating on their platform.

A loud chime echoed through the stadium.

"Black and Crimson Team wins the Duel of Einherjar! Competitors, you now have one hour before the next round begins. Use this time wisely—recover, strategize, and prepare for what's ahead!"

As Eirik stepped onto our platform, breath still uneven, he dragged a hand through his sweat-dampened hair. He was grinning, of course.

"Not bad," Magnus said, arms crossed. "But not first."

Eirik scoffed, stretching his arms behind his head. "Second place isn't a loss. It's just a delayed victory."

Fenja rolled her eyes, but I caught the small smirk she tried to hide.

I kept my thoughts to myself. The whole match had been brutal, but watching Eirik wield his shadows alongside that sword? It was a reminder—like I needed another one—that he was dangerous.

Eirik collapsed onto one of the benches lining our waiting area, rolling his shoulders. "Finally. I need food."

"You always need food," Fenja muttered.

Magnus grabbed a water flask from the supply rack and tossed it to him. "Hydrate first, then eat."

Eirik rolled his eyes but took a long drink anyway.

Thyra, however, wasn't paying attention to any of it. She stood at the edge of our platform, arms crossed, her gaze locked on the shifting arena below.

I followed her line of sight.

The labyrinth.

Of course.

We had known what was coming next, but now, with the

battlefield reforming before our eyes, it was real. Thyra flexed her fingers at her sides, her expression unreadable, but the tightness in her jaw gave her away. She wasn't rattled, exactly—just focused.

I rubbed the back of my neck, trying to ground myself. "You good?"

She nodded once. "Just thinking."

"Don't get lost in there," Eirik said lazily, leaning back against the railing. "I'd hate to have to explain to the Chairman that our strategist got outsmarted by a rock wall."

Thyra didn't even look at him. "If you went in, you'd be running in circles within five minutes."

Magnus smirked. "Five's generous."

Eirik scoffed. "You all underestimate my genius."

Fenja leaned toward me and muttered, "We don't."

I huffed a quiet laugh, but my focus was still on the arena.

The hour ticked by in a blur of water breaks, whispered strategy discussions, and the occasional bickering from Eirik and Fenja.

Then, another chime rang through the air. The ground trembled.

I turned my attention back to the arena just as the smooth black surface twisted and shattered apart, morphing into a labyrinth of jagged stone. The walls groaned as they rose like ancient monoliths, shifting and rearranging, as though they were alive. The air rippled unnaturally, a clear sign of illusion magic already at play.

A maze designed to deceive. And Thyra was about to walk straight into it.

The announcer's voice rang through the arena, brimming with anticipation.

> *"The trickster god Loki is known for his love of mischief, and today, our competitors will step straight into his web! In this challenge, they must navigate an ever-shifting maze, where nothing is as it seems! But beware—every step could lead them deeper into deception, and some tricks are more deadly than others. The goal? Retrieve the golden apple from Idunn's grove—if they can make it that far! But*

tread carefully, warriors... for the air itself carries the breath of Helheim."

Thyra flexed her fingers once, then let them fall to her sides. "Just a maze."

"Not one built by Loki," Fenja warned.

A faint twitch of Thyra's brow said she'd heard. She adjusted the clasp at her collar, the smallest flicker of tension in her shoulders. Then, without another word, she walked to the starting podium.

The holo-screen countdown began its slow descent.

Three.

Two.

One. ***Go*.**

The moment she crossed the threshold, the maze sealed itself behind her, locking her inside. At the same time, similar labyrinths formed around the other competitors, each contestant trapped in their own twisting nightmare.

From the outside, I could see the mazes shifting constantly, entire sections folding inward, others stretching taller, the walls morphing as though they had a will of their own.

Then came the first sign that something was wrong.

A strange, light-yellow tint began bleeding into the air, subtle at first—just a faint haze, threading through the corridors, curling around the stone walls. It drifted unnaturally, its edges blurred as though it wasn't fully real.

The tint thickened, spreading faster—a creeping, deadly tide.

Then came the screams.

The first competitor to react was a woman from the Blue Team—she barely took three steps before she stumbled back, clutching her throat.

My stomach twisted.

A low, strangled gasp echoed from another maze—a contestant from the Ruby Team. He dropped to his knees, gripping the ground as if he could keep himself from falling deeper into whatever had overtaken him.

Thyra, still moving cautiously, paused.

She must have heard the screams from the other mazes.

For a moment, she didn't move. Then, she carefully extended her hand, sending a small burst of controlled air through the corridor in front of her.

The strange haze curled and shifted in response—and then lashed forward like a striking serpent. Recognition flickered across her face.

This wasn't just some trick of the light.

This was poison.

A creeping, insidious toxin that didn't strike instantly but spread like a slow death, winding its way into the lungs, choking, burning, suffocating. The breath of Helheim—lingering in the maze like an invisible executioner.

Loki's trick wasn't the maze itself—it was that every breath could be their last.

Thyra's hands clenched into fists.

She adjusted immediately, summoning a stronger current of air, wrapping it around herself like a second skin, keeping the poison at bay.

Other competitors weren't so lucky.

From where we stood, I saw another figure collapse inside the maze, their form flickering as they were forcibly removed from the Challenge—disqualified before they even had a chance to escape.

Despite the gasps and cries from spectators and other competitor platforms, Thyra didn't stop moving.

Other teams interfered immediately. A member from the Green Team flicked their fingers, layering more illusions over the maze, creating duplicate pathways and false openings that led nowhere.

Thyra adjusted quickly to the interference. Instead of relying on sight, she listened. Then, with a subtle shift of her fingers, she sent out a controlled burst of air down the corridors, testing the path.

Where the air bounced back—invisible walls. Where it moved freely—a real path.

Magnus grunted in approval. "Smart."

The Black and Crimson Team weren't about to let her through without a fight. They made their move. Their illusionist, stationed in their viewing area, flicked his fingers, warping the runes along Thyra's labyrinth. The walls blurred, distorted, making it nearly impossible to tell what was real and what was a trick.

At the same time, their wind manipulator unleashed a sudden, forceful gust, trying to shatter Thyra's protective barrier—pushing the poison closer.

Thyra's teeth clenched. The wind slammed into her barrier, the toxin curling closer. Too close.

She braced, fingers flicking as she tried to control the currents—but the pressure was too much. The gust nearly buckled her shield.

Then, before any of us could do anything to counter, she pivoted.

Instead of resisting the gust, she moved with it. She shifted her fingers subtly, threading her own air currents into the opposing wind, weaving control into the chaos. With a sharp flick of her wrist, she shaped the swirling gusts into a cyclone, absorbing their attack and hurling the force right back at them.

A sharp crack echoed through the stadium as the force of Thyra's counterattack shattered the illusions clouding her path. She had turned the Black and Crimson Team's interference against them, unraveling their wind manipulator's trick. For a brief moment, their Illusionist's magic faltered—just long enough for Thyra to spot the true path forward and press on.

With the poison whipping at her heels, Thyra sprinted forward, dodging the last of the traps. And then, at the heart of the maze, a glow appeared.

A grove shimmered into existence. Idunn's grove.

I sucked in a breath. *I had heard the stories—everyone had.* Idunn, the goddess of youth and renewal, keeper of the golden apples that granted the gods their immortality. The grove was sacred, untouched by time, a hidden sanctuary in the old myths.

Here in the *Leikr*, the trees were pale gold, their branches reaching upward as if stretching for the sky. The golden apple rested on a stone pedestal, gleaming under the flickering runes.

With one final burst of speed, Thyra grabbed the apple just before the maze could shift again. The moment she did, the toxic haze vanished instantly, and the labyrinth disintegrated in a massive burst of golden dust as if it had never been there.

Thyra didn't move right away. She stood still, her back rigid, fingers locked around the golden apple like she expected it to disappear. The sharp lines of her shoulders, the way her breath hitched—it wasn't relief. It was something else.

The holo-screens blared: "**Gray Team: Challenge Complete!**"

The crowd roared. Thyra blinked once, then turned sharply, walking toward us with even strides, her expression unreadable. Too controlled.

As she strode back toward us, she flexed her fingers, shaking out the tension, the only sign of exertion a faint sheen of sweat on her brow. She hadn't needed any of us—hadn't hesitated, hadn't faltered. It was impressive. And maybe just a little unnerving.

"And there you have it, warriors! The Gray Team emerges victorious, proving once again why they are a force to be reckoned with! But victory comes at a cost. This round has claimed two teams—Blue and Ruby have been eliminated from the Leikr.

Regretfully, we report that the Blue competitor suffered grievous injuries and was unable to complete their trials. They have been removed from the field for urgent medical intervention. As for the second..."

The announcer's voice dropped slightly, just enough to give weight to the words.

"The competitor from the Ruby Team... did not make it out."

A hush rippled through the crowd, even among the most ruthless competitors. It was the second life the *Leikr* had claimed, and every time it happened, it sent a chilling reminder through the arena—this was no game.

"And so the Leikr continues! With another trial conquered and the battlefield narrowing, who will remain standing by the end? Stay with us as we move to the final challenge of the day—Naglfar's Passage!"

Thyra stepped onto our platform, shaking the last remnants of the golden dust from her shoulders. Her expression was unreadable, her gaze fixed ahead rather than meeting anyone's eyes.

Fenja was the first to break the silence. "That wasn't just illusion magic," she said, arms crossed. "That yellow air—"

"Poison," Magnus finished, his jaw tight. "I heard them. The other competitors. Some of them didn't make it out before it overtook them."

Eirik let out a low whistle. "The creators really went all in for that one."

I exhaled, forcing my fists to unclench. I'd heard it too—the coughing, the panicked cries that had echoed from other mazes. Some had been pulled out before it was too late. One hadn't.

Thyra was oddly quiet.

"You knew," I said finally, studying her.

She didn't look at me. "Figured it out just in time."

Glancing at the leaderboard flashing on the holo-screens, I asked, "What happens now that two teams have been eliminated instead of just one?"

Fenja shrugged, arms crossed. "No telling what the administrators will do. Might cut a round. Might add another." Her gaze flicked to the holo-screens. "One thing's for sure—however they adjust, the number of days stays the same. This is about entertainment, after all."

A heavy silence settled over us.

I looked down at my hands, flexing my fingers to shake out the tension creeping into them. Blue and Ruby were out. One was carried off the field—one never left at all.

And now, it was my turn.

I had spent the last two rounds watching from a safe distance, defending, interfering—but soon, I would be the one down there. Alone. Facing whatever the *Leikr* had waiting for me.

Naglfar's Passage.

My stomach twisted, but I forced my shoulders back, standing straighter. I couldn't let them see hesitation. Not the crowd. Not the Chairman. *Not my team.*

I barely knew what to expect. The myths painted it as the ship of the dead, crafted from the nails of the unburied—something destined to bring ruin when it finally set sail. It wasn't a story with a happy ending.

A cold weight settled in my gut.

If my family were here, what would they say?

My father would probably tell me to trust my instincts, to keep my mind sharp, no matter how the battlefield changed. My mother would remind me that navigation wasn't just about knowing the path—it was about feeling it, adapting with every step.

And Claire? She'd probably make some joke about how I should have studied more maps. Edvin would just tell me to run fast and not die.

A small smirk tugged at my lips, despite everything.

I clenched my fists. *Focus. Breathe. Move.*

"We can be heroes... just for one day." David Bowie's line surfaced uninvited, the echo of an old song that had made it into my collection—back from when being a hero felt like a choice, not a curse.

I would get through this. I had to.

But one thing was clear, after what happened in the last round—*if I made a mistake, there would be no second chances.*

SIXTEEN

The Naglfar

AEDAN

My pulse kicked up a notch.

My turn.

The moment the holo-screens flickered, signaling the next challenge, the stadium's floor trembled. A deep, groaning creak echoed through the arena, and the black ground beneath the central competition ring seemed to dissolve into an abyss of churning, dark water. A hush fell over the spectators as an enormous, ancient-looking ship began to rise from the depths.

No, not a ship. Pieces of a ship.

Broken, jagged remnants of what must have once been a massive vessel—splintered wooden beams, rusted chains, shattered hull fragments—all floating in the eerie black expanse, connected only by narrow, unstable-looking planks. Ghostly mist coiled between the floating debris, and for a second, I swore I saw something move beneath the surface.

The weight of the moment pressed down on me like an iron hand as I stood at the edge of our platform, staring out at the churning abyss that had swallowed the competition floor. The dark waters, thick and sluggish like oil, lapped hungrily at the jagged remains of a once-great ship—Naglfar, the vessel of the dead, said to carry the forces of *Ragnarök.*

A fitting place for a trial. A death trial, that is.

I clenched my fists, my pulse hammering beneath my skin. This was my turn to prove myself—or fail in front of thousands. A part of me had hoped for something straightforward—following runes, reading patterns. Instead, I got deadly water, a floating graveyard, and a stadium full of people watching.

"You can't always get what you want..." Mick Jagger's voice surfaced in the back of my mind, dry and smug as ever.

I huffed out a breath.

But maybe—just maybe—I'd get what I needed. If I was lucky.

I pushed the lyric aside and anchored my attention on the shifting arena.

This battlefield wasn't just dangerous—it was alive. Constantly fluctuating. Platforms drifted, some bobbing unsteadily, others crumbling before my eyes. Jagged ship fragments jutted out at odd angles, forming makeshift bridges. *But the worst part? The water.*

A swirling mist veiled the wreckage, distorting the battlefield, making it impossible to judge distance with certainty. I hesitated, my gaze flicking upward for the briefest moment. The artificial sky above the arena wasn't a reflection of the dark abyss below—it was eerily clear, speckled with stars. It was strange, almost too real, but there was no time to dwell on it. I forced my focus back down.

And I was right. It wasn't just water. The longer I looked at it, the more I saw—hands. Pale, elongated fingers reaching up from the depths, grasping for anything they could pull down.

The Naglfar's dead.

I dug my nails into my palms, pushing aside the gnawing unease curling in my gut. *Focus.*

"You've got this," Thyra said beside me, voice steady. She didn't offer false reassurance, just a firm nod. "Trust your instincts."

Eirik smirked. "And if you fall in, at least you'll be in good company."

I shot him a dry look. "Yeah? I'll make sure to tell the dead how much you admire their work."

Eirik chuckled. "Oh, they'd love me."

"Doubt it. Even restless spirits have standards," I muttered under my breath, earning a smirk from Eirik.

Magnus crossed his arms, nodding toward the wreckage. "It's a test of navigation, not brute force. That's your advantage."

Einar was watching me closely, his gaze assessing. "Watch for the real path. The rest is just a trick."

Fenja cracked her knuckles. "And don't fall in."

I let out a slow breath, trying to settle the storm brewing inside me. But the doubts were merciless.

Somewhere out there, my family might be watching. If Elin had found them, would they understand what I had to do—or would they only see the Chairman's uniform?

And the Chairman...

I felt the unnatural energy still humming beneath my skin. Whatever he had done to me, it was still working, making my reactions sharper, my *megin* stronger. But it wasn't mine.

Before I could dwell too much on the slow churn of dread tightening in my stomach, Thyra's voice cut through my thoughts.

"It's time," she said firmly. "Just focus on the navigation. We'll handle any interference."

I nodded, exhaling slowly. *No more overthinking. Just move.*

Climbing off our platform, I made my way toward the competition ring, my boots landing solidly on the ground. Then—it hit me.

Something was different. Very different.

There was no separate battlefield waiting for me. No individual arena like the previous rounds.

Instead, one enormous arena stretched before us, a vast abyss of black water with a single, broken ship rising from its depths. *And I wasn't alone at its edge.*

Every competitor stood on their own starting podium, forming a circle around the same massive wreck.

This wasn't a solo Challenge.

We were all in it together.

The announcer's voice crackled through the air, brimming with excitement.

"Warriors! The final round of the day brings something truly special! Unlike previous rounds, all competitors will face this Challenge in the same arena! That's right—each of you will step onto the cursed wreck of Naglfar and attempt to find your path to salvation. But be warned! The ship is not a passive graveyard—it shifts, it deceives, and it seeks to claim those who tread carelessly! Only those who can navigate its treacherous passage will survive! The rest? Well... the dead are always eager for company!"

A murmur rippled through the crowd. *This wasn't normal.*

I adjusted the straps of my shield and sword. A shared arena meant more chaos. More interference. More chances to screw up.

I could hear Eirik somewhere above me say, "At least this means we get a front-row seat to everyone else's failures."

Great, just what I needed—another distraction in the challenge.

I rolled my shoulders, trying to shake the tension out of them. *Too late for that.*

A hush fell over the stadium.

The holo-screen flashed "**Competitor Ready.**"

The countdown began.

Three.

My *megin* hummed beneath my skin, ready to react.

Two.

The first step mattered. If I hesitated, the shifting planks would make me second-guess everything.

One.

The signal flashed. ***Go***.

I launched forward, landing hard on the first platform—a waterlogged plank that immediately groaned under my weight. The moment I pushed off toward the next, the wood vanished beneath me.

"Son of a—"

I barely managed to yank a nearby plank toward me with telekinesis, landing on it just as my boots would have hit open water. *That was too close.*

The battlefield wasn't just unstable—it was deceptive. Some platforms flickered like mirages at the edges of my vision, while others crumbled the moment someone stepped on them. The Teal team's competitor to my left leapt onto a beam, only for it to dissolve beneath them. Luckily for him, his Hyperelasticity ability saved him from plunging into the restless water. But anyone could be gone in an instant with one false move. That was the trick. Naglfar's illusions.

I focused, narrowing my gaze at the scattered debris. Somewhere among them was the true path forward. I just had to find it. But every path ahead flickered, teetering, altering beneath the mist. No clear way forward.

Gritting my teeth, I picked the most solid-looking plank and vaulted. The moment my boots hit the surface, the plank tilted violently. My stomach lurched as the wood buckled beneath me, vanishing like a mirage.

Blast!

I twisted midair, barely catching the edge of a half-sunken beam with my telekinesis, yanking it toward me just in time to land on it. But the reprieve was short-lived. The plank I clung to trembled, then shattered under my weight.

Panic flashed through me. I threw myself toward the next closest platform—only for my foot to slip right through it.

It wasn't real.

A sharp jolt of fear surged up my spine as gravity took hold. At the last second, I wrenched myself sideways with a desperate burst of telekinesis, slamming onto a nearby mast with enough force to send pain jolting up my arms.

That was too close!

My breath came out in bursts from the frantic exertion. I was guessing, and it was going to get me killed. Every second I hesitated, the battlefield shifted again, erasing whatever path I thought I saw.

I clenched my jaw, scanning ahead, but nothing made sense. The wreckage was twisting, alive in its deception—no stable path, no pattern I could trust. The mist thickened, swallowing the debris before I could track their movements.

Come on, Aedan. Think!

And then, just as frustration boiled over, I caught something out of the corner of my eye.

Not below.

Above.

The stars still burned bright above me, untouched by the chaos below. That's when I saw it.

The constellations weren't random. *They were familiar. Too familiar.* The same ones sailors had used for centuries, guiding ships through uncharted waters. My father's voice echoed in my mind from our boating lessons, unbidden: *"The sea is never empty, Aedan. The stars will always show you home."*

A shiver ran through me, but this time, it wasn't from the cold. If the Challenge was designed as a navigation test, then there had to be a real path hidden in plain sight. And if this was a shipwreck, then it stood to reason that the designers had accounted for how Viking sailors once found their way.

I aligned myself with the constellations above, scanning the debris below through a different lens. That piece of mast—it followed the same axis as the North Star. That next beam—the angle matched the direction of the Pleiades. My pulse quickened. It wasn't just scattered wreckage. It was a map.

Got you.

Around me, competitors scrambled across the wreckage, each

using their own methods to navigate. Some were thriving—others, not so much.

The Teal team's competitor with Hyperelasticity vaulted effortlessly from beam to beam, limbs stretching unnaturally to cover distances no normal human could. The Magenta team's player, using Geokinesis, stabilized a floating plank by wrapping it in stone, turning it into a solid stepping platform.

Then there were the ones struggling.

The Brown team's participant tried to send arcs of energy across the wreckage to map out safe paths—but he miscalculated. A plank disappeared beneath him, and before he could react, the black water swallowed him whole. A gurgling wail rose from below.

A woman from the Vermilion team on the opposite side had made better progress at first, moving fast, her instincts sharp. But the battlefield wasn't just changing—it was fighting back. A gust of unnatural wind knocked her off balance, and when she tried to recover, a chunk of debris—probably launched by an opposing team—slammed into her side. She staggered, grasping desperately at a loose beam.

For a second, I thought she might save herself. But then the plank she was holding onto shifted on its own, as if something had yanked it away. Her scream rang through the mist as she plunged into the abyss. The black water churned violently as the dead dragged her under.

I swallowed hard.

This wasn't just about finding the right path. It was about keeping your footing long enough to survive.

I forced my focus forward. The platforms were volatile, shifting constantly. I had to keep moving.

Another jump. Another telekinetic pull. A wild scramble over a crumbling mast.

Then, out of sheer desperation, I tried something different.

I flicked my shield to life and projected it onto the next plank. Then, I took a leap of faith onto it.

For half a second, I fully expected to fall straight through.

Instead, the energy barrier beneath my feet held.

I blinked. *Wait. This works?!*

I jumped again, letting the shield carry me forward like a floating platform along the path mapped by the stars.

It wasn't smooth—I nearly lost my balance twice—but it worked.

Unfortunately, other competitors noticed.

Within seconds, one of them—the Emerald team competitor—copied the move, using their own shield to do the same thing. Then the Red competitor with Adaptive Physiology adjusted their abilities mid-jump to mimic the technique.

I groaned. Should've kept that trick to myself and fully trusted the star path.

Then, the sabotage began.

A sudden gust of wind slammed into me, sending my shield flying off course.

Black and Crimson.

Before I could fully recover, a jagged harpoon shot toward me, aimed straight for my landing spot.

I barely got my sword up in time, activating its energy edge. The blade ignited, slashing through the projectile before it could strike me.

"Sniveling *argrs*," I muttered, borrowing Fenja's word—an old Norse insult for the cowardly and dishonorable.

They weren't letting up.

The Black and Crimson team was incessant. Every gust of wind, every projectile, every illusion was calculated, precise. But they weren't the only ones.

The other teams had caught on. It wasn't just one group trying to throw me off course anymore—it was several. A spike of rock erupted near my feet. I barely jumped in time, rolling mid-air and landing hard on the next wobbly plank. A second later, another team sent a flash of blinding light straight toward me. I clenched my jaw, blinking rapidly to clear my vision before my next step.

And still, the Black and Crimson's wind manipulator was waiting.

He was baiting me—pushing me, making me focus on everything else. I didn't realize it until too late.

I caught a flicker of movement from our platform where my team stood. They were inundated by the sheer volume of interference.

Thyra, fighting off a rival wind attack meant to throw me completely off balance.

Eirik, countering shadows creeping across the shipwreck, trying to pull me into a trap.

Fenja, sending shards of metal flying to block another incoming projectile.

Einar, his Spectral Perception flickering like a beacon, shouting something I couldn't hear—but he wasn't looking at me. He was focused on something else.

They were overwhelmed.

And that's when the wind manipulator struck.

The gust slammed into me—a brutal, focused force aimed right at my back.

I had no way to stop it.

I stumbled—arms pinwheeling—my footing vanished.

The last thing I saw was the cold, black abyss below.

And then—*water*.

The moment I hit the surface, the cold burned. It wasn't just the temperature—it was wrong. The water latched to me like tar, thick and suffocating, as if it had a will of its own.

My lungs seized. Every muscle locked as if flash-frozen. The pressure crushed against my chest, squeezing until spots danced at the edges of my vision. My heart stuttered, then thundered against my ribs like it was trying to escape.

Then they came.

A chorus of rasping voices slithered through the darkness, speaking in a language older than time. My limbs seized as skeletal hands—no, not skeletal. Shadowy, wraith-like fingers—clawed at my arms, my waist, my legs. The drowned warriors of Naglfar.

They knew me.

"Blood of the exiled. Flesh of the fallen. You do not belong here."

I thrashed, kicking wildly, but they coiled around me, pulling me down. The abyss opened beneath me, swallowing the last traces of light, pressing in on my chest. My lungs screamed for air. The roar of the stadium above faded into nothing, the world shrinking to this nightmare beneath the surface.

No.

I am not dying in this gods-forsaken trial.

I wrenched an arm free, reaching for my sword. My fingers barely curled around the hilt before the wraiths tightened their grip. My vision blurred, the icy burn of the water creeping into my mind, whispering, lulling. *Let go.*

I bit down hard on my tongue. Pain cut through the haze.

I struggled against the binding hands around me. Until I remembered that I didn't need to.

I called on my telekinesis.

The sword responded instantly with a swing, igniting with a blue blaze.

A pulse of raw energy erupted from the blade, not a burst of fire, but something more primal—a ripple through the water, an undeniable command.

The dead shrieked.

Their forms flickered, unraveling at the edges. Their grip loosened. It was enough.

I kicked, pushed, forcing my body upward, willing myself back to the surface.

Above me, the battlefield was still in chaos. Platforms crumbled, mist choked the air, and competitors struggled to stay upright. I caught a glimpse of my team. They were still fighting—Thyra and Fenja countering attacks from multiple directions, Eirik's shadows lashing out to shield me from another incoming projectile.

For a minute, I thought I was on my own until a platform of gleaming metal suddenly shot into place.

Fenja.

I threw myself forward, arms screaming as I grasped the edge. My boots slammed against the slick surface, my body heaving with the effort as I hauled myself up.

The moment my knees hit solid ground, I gasped for breath, coughing up seawater. Every inch of me was soaked, trembling from the cold and the sheer fight to get back up.

But there was no time to rest. The final stretch was ahead.

I pushed to my feet, shuddering as the icy grip of the dead clung to my limbs like phantom chains. My breath came in ragged gasps, but I had no time to shake off the cold. The final stretch loomed ahead—a jagged, fractured bow of the ship, rising like the prow of a ghost vessel, its splintered edges curling toward the abyss. The battlefield was collapsing, the wreckage groaning as it fought to drag us all down with it.

Still, I forced myself forward. Every instinct screamed at me to keep moving, to focus on the teetering planks beneath my feet. But for the briefest moment, something pulled my gaze upward.

The stars still burned bright above me, untouched by the chaos below. Fixed. Unwavering. My path had been written there from the start—I had just needed to see it. My father had been right. The sea was never empty.

And neither was this battlefield.

At the ship's heart, shimmering faintly in the mist, sat the prize. Six large otherworldly discs. Eight teams had started this Challenge, but now only six remained. And all those players were converging at once.

The competitors surged toward it, each racing across the collapsing wreckage, vaulting over debris, pushing through the relentless onslaught of wind, interference, and the grasping hands of the dead. The battlefield was pure frenzy now—bodies twisting mid-air, beams falling like axes, weapons clashing as teams fought not just against the Challenge but each other.

I forced my focus forward. A massive mast had broken free ahead, crashing down at an angle that cut off the shortest path to the final platform. It was too far to jump, and with the dead swarming below, I had no margin for error.

I clenched my fists.

Move.

I barely had time to register the thought before my telekinesis snapped into action, wrapping around the enormous mast's broken end, twisting it midair just enough to realign its fall. It landed with a deafening crack, forming a temporary bridge.

I leapt onto it, feet skidding against the slick wood. What I'd just done hit me all at once—my *megin* alone wasn't normally enough to move something that heavy, not at that speed, not at that angle.

I wasn't just stronger—I was something else. Something more.

The injection.

I ground my teeth and shoved the thought aside. Whatever the Chairman had done, I didn't have the luxury of hesitating now.

The final platform was just ahead, and I wasn't alone.

Two competitors were already there—one from the Black and Crimson team, the other from the Red team. Both dove for the first disc at the same time.

It was close. Inches. A fraction of a second.

The Red competitor's hands wrapped around the artifact just as the Black and Crimson warrior's fingers brushed its surface. A flash of blue light surged outward, sealing the first victory.

The Black and Crimson fighter snarled, twisting mid-motion to snatch another one—but so did the next closest competitor.

The moment turned vicious. A strike, a counter, a desperate scramble for control. The Black and Crimson fighter slammed their elbow into their opponent's ribs, sending them staggering back just enough for them to seize the second disc. Another pulse of blue light flared.

Two down.

I was next.

I crouched, muscles coiling. I needed to move—now.

The mast groaned beneath me, see-sawing, tilting. The jagged beams ahead blurred at the edges, swaying like they weren't solid. The wind screamed. Or maybe that was something else.

Jump, Aedan. Move.

I forced my breath steady and lunged off the mast, muscles screaming in protest. The beam collapsed beneath me just as I vaulted, the sudden drop ripping the air from my lungs.

The abyss yawned. The void below stretched endlessly, and for a second—a heartbeat, maybe—I thought I'd miscalculated.

I wasn't going to make it.

Then—impact. My boots slammed into the platform's crumbling edge. I scrambled forward.

The instant I was on solid surface, another competitor crashed down just behind me—one of the Emerald Team's, their hands sparking with raw energy. I didn't give them the chance to recover.

I spun, igniting my blade, forcing them to veer away.

No time.

I dropped my sword into a defensive stance and used my telekinesis to bring the disc closer. My fingers stretched, reaching for the third disc.

For one gut-wrenching second, I thought I wouldn't make it. That someone faster, stronger, would tear it from my grasp.

I lunged. Too slow. The Emerald competitor was right behind me.

No time. No margin for error.

I wrenched the disc toward me with a final burst of telekinesis, the force nearly yanking me off balance. My competitor reached—just a fraction too late. My fingers slammed down over the surface.

Blue light.

The disc pulsed beneath my touch, and the holo-screens

exploded with the announcement: "**Gray Team: Challenge Complete!**"

For a split second, I barely processed it.

I had it. I'd won.

Then the moment shattered.

Shouts. Clashes of weapons. Desperate scrambles from the remaining competitors for the last discs.

I stumbled back, my fingers tightening around the prize, my pulse still hammering.

The battlefield was still collapsing. The ship continued to splinter and sink, dragging down those who weren't fast enough.

I turned just in time to see a near disaster—one competitor from the Magenta Team jumped too late, their footing slipping as the platform beneath them crumbled. For a heartbeat, it looked like they were lost to the depths. But at the last second, they caught hold of a jutting beam, hauling themselves up with a desperate burst of strength.

The remaining discs vanished one by one in flashes of blue light.

It was over.

But the sinking wreckage behind me, the crumbling battlefield, the sheer brutality of it—

It was a warning.

This wasn't the end.

My legs nearly buckled as I stood there, every muscle trembling from exertion. The icy grip of the dead still ghosted across my skin, phantom hands pulling at my limbs. Each breath burned in my lungs, tasting of salt and decay. Their voices echoed in my mind: *Blood of the exiled. Flesh of the fallen.*

I pressed my palms against my thighs to stop their shaking. Whatever the Chairman had injected into me had gotten me through, but the cost of that power sat like lead in my stomach. I'd moved that mast, controlled the debris with a strength that wasn't natural—wasn't mine. The knowledge of what that meant would have to wait.

I let out a ragged breath, running a hand through my dripping hair, my pulse still hammering in my ears. The roar of the crowd felt distant, almost muted beneath the weight of what had just happened.

And then, cutting through the noise, the announcer's voice boomed once more, commanding the stadium's full attention.

"What. A. Finish! Ladies and gentlemen, warriors and spectators, what we just witnessed was a battle of sheer determination, strategy, and survival! Naglfar's Passage has claimed its victims, but for those who endured, victory is theirs!

And the results are in! Ten teams entered this round, but only eight will move forward.

Yet this victory comes at a cost. The Vermillion and Brown teams were unable to escape the clutches of the dead—taken by the cursed spirits of Naglfar's abyss, their journeys in the Leikr coming to a tragic end. Their sacrifice serves as a reminder that these trials are not just games; they are a test of true warrior ability, where the weak are left behind, and only the strongest endure. We honor their fight."

A moment of respectful silence hummed through the stadium before the announcer continued, voice sharp and commanding.

"And with that, warriors, the Challenge Rounds are officially COMPLETE! You have faced trials of strength, agility, endurance, combat, strategy, and navigation—pushing yourselves to the very limits of what it means to be a competitor in the Leikr! But the real competition? It begins now.

So, listen up, warriors, because here's how the Obstacle Rounds will play out! Each round, teams will go head-to-head in brutal, unforgiving obstacle courses. The first team to complete the round wins—until only two teams remain for the final showdown!

But with eight teams still standing, the bracket isn't straightforward. In Rounds 8 and the semi-final, whoever loses the first match will have to fight for survival against the lowest-ranked remaining team in a second matchup.

That means no one is safe. Every second, every point, every move matters. Fight for your place, or get left behind!"

The crowd erupted in a mix of cheers and murmurs, but I barely heard any of it. My chest still heaved from the effort of the challenge, my skin damp with seawater and sweat. As I turned, scanning the endless rows of spectators, a single thought cut through the exhaustion. The same questions that had been nagging me since the *Leikr* began.

Was Elin watching? Had she seen what I just did?

Had my family? Would they be proud—or would they see the Chairman's colors on my uniform and wonder whose side I was really on?

I dragged a hand down my water-beaded face, shoving the questions into the corner of my mind. There were no answers to be had—not yet.

Climbing the platform where my team waited, I barely had time to steady myself before Magnus clapped me on the back, his grin wide. "Not bad, navigator."

I rolled my eyes but couldn't suppress the smirk tugging at my lips.

"Thought we were gonna have to fish you out for a second there," Eirik said, arms crossed. "The way you flailed in the water? Not your best moment."

I shot him a glare. "Next time, you can take a swim with the dead and tell me how graceful you look."

Fenja snorted. "He'd just use his shadows to cheat."

"Obviously," Eirik said with an exaggerated shrug. "That's called strategy."

Thyra, who had been uncharacteristically quiet, finally spoke, her gaze still locked on the remains of the battlefield. "It wasn't just luck that got you through," she said, her tone measured. "You adapted."

I met her gaze, sensing the weight behind her words.

"You knew the attacks were coming, and you kept moving," she continued. "That's what'll matter in the obstacle rounds."

The mention of the next phase sobered everyone.

"Speaking of which," Magnus said, rolling out his shoulders. "Round eight and the semifinals just got a lot messier."

I frowned. "Because of the odd-numbered teams?"

Fenja nodded. "Exactly. The lowest-ranked team from round seven will have to run a second course against the lowest-scoring team from the first set of matches in round eight. They'll be at a serious disadvantage."

Eirik grinned. "Which means more chances to eliminate the weak links."

"Or more chances for us to get targeted," Thyra countered, crossing her arms. "It's not just about winning anymore—it's about making sure we don't land at the bottom of the board."

Magnus cracked his knuckles. "Then we make sure we don't."

My fingers curled into fists. The course was behind me, but the weight of the next round already loomed.

The battle wasn't over. Not yet. We had survived the Challenges. But now came the real fight.

The obstacle courses.

SEVENTEEN

The Archives

TRISTAN

The Internal Affairs command center was unusually restless, tension threading through the air like an invisible force. The *Leikr* obstacle rounds had begun, and every holo-screen along the walls flickered with live footage, immersing the room in shifting gold and electric-blue light.

Clusters of IA officers and troopers gathered around the screens, some standing with arms crossed, others leaning on cubicle walls, murmuring in hushed but urgent tones. Some muttered bets on the outcome, others debated the Magenta Team's dirty tactics, but all were riveted to the match. It was the trials' seventh round—the first obstacle course.

I ignored the chatter, barely registering the voices around me.

My eyes were locked on the largest central screen, which displayed Thyra's team at the starting line, clad in their signature gray uniforms. At the forefront stood Fenja and Magnus, the two selected —not by their captain, but by the committee's new arbitrary pairing rule.

I knew them well enough. They had been part of our team on Auor Island when we'd attempted to capture the Unregistered's family and Elin. Magnus, a brute-force warrior with the endurance of a storm-battered mountain. Fenja, precise and strategic—a master of playing the long game. Together, they were a dangerous combination.

A bitter taste settled in my mouth. *I should be out there.*

I had trained for this. Endurance, strategy, skill—I had spent years honing all of it, pushing myself past every limit. *And now? A spectator.*

My jaw tightened.

And yet, there was another part of me—one I didn't particularly like—that was relieved.

The *Leikr* obstacle rounds were some of the most punishing in the games. Unlike earlier events, these were direct head-to-head battles between teams, where no outside interference was allowed. Teammates couldn't step in to help, and no one could sabotage from the sidelines.

But the competitors weren't bound by the same restrictions. Slowing down, tripping up, or outright attacking your opponents was all fair game. And more often than not, these matches turned into brutal fights for survival.

I clenched my fists.

It was a test of true warriors. And I had been denied the chance to prove myself.

But hadn't I already proved myself?

The thought crept in uninvited, laced with bitterness. Capturing Gabriel was a victory—the kind of achievement that should have earned me something. Recognition. Respect. Instead, it had amounted to nothing.

He had been silent under interrogation, refusing to break or even engage. It was infuriating. Even now, locked away in a detention cell, he remained completely unshaken, as if the entire world moving against him was nothing more than an inconvenience.

For all my training, for all my victories in the field, I had delivered a high-value prisoner, and yet...

It hadn't mattered.

Not in the way I wanted it to. No promotion. No reassignment back to Protective Services. It hadn't been enough.

If I wanted to change that, I needed Elin and the Unregistered's family. They were the key. Capturing them would prove my worth, it would finally get me where I needed to be.

And I had a lead.

A single thread to pull—one that might unravel everything.

I just had to follow it.

I flexed my hands at my sides, dragging my focus back to the holo-screen.

The view zoomed in on the competitors.

Magnus and Fenja stood at the starting gate, their expressions grim but determined. On the other side, their opponents stepped forward—Varis and Kara, representing the Magenta Team.

I recognized them both instantly.

Varis, a towering brute with enhanced durability, built to withstand punishment and keep going. Kara, a swift, acrobatic fighter, specializing in environmental manipulation—deadly in a terrain-based event.

The obstacle course stretched before them, a sprawling serpentine labyrinth of shifting platforms, icy ridges, and treacherous metal conduits designed to move like a snake's endless body.

The announcer's voice boomed through the holo-screen.

"Inspired by Jörmungandr, the great serpent that encircles Midgard, this challenge will test our warriors' ability to endure the storm! The ground beneath their feet is treacherous, the air filled with venomous mist, and at the final gate—Jörmungandr itself awaits! The first team to reach the gate gets the first strike against the beast. If they succeed, they win the round!"

I leaned forward slightly, instincts flaring.

At the blare of the starting gong, the competitors took off.

The platforms groaned as they twisted and undulated, forcing the competitors to adapt in real time.

Magnus plowed forward, his Stonebound *megin* activating as his fists hardened into rock, slamming into the shifting ground to stabilize Fenja's footing.

She moved swiftly, spinning threads of metal into grappling hooks, anchoring herself before the terrain twisted beneath them again.

But the Magenta Team wasn't just running—they were attacking.

Varis, using his near-invulnerable frame, slammed his weight onto the fluctuating platforms ahead of Magnus, causing them to tilt wildly, attempting to throw him off balance.

At the same time, Kara flicked her wrist, manipulating the air pressure, making the venomous mist swirl toward Fenja's path, obscuring her vision.

I smirked despite myself. *Good tactics.*

But Fenja wasn't easy prey.

She extended a blade-like filament of metal, hooking it into the wall and using it to swing wide, narrowly avoiding Kara's trap.

Magnus, on the other hand, met brute force with brute force.

As Varis lunged, Magnus planted his feet and shoulder-checked him midair, sending him skidding across the shifting platforms. The impact rattled the course, forcing both teams to adjust—momentarily locked in a battle of momentum and control.

The officers around me reacted instantly, their collective tension spilling into the air.

Shouts erupted from the officers clustered around the holo-screens, some cheering, others cursing as Fenja and Magnus fought to stay ahead, their struggle mirrored in the room's energy. Even Kolve, who usually found a way to annoy me at every opportunity, was too engrossed in the match to bother with his usual jabs.

Good.

I pushed back from my station, keeping my movements casual,

masking my real intent beneath the illusion of disinterest. The energy in the command center remained locked on the holo-screens, the tension thick, every officer too absorbed in the *Leikr* to spare a glance my way.

I forced myself to walk at a measured pace, despite the tightness coiling in my chest.

Act normal. Don't rush.

No one noticed as I slipped through the side door. The cheers and curses from the command center faded, swallowed by the hush of the corridor.

The temperature shift hit first—colder here, the air crisper, untouched by the body heat of the packed room behind me. The sound of distant footfalls echoed somewhere deeper in the building. *Security patrols? Maybe.* The IA facility never slept.

A low hum filled the space—the whir of security cameras tracking their designated zones. I kept my pace even, my breathing controlled. No sudden movements. No hesitation. Any officer walking past now would see a man headed somewhere with purpose. Not someone sneaking where he didn't belong.

Still, I kept my head down.

Anyone catching me out here now, alone, would ask too many questions.

I blew out a breath, trying to steady my pulse.

I had been waiting for this moment. Waiting for an excuse to dig deeper into something I never should have seen.

This wasn't rebellion. I wasn't looking for trouble.

This was about Elin. The Unregistered's family. If I found them, if I brought them in, everything would fall into place. My standing. My future.

That was why I was here.

Wasn't it?

The thought tightened like a snare. *If that was true, why did my hands flex at my sides, anticipation curling in my gut?*

Why did it feel like I was looking for something else entirely?

Something I wasn't ready to name. Something that had been gnawing at the edges of my thoughts since—

Gabriel.

He had been silent under interrogation, offering nothing. But something about him had unlocked a memory I hadn't realized I had buried.

During the fight where I captured him, the powerful Illusionist in his group had tried to stay hidden, lingering at the back of the battle, shrouded in deception. But for the briefest second, I had caught a glimpse of his real face before he masked himself again.

It had nagged at me ever since. Because I had seen that face before.

It was older. Wearier. But familiar.

Not in person.

But on the Chairman's screens.

The file on the Chairman's screens had been outdated—a relic from days long past. Not something pulled from an active database, but something buried. Forgotten.

I hadn't pieced it together. Not right away.

But recalling the Illusionist's aged face—it had finally clicked.

If that file had been pulled from history, then any other documents connected to the man wouldn't be in the modern *Stórmenni* system either.

They'd be in the archives.

But the IA archives weren't just some open database tucked away for casual access. The security was tight—far beyond standard clearance levels. Even as an investigator, my access was limited, restricted to files deemed necessary for my work.

If I got caught there, pulling unauthorized records…

I clenched my jaw, forcing the thought aside.

Tonight, I wasn't here for what I was allowed to see.

I reached the reinforced doors, their glossy black metal reflecting the dim overhead lighting. The small entry panel blinked red, waiting for the right authorization. If I failed this, alarms would trigger instantly.

I swallowed hard.

The hall remained empty—for now. But at any moment, a patrol could pass through.

A cough echoed from somewhere down the corridor—a distant officer, perhaps, but too close for comfort. My fingers itched to move faster.

Don't rush. Don't panic.

I needed an override.

Sliding my Communicator from my belt, I flicked through the interface, bringing up a mirror clone of an active session—a trick I had used back in my Clan Hunter days, pulling restricted reports off-grid.

The system needed to think I was someone else. Someone with higher clearance.

To the scanner, I wasn't Tristan, the investigator poking around where he shouldn't be.

I was Kolve.

A single beep.

A pause.

Then, the panel blinked green.

I nearly let out a breath of relief.

The door slid open, the air inside colder still, sterile. The large room was sleek, lined with towering holo-terminals, their interfaces glowing a cold, impersonal blue. The hum of their processing power filled the silence. Surveillance nodes blinked in the ceiling, scanning for unauthorized activity. No visible guards, but that didn't mean I was alone. The system itself was watching.

I lingered on the threshold for a beat longer than necessary, listening—half expecting footsteps to echo behind me, a voice demanding what in the *Muspell* I was doing here.

Nothing.

For now.

I slipped inside.

The door closed behind me, wrapping the cold air around me. I resisted the urge to glance at the security interface to my left. If the patrol logs refreshed while I was in here, I'd have seconds to react. Seconds before my access was flagged and the doors sealed.

I settled into a holo-terminal near the back, the translucent interface hovering in the air before me, its soft blue glimmer casting weak shadows across my hands.

With a flick of my fingers, I spread the data screen wide, panels sliding apart in a seamless motion. My hands moved without hesitation, swiping through menus, keying in commands with subtle flicks of my wrist.

Every second here was a risk.

I rotated my palm, enlarging the security console, my movements swift and controlled. The wrong input, the wrong flag, and someone in the command center might see a flashing alert—a breach notification screaming across their own screens.

Tension pulsed in my neck as I adjusted the search field with a smooth pull of my fingers. The system flashed red.

Restricted Files.

My jaw tightened.

Odin's beard!

I twisted my wrist to expose the recalibrating filters and tried entering Kolve's override command that I had pinched from his desk earlier. The old fool kept a paper taped to the bottom of his desk with the code written on it.

I held my breath.

The system compiled within seconds, the menu reappearing without restrictions.

With a flick of my fingers, it expanded.

Clan assembly records. Former Clan leaders. Security alerts on unregistered members.

I quickly initiated searches through each, but nothing.

I flicked a glance over my shoulder.

No movement. No alarms blaring.

But I could feel time slipping away, the weight of every second pressing against my ribs.

I lifted my hand and swiped downward to close the session—when something stopped me.

A single flagged entry, concealed under a false tag—hidden in a mislabeled archive of expired arrest warrants.

That wasn't standard procedure.

I hesitated, my breath slowing.

Someone had tucked it away here deliberately.

A warning flared in the back of my mind, telling me to leave it alone.

But I didn't.

I tapped the floating entry, pulled it toward me, and flicked my fingers to expand it into full view. For a moment, the system lagged as if resisting the request. Then, the file unfolded like a map, layers of data blooming outward, each segment a broken piece of something much larger.

This wasn't an arrest warrant.

It was an administrative record. An old one.

The file flickered, portions of it corrupted and overwritten, segments manually scrubbed from existence. But as I moved my hands, dragging, twisting, and realigning the broken pieces, a name emerged from the fragments.

Liam Jarnulf.

A chill rippled down my spine.

I lifted my fingers and snapped them apart, expanding the corrupted record further, forcing the system to stitch together what it could.

A broken link to an image file surfaced—a photo reference, but damaged.

I tapped it, swiped left, and followed the web of missing data that stretched across different concealed logs. The holo-screen glowed in warning, resisting my attempts to retrieve it.

A final command. A forced bypass.

The image snapped into view.

And there he was.

The same man I had seen on the Chairman's screens. The same haunted face—but this time, with a name.

Liam Jarnulf.

My pulse pounded in my ears.

I pushed my palm forward, opening all remaining fragment files, dragging them into a separate cluster so I could read them simultaneously.

The pieces were old—far older than they should have been. Redacted notes bled across the screen, entire sections blacked out or erased. But what remained painted a dangerous picture.

Liam Jarnulf was a part of the Protective Services and a former Advisor to the Chairman, which made him a member of the Chairman's inner circle.

His official records had been wiped clean.

He had been listed as "deceased" in multiple reports—but clearly, that wasn't true.

Someone had gone to extraordinary lengths to erase him.

My fingers curled into a fist, the holo-screen shifting slightly in response to my tension.

Two things were certain.

Liam Jarnulf was the Illusionist I had fought in the alley.

And he was alive.

If the Chairman had been searching for him all these years... it meant Jarnulf was more than just a fugitive.

He was a threat.

I exhaled through my nose, flicking my hand sharply to begin closing the system. I needed to get out of here. *Now*.

I moved to shut down the console, my hand hovering over the exit command.

But in my haste, my finger slipped.

The holo-screen shifted sideways, scrolling past another flagged document.

I frowned.

It wasn't related to Jarnulf.

And I hadn't been looking for it.

But something about the tag caught my attention.

My gut twisted.

I lifted my fingers, pulling the document toward me, rotating it slightly as I read.

It was a border security report—one that had been classified and buried deep within the archives.

A soft red light pulsed along its edges, indicating a highly restricted security layer.

I entered the override command again, my Communicator still masquerading as Kolve's access ID.

The barriers flickered, then collapsed.

The document loaded, displaying a log of an incident at the shield wall.

Incident Report: Unauthorized Entry Attempt
Date: 3 Years Ago
Summary: A group of unregistered individuals—approximately twenty men, women, and children—approached Falinvik's shield wall, requesting safe passage.
Status: Turned away.

My pulse skipped a beat as my eyes locked onto the last line of the document.

Identified Affiliation: Sudri Clan.

I froze.

The Sudri Clan.

They had been wiped out.

That was the official history, the one I had been raised to believe —that the Nordri, now *Stór-menni*, were the last survivors.

But this was not propaganda. This was an official, classified document.

No.

The word formed instantly, instinctively. A rejection. A refusal.

Because it couldn't be true.

And yet...

The words on the screen didn't shift. They didn't warp or dissolve into something I could explain away.

Identified Affiliation: Sudri Clan.

My breath came too sharply, too fast. The soft blue glow of the interface pulsed beneath my fingertips, steady and unbothered—as if I hadn't just unearthed something that shattered the foundation I stood on.

The Sudri were gone.

That was history. That was fact.

We had been told—since childhood, since the first lessons of who we were and why we fought—that the Nordri were alone. That we had survived because we were the strongest, the only ones left.

The Sudri were gone.

And yet, here they were.

I swallowed hard, my vision tunneling in on the cold, clinical words on the screen.

My hands clenched, fingers tightening against the holo-interface. I forced myself to look away, just for a second. The Archives were still silent, the security lights still blinking in passive cycles. The world hadn't changed. *But I had.*

If this was real... if a group of Sudri had made it to our border just three years ago... then that meant...

Elin had been right.

Her voice from Auor Island clawed its way back into my memory, sharp and defiant:

"Your Chairman lied. The other Clans are alive and well."

I had dismissed her then, calling it a Resistance lie.

But this was not a rumor.

This was an internal *Stór-menni* security report. And it meant that everything I had been told about the fate of the other Clans was a lie.

I swallowed hard, my mind struggling to process everything I had just uncovered.

Liam Jarnulf was alive.

The Sudri Clan still existed.

And the Chairman had hidden both truths.

And now? I knew.

A chill settled into my spine, not from the cold air of the archives but from the realization that I had just stumbled across something I was never meant to see.

I leaned back in my chair, my mind spinning with implications. I had no idea what Liam Jarnulf meant to the Chairman, but the lengths taken to erase him from history told me everything I needed to know.

This wasn't just an old enemy resurfacing.

This was personal.

And the Sudri report?

I swallowed hard.

My father's bloodline was Sudri—a fact that had once meant something, long ago. I still remembered the scent of spiced tea in my grandfather's coat, the quiet hum of Egyptian slipping between rooms during his visits. He'd always brought small gifts and stories, his voice warm and animated in a way that made the air feel less heavy. But that all faded when I was placed under my mentor Henric's care. From that moment on, I was raised as *Stór-menni*—shaped into what the Chairman's world required. Henric had drilled one truth into me: the other Clans were weak, obsolete, relics of a past that had no place in the future. And I had believed him.

But if the Sudri were alive...

Then what else had the Chairman lied about?

A hollow feeling settled into my chest, like a weight pressing against my ribs.

I had come here searching for one answer. Instead, I found two.

And both of them had the potential to destroy everything I thought I knew.

My hand moved to my Communicator, fingers hovering over the copy command.

But then I hesitated.

If Liam Jarnulf had been erased once, what would happen if someone found out I was looking for him?

If the Sudri still lived, what would happen if the Chairman realized one of his own officers, without clearance, had seen proof?

For the first time in a long while, I felt something sharp and cold settle into my gut.

If the Chairman had hidden these truths...

Then what would he do to me if he found out I knew them?

I clenched my fists, forcing a slow breath through my nose. There was no time to dwell on it now. I had already spent too long here—too many minutes unaccounted for. *If someone noticed my absence, or worse, checked the archive logs...*

No. I couldn't afford to think like that.

I lifted my fingers, sweeping the holo-screen shut, wiping the session clean, erasing any trace of my search. Then, I rose from my seat.

The sterile air of the archives suddenly felt suffocating, the walls pressing inward. My movements were careful but quick as I slipped out of the room, heart hammering in my chest.

The corridor was as empty as when I had left it—but now, every shadow felt deeper, every sound sharper. I forced myself to move at a measured pace, ignoring the instinct screaming at me to run.

Act normal. Keep your breathing steady.

As I neared the command center, the muted roar of voices met my ears, growing louder with each step. I slid through the side door, blinking against the sudden brightness of the holo-screens.

No one noticed my return.

Every officer remained glued to the massive displays, their focus locked on the match as the final stretch of the seventh round played out in front of them.

I swallowed hard, my thoughts still spinning, my pulse still too fast—but I willed myself to watch, to blend back into the room as if nothing had happened.

On the holo-screens, both teams neared the massive wooden gate, the final obstacle between them and Jörmungandr's lair.

At its center, a giant iron ring knocker waited.

The first team to seize it would earn the right to face Jörmungandr first—and, if they succeeded, win the round.

On one side, Magnus and Fenja pushed forward with unwavering determination. On the other, Kara and Varis of the Magenta Team fought to close the gap.

Kara's eyes narrowed, sensing the momentum shifting in favor of the Gray Team. Desperate to turn the tide, she flung another burst of wind, aimed directly at Fenja, trying to slow her down before she could reach the gate.

But Fenja was ready.

At the last second, she twisted, using the wind's momentum instead of fighting it, launching herself forward—her hand closed over the ring knocker just before Varis could reach it.

The Gray Team had won the first strike.

The moment Fenja's fingers wrapped around the knocker, a deep tremor shook the battlefield.

A monstrous hiss erupted from the depths.

The massive gates opened, allowing Fenja and Magnus to enter. The moment they did—it rose.

The Jörmungandr construct loomed before them, a titanic

serpent of shimmering scales, its twisting body coiling around the final stretch of the obstacle course. Runed fangs dripped with venom, each drop sizzling as it hit the ground.

Its glowing yellow eyes locked onto the competitors, scanning for its first target.

"And there it is—Jörmungandr! Will our warriors slay the beast, or will they be swallowed whole?"

The announcer's voice boomed through the holo-screens, sending a ripple of anticipation through the watching officers.

The serpent lunged.

The crowd reacted instantly, voices rising in a mix of cheers and curses as the battle began in full force.

And yet, despite the action unfolding before me, I felt the hairs on the back of my neck prickle—not from the game, but from something else.

A presence.

A shift in the air beside me.

A voice, slow and knowing.

"I'd ask what's so fascinating, but I can guess."

I didn't need to look.

Kolve.

The IA Watch Commander leaned against a nearby console, arms crossed, his smirk dripping with condescension.

"Must sting, huh?" he continued. "Watching from the sidelines?"

My jaw clenched, but I kept my posture relaxed, my expression unreadable.

Was that just his usual needling? Or was there something beneath the surface?

I forced my eyes back to the screen, keeping my voice even. "The trials are mandatory viewing, aren't they?"

Kolve shrugged, his gaze lingering on me just a little too long. Sizing me up.

"Just saying, you look like you'd rather be down there."

A slow, creeping sensation coiled at the back of my mind, pressing against the weight of what I had just done.

Did he know?

Had someone noticed my absence?

Had I left some trace, some small slip in the archives that I hadn't accounted for?

Silence.

Kolve exhaled, shaking his head. "You really don't make things easy, do you?"

The words landed too deliberately, like he was waiting for me to react.

I arched a brow, keeping my breathing steady, waiting.

Then he waved a hand, begrudgingly.

"The Gabriel capture. I'll give you that one. Not bad."

That surprised me.

Kolve had never trusted me. He still didn't. But begrudging praise was rare from him.

I studied his expression, looking for something—some sign that this was more than just his usual antagonism.

Still, his smirk faded into something sharper.

"Not that it matters now. He's being transferred."

The topic shift should have settled my nerves, but it didn't.

My mood darkened instantly. "Gabriel still isn't talking?"

Kolve sighed. "Not a word. He won't break, won't bargain. Just sits there, staring at the wall."

I frowned. "We've handled tougher cases."

"This one's different." Kolve's voice dropped slightly. "It's like he doesn't care what happens. No fear, no leverage. Just... waiting."

I didn't like that.

We'd caught a high-value Resistance operative, and yet—he acted like he had already won.

That same feeling twisted in my gut again.

First, the archives, the truths I had uncovered. Now, Gabriel, unshaken in his cell, waiting. *For what?*

"That's why we're done wasting time." Kolve's voice cut through my thoughts. "He's being transferred."

My shoulders tensed. "Where?"

"Skjoldur." His tone was matter-of-fact, but there was something else in it. "The interrogators there will take over."

A chill settled in my spine.

The IA's methods were harsh, but the Skjoldur detention center... that was different. It ripped answers from people, whether they wanted to talk or not.

My fingers curled tightly into my palm before I forced them to relax. "You're handing him over already?" I asked carefully.

Kolve didn't hesitate.

"The Chairman made the call." His voice was blunt, final. "Gabriel leaves tomorrow morning."

I didn't respond.

I should have felt satisfaction. Instead, the unease gnawed deeper, a shadow stretching in the back of my mind.

Gabriel wasn't panicking. He wasn't negotiating. He was waiting.

Why?

That realization settled in my chest like a lead weight, pressing deeper with every passing second.

On the holo-screen, the Jörmungandr challenge reached its climax. Magnus and Fenja launched their final strike—Magnus shattering the serpent's skull, Fenja's metal tendrils coiling around its throat.

A loud cheer erupted around me as they claimed victory, but the sound barely registered. The true battle wasn't here on the screens—it was happening in the shadows, behind locked doors and buried files.

And I had just stumbled into the middle of it.

I quieted the impulse to move, forcing myself to stay still. To blend in.

Kolve was still watching me. Assessing.

I gave him a curt nod, forcing a smirk I didn't feel. "Guess Gray Team pulls through after all."

He snorted, shaking his head. "For now."

He turned back to the holo-screen, but I didn't miss the way his eyes lingered just a second too long, like he was waiting for something.

I needed to be careful.

I needed to be sure I hadn't left any trace in the archives.

I needed to figure out why Gabriel wasn't afraid.

As the room erupted in post-match analysis, officers broke into good-natured arguments about the round. Some officers muttered curses at losing their bets; others clapped, trading comments on Magnus and Fenja's strategy. One group near the center console had already moved on, analyzing how the next round's competitors would stack up.

The energy was shifting, the focus redirecting. *Perfect.*

I took a slow step back, then another, letting the movement blend into the natural shuffling of the room. The best way to disappear wasn't to sneak—it was to move like I belonged.

Not too fast. Not too obvious.

Just enough to disappear into the crowd, to slip out of the room—before I gave something away.

Because tonight, I had found two impossible truths.

And if I wasn't careful, I'd be the next one erased.

EIGHTEEN

The Two Plans

ELIN

The distant hum of machinery vibrated through the subway walls, mixing with the damp scent of concrete and geothermal minerals. Dim lights flickered overhead, casting fractured shadows along the narrow corridor. I pressed my back against the cool stone, steadying my breath. The ghost of the Chairman's presence still clung to my mind, like smoke that refused to dissipate. But the last thing I needed was for Nodin to see how rattled I truly was.

"Tell me you're still you." Nodin's voice was quiet but urgent, his hands gripping my shoulders, grounding me. His dark eyes searched mine, looking for something—anything—that would confirm I was still myself.

I exhaled sharply, my pulse hammering in my ears. "I'm fine. I'm me, Nodin."

His grip tightened for a fraction of a second before he let go, but he didn't step back. He was close—too close—his warmth pressing against the chill that had seeped into my bones. His fingers twitched —hesitant, uncertain. Like he wanted to pull me closer, but knew he shouldn't.

"What happened?" His voice lower now, rougher.

I hesitated, my skin prickling under his scrutiny. "I saw Aedan. Just for a moment. But the Chairman—he found me too fast. He was waiting. Like he knew I'd try again."

Nodin's jaw clenched, and his expression darkened in a way I rarely saw. "That's not good."

"No kidding." I crossed my arms, trying to shake off the lingering dread, but his eyes locked onto mine, pinning me in place.

"Elli, are you sure?" His voice was barely above a whisper now, but there was something in it—something deeper, more personal. "You feel the same? Like... nothing changed?"

My breath caught. He wasn't just asking if my mind was intact. He was asking if I was still me—the me he knew, the one he trusted. The one he—

I shoved the thought away, swallowing hard. "I swear. I'm still me."

His expression remained unreadable for a beat too long, and for a second, I thought he was going to say something—something that would tip the balance between us. But instead, he raked a hand through his dark hair, shoulders easing just slightly. "Then we keep it to ourselves."

Relief coursed through me. "You agree?"

He nodded, though his shoulders stayed tense. "For now. But if anything feels off—"

"I'll tell you," I promised, though the words felt heavy on my tongue. I wasn't sure I even believed myself.

Nodin held my gaze a moment longer, searching for something—reassurance, perhaps, or confirmation that I was telling the truth. Whatever he was looking for, he seemed satisfied enough to let it go. With a slight nod, he stepped back.

"Actually, that's why I came looking for you." His tone shifted to something more casual, as if deliberately moving past our moment. "McHaill just got back to base. Sounds like he has news about Gabriel."

I straightened immediately. "What kind of news?"

"Don't know the details," Nodin replied, already turning toward the main corridor. "But no one ever calls an emergency meeting to say, 'Hey, turns out everything's fine.' Everyone's gathering in the strategy room now."

My mind instantly refocused, the lingering presence of the Chairman pushed aside by a more immediate concern. If McHaill had information about Gabriel, that could change everything.

We hurried through the winding tunnels of the base, the damp air cool against my face. Resistance members rushed past us, carrying equipment and data chips, their expressions tense with purpose.

"Whatever it is," Nodin said as we approached the strategy room, "it's big."

The room fell silent as we entered. All eyes turned toward McHaill, who stood at the center table, his expression unreadable but his posture rigid with tension.

"We got word," McHaill said, his voice clipped. He pulled a data chip from his pocket and placed it on the table. "Gabriel's transfer is confirmed. He's being moved to Skjoldur."

Silence. The weight of his words pressed down like a vice, the thrum of the holo-table the only sound in the room.

Across from me, Mrs. Grady's hands pressed together. "When?" Her voice was tight, controlled, but her shoulders tensed as if bracing for impact.

McHaill gave a short nod, tension coiling in his expression. "Soon. Within the next couple of days. They're accelerating the process." He tapped the data chip, the small click unnaturally loud. "Something may have spooked them."

Mr. Grady let out a slow breath, running a hand down his face. His gaze flickered toward his wife, a silent conversation passing between them before he spoke. "That's both a curse and a blessing."

"We already have the Skjoldur layout from the holo-lounge," Sigrid said, leaning over the table, arms folded. "But timing will be everything."

Yrsa stepped forward, rolling her shoulders as if preparing for a fight. With a flick of her wrist, the holo-screen activated, casting a cold blue light across her face. The three-dimensional model of Skjoldur expanded outward, its sharp digital edges flickering against the dimly lit room.

"Our window is small," she said, sweeping her hands outward. Security schematics spun into place, their patrol routes glowing red. She pinched two fingers together, dragging the timeline forward, her movements precise, methodical. "The only real opportunity we have is during the Final *Leikr* round." Security patterns visibly thinned as she manipulated the data.

As she spoke, McHaill frowned, arms crossed. "You're banking everything on the Chairman prioritizing security at the games."

Yrsa shot him a look. "I'm banking on the Chairman's arrogance. And it's the best shot we'll have at infiltrating the detention center."

My stomach twisted. "So Aedan will have to fight the rest of the tournament," I murmured, my voice barely above a whisper. "He'll have to keep surviving until then."

Mrs. Grady closed her eyes for a moment, as if steeling herself against the thought. "We don't have another option. Without Gabriel, there's no way to remove his *Hepta Baugr*."

The words sent a splintering jolt through my chest.

I swallowed hard, but it did nothing to steady the storm surging inside me. A rush surged beneath my skin, my fingers tightening around the edge of the strategy table as the weight of reality sank in like an anchor.

Aedan wasn't just trapped. He had to keep fighting.

The Leikr wasn't over.

Round after round, trial after trial—he would have to push through all of it. Injuries. Exhaustion. The relentless brutality of opponents trying to beat him down, break him.

And if he lost? If he slipped for even a second?

I squeezed my eyes shut. No. I couldn't think about that.

My breath hitched, each inhale tight and uneven. Aedan—battered, bleeding—forced to stand, again and again. The *Stór-menni* circling like wolves, waiting for him to fall.

I took a step back, barely aware that I was moving, the weight in my chest making it impossible to stay still. A sharp pressure built behind my eyes—a warning, a demand.

No, not now. Not here.

But my body ignored me.

My *megin* surged, hammering against my medallion like a war drum, too loud, too strong, too much. The edges of the room wavered, distant voices stretching into distant, distorted echoes.

I gritted my teeth, trying to hold on, but the Resistance base was already slipping away, pulling me under like a riptide.

Then—

The scent of roasting meat and damp wood filled the air, mingling with the metallic tang of geothermal steam rising from the pipes beneath the cobblestones. The glimmer of neon signs danced across wet pavement, distorted in puddles of melted snow.

Baldur Street.

A shiver crawled up my spine—not from the cold, but from the sudden, eerie familiarity of it all.

I know this moment.

And there—just ahead—stood Aedan.

My breath caught. He stood wrapped in a heavy gray cloak, his dark hair tousled by the wind, his face sharper—more tired—than I remembered. But that was the thing. I did remember.

He moved toward me just as he had before. The exact same way.

My pulse skipped.

This wasn't new. This had already happened.

"Elin?" His voice was low, urgent, just as it had been that night. The sound of it wrapped around me like a tether, pulling me deeper into the vision.

I barely had time to nod before he pulled me into a tight embrace, the warmth of his body a stark contrast to the cold air around us. I felt his breath against my cheek, the steady rise and fall of his chest against mine.

I wasn't just seeing the past—I was reliving it.

Everything unfolded exactly as it had before. My words. His words. The way his hands gripped my arms, as if trying to make me understand.

I had no control.

I wanted to scream, to shake myself free of this moment, but I was locked inside it, forced to watch it play out again.

"Aedan," I whispered, gripping his cloak as if I could anchor him in this moment. "Are you okay? What are you doing here?"

His short, breathy laugh. His wary glance over his shoulder.

I know what's coming next.

"What am I doing here? What are *you* doing here, Elin?" He pulled back slightly, scanning the street. "This isn't safe—you shouldn't be here."

"I know," I admitted. "But we came for you. We've been searching for a way to get you out. And then I saw you, right here. I couldn't just—"

"Elin, I can't go."

The same gut-punch as before. The same helpless frustration washing over me.

I tried to brace myself, but the words still cut through me like a blade.

"What do you mean, you can't go? We're here—we have a plan—it's gonna—"

He lifted his wrist, and there it was. The *Hepta Baugr*. The small, blinking red light. The thing keeping him chained to the Chairman's will.

The light in his eyes dimmed.

"You have a *Hepta Baugr*," I breathed.

It was happening exactly the same way.

And yet—this time, I saw it differently.

Before, I had been so consumed by despair that I hadn't fully absorbed the truth buried in Aedan's next words.

"Well, you didn't think they would just let me wander around the streets free, did you?" A weak smile tugged at his lips. "And if by last time, you mean in the *Leikr* training room—then yeah, training is the only time they remove it."

I froze.

My heart lurched, as if the realization had physically slammed into me.

This is it. This is the part I missed before.

The market noise seemed to muffle as his words echoed through me.

They take it off for training.

The last time I had lived through this moment, I had been too overwhelmed, too desperate to see what was right in front of me. But now? Now it was blindingly obvious.

If they removed it for training... then he wouldn't have it on during the *Leikr* either.

Oh, gods.

Aedan didn't seem to notice my shift in expression. "It interferes too much with my abilities," he muttered, rubbing his wrist absently.

I felt sick. Not because of the vision itself—but because of how long it had taken me to see what should have been obvious.

We didn't have to break into the Chairman's tower. We didn't need Gabriel to unshackle Aedan.

We just had to get him during the Leikr.

Before I could react—before I could change anything—the moment ripped away from me.

The blinking on his wrist sped up. Aedan stiffened. "They're tracking me. I have to go."

"No—wait," I whispered, reaching for him, but the moment was already slipping.

I wanted to hold on, to make him stay, but Nodin's voice cut through the air. "Elli, now. That's a *Stór-menni* squad leader heading this way."

And, just as before, Aedan hesitated for the briefest second—then he was gone.

The vision shattered.

A ragged gasp tore from my lips as the world around me reassembled itself—the dim glow of the Resistance base, the worn edges of the strategy table a few feet in front of me, the low murmur of voices pressing back in like a tide. My heart pounded against my ribs, my breath uneven as I blinked away the last traces of Baldur Street.

I wasn't there anymore. Aedan was gone.

But his words weren't.

A presence stirred beside me.

I turned slightly, my heartbeat skidding, and found Nodin watching me. He stood just a step away—close enough that I could feel the steady weight of his presence. His hazel eyes, usually laced with amusement, were unreadable now, scanning my face with something quieter. Something I couldn't quite name.

His gaze shifted over me, his brows drawn together in the barest trace of concern. *Was he making sure I was okay—or afraid I wasn't?*

A faint prickle ran down my spine, but it wasn't fear. It was the way he noticed things no one else did.

Of course, he had seen the way my features changed when I had a vision.

He always did. He was probably paying even closer attention since I told him about the Chairman breaking into my visions. But now, his expression wasn't just watchful—it was hesitant, conflicted. His fingers flexed at his sides, like he wanted to reach for me but wasn't sure if he should.

I let out my breath shakily, forcing my grip to loosen where my hands had curled into fists.

Nodin's fingers twitched, his stance shifting as if he was waging an internal debate. Then, barely above the room's thrum, he said, "You with me, Elli?"

His voice was steady, but there was something beneath it—something raw.

I nodded, though the movement felt unconvincing. "Yeah. I just—" My words hitched. "That one wasn't supposed to happen."

His brow furrowed. "What do you mean?"

I drew my arms around myself, grounding against the cold throb beneath my skin. "I didn't try to look. I didn't reach for it. It just... took me." The words sounded distant even to me. *It didn't make sense. I had my medallion. Wasn't that supposed to stop this? Wasn't I supposed to be in control now?*

Nodin went still, his expression unreadable, but there was a shift—subtle, careful. His hands, which had been hovering like he wanted to steady me, curled into loose fists instead. He was thinking about something.

After a pause, he spoke, voice quiet but certain. "Strong emotions can do that sometimes."

Heat flushed through my cheeks, sudden and sharp. *Strong emotions.*

The weight in my chest had been unbearable just before the vision took over. *Aedan. The Leikr.* The fact that he had to keep fighting, again and again, with no way out.

A part of me wanted to argue—wanted to say it wasn't about that, that my abilities weren't that unstable. *But... weren't they?*

Nodin's gaze drifted over me again, slower this time, as if seeing something he hadn't fully processed before. His usual smirk was absent, his shoulders tense—not in suspicion, but in understanding. He knew what had triggered me.

His fingers flexed again, almost like he wanted to reach for me, but he didn't. Instead, his voice softened, careful in a way that made my throat tighten.

"It's over now."

I nodded, my throat tightening around the words I couldn't say, but my mind was already racing back to what I had just seen—*what I had just realized.*

I staggered forward to the edge of the table, where the others were still discussing the situation.

"Wait."

The word left my lips before I fully grasped its weight.

All eyes snapped to me.

I barely registered their stares. "Aedan," I said, hurriedly. "They take his *Hepta Baugr* off for training."

A flicker of confusion passed through the room.

I swallowed, my pulse hammering. "That means..." The words stuck in my throat, the weight of them suddenly immense. "That means he doesn't wear it during the *Leikr* either."

Silence.

A sharp, electrified pause—then chaos.

"Of course!" Mr. Grady surged forward, his chair scraping against the floor. "We should have thought of it sooner. That's the perfect window. Are you sure?"

"I'm sure," I said, the image of Aedan's bare wrist seared into my mind. "Every time he trains, they remove it. They have to." A shiver ran down my spine, the truth crashing down on me even as I spoke it aloud. "And in the final rounds... he'll be unshackled."

The realization rippled through the room like a thunderclap.

Claire's breath hitched. "Then we could get to him."

Edvin rubbed the back of his neck, his usual smirk nowhere to be found. His voice was quieter, but dead certain.

"Not just get to him," he said. "We could get him out."

Nodin, leaning against the wall with his arms crossed, let out a low whistle. "Love that for us. Two rescues at the same time? Bold. Reckless. Possibly stupid. But hey, I'm in."

Yrsa frowned, arms crossed. "Let's not pretend this isn't a logistical nightmare." She gestured toward the holo-table. "Skjoldur and the stadium are in completely different sectors. The timing has to be exact, or one mission could sabotage the other."

McHaill grunted. "Not to mention resource strain. We don't have endless people to throw at both operations. If one team gets caught, we risk blowing the whole thing."

My nails bit into the table's edge. "We don't have another choice. If we wait to do them separately, we lose our best shot at both."

Edvin let out a dry scoff, shaking his head. "Right, because a 'best shot' with a 90% chance of failure is very comforting."

Mrs. Grady glanced at her husband. "Could we stagger the timing?"

Mr. Grady considered the holo-display. "It's possible, but not by much. Aedan will be unshackled only during the *Leikr*. We can't afford to miss that window. And we need time to plan. As for Gabriel's..." His gaze flicked to Tibadeau.

Tibadeau adjusted his sling with a wince. "If we stall even a little, we lose the only window where security is stretched thin because of the *Leikr* final. There won't be another shot."

Yrsa sighed. "Then we synchronize. Both teams move in tandem, no deviation."

McHaill's brow furrowed. "And if something goes wrong?"

Nodin smirked. "Then we improvise. Which, let's be real, is already part of the plan."

Yrsa rolled her eyes. "Not exactly reassuring, Nodin."

Edvin shrugged. "I mean, it's realistic."

Sigrid turned to Mr. Grady. "We'd need a distraction at the *Leikr*. A big one."

Mr. Grady didn't react right away. Instead, he adjusted his cuffs, glancing at the holo-display with a considering look—like he was sizing up an opponent. Then he nodded. "Leave that to me."

Nodin smirked. "Should we be worried?"

"Probably," Mrs. Grady murmured, but her lips twitched slightly.

For the first time since the meeting started, hope sparked in the air—but only for a moment.

Because the next thought hit me like ice water.

He doesn't know.

Aedan didn't know we were coming. He didn't know that there would be a chance to escape. That if he fought his way to the finals, he'd be fighting toward something more than just survival.

And if he didn't know, he might not be ready.

A chill ran down my spine. We could have the perfect plan—but if Aedan wasn't expecting it, if he didn't know when or how to act, *we could lose our only chance.*

Mrs. Grady must have caught the shift in my expression. "What is it?"

I hesitated. "Aedan needs to know. He has to be ready when the moment comes."

Sigrid sighed. "We can't risk a message. Too many eyes, too many ways for it to be intercepted."

"She's right," McHaill said. "The Chairman has locked down all external communications for the competitors."

Mrs. Grady pressed her lips together, her expression drawn tight. She looked at her husband, as if searching for another solution, another option. But in the end, she only nodded.

"It's too dangerous," Mr. Grady said, voice firm. "We need to trust Aedan will be able to react in the moment."

That was it. The matter was closed.

Except it wasn't.

The adults weren't wrong. Logically, this was the right call. It was reckless. The kind of thing that could get us both caught. But logic wasn't enough.

I swallowed hard, scanning the room. No one else was going to do it.

But I wasn't ready to give up.

Nodin shifted beside me, the movement subtle—but when I turned, I found his gaze already locked on mine. Sharp. Expectant.

A silent conversation passed between us.

Everyone else was moving forward—locking in strategy, refining logistics, shoring up the plan. We were about to go off-script.

I tipped my head a fraction toward Nodin, just enough for him to notice. A cue, invisible to anyone else.

His lips quirked at the corner, a smirk flickering into place just long enough for me to see it before he tipped his chin down and muttered, barely above a whisper—

"So, when do we start ignoring all reasonable advice?"

A jittery pressure built behind my ribs, like I'd already leapt—and was just waiting to land.

"Now."

NINETEEN

The Strategy

ELIN

The underground base had transformed into a hive of activity. Tables were crowded with holo-screens, maps, and lists of resources. Resistance members moved between stations, voices overlapping in bursts of urgency. The air was thick with the scent of oil and dust, the mechanical whirr of holo-devices providing a constant backdrop to the murmured strategizing.

Three days. That was all it had been since we first pieced this plan together, but it felt like a lifetime. In those seventy-two hours, the situation had only grown more urgent. Gabriel's transfer had been confirmed. Aedan was still fighting in the *Leikr*—his team was now in the quarterfinals up against the Mauve team.

And *still*, I hadn't found a way to get to him.

I clenched my jaw, my fingers drumming against the table's edge as I scanned the latest updates. The clock was running out, and Nodin and I were still in a waiting pattern, looking for any crack in security, any opportunity that wouldn't get us immediately caught. But we couldn't exactly waltz into the stadium, and the Chairman's tower was out of the question.

Which left nothing.

Every hour that passed tightened the vice around my ribs. Aedan had no idea we were coming. No idea that if he pushed through to the finals, there would be a way out.

A tremor ran through me before I forced it down. I couldn't let the panic take over. Not now. We had to find another option—but until then, I needed to stay sharp, to focus on what we could control.

The mission planning continued around me, an unrelenting rhythm of strategy and precision. The rescue plans for Gabriel and Aedan were unfolding, each moving part critical, each second accounted for.

One corner of the room was dedicated to Skjoldur's infiltration team—Bae, Mr. Tibadeau, and a handful of Resistance fighters gathered around Yrsa as she laid out the center's security. The table in front of them was illuminated with a three-dimensional model of Skjoldur. Yrsa ran her hand through it, creating ripples in the blue light.

"The detention center has three layers of security," she explained, her fingers tracing each ring. The hologram responded to her touch, highlighting sections in red. "Outer perimeter drones, middle layer guard rotations, inner core biometric locks."

"Given that security, a direct assault is the only way," Knud said, his voice gruff, edged with impatience. As one of the Resistance's most experienced fighters, he had been assigned to Gabriel's team by Yrsa. He jabbed a thick finger at the holographic map, disturbing the projection. "We hit them hard and fast at the north entrance. Don't give them time to react."

"Or," McHaill drawled, leaning back with an unimpressed look, "we could try something that doesn't get Gabriel executed immediately. These aren't amateur guards, Knud. They have protocols for uprisings."

Knud snorted, clearly irritated. "And sneaking in leaves too many variables," he countered. "One wrong step, one unexpected patrol—"

"Which is why we don't step wrong," Bae cut in smoothly, adjusting her utility belt with practiced ease. "Come on, Knud.

You're all brute force, no finesse," she continued with a grin. "A little patience won't kill you."

"Patience is for people who have the luxury of time," Knud shot back.

"Both approaches have merit," Yrsa interrupted, her calm voice cutting through the tension. "And both have flaws."

She manipulated the hologram to zoom out, giving a fuller view of both the detention center and the city grid around it.

"What if we do both?" she suggested. "Not an assault, but a distraction. Here." She pointed to the power distribution center two blocks from Skjoldur. "A controlled explosion. Nothing that will harm civilians, but enough to draw attention and resources away from the detention center."

"Meanwhile, our infiltration team slips in through the reduced security," Bae added, catching on.

Knud and McHaill exchanged a look, their mutual stubbornness softening into consideration.

"It could work," McHaill admitted.

"If the timing is perfect," Knud qualified.

"Which it will be," Yrsa said, with the quiet confidence of someone who had done the impossible before. "Because we'll make it so."

"So, what's our play on the inside?" Bae asked.

"Conventional wisdom says enter from above or below," Tibadeau added, adjusting his sling with a wince. "But they'll expect that. We're going through here." He pointed to a maintenance tunnel, and the hologram zoomed in, revealing a narrow passage. "Used for geothermal pipe access. Guards avoid it due to the steam and heat."

"Right," Yrsa confirmed. "Once inside, Tibadeau, your job is to breach the mainframe and keep the security loops running. Bae, you and the team will secure Gabriel and get him out before they catch wind of us."

"And the timing?" McHaill asked.

"Guard rotation on the hour every hour," Sigrid answered. "Plus an automated system. The team will have exactly seven minutes before the system runs its security sweep."

Tibadeau nodded grimly. "If we're not in position by then, the mission fails before it begins."

A heavy silence settled over the room. Seven minutes. No margin for error.

Yrsa rolled her shoulders back, her sharp gaze sweeping over the team. "We need this tight. No missteps. Let's run it again."

The holographic figures representing the Skjoldur infiltration team flickered to life, moving through the detention center's corridors with practiced precision, each member hitting their marks perfectly.

Until—

"Stop." Bae pointed to the security panel near Gabriel's cell. "The timing's off. See how the patrol and the system check overlap? We'll be caught in the crossfire."

Tibadeau leaned forward, manipulating the simulation's timeline. "If we delay our entry by forty-seven seconds..."

"We miss our window at the exit," Knud finished, frowning.

"Unless..." Bae's eyes lit up. She gestured to another corridor—a narrow maintenance shaft barely wide enough for a person. "We split the team. Two through the main route, one through here."

"That's practically a ventilation duct," McHaill objected. "And it runs directly beneath the guard station."

"Exactly." Bae grinned. "They never check what's under their feet. I can place a signal disruptor there that will buy us the extra minute we need at the exit."

Tibadeau nodded slowly, seeing the logic. "It might work."

Yrsa ran the simulation again. This time, the holographic team extracted Gabriel successfully, their escape route clear.

"That's better," she said approvingly.

While the others finalized Gabriel's mission, our team gathered around a separate projection—one showing the *Leikr* stadium's inner workings. The Gradys, Nodin, Reo, Sigrid, and I hovered close, studying the shimmering layout of gates, contestant zones, and exits.

Mrs. Grady manipulated the hologram. Her hands moved with practiced grace, sections of the arena lighting up in sequence.

"The Chairman's box will be here," she pointed to an elevated platform overlooking the arena. "Heavily guarded, but all attention will be focused outward—on the competitors, on the crowd, on potential threats from outside."

"Not on threats already inside," Claire added, a small smile playing at her lips.

"Exactly," Mrs. Grady confirmed. "Meanwhile, Aedan will be here." The hologram shifted, highlighting the competitor platforms. "Once the competitors are in the arena, security relaxes around them—they're focused on guarding the perimeter and the Chairman, not the teams."

"Liam, we'll need your distraction to hold long enough to keep the Chairman's eyes on you," Sigrid said, tapping the display where the Chairman's private seating was highlighted in red.

Mr. Grady exchanged a look with his wife before nodding. "Oh, I'll make sure it's interesting enough for him. He won't be able to resist."

"We'll need to manipulate the arena's holo-feed, too," Mrs. Grady added. "That way, the distraction holds even if they start to suspect something's off."

"And when the distraction is in full effect, Claire and Edvin sneak onto Aedan's platform, get him clear of his team, and we get him out." Sigrid's tone was firm, resolute.

Nodin glanced between the two groups. "We're balancing on a knife's edge here. Two simultaneous rescues...One slip—"

"We won't slip," Sigrid cut in. "We execute perfectly, or we fail. There's no in-between."

No one argued. Instead, the conversation fractured into smaller side discussions—final refinements, what-ifs, worst-case scenarios. Every possible angle was scrutinized, weaknesses shored up.

By the time the groups merged back together, the air was thick with unspoken tension, the weight of what we were about to attempt pressing down on us.

I exhaled, pressing my fingers to my temple, but the gnawing doubt remained.

"What if they change Gabriel's transfer schedule?" I asked, voicing the question that had been gnawing at me since we began.

"They won't," McHaill said confidently. "The Chairman runs this city on precision. Deviate from the schedule, and you draw attention. The last thing they want during the *Leikr* is attention on a prisoner transfer."

"And if they do?" I pressed.

Yrsa's expression hardened. "Then we adapt. Tibadeau has built three signal jammers that can disrupt any vehicle within half a kilometer. If the transport changes course, we'll force it to stop."

"And the stadium?" Nodin asked, leaning against the wall. "What if Aedan's team is watching him too closely?"

"That's where this comes in," Sigrid said, placing a small metallic disc on the table. "Electromagnetic pulse, modified to affect only *Stórmenni* communication devices. When activated, it'll create a short window of confusion—just enough time for Claire and Edvin to make their move."

"What about the Chairman?" Reo asked, his voice quieter as he turned to Mr. Grady. "How long can you hold your illusion and keep his attention?"

The room grew still. Everyone knew the Chairman's mind intervention abilities made him the most dangerous variable in their plan.

"An illusion that big? Three minutes," Mr. Grady answered after a thoughtful pause. "Maybe four. But it should be enough—his focus will be split between my illusion and the final match festivities."

"It has to be enough," Mrs. Grady said with finality.

As the planning continued, I found myself drifting toward the corner where a small holo-display showed footage from the *Leikr's* previous rounds. Aedan moved across the screen, his face set in concentration as he navigated Naglfar's challenge. The recording looped just as he grabbed the victory disc, exhaustion and relief briefly breaking through his guarded expression.

"We're going to get him back," Claire said quietly, appearing at my side.

I nodded, unable to look away from the screen. "And Gabriel."

"And Gabriel," she echoed.

Across the room, Mr. Tibadeau stared at his own display—a security still from the IA headquarters showing Gabriel being escorted to a holding cell. His nephew's face was calm, even as guards flanked him on both sides.

Mr. Grady crossed the room to stand beside him, placing a gentle hand on his shoulder. "He knew the risks," he said softly.

"He did," Tibadeau agreed, his voice rough. "We all do."

The weight of what we were attempting settled over the room. Not one mission but two, intertwined and inseparable. Two people we couldn't leave behind, no matter the cost.

Before anyone could break the silence, the door burst open.

McHaill, who had briefly left the room, rushed back in, his expression grim. "We have a problem."

All activity ceased as heads turned toward him.

"New intel from our source." He slapped a data chip onto the central table. The hologram flickered, revealing security footage of a familiar figure being escorted through a high-security corridor.

"Tristan," I breathed, my blood running cold.

"He's been assigned to Gabriel's transfer team," McHaill confirmed. "And that's not all. He's requested additional security for the prisoner transport—not standard protocol. Which means more guards at the detention center."

"He knows something," Mrs. Grady said, her voice tight.

"Or suspects," Mr. Grady corrected. "If he knew, we'd already be compromised."

Sigrid studied the footage, her eyes narrowing. "This changes our approach. We can't risk a direct interception with him involved."

"Is he psychic? What's his ability?" Knud asked, already recalculating.

"Fire manipulation," I answered, remembering all too well the flames that had licked at my heels during our last encounter. "And he's dangerously good at it."

"So we adapt," Yrsa said firmly. "We change the timing on the initial distraction—we wait until they leave. As long as he and his extra guards are only part of the transport and don't stay at the detention center, our plan still works." She turned to Elin. "Think you can keep an eye on him through your visions without alerting the Chairman?"

I hesitated, the phantom touch of the Chairman's presence still lingering at the edges of my mind. "I can try."

"That's not good enough," Yrsa replied, not unkindly. "We need certainty."

"I can do it," I amended, straightening my shoulders. At Nodin's meaningful stare, I added, "I doubt the Chairman is 'watching' Tristan. But to be safe, I'll do short bursts."

"Good." Yrsa nodded. "Because now we're not just avoiding standard security—we're dealing with someone who has tangled with us before and captured one of us."

The room fell silent as the implications sank in. The stakes had just gotten higher.

Then, almost on cue, the holo-screens shimmered, shifting from strategy schematics to a live feed.

The team had planned it this way—timed the display to show the broadcast of the quarterfinals' final moments. There was no point in guessing. We needed to know.

If Gray team lost, there was no rescue. No way to get Aedan out.

I barely breathed as the *Leikr* quarterfinals overtook the main display, casting a stark glow across the room.

The Muspelheim-themed arena roared to life on screen, waves of simulated ash and steam rising in glistening heat waves. The camera panned across the battlefield—a hellscape of fire, lava, and stone—before zeroing in on the final stretch.

At the center of the battlefield, a narrow basalt bridge loomed over a chasm of molten rock, the final obstacle between victory and elimination. At the far end, a jagged obsidian pillar stood against the inferno, the sigil stone pulsing atop it, waiting to be claimed.

Aedan's team, Gray, was locked in combat with Mauve.

Blades hissed as they clashed, sparks bursting in the superheated air. The crowd roared as the four warriors battled for control of the bridge, neither side willing to yield.

A Mauve fighter lunged first, his Clan-forged sword arcing toward a gray-clad opponent. The impact sent both combatants skidding backward, their boots barely finding purchase on the fractured rock.

The holo-camera zoomed in, catching the moment as the second Gray warrior pivoted, her shield absorbing a crushing blow before she countered, her sword carving a swift, two-handed arc. Her opponent stumbled, nearly losing their footing on the unstable terrain.

The announcer's voice boomed over the stadium, excitement crackling through the speakers.

> *"And there it is! Excellent blade control from—wait—confirmation coming in—Thyra Bjorndóttir of the Gray team, executing that counter with remarkable precision! And alongside her, Einar Haldorsen, wielding a defensive stance as unshakable as his namesake! Both teams are neck and neck! Whoever claims the sigil stone first secures their spot in the semifinals!"*

The tension in the Resistance base was suffocating.

I held my breath, my pulse hammering in time with the flashing holo-feed. We needed the Gray team to advance—Aedan had to make it to the finals.

Nodin stood beside me, arms still crossed, but his fingers tapped an uneven rhythm against his bicep. "Alright, we just need them to not die before they get the sigil."

McHaill grunted. "Easier said than done."

Onscreen, the Mauve warrior launched into a rapid offensive, striking high and fast. Thyra dodged with sharp precision, slipping just out of reach before twisting and bringing her sword up in a fluid counterattack.

A blade slashed toward her ribs—she twisted, just barely avoiding the edge. She responded with a sudden counterstrike, her sword carving upward, forcing her opponent to stumble.

The bridge trembled beneath them.

Tibadeau's voice was grim. "That bridge isn't going to hold much longer."

Then—a flicker of movement from the second Mauve fighter.

A sudden charge, blade angled low.

My heart stopped.

Einar saw it at the last second.

The Mauve warrior aimed for Thyra's back, but Einar stepped in, shield bracing against the full force of the strike. The impact reverberated through the screen, the force so intense that cracks splintered across the bridge's surface.

Chunks of molten rock broke free, plunging into the lava below. The Mauve fighter staggered, thrown off balance—an opening.

Thyra took her chance.

With one sharp inhale, she sprinted past the fighter toward the obsidian pillar.

The sigil stone was out of reach, perched atop the final ledge—but Thyra didn't slow.

At the last second, she threw out a hand, sending a controlled burst of air that tilted the glowing stone off its pedestal. It tumbled forward—she snatched it mid-air.

A hush.

Then—

The holo-screen blazed with a verdict: "**GRAY TEAM ADVANCES.**"

The Resistance room erupted in a collective cheer.

My chest tightened as the realization sank in. One more step. One more match, and Aedan would be in the finals.

Nodin let out a low whistle. "Well, that was dramatic."

Sigrid folded her arms, still eyeing the holo-screen. "Too close."

I could only nod, my knuckles white against the table. *Too close indeed.*

As midnight approached, the planning transitioned into preparation. Equipment was distributed—communication devices no larger than a thumbnail, weapons disguised as everyday objects, identity shields that would mask our faces from recognition software.

"One final thing," Yrsa said, her voice cutting through the activity. "The *Leikr* finals coincide with the Chairman's address to the city. Every screen in Falinvik will broadcast his speech before showing the match. At precisely that moment, every *Stór-menni* guard will stand at attention for the Chairman's oath. That's our window."

"Thirty seconds," Sigrid added. "That's how long we have before anyone realizes what's happening."

"Thirty seconds to start a revolution," Nodin murmured.

"Not a revolution," Mr. Grady corrected, his eyes meeting his wife's across the room. "A *rescue*. We're not here to change Falinvik—not yet. We're here for family."

Claire nodded, her hand resting on the edge of the table as if grounding herself. "Then let's bring them both home."

I took in the people around me—some I'd known for months, others for mere days. But in this moment, we were bound by something stronger than time. A shared purpose. A promise.

"Everyone clear on their roles?" Yrsa asked, scanning the room. Nods all around. "Then get some rest. In 24 hours, we either make history or become part of it."

As the room began to empty, I lingered, staring at the dual

holograms—Skjoldur and the *Leikr* Stadium, twin fortresses we were about to breach. Two impossible missions. One chance to get it right.

Around me, quiet conversations faded as the others moved off to prepare. Weapons were checked. Supplies were accounted for. Plans were set into motion.

But my thoughts remained elsewhere.

Aedan didn't know.

We could have the perfect timing, the perfect strategy—but if he wasn't expecting it, if he wasn't ready to act when the moment came, we could lose everything.

I drew in a slow breath, pressing my hands against the table's cool surface. *How were we supposed to warn him?* A message was out of the question. The Chairman had locked down communications, and even if we found a way to slip one through, there was no guarantee Aedan would see it in time.

We needed another way.

A shadow passed over the table.

I looked up just as Nodin sauntered toward me, hands tucked into his pockets, wearing an expression that was far too casual for the tension wrapped around my chest.

"So," he said casually, resting his elbow on the table. "How do you feel about a party?"

I blinked once. Twice. "What?"

"A party," he repeated, smirking. "Drinks, music, poor life choices —you know, all the good things in life."

I rolled my eyes. "Unless you've suddenly forgotten we're in the middle of planning a rescue mission, I'm going to assume you have a point."

He tipped his head toward the far side of the room, where a handful of Resistance members were talking in hushed but animated voices. "I overheard something interesting. Apparently, every year the finalists in the *Leikr* get a special... let's call it a reward. The higher-ups throw them a little party at one of the local taverns."

My pulse kicked up a notch. "Aedan's team is in the semi-finals."

"Exactly." Nodin's smirk was edged with anticipation. "Which means, if they make the finals, which we need them to do for the rescue to move forward, he's going to be there."

I stared at him, the implications snapping into place like puzzle pieces. *This was it.* The opening we had been waiting for—somewhere outside the stadium, outside the Chairman's tower. Somewhere we could actually reach him.

"We just have to figure out which tavern," I said.

Nodin tapped a knuckle against the tabletop, thoughtful. "It won't be public knowledge. The last thing the *Stór-menni* want is a security mess with all their 'star players' out in the open. But if the Resistance knows about it, that means someone has intel."

I inhaled sharply, the weight in my chest shifting. For the first time in days, the problem wasn't just a wall in front of me—it was something we could climb.

"We find the tavern," I murmured, meeting Nodin's gaze. "And we find Aedan."

His grin widened. "Now you're getting it."

I let a flicker of hope take root. It wouldn't last long. Not unless we moved fast—before someone else took Aedan's fate out of our hands for good.

TWENTY

The Partner

AEDAN

The *Leikr* Stadium was a beast of stone and sound, its very foundations quaking beneath the weight of the crowd. If the first obstacle round had been nearly packed, the semi-finals had pushed the arena past its limits, bursting at the seams with spectators crammed into every available seat. Even the overflow stands—temporary structures erected along the upper tiers—were filled with eager onlookers, their cheers blending into a deafening roar that vibrated in my chest.

The air pulsed with heat, sweat, and electric anticipation, a living force pressing in from every side. The *Leikr* announcer's voice boomed overhead, declaring that

"this was when warriors would rise. And the weak? They would fall."

Above, the massive holo-screens hovered effortlessly, projecting rapid flashes of the past battles—victories, failures, near-deaths—each one fueling the energy of the arena. Every spectator, from the lowest-ranked Clan member to the highest-ranking *Stór-menni* officials, leaned forward, waiting for the next spectacle.

Even the Chairman had returned to his private box, a shadowed balcony that loomed over the highest tier. Though I couldn't see him from where I stood, I could feel his presence—like a blade pressed to the back of my neck.

I took a slow, measured inhale, turning my eye skyward away from his box.

The stadium's high domed ceiling, a masterpiece of steel and glass, stretched above us like the ribcage of the giant beast, barely holding back the turbulent sky. The jagged storm clouds shifted overhead, their pale light slashing through the gaps, casting an eerie glow across the arena floor.

Everything felt heavier. The noise. The heat. The pressure.

Somewhere in the back of my mind, a Jim Croce lyric surfaced—uninvited, but stubborn. "*This is it—this is life on the edge of a knife.*"

I exhaled slowly, rolling my shoulders as if I could shake off the tension settling in my bones. *It was just nerves.*

At least, that's what I told myself. The truth was, I hadn't felt the same since the injection.

A sharp ache pulsed at the base of my skull, an aftershock of whatever poison, drug, or enhancement the Chairman had forced into my system. I still didn't know exactly what it was.

Every time I thought the effects had finally faded, it came crawling back—a lingering burn in my veins, a whisper of something wrong beneath my skin.

Would it ever go away? Or was this permanent?

And then there was the medallion he had given me.

It rested against my chest, cool and unmoving beneath the collar of my tunic. The Valknut engraved in its surface—the Chairman's emblem—pressed into my skin like a brand.

I couldn't take it off. It was the only thing helping to stabilize my *megin*. So, as much as I hated it, I also needed it.

Between the injection still burning in my veins and the medallion's weight against my chest, I couldn't shake the feeling that part of me belonged to him now.

And maybe that was the worst part.

Because deep down, I knew—

The Chairman's injection. The medallion. They were helping me survive the *Leikr*.

I couldn't afford to dwell on what that meant. Not now. Not on what it was doing to me. Not about Elin, or my family, or whether they were even still alive. If I let that weight creep in now, I'd crack. So I locked it down. I had to.

I flexed my fingers, forcing the thoughts away. *Focus.*

The six of us stood together on the platform, waiting. The layout of the platforms had changed for the Obstacle rounds in the *Leikr*. Each team platform had a central staging zone. Once the participants were named, they stood on a circular section, which detached from the platform and lowered into the depths—an elevator straight into the unknown.

The *Leikr* Committee—a group of shadowed figures behind the obsidian screens above the arena—were about to announce the next pairing for the semi-finals.

And I knew I was about to be called. *I had to be.*

Everyone else on the team had already competed in one of the previous Obstacle rounds. Fenja and Magnus had stumbled back from their round two days ago, bruised and covered in dirt after barely escaping Jörmungandr. The next day, without time to recover, Fenja was forced back into action, this time alongside Eirik, battling through Niflheim's treacherous, ice-laden cliffs in round eight. Then came Einar and Thyra's quarter-final, where the Muspelheim collapsing bridges had nearly sent Einar into molten lava, and it had taken precise footwork, air manipulation, and sheer determination to survive against the landscape and their opposing team's attacks.

Now, I fully expected it to be my turn.

For some reason, I had been held back for this moment, kept in reserve while the others fought their way through the quarter-finals. That meant one thing: *I was about to be thrown into the most brutal match yet.*

And whoever they paired me with could determine whether I survived it or not. The only question was who would be my partner. And that was what had my stomach in knots.

From the corner of my eye, I saw Eirik, standing slightly apart from the group. His expression was unreadable, arms crossed over his chest, weight shifted onto one foot like he was simply waiting for the inevitable.

I had spent enough time around him to know he was never easy to read. His movements—fluid and deliberate—held an effortless control, and his arrogant words were always chosen with precision as if he were calculating every outcome before making a move. Always two steps ahead.

It was a skill I'd seen before.

I glanced toward Thyra, expecting indifference, but her expression was tight, unreadable. Not the usual steel-edged focus, but something more thoughtful. She wasn't watching Eirik. She was studying him.

I didn't know if that was a good thing—or a very bad thing.

The arena bell tolled, a deep, resonating sound that sent a ripple of anticipation through the crowd.

Above us, the screen flickered, displaying the official seal of the *Leikr* Committee, radiant white-hot against the black.

Then, the voice.

"For the next semi-final pairing...for the Gray team..."

I exhaled slowly, bracing myself.

"...Aedan Grady."

No surprise.

But then—

"...and Eirik Sigvardsson."

A hush fell over our group.

Beside me, Magnus let out a low chuckle. Fenja raised an eyebrow, glancing between me and Eirik with mild curiosity. Einar's expression was carved from stone, giving nothing away.

And Thyra—

For the first time since I met her, she frowned. It wasn't doubt, but something close to irritation—except her eyes snapped to me, not Eirik. A brief, subtle shift, like she was weighing something. Calculating.

And in that flicker of hesitation, I thought I saw something else. *Concern?*

Before I even turned my head, I felt the weight of Eirik's gaze shift toward me.

And when I did—

He was smirking.

Figures.

"Looks like it's you and me," he said, adjusting his weight like this was nothing more than a routine sparring match.

Before I could respond, Thyra's voice cut through the tension.

"Stay focused," she said—but her gaze held mine just a moment longer than it should have. Not quite a warning. Not irritation, either. Something quieter.

I turned to her, expecting more—a follow-up, a sharper edge, anything to explain the way her eyes had shifted. But she just nodded once, almost imperceptibly, then turned away.

I didn't bother answering Eirik. I was too busy pushing aside my initial reaction.

Why him? Why not Einar, precise and methodical? Or Magnus—predictable, at the very least?

But Eirik? He was a wild card—and wild cards either saved the game or burned the whole table down.

I had seen him fight. He was fast. Strategic. And he never revealed his hand too soon as if he were always holding onto a secret no one else knew.

Just like Thyra.

I glanced back, but she was already walking away—no parting words, no explanation. But something about the way she turned—shoulders tense, jaw tight—made me wonder if she'd wanted to say more. And didn't.

Whatever lay ahead, one thing was certain—I needed Eirik. Like it or not, we had to be on the same side for this round.

We both moved to the section dedicated to the chosen participants.

Eirik tilted his head slightly, watching me with an expression I couldn't quite place. "You seem... thoughtful," he said, his tone casual, though I knew it was anything but.

I met his gaze, steady. "Just making sure we're on the same page."

The corner of his mouth lifted. "And are we?"

I didn't hesitate. "We need to be. Because if we're not, we both lose."

Before either of us could say more, the platform beneath us shifted, the metallic floor beginning to descend toward the arena floor.

No time to second-guess.

The semi-finals were about to begin.

And whether I liked it or not—Eirik and I were in this together.

TWENTY-ONE

The Semi-Final

AEDAN

The platform groaned as it lowered toward the arena floor, metal grinding against stone. The crowd's deafening roar grew even louder, the stadium pulsing with frenzied energy as the semi-final obstacle course revealed itself on the floating screens above us.

"THE VEIL OF SVARTALFHEIM"

The words glowed in eerie silver, morphing into twisted runes that flickered before turning into the outline of a massive labyrinth—walls of jagged black iron, twisting like the tunnels of the deep. Shadows slithered along the passages, shifting and curling like living things.

For half a second, my brain conjured AC/DC's "Highway to Hell." *Not helpful, but not wrong either.*

The announcer's voice boomed over the stadium:

"Two teams enter the Labyrinth of Svartalfheim, where the dark elves forged their domain in the depths of the earth. Inside, the paths will shift, illusions will deceive, and unseen hunters will strike from the shadows. Only those who master the darkness can claim the way forward. But beware—at the heart of the labyrinth, something stirs,

something ancient, something hungry. Who will escape, and who will be lost in the dark?"

The crowd erupted in a feverish chant as the platform locked into place, the ground rumbling beneath our feet. The air was thick with the scent of damp stone, decay, and something darker—something ancient.

My heartbeat hammered in my ears.

Beside me, Eirik stretched his arms, rolling his shoulders, his expression unreadable as ever. "Well," he muttered, "this should be fun."

I barely resisted the urge to glare at him.

Across from us, on the opposite platform, our competitors stepped forward—two warriors clad in deep crimson and black, their medallions flaring with energy. I recognized them immediately.

Viggo and Ragna—two of the Black and Crimson's most ruthless competitors.

Of course, it had to be them.

Eirik scoffed, cracking his knuckles. "Well, I guess we're making some new friends."

I flexed my grip on my sword handle, shifting my weight forward. "They're not here to make friends."

A horn blasted through the stadium, the signal that the round was about to begin.

A low, mechanical grinding noise echoed as the massive iron gate in front of us slid open, revealing the entrance to the labyrinth.

A tunnel of twisting, shifting metal, its walls pulsing faintly with an unnatural luminescence. Beyond it, the passageways were shrouded in dense, creeping smoke.

Then the shadows began to move.

My grip tightened on my sword and shield, my *megin* thrumming beneath my skin, ready for whatever horrors lay inside.

"***BEGIN!***"

The horn blasted again, and we ran.

I sprinted forward, matching Eirik's pace as we plunged into the maze. As soon as we crossed the threshold, the air shifted—thick and suffocating, as if the shadows themselves had weight. The scent of damp earth, rusted metal, and something acrid filled my lungs, burning at the edges. My breath curled in the air, dissolving like smoke.

The walls groaned and shifted.

Not stone. Not bone. Dark iron.

Jagged, interwoven metal stretched upward, twisting into impossible, spiraling formations. The walls radiated with an uncanny blue color, runes stuttering in and out of existence like the dying embers of a fire. Shadows slithered along the passageways, moving in ways that weren't natural. They didn't follow the flickering torchlight hanging from rusted iron sconces—they avoided it, recoiling like living creatures.

Somewhere on the other side of the maze, Viggo and Ragna moved towards us, their footsteps lost in the labyrinth's unnatural silence. They wouldn't attack yet—not until we were deeper inside, where Svartalfheim's darkness would test our resolve.

Illusions. Traps. The announcer had said. The hidden horrors of the dark elves.

I had no idea what was waiting for us, but I could *feel* it.

Eirik moved with effortless ease, his steps barely making a sound against the cold metal floor. "Watch for illusions," he muttered. "Svartalfheim doesn't play fair."

The moment he spoke, the walls shifted.

The iron corridors distorted before my eyes—elongating, contracting, twisting. The passage ahead melted away, replaced by a jagged dead end, the walls curling inward like grasping hands.

I skidded to a stop, heart pounding.

"That wasn't there before," I whispered.

"Exactly," Eirik muttered. He raised a hand, his shadows rippling out, distorting the air around the illusion. The instant they touched the wall, the iron shuddered—two versions of reality layered over each other like overlapping memories.

I stepped closer, not rushing. My eyes scanned the distortion—how the light bent differently across each version, how the runes shimmered in opposite rhythms. The scent of rust and heat drifted faintly from one side, but not the other.

"You see it?" Eirik asked, voice low.

"I see enough," I said, tightening my grip on my shield. "One of them looks too perfect. Like it wants us to believe it's real. The other's wrong... but it feels honest."

I hesitated for only a heartbeat, then angled toward the flawed path—the one that didn't try so hard to hide what it was.

I stepped through.

For a second, the world *twisted.*

Then I was on the other side.

Eirik followed at a slower pace.

I barely had a second to see what was in front of me before the *ground lurched beneath me.*

A sharp *click* echoed beneath my boots.

I froze.

Eirik's eyes darted down just as I realized—the floor wasn't *real.*

It was a mirage. A projection of stability over nothingness.

Before I could move, the illusion vanished, and the metal floor beneath me collapsed into darkness.

I had a split second to react—throwing myself sideways, my fingers just catching the rough edge of the wall.

But the abyss below was not empty.

Figures moved in the blackness—warped, twisted creatures, their skin dark as the void, eyes burning like blue embers. They clung to the walls of the pit, watching, waiting. Their elongated limbs stretched unnaturally, fingers like iron claws, reaching upward.

The beings were pulled straight from my mother's recount of Norse legends. Dark elves. *The Dökkálfar.*

"Move!" Eirik barked. I lunged as he yanked me up just as one of the creatures jumped, its clawed hand slashing at the air where I had been.

The moment my boots hit solid ground, my legs nearly buckled beneath me, the raw adrenaline crashing over me like a wave. My lungs heaved, chest burning, hands still clenched from the sheer force of my grip on the jagged ledge. The sensation of falling lingered in my bones, a sickening aftershock that refused to let go.

Behind me, the pit snapped shut with a metallic groan, erasing all evidence that it had ever been there. But my body still felt it—the gaping void beneath me, the claws reaching from the dark.

I swallowed hard, trying to force down the tremor in my limbs, but my heart still hammered against my ribs when Eirik's voice cut through the silence.

"Like I said, Svartalfheim doesn't play fair," he said, as if we'd just sidestepped a puddle instead of near death. "You need to watch yourself."

I whipped toward him. "Watch myself? That's your takeaway? I nearly got dragged into whatever nightmare is lurking down there."

Eirik shrugged. "But you didn't."

I took a step closer, glaring. "You knew. You saw the illusion before I did."

He gave a half-shrug, his tone dry and maddeningly casual. "Maybe."

I clenched my jaw, forcing my hands to steady. "Next time, how about you actually say something instead of waiting to see if I'll figure it out before I die?"

Eirik tilted his head slightly, considering. Then, with that same infuriating ease, he said, "But where's the fun in that?"

I let out a sharp exhale, trying to shake off the lingering tension. "Alright. Next time, I'll let you fall first."

His grin widened. "That's the spirit."

We kept moving, the corridors narrowing, the air growing heavier. The oppressive darkness wasn't just around us—it was watching us.

Then the whispers began.

Soft at first, curling around me like threads of silk.

Then louder. *Stronger.*

"Aedan."

I froze.

A voice—low, familiar, calling my name.

I turned—and saw her.

Elin.

She stood at the edge of the corridor, her form fluttering, half-shadow, half-real. Her amber eyes were wide, desperate. Her lips parted, forming words I couldn't hear. Calling to me.

"Elin?" My voice barely escaped my throat.

She reached for me.

Eirik grabbed my wrist and yanked me backward.

"Whoever you think that is, it's *not* her," he snapped.

As he said it, Elin's form *rippled*—her mouth stretching unnaturally wide, her eyes burning an unnatural blue, and suddenly she was lunging at me.

I barely raised my shield in time.

The *illusion shattered,* dissipating into curling smoke, but the whisper of my name still echoed through the labyrinth.

The maze knew my name. It knew Elin. But how?

It had to be reading us somehow, peeling back our minds, twisting our thoughts into weapons against us.

Which meant they knew Eirik, too.

I didn't even have a second to process what had just happened before Eirik went rigid beside me. His usual sharp, fluid movements halted, drawn tight like a bowstring.

Then I heard it.

A voice—not Elin's this time.

"Eirik."

The air around us vibrated, like something unseen had just breathed the name into existence. It was soft, but filled with something sharp beneath it, like an edge hidden in velvet.

And then I saw her.

Thyra.

Eirik's entire body was still. Not like when he was preparing to dodge, or waiting for an attack. No—this was different. He didn't move—caught in a stillness, like time had folded around him.

The illusion—Thyra—wasn't attacking yet. She just stood there. Watching him. Not desperate, not screaming, not broken like Elin's illusion had been. But judging. Waiting.

A flash of something crossed Eirik's face. His grip on his daggers tightened, but he didn't strike.

He wasn't sure.

This wasn't just a memory. It was a *wound.*

For the first time, he hesitated.

I stepped forward, voice low. "Eirik."

His eyes darted to me just for a second. But it was enough. The illusion snapped toward me, its eyes blazing cold blue—

That was all Eirik needed.

The stillness broke. In a blur, he twisted, his dagger flashing up in an arc of blackened steel, slicing clean through her throat. No hesitation now. No flinch. Just action.

The illusion had hardly opened its mouth before it disintegrated into curling black smoke, vanishing into the walls of the labyrinth.

But Eirik's dagger was still poised midair. A muscle ticked in his jaw.

Then, finally, he let out a slow, deliberate breath and shook the lingering smoke from his blade like it meant nothing.

But it had. And we both knew it.

The air felt too tight in my lungs, but I kept my voice even. "You knew about the illusions."

Eirik's face gave nothing away. His usual smirk wasn't there. His voice was quieter than before. "I've encountered them before...nasty things. But they don't create something from nothing."

A chill crawled down my spine. If that was true, then the illusion

—Thyra's face, her voice, the way she had looked at him—had been pulled from something real.

Which meant I wasn't the only one being haunted.

Eirik shook his head, dispelling whatever thoughts were clawing at the back of his mind. "We have to keep moving."

I forced myself to nod, though my legs felt heavier than before.

As we walked deeper into the maze, a low vibration hummed against my boots. Not just in the walls—something deeper. Beneath the metal floor. Subtle. Rhythmic.

Like breathing.

I glanced at Eirik, but if he noticed it, he didn't say anything.

Maybe it was nothing.

But then—the labyrinth stilled.

The shift was so sudden, so unnatural, that it made me hesitate mid-step. For the first time since we had entered, the twisting iron walls didn't groan, shift, or oscillate with shadows. The jagged paths that had been closing around us like a living thing now sat uncannily silent, as if watching. Waiting.

I steadied my grip on my sword handle. The only sounds were my pulse echoing in my ears and the faint hum of Eirik's shadows curling at his feet.

He glanced around with a slight frown on his features. "I don't like this."

"Me neither," I admitted.

Eirik twirled a thread of shadow between his fingers, the tendrils coiling restlessly. He scanned the walls, his expression sharp. "Whatever this is, it's not rest."

I turned in a slow circle, studying the open space. The walls hadn't just stopped moving—they seemed to have drawn back, creating a small clearing. *A trick? Or mercy?*

I shot him a look. "Yeah, it's messing with us, alright. This—" I gestured at the open space around us, "—feels like an illusion. Or worse, bait."

Eirik hummed in thought, his gaze flicking upward toward the jagged iron ceiling, where the shifting blue shine of runes glistened uncertainly, like a dying ember.

"I say we don't stand here long enough to find out," he said finally.

I nodded. "Then let's find the way forward."

He fell into step beside me, shadows shifting across his face. "You really think it's going to let us go that easily? There's always another nightmare waiting in this place."

My fingers curled tighter around my sword. "Then we don't wait for it. We face it head-on."

A beat. Then Eirik let out a quiet chuckle, stepping forward. "See how much you've grown? This is why you're the fun one now."

I rolled my eyes and turned toward the nearest passage. "Let's go before the—"

The shadows moved.

Not a twitch, not a trick of the dim light—they surged forward all at once.

A ripple of black mist unfurled from the walls, not just darkness but something alive, something breathing.

Eirik reacted first, his daggers spinning into his hands. "And there it is."

The labyrinth hadn't stopped. It had just been waiting for the right moment to strike.

They came from every direction, emerging from the darkness like wraiths. Not undead warriors, but *Dökkálfar*—the shadow elves of Svartalfheim.

Their bodies quivered like mirages, shifting between solid and incorporeal, making it impossible to tell which ones were real. Some wore tattered armor, their faces hidden behind masks of black iron, while others were nothing but silhouettes with gleaming pale-blue eyes, watching, waiting. They moved with chilling precision, their daggers curved like fangs, their spears impossibly thin and sharp—silent killers forged in the abyss beneath the mountains.

I heard the hiss of Eirik's daggers igniting and a faint blue glow beside me. I quickly pulled out my sword handle and flicked my wrist. My sword blazed into life—its sleek, energy-infused blade shimmering with light.

Then, out of nowhere, a spear jerked toward me like a flash of moonlight. I snapped my shield up just in time, the impact rattling up my arm. Twisting, I lashed out with a burst of telekinetic force, slamming the creature back into the shifting dark.

The *Dökkálfr* shattered into wisps of black mist.

It hadn't been real.

The whisper of shifting metal was the only warning before another lunged from my blind spot. This one was real.

I spun, meeting the curved dagger with my sword—but not before its tip raked across my shoulder. The fabric scorched, the skin beneath burning. I bit down hard, ignoring the sting as the clang of metal echoed through the labyrinth. The creature didn't flinch, didn't grunt, didn't breathe—just attacked again, faster than before.

Eirik was already gone, moving like a shadow among shadows. I caught glimpses of him—his daggers slicing through *Dökkálfar* warriors, his form shifting as he weaved through real enemies and illusions alike.

More of them materialized from the darkness.

Two. Three. Five.

Behind us, the clang of swords and shouts told me that the Black and Crimson Team had joined the fight.

I caught sight of Ragna's axe cutting through one of the *Dökkálfar*, the blade passing through empty air before she spun and struck again, this time hitting solid flesh. Viggo was close behind her, his broadsword flashing in the dim light, carving through illusions and reality with ruthless efficiency.

But the *Dökkálfar* were relentless.

Their curved daggers struck from impossible angles, phasing in and out of reality like candle flames. For every shadow we cut down, another took its place.

And that's when I realized—

They weren't just attacking.

They were driving us backward.

Forcing us deeper into the labyrinth.

I was still processing the thought when something heavy slammed into my shield. The impact nearly knocked me off balance, my boots skidding against the cold metal floor.

I gritted my teeth and shoved back, twisting to see—

Viggo.

His broadsword pressed against my shield, his smirk barely visible beneath the dim sheen of the labyrinth's ghostly blue light. He had waited for this.

"Getting tired, Gray team?" he sneered, voice deceptively light. His grip on his weapon never wavered.

Before I could respond, he suddenly twisted, dropping low and hooking my ankle with his boot.

I scarcely managed to telekinetically shove him back before he could take me to the ground, the force sending him skidding across the floor, but the movement gave him exactly what he wanted.

Space.

I was being forced back. Away from the path forward.

The instant I staggered, the *Dökkálfar* swarmed. Spears lunged toward me—I raised my shield, bracing for the impact—then caught a glint of silver at my side.

A dagger.

Too close.

I didn't think. I *reacted.*

A raw energy tore through me, and I threw out my arm with a shout—unleashing a telekinetic shockwave in all directions. The air cracked like thunder. Stone groaned. The ground shuddered beneath my boots as an invisible force exploded outward from my core.

The nearest *Dökkálfar* didn't just stumble—they were hurled backward, limbs flailing, their silhouettes spasming between solid flesh and smoky illusion as they slammed into the walls with bone-jarring *thumps.*

The energy that tore from me wasn't just instinct—it was power, raw and unchecked. Too strong. As soon as it left my body, I felt it—like my *megin* had been stretched, augmented beyond what I knew. The medallion thudded against my chest, slightly warm. I didn't know if it was containing the power—or feeding it. I staggered slightly, my pulse hammering as the *Dökkálfar* shattered like smoke in the wind.

That shouldn't have been possible. Not like that. Not at that scale.

The heat burned in my veins again. The Chairman's voice echoed in the back of my mind—*"Consider it an enhancement."*

I whipped around, scanning the chaos. Eirik wasn't far from me, his blades flashing in the dim light as he weaved through the shifting shadows. Even he wasn't untouchable—not here, not against this many.

A dagger grazed his arm, cutting through the fabric of his cloak and slicing a shallow line across his forearm. Blood beaded and darkened the sleeve, but he didn't miss a beat—just moved faster, more vicious, like the pain sharpened his focus. He twisted to drive his knife into the *Dökkálfr's* side.

My moment of breath was shattered as a new shadow surged toward me—Ragna.

She lunged at me, her massive axe arcing toward my head.

I dodged, the edge of her blade slicing past my cheek, close enough to leave a burning cut that streaked across my cheekbone. Blood mixed with sweat, the sting making my vision blur for half a second—but I held my ground. She recovered instantly, using the momentum to swing again—faster, stronger.

I caught the strike against my shield, my arm buckling under the sheer force. Pain shot up my elbow into my shoulder—nothing broken, but the impact had rattled the joint enough to slow me. I shifted my grip, adjusting for the dull throb.

"She's strong," I muttered, holding my ground.

"She's precise," Eirik corrected, now closer to me—barely

ducking as Viggo's sword cut through the space where his neck had been.

Ragna was already swinging again. I had no time to recover—

So I didn't.

Instead, I let go of my stance, rolling with the force, twisting at the last second to use my own momentum to slam my shield into her gut.

She grunted, staggering back a step. Not much, but enough.

A moment. An opening. I drove my sword forward.

She twisted, catching the blade against the haft of her axe, but I was already moving—telekinetically yanking her foot out from under her.

She stumbled—not down, but off balance.

That was all I needed.

I surged forward, slamming my shield into her again, this time with enough force to send her crashing into the wall.

The impact knocked the air from her lungs, her head snapping back against the metal before she hit the ground in a crouch.

I readied myself for her counterattack—

But she didn't come at me.

She smiled.

Why is she smiling?

Viggo suddenly slammed his boot down onto a rune-etched plate on the ground. The entire labyrinth groaned.

A trap.

The *Dökkálfar* vanished into the walls.

So did the path forward.

The metal beneath us lurched—and then the entire corridor shifted.

I barely caught my footing before I saw it—

The walls between us and the exit—closing.

I heard Eirik curse under his breath. He moved first, cutting through a shadowy *Dökkálfr* that lunged at him from the churning mist, but the trap had already been sprung.

Viggo and Ragna weren't trying to kill us.

They were trying to block our way forward—to trap us behind the *Dökkálfar* while they got to the final challenge first.

The walls continued shifting, closing like massive iron jaws.

Eirik's gaze darted toward me—just a second of unspoken calculation.

There was no more time for hesitation.

I reacted. And yet, I felt it again—like my body knew the answer before my mind did. A raw, overwhelming certainty that I could rewrite the outcome.

"Eirik!"

The second I called his name, I acted—not just with strategy, but with something deeper, something newly awakened.

My *megin* surged, but it was different this time—more precise. I didn't just throw out a shockwave, I controlled it. I grabbed hold of Eirik and hurled us through the closing gap, the force threading us between the collapsing iron walls in a split-second maneuver I shouldn't have been capable of.

For a breathless moment, we were airborne, sailing over the collapsing corridors, over the shadows still writhing beneath us.

I hit the ground hard, rolling once, landing harder than I meant to. My ribs screamed in protest, something pulled—maybe cracked—but I forced myself upright.

I sucked in air, each inhale scraping raw against my chest.

Eirik landed beside me, but this time, he didn't immediately move.

His daggers were drawn, but he wasn't looking at Viggo and Ragna.

He was looking at me.

I was still catching my breath, but I could feel it—the lingering hum of raw power beneath my skin. The energy had surged beyond anything I'd done before, bending the world around me, letting me reshape our fate from the trap.

Eirik had seen it.

For once, his usual smirk was nowhere to be found. Instead, his gaze flicked between me and the shrinking gap in the walls, calculating, reassessing.

"You—" His voice was quieter than before, unreadable. A faint scoff escaped him as he shook his head. "Well. That's new."

It wasn't sarcasm. It wasn't amusement. It was something sharper. Something closer to concern. And that unnerved me more than anything.

The loud grinding of metal broke my thoughts.

I turned—just in time to see Viggo and Ragna staring at us through the closing wall.

They had planned to trap us. Instead, they were the ones stuck. For the first time, Viggo's smirk disappeared. The gap between the shifting walls shrank, and I could barely hear him over the metal gears.

But I saw his lips move.

"See you on the other side."

Then the maze swallowed them whole.

I half expected the labyrinth to conjure another illusion, one final trick. But the shadows held still. For once, there was no whisper. Just the aftermath.

Relief barely brushed the edge of my nerves as I turned to Eirik. "We need to move."

Eirik dusted off his cloak, adjusting the grip on his daggers. "Agreed."

The final challenge was still ahead of us.

And if we won—the Black and Crimson Team wouldn't get a second chance.

Before we could move, a low hum began to rise from the center of the arena. Beneath our feet, the stone trembled.

Then, with a sudden burst of blinding light and an ear-splintering *crack*, the wall ahead split down the middle—runed iron peeling back like the petals of a mechanical flower. From the heart of the labyrinth, a gate emerged.

Towering. Obsidian. Veined with threads of molten crimson that throbbed like a heartbeat. Runes slithered across its surface, fluttering as if waking from centuries of slumber. The air turned sharp, brittle with frost and static.

We didn't hesitate. Eirik and I sprinted toward the newly revealed gate. As soon as we passed through it, the ground shook violently, and the walls groaned as something ancient and massive stirred in the deep.

And from the depths of that darkness, a pair of glowing red eyes snapped open.

Without losing a second, the beast lunged. Its blackened fangs dripping with venom, its massive body coiling through the labyrinth, tearing through walls of dark iron like they were paper.

Nidhogg.

The corpse-eater. The devourer of the damned. Another legend reborn from my mother's stories.

The dragon's scales were not just black—they seemed to absorb the very light around them, swallowing the glimmer of the runes etched into the walls. A stench like rot and sulfur choked the air, each breath from its maw rolling out in waves of decay.

And it was watching us.

The final gate—the way out of the labyrinth—was behind it.

We had one chance to get through.

I tightened my grip on my sword—the blade pulsing as if alive. My shield hummed at my side, its translucent barrier gleaming, ready to absorb the beast's first strike.

Eirik stood beside me, his shadow curling at his feet like an eager predator. His daggers glinted in the dim light, but it was the darkness itself that would be his weapon.

"Tell me you have a plan," I muttered.

Eirik's smirk was razor-sharp. "Survive?"

Great.

The dragon struck first.

Its tail whipped through the air, the sheer force of it collapsing the nearest wall, sending shards of metal and rock flying like daggers.

Eirik and I split in opposite directions.

He moved first, slipping into the darkness, his form vanishing in the shimmering light.

Nidhogg roared and lunged toward me—its massive claws slamming down, its venom-dripping fangs bared.

I threw out my telekinesis—not to attack, but to launch myself backward, the force propelling me out of its reach just in time. As my boots hit the ground, I braced and lashed out with my sword, aiming for the nearest gap in its scales.

The blade bit in—just barely.

Nidhogg recoiled, but it wasn't wounded.

It was laughing.

A low, guttural rumble vibrated through its chest, reverberating through the walls.

It wasn't going to make this easy.

Eirik struck next.

From the shadows behind the dragon, his daggers sliced through the air, leaving behind afterimages—duplicates of himself weaving around the battlefield.

The dragon reacted, snapping at one illusion—only for its fangs to close around nothing.

A second later, Eirik was already moving again, his real form darting between the dragon's blind spots, stabbing for the soft tissue near its legs.

Nidhogg bellowed in fury, whipping around, but Eirik was already gone—a shadow among shadows.

But we needed more than distraction.

We needed damage.

Nidhogg exhaled, and the air turned toxic.

A black, rotting mist curled through the air, its foul stench searing my lungs. The metal walls of the labyrinth didn't just corrode—they melted, hissing and warping like flesh seared by fire. The very air around us trembled with decay.

I had seconds to react before the mist surged forward. My shield flared to life, a shimmering wall of energy standing between me and oblivion. But even as it held, the pressure was suffocating. My boots scraped against the shifting ground, the force pushing me backward—toward the walls. Toward the dead end.

The impact jarred my side, sending a fresh spike of pain through my ribs. I gritted my teeth. Whatever I'd pulled when we hit the ground hadn't healed, and now it screamed with every shift of my torso. But there was no time to stop. No time to hurt.

Out of the shadows, Eirik slid in beside me, his shield blazing against the rot-mist, its light warping under the pressure. He was panting, face streaked with ash and fury.

He cursed under his breath. "Now would be a great time for a brilliant idea, Aedan."

My jaw clenched. *Defense wouldn't save us. We needed to go for something vital.*

Nidhogg's throat.

The runes on its scales pulsed, the gleam thrumming like a heartbeat. *A weak point? Or a trap?*

It didn't matter. It was the only shot we had.

But was it enough?

I could feel it now—the energy coursing beneath my skin, coiling in my chest, waiting. This power had been lurking beneath the surface ever since the Chairman's injection, showing itself in bursts I couldn't fully explain. I had ignored it, pushed it aside, pretending it wasn't changing me.

But now—now I needed it.

I had spent so much time fearing what he had done to me, but in this moment, the truth settled in my bones. It wasn't just something done to me. It was mine now. And if it was mine, I could use it.

The weight of hesitation snapped away like a tether cut loose. Resolve settled into its place, clean and final.

"*Eirik,*" I called, my mind already forming a plan. "I need an opening!"

Eirik didn't hesitate. His shadow expanded, curling upward like black smoke before splitting—forming dozens of shifting afterimages around the dragon.

Nidhogg snapped at them, thrashing in confusion.

That was my moment.

I threw everything into my telekinesis—not just to propel myself forward, but to control the space around me. The air itself seemed to bend as I launched toward Nidhogg's throat, like I was moving through the battlefield rather than just across it.

It wasn't an effort, wasn't a struggle. It was control. The threads of energy that bound the world together—air, momentum, impact—I could feel them, manipulate them with a single thought.

This was what the Chairman had wanted from me.

For once, I didn't fight it. I didn't let hesitation steal my control.

Nidhogg's eyes snapped to me—too late.

I reversed my momentum at the last second, angling myself downward, sword in hand. My injured ribs screamed at me. But this time, I didn't just let gravity do the work. I pulled the force around me, gathering it, compressing it, letting the weight of my strike become something more.

Something unstoppable.

The moment I was above it, I swung. The blade burned with light as it drove into the soft space between its scales. The impact shook my bones.

The dragon screamed.

A blast of energy erupted from the wound, the force hurling me back across the battlefield. I barely twisted in time to land on my feet, skidding across the ground as Nidhogg burst into a mass of sparkling dust.

The air was still, except for the shower of golden flakes falling around us.

The only sound was my own ragged breathing. I could still feel it

—the echo of the power I'd unleashed. It coiled under my skin like a storm waiting to break again. It didn't feel like a gift. It felt like a fuse.

Eirik stood nearby, his posture relaxed—but his expression unreadable.

Then, the gate behind the dragon began to rumble open.

A voice boomed over the arena—

"GRAY TEAM: ADVANCES!"

The labyrinth shook as the doors swung wide.

The crowd roared, the cheers and jeers of thousands echoing through the arena.

I turned, my heart still racing, as the opposite side of the labyrinth remained oddly quiet.

Then—movement.

A second later, Viggo and Ragna emerged, staggering onto their platform, faces pale, armor scorched and darkened with soot.

The holo-screens shifted, a new message appearing in bold silver letters:

"Black and Crimson Team: PREPARE FOR ROUND TWO."

A chill shivered down my spine. They had to run the course again.

Eirik let out a low whistle. "Well, that sucks for them."

I nodded, watching as Viggo and Ragna barely had a moment to recover before the gates of a second labyrinth opened before them.

The round wasn't over. Not for them.

And yet, something about the way Viggo looked at us—cold, assessing—sent a ripple of unease through me.

I turned away, pushing the thought aside. For now, we had won.

But the finals were still ahead.

I slowly let out a deep breath, but it didn't ease the tightness in my chest. My ribs ached something fierce. My shoulder burned. My *megin* still hummed, raw and unsettled beneath my skin.

We'd survived.

But the relief didn't come. Not fully. Just a glimpse—sharp and breathless—before the weight of what I'd done settled over me. What I'd become.

The Chairman's medallion still hung heavy against my chest, echoing every heartbeat. We'd made it out. But part of me wasn't sure I had escaped anything.

Eirik stood a few paces away, silent. Still. He didn't say anything —but his eyes flicked toward me, lingering for a second too long. Not in a challenge. Not in calculation. But recognition.

Whatever he'd seen back there, whatever I'd become in that moment—he knew.

And for once, he didn't smirk.

He just nodded once. Small. Almost imperceptible.

And somehow, that said more than words.

TWENTY-TWO

The Party

ELIN

I had to admit—Nodin was infuriatingly good at sneaking out. Not that I was bad. Weeks of dodging *Stór-menni* patrols and navigating the labyrinth beneath Falinvik had sharpened my instincts. But Nodin? He moved like shadows made room for him. Effortless. Unhurried. Like he belonged in the spaces no one else could see.

But it was more than that. It was the way he made it feel like we weren't doing anything wrong, even as we slipped past guards and out through the old utility passage near the geothermal shaft. Like we were just two kids ducking out for air, not risking everything to spy on a party we had no business being near.

"Are you *sure* no one saw us?" I whispered as we slipped deeper into the unused subway tunnel, boots crunching softly on frost-covered concrete.

He grinned in the low glow of his Communicator. "Elli, *please.* Have some faith. If anyone noticed, it's because you were muttering loud enough to wake the geothermal pipes."

I elbowed him lightly, earning a quiet laugh as we pressed further down the passage. The scent of mineral water and old oil filled the air, mingling with the faint hum of power still pulsing through long-forgotten rails.

"I still don't get how you found out where the finalists' party is happening," I said, trying to keep my voice even. "It's not like the *Stór-menni* post invites on community bulletin boards."

He shrugged all casual charm and shadows. "I have my ways."

"That's not an answer."

"Exactly," he said, giving me a wink before hopping over a pile of rusted metal debris. "Let's just say a little bird chirped in the right direction."

I rolled my eyes, but let it go—for now. Still, it gnawed at me. Nodin had been vague about a lot of things lately. Casual, yes, but *too* casual. *How had he found out the exact location where the finalists were going to celebrate? And why hadn't anyone else at the base known?*

We reached the old maintenance ladder. He climbed first, pushing open the heavy grate with practiced ease. Moonlight and frost-laced air spilled down into the dark. When he reached the top, he glanced down at me, his eyes catching just enough light to look silver.

"After you, troublemaker," he whispered.

"Flattery won't get you out of latrine duty next week," I muttered, climbing past him.

His quiet laugh followed me up.

We emerged into the glittering artificial shine of Falinvik's modern district. Glass-and-metal towers gleamed under the starlight, every surface inscribed with softly glowing rune-work. Even the floating streetlights pulsed with lightwoven sigils, humming dimly. The whole city looked like it had been forged from myth and circuitry.

And tucked between two tech giants was *Sigrhall*.

A modern tavern done up like a digital fever dream of the Viking age. It was part monument, part mirage—its obsidian glass frame echoing the silhouette of an ancient mead hall, complete with dragon-headed steel beams that jutted from the rooftop, their etched runes pulsing faintly like a heartbeat.

Above the wide entrance, a holographic Valkyrie drifted through the air with wings of mist and pixel-light. Beneath her, the doorway itself gleamed with gold-etched runes that rearranged themselves every few seconds, displaying the tavern's name in ever-shifting fonts: *SigrHall*. Victory Hall.

I barely had time to absorb it before a sleek hover vehicle turned onto the street and slowed in front of the tavern. Nodin and I ducked behind a delivery kiosk, crouching low as the vehicle came to a soundless stop.

The doors of the vehicle hissed open, and my breath caught.

Aedan stepped out. Blindfolded.

I gripped Nodin's sleeve instinctively, the cold knot in my chest hardening. But Aedan was smiling—laughing, even—and for a moment, I just watched him as I had during the *Leikr* broadcasts, the flickering projections in the Resistance base our only window into that brutal world.

I'd learned all of Aedan's teammates' names by now. *Magnus*, with the mountain-sized frame and blunt sarcasm. *Fenja*, sharp as her metal-shifting megin. *Einar*, quiet and lethal, with those eerie eyes like he could see through solid stone. And *Eirik*—arrogant, sharp-tongued, and wielding shadows like they were part of him.

But it was Aedan I couldn't stop watching.

I hadn't realized how tightly I'd been holding that image of him at the end of the semifinals—bloodied, staggering, still standing when everything said he shouldn't be. I remembered how my stomach had dropped when he fell to one knee. How my whole body tensed waiting to see if he'd get back up.

He had. Of course, he had.

But seeing him now—whole again—was like seeing the ghost of someone I hadn't been ready to lose.

As if reading my thoughts, Nodin's voice was soft beside me. "The *Stór-menni* bring in healers for the winners. Some with *megin* strong enough to patch up broken ribs and torn muscles in minutes. He probably saw two or three within an hour of the match."

"And the losers?" I asked.

"They get what's left. If anything. Healers spend their *megin* carefully—it takes a toll."

I nodded, eyes still locked on Aedan. His walk was steady. No limp. No wince. The only hint of everything he'd been through was in the way his team kept close—Magnus hovering like a bodyguard, Fenja sharp-eyed, Einar silent but alert, and Eirik close to his side.

Then came Thyra.

She stepped out last, her stride already too familiar. She said something low to Aedan—something that made him laugh again—and then reached out, guiding him forward with a light touch at the elbow.

Just for a second, I froze.

It was... nothing. She was his captain. She probably helped all her teammates like that. And I'd seen them interact before, during the trials. They worked well together. Trusted each other.

But that touch. That moment.

Her hand on his arm wasn't possessive, exactly. But it didn't need to be.

It lodged somewhere behind my ribs and stayed there.

"She's always so close to him," I murmured, trying to sound neutral. I didn't quite manage it.

"She's his captain," Nodin said with a shrug. "Probably making sure he doesn't run into any walls."

"Right."

The word felt heavier than it should have.

I glanced sideways. Nodin's eyes were still on the tavern door, but his jaw was tight, his expression unreadable. For once, he wasn't smirking.

The door slid shut behind the last of them, music pulsing outward—a mix of pounding drums and digitized fiddle. Inside,

Aedan was being led into a celebration. A moment of joy after surviving something none of them should've walked away from.

I should've felt relief. I *did*. But it was tangled with too many other things—uncertainty, worry, and the weight of two connections I wasn't quite ready to fully examine.

Beside me, Nodin finally let out a breath. "We should move before the street patrol loops back."

But neither of us moved.

We crouched there a while longer, shoulder to shoulder in the frozen dark, watching the shadows flicker behind the tavern's shimmering glass. It all felt so... complicated. The laughter inside, the knot in my chest, the way Nodin hadn't said a word in minutes.

Finally, without speaking, he motioned me to follow.

We crept around the side of the building, keeping close to the shadows cast by the sleek high-rises surrounding *SigrHall*. The tavern's main entrance was impossible—two armed *Stór-menni* guards flanked the door, their helms reflecting the glow of rune script overhead. No one passed them without clearance.

Nodin pulled me back behind a support column just as one of the guards shifted.

"Front's locked up tighter than Ginnungagap," he muttered, eyes scanning the alley behind the tavern. "But there's always a back door. Even the *Stór-menni* need to sneak out for a smoke or a breath of air."

I looked at him. "You're suggesting we wait? Just hope someone decides to take a break?"

He grinned. "Not hope. Trust probability."

I narrowed my eyes. "You just made that up."

"Probably."

But we stayed. Tucked in the narrow alley behind the tavern, backs pressed to the cold wall. The steady thump of bass and strange vocals pulsed through the building, vibrating slightly against the concrete. Time passed. Not much, but enough for my nerves to start crawling up my spine. But before I could say anything—

The side door cracked open.

A young Clan member—barely older than us—stepped out, rubbing his temple. He muttered something under his breath about the noise and leaned against the wall, lighting a sleek, smoldering inhaler between his fingers.

Nodin gave me a look.

We moved fast—silent. I kept my hood low as we crept behind the crates stacked beside the door. When the Clan boy turned to exhale, Nodin slid forward and caught the door before it closed.

With a two-fingered salute behind him, he pulled me inside.

The sound hit me like a wave. Music roared through the space—modern bass lines woven with ancient drum rhythms and streaks of what sounded like throat-sung chants, all pulsing beneath shifting lights that moved like starlight caught in smoke.

Inside, *SigrHall* felt like the belly of a ship carved out of legend and glass. Curved walls etched with runes shimmered faintly under each beat. Stark iron beams arched overhead like ribs. Columns of luminous mist drifted between elevated platforms where *Leikr* participants and their hangers-on leaned over balcony railings, laughing or toasting from silver horns. Holo-projections filled the space above them, flickering with victorious moments from the Challenges.

The crowd was dense. Most were young—warriors, tacticians, and *Leikr* fanatics. Their cloaks shimmered with faction colors and status badges, but there were no weapons in sight. This was a time to celebrate, and they were determined to make it count.

I stayed close to Nodin as we hugged the back wall, our eyes scanning the moving silhouettes.

"See him?" I asked.

"Not yet." Nodin tilted his head toward a glowing mezzanine above. "They might've dragged him up top. Team perks."

We moved together, slowly. I could feel the tension buzzing in my chest like a held breath—not just because we were somewhere we absolutely shouldn't be, but because *he* was here. Somewhere in this haze and noise. Laughing. Alive.

I hadn't seen him in person since that brief, heart-stopping moment on Baldur Street. Now he was close enough to touch.

We turned a corner, pushing past a pair of drunken teammates arm-wrestling over a table made of projected crystal. I reached out instinctively to steady myself—and grazed against Nodin's arm.

His posture stiffened for a half second. Then—

"Elli," he said suddenly, voice low.

I turned toward him.

His eyes weren't on me.

Across the crowd, something—or someone—had caught his attention. The grin he'd been wearing since we left the tunnels vanished, replaced by a look I couldn't read.

He leaned in close, close enough that his breath brushed the edge of my hood. "Stay here," he said. "By the wall. I'll be right back."

"What?" I blinked. "You're *leaving* me here?"

But he was already gone—disappearing into the crowd like smoke through mesh. I started to follow, but something in his voice stopped me.

I stood frozen for a moment, the crowd surging in front of me. The edge of the room pulsed with light, and the rune-carved columns near the rear twinkled in waves. I tried to spot Nodin again but saw only the blur of cloaks and shifting faces.

That's when I saw him.

Aedan.

He was at the far edge of the main floor, talking to Einar and Fenja, a drink in hand, his dark hair pushed back, the cut of his smile so familiar it made my stomach twist.

I didn't think.

I pulled up the hood of my cloak—black, nondescript, a shadow among shadows—and stepped forward, moving quickly through the crowd, slipping between clusters of *Stór-menni* like a ghost.

As I passed him, I turned just enough.

Just enough to let him see the curve of my jaw. The glint of my eyes beneath the hood. Nothing more.

I didn't stop. Just walked past, heart pounding, toward a dark alcove along the back wall—a quiet nook tucked behind one of the curved support columns.

And then I waited.

Hoping he'd follow.

Hoping he'd *seen* me.

Hoping this wasn't a mistake.

The music still pulsed through the floor, rattling up through my boots. The crowd blurred into motion, color, and static. I kept fidgeting—glancing back toward the mezzanine.

My heart had been racing since I passed him, hoping—praying—he'd seen me. But now that I was here, tucked into this shadowy corner, the doubts began to claw their way in.

What if he didn't see me? What if I moved too fast? What if he thinks it was nothing?

Or worse, what if he saw and couldn't come?

I shifted my weight from one foot to the other, peeking out from beneath my hood every few seconds, scanning the crowd for familiar shoulders or dark curls or anything that looked like him. And there was still no sign of Nodin either. He'd vanished like a puff of smoke, and with every passing minute, that ache of uncertainty in my chest doubled.

Where are you? Either of you.

Then—

"Aedan," I breathed.

He was moving fast, slipping past the edge of the crowd with that same quiet control I'd seen in the arena—shoulders tense, eyes sharp, every step precise. And when he saw me in the alcove, really saw me, he froze.

"Elin?" His voice was low, almost hoarse, like he didn't quite believe I was real.

I stepped forward. "You saw me."

He grabbed my wrist—not rough, but urgently—and pulled me deeper into the shadows.

"You shouldn't be here," he whispered fiercely. "Elin, you don't understand. The Chairman could show up any minute. If he sees you—"

"I had to come," I said, my voice breaking despite everything I'd told myself. "I've been going out of my mind. Watching you on those screens. Seeing you fall in the semifinals. Aedan, I thought—" I stopped. Swallowed. "I had to know you were okay."

His face softened, just for a second. But he didn't let go of my wrist. "Elin... you have no idea how much I've wanted to see you. I just—" He glanced back toward the crowd, then lowered his voice further. "I'm not supposed to know anyone in Falinvik. If someone sees us... if they report this... They'll know you're here."

"I can take care of myself," I said, maybe a little too fast.

His eyes met mine. "That's not the point. I can't risk you."

I felt the tension between us, thin and electric—like the world had gone quiet around our small sliver of space. He looked like he wanted to reach for me. But he didn't dare.

And it broke my heart a little.

I wasn't sure how long we stood in that pocket of shadow, just the two of us pressed into the quiet between heartbeats and danger. Aedan's hand still hovered at my wrist—barely touching me now, but he hadn't let it fall away either.

His eyes searched mine like he was trying to memorize every part of my face.

I took a breath, grounding myself. "Listen. We're planning something. The Resistance. We're going to get you out during the finals."

His eyes widened. "What?"

I nodded. "We can't remove the *Hepta Baugr*, not with the grid active. But during the final trial, they remove it, right? Just like they did for the other rounds."

He glanced down instinctively at his wrist. The *Hepta Baugr* was there, silver and seamless, wrapped around his skin like a shackle masquerading as jewelry. He covered it quickly with his sleeve.

"Yeah," he said, voice low. "They'll take it off before the final starts. That's the only window."

"Exactly. That's when we'll strike."

He ran a hand through his hair, visibly rattled. "It's a good plan. It is. But the finals are tomorrow, Elin. That doesn't give you much time."

I met his gaze and held it. "We've been planning. We'll be ready. Just... keep surviving, okay? Be ready."

His expression cracked, just slightly, and he stepped half a pace closer.

The space between us dissolved.

We weren't touching, not quite. But I could feel the heat of him—his presence like static, like a storm trying to hold still. His eyes dropped to my mouth for the briefest second before flicking away again, like he was punishing himself for the thought.

"I wanted to believe you were okay," he murmured. "But part of me didn't let me. After Ginnungagap... and my family."

I reached up—slowly, hesitantly—and touched his sleeve. "Aedan... they made it out."

He blinked.

"Your family. Claire, Edvin, your parents—they made it out. They're safe. They're with us. With me. At the Resistance base. They've been helping us plan your rescue."

A beat of silence.

Then Aedan staggered back a step like the words had physically hit him. His voice cracked. Just two words, but they nearly undid me.

"They're... alive?"

I nodded, my throat suddenly thick.

His hands pressed to his mouth for a second, as if holding something in, and when he dropped them, his whole face had changed. The lines of tension were still there—but something else had broken through.

Relief.

Real, shaking relief.

He stepped back toward me, almost reaching for me again, but caught himself. "Thank you," he whispered, eyes locked on mine. "You have no idea what that means. I've been trying not to let myself hope."

"I know."

We were close again—closer than before. I didn't move. Neither did he. And it felt like we were standing on the edge of something, balanced between everything unsaid and everything we didn't dare do. My heart beat hard enough to shake my ribs.

His hand lifted, brushing a stray curl that had fallen from my hood.

He didn't touch me. But he didn't seem ready to let go of the moment, either.

"I want to—" he started, voice low, "but I can't. Not here. If anyone sees us—if they report it—I don't know what the Chairman would do to you."

"I don't care."

"I do," he said, firm but quiet. "Too much."

The ache between us was almost unbearable. For a second, neither of us spoke. The silence settled like a breath between glass.

He hesitated, then spoke more quietly, like he needed me to hear it—really hear it.

"Elin... there's something I need to tell you. But first, I need you to know—I'm okay. Or at least, I think I am." His voice dropped even lower. "The Chairman gave me an injection... whatever it was, it's been stabilizing my *megin*. Amplifying it, maybe. I don't know. It's not natural, but it's kept me on my feet in the *Leikr*."

I blinked. "Injection?"

Aedan tensed. His gaze flicked toward the shadows, jaw tightening. "Later," he muttered, eyes narrowing like he'd just sensed something.

But it was already too late.

A voice came from the shadows.

"Injection?"

The voice was sharp. Precise. And unmistakable.

Aedan turned toward the sound, already bristling. "What's *he* doing here?"

I spun around to find Nodin stepping from the dark like a spectral image. His braid was half-loosened, his expression unreadable—but his eyes, when they locked on Aedan, burned with something deeper than curiosity.

"He came with me," I said, my voice quieter now. "He's the reason I got in at all."

Aedan's jaw tensed. He gave a small, almost imperceptible shake of his head—but he wasn't looking at me. He was still staring at Nodin.

"Figures," he muttered.

The word landed harder than it should have. My chest tightened, confusion flickering beneath the sting. *Was that resentment? Jealousy? Distrust?*

"You know," I said cautiously, trying to keep my voice steady, "he's been risking just as much as the rest of us."

That made Aedan finally look at me. But there was no warmth in his expression.

"Of course he has," he said—sarcastic now, low and bitter. "He's always with you, isn't he?"

I froze. The words hit deeper than I expected. It wasn't just suspicion. It was hurt.

My breath caught, and before I could stop myself, the words slipped out—soft but sharp. "Oh. And Thyra? She's just part of the team?"

His jaw clenched. "That's not—"

"*What* injection?" Nodin cut in, eyes never leaving Aedan. "You said the Chairman gave you something."

Aedan's jaw set. "It's nothing. Doesn't matter."

Nodin didn't move. "If the Chairman injected you with something that altered your *megin*, it matters."

"You sound *very* interested," Aedan said, his voice going colder. "Why?"

Nodin stepped forward, his gaze unreadable. "Because I've seen what he's capable of. And because I don't think you understand what's been done to you."

"Oh, trust me...I understand enough," Aedan bit back.

"Do you?" Nodin asked, voice deceptively quiet.

"Since when are you a part of this, anyway?" Aedan echoed, voice low, eyes narrowing.

I touched Aedan's sleeve, trying to calm the storm rising between them. "He's helping us, Aedan. He's been—"

But Aedan pulled his arm away, gaze still locked on Nodin. "Right. Of course, he is. Just happened to be around to escort you into the lion's den?"

Nodin didn't flinch. "Someone had to."

"Funny," Aedan said tightly. "Didn't realize the Resistance handed out personal bodyguards now."

Nodin's voice stayed cool. "You might've needed one—especially if you're letting the Chairman inject you with whatever he's cooking up in those labs."

Aedan bristled. "Letting him—"

"Can we not do this right now?" I cut in, the words sharper than I intended. My pulse thudded in my ears as I looked between them. "Nodin, what are you talking about? How do you even know anything about that?"

His eyes flicked to me, just for a second—something cracked open there, like he was on the verge of saying more.

But then—

The music shifted. The air thickened. Conversation dipped. Every head on the upper level turned toward the stairs as a new figure descended.

The Chairman.

His cloak trailed behind him like falling ink, his steps measured and quiet. But even from across the room, I could feel the silence he commanded. His eyes scanned the crowd.

"Go," Aedan hissed. "Now. Both of you."

I hesitated—just for a second. "Don't forget, Aedan. Be ready tomorrow."

Aedan gave a brief nod. Then Nodin's hand found my elbow, steady and firm.

"This way."

As we slipped back toward the rear corridor, I risked one last glance over my shoulder.

Aedan was already gone.

Or maybe he'd just turned away before I did.

The moment hung there, suspended and silent. Then it vanished like dew at dawn.

Nodin tugged me along the corridor behind the club's back wall, his grip firm but not rough, threading us through the throb of music and murmurs of the crowd. The emergency exit glowed ahead—just a door away.

Then the world spun.

A sudden chill pressed against my skull, cold and coiling like fingers dipped in frost slithering across the edges of my mind. This wasn't a vision.

I stumbled.

"Elli?" Nodin glanced back.

But I wasn't really hearing him anymore.

Something—*someone*—was inside.

A voice without sound. A presence, slick and calculated. It slithered between thoughts like oil. Cold gray eyes flickering behind my eyelids.

Leaving so soon?

My heart pounded. No. No, no, no—this wasn't happening.

I dug in my heels, my hand shooting to press against my eyes.

The Chairman.

Of course, he would've noticed. His mind had brushed mine

before, at a distance. But this was different. Focused. Intent. He wasn't trying to glean information—he was *pushing*. Invasive. Rooting around like he already owned the space.

"Elli?" Nodin said again, louder now. His voice sounded like it was underwater.

You hide well, the voice said, calm and chilling. *But not well enough.*

I tried to pull back, to shut him out.

Mr. Grady's recent lesson flashed through my mind. *When you feel someone pushing in, find a thread—something that grounds you. Poetry. Music. A story. A memory.* Distraction was resistance.

I gasped in a breath and forced myself to speak. Not aloud—just in thought.

"*Not all those who wander are lost...*" I whispered, clinging to the words like a lifeline.

The pressure hesitated.

It was a poem from Ander's favorite book—*The Fellowship of the Ring*—something he used to recite when I felt adrift. I didn't know why it surfaced now, only that it did. So I kept going.

"The old that is strong does not wither..."

The Chairman pressed harder, like ice seeping into cracks.

"Deep roots are not reached by the frost."

Still there. Still pushing. My vision was tunneling.

He's stronger than before.

He knows I'm here.

My knees buckled. Nodin caught me just before I collapsed, one arm wrapping around my waist.

"Elin—what's happening?"

"I—I think he's inside my head," I whispered, the words barely making it past my lips.

Nodin's face paled.

I gritted my teeth and reached for my medallion. My *megin* wasn't enough. I was going to lose this fight. The Chairman's full focus was on me.

And he was powerful, too powerful.

My fingers closed around the cool metal. I needed more. *Come on. Come on, please.*

I summoned my *Ljós*.

It flared to life beneath my skin, a low, humming thrum like a deep note held in a vast hall. It rushed up my chest, into my throat, behind my eyes. I felt it rise—a bright, blinding light pushing outward.

GET OUT! I screamed in my mind, unleashing it in a burst of internal radiance.

The presence recoiled.

The pressure snapped back so violently that I nearly screamed.

He was gone.

But so was my strength.

The air around me felt scorched and cold at the same time—like the world didn't know what season it was anymore. Everything went gray at the edges.

My legs gave way, and I slumped into Nodin.

"I got you," he said, one arm tightening beneath my knees, the other behind my shoulders. He lifted me effortlessly.

I tried to protest, but my body wouldn't cooperate.

His voice was tense now—quiet but raw. "You used *Ljós* to force him out, didn't you?"

I nodded weakly, my breath shallow. "I had to."

"Idiot," he muttered, but it didn't sound angry. Just terrified.

He shifted me closer to his chest, his jaw clenched tight, and bolted through the exit door. The cold night air slapped my skin like a second shock. Down the alley. Toward the tunnel entrance.

Every step was a blur. The lights overhead warped and bent, my head dropped against his chest. But I was still aware of him—of the thundering of his heart, of the way he cradled my body like I might slip through his arms if he didn't hold on tight enough.

I wanted to speak. To tell him I was okay. To ask what he'd seen inside *SigrHall.* What he knew about Aedan's injection. But no words would come.

As he kicked open the old gate to the metro stairwell and hurried down the steps two at a time, I saw his face under the emergency light—drawn, pale, haunted.

Not just because I was in danger.

There was something else in his eyes—recognition, maybe. Regret. Or something that looked like guilt sharpened into something else I couldn't name.

And I was too weak to ask what it meant. My eyes closed, but the feeling in his eyes followed me into the dark.

TWENTY-THREE

The Confirmation

TRISTAN

The corridors outside IA's high-security cells were always cold—but today, it felt like the walls themselves had turned against me. Too still. Too quiet. As if they could sense that I didn't belong here anymore. That something had shifted inside me.

The vibration of the overhead lights was steady, the dull drone of the ventilation system unchanged, but every sound scraped at my nerves. The click of my boots. The whir of climate control. The ghost of my own heartbeat drumming against my ribs.

I shouldn't be here. Not after what I'd seen.

But I couldn't stay away.

Not with the memory still burning in my head—those words, pulsing red at the bottom of a forgotten border report: Identified Affiliation: Sudri Clan.

The Sudri were gone. That's what they told us. That's what we all believed. That was *history*.

But the file was no trick. It was real.

And now I couldn't look at the world the same way.

I had tried to forget it. Had tried to tell myself it was a clerical error, a technical flaw. But I couldn't unsee the redacted tags. The deliberate suppression. Someone had buried that truth deep.

Just like someone had erased Liam Jarnulf from the records—and from the Chairman's own past. And I had stumbled right into the rot at the center of both lies.

Now, I needed something more than pixels on a holo-screen. I needed *confirmation.*

I had waited until the IA command center's attention shifted to another *Leikr* round broadcast before I slipped away. No one questioned my absence. And that was just how I liked it.

As I stepped through the final checkpoint, the security camera blinked rapidly red three times. A perfectly timed glitch, momentarily scrambling the camera's feed, courtesy of the same little code slip I'd lifted from Kolve's console earlier. I'd planned it that way. No one could know I was here. Too many questions would follow—ones I wasn't ready to answer.

I activated the mirror clone on my communicator again, using Kolve's code. To anyone watching, it would look like *he* had come for another visit.

A soft green blink. Entry granted. I stepped through.

The cold hit like a slap—sharp, surgical. The air smelled faintly of metal and disinfectant, clean in a way that felt unnatural. *Megin-*dampeners buzzed against my skin, not just curling under it, but burrowing, like a low-grade current worming through my nerves. Every breath stung.

Gabriel's cell came into view.

Like the others, it was more sterile than cruel—an efficient cube of clean lines and quiet containment. Every surface gleamed in soft, matte-gray alloy, seamless and precision-crafted. A recessed bed jutted from one wall, its surface contour-shifting slightly to match the occupant's posture, powered by adaptive pressure tech. A transparent toilet unit was folded flush into the opposite wall—sleek, sensor-activated. The only sink was a thin silver slit in the corner that projected a stream of purified water when cued by a flick of the wrist. Above it all, the ceiling pulsed with a steady ambient light calibrated to the occupant's circadian rhythm, unchanging unless commanded otherwise.

To most people, the cell would've looked like a clinical marvel—a symphony of *Stór-menni* technology meant to contain without comfort. To me, it was just another IA standard-issue box. Built to minimize resistance. Designed to erase individuality.

Gabriel sat in the far corner, as always. Perfect posture. Uncuffed. He didn't need restraints in the cell. And that quiet calm of his was more dangerous than most people's rage.

His face was still. Eyes lowered. A man carved out of silence.

But I knew better now.

Gabriel wasn't just a silent prisoner. He was Resistance. And, judging by his features—his bloodline—he was *not* Nordri.

And maybe that was why I'd come. Because he might be the only person I had access to who knew whether the Sudri still lived.

I paused just outside the energy barrier, locking him into the cell. My breath ghosted faintly in the cold air.

He didn't look at me. Didn't blink. Didn't move.

"Gabriel," I said quietly.

No response.

"You've been here for days. Not a word. Not to anyone."

He stayed perfectly still. Staring at the floor like the concrete had secrets worth more than anything I could say.

"Either you're the most disciplined operative I've ever met," I murmured, "or you know we won't break you."

I hesitated, then added—"But you are underestimating the interrogators at Skjoldur. And that's where you're headed next."

That landed.

A flicker—barely noticeable. His eyes shifted. Just a glance. Toward me. Then back to the floor.

I hated how much that tiny movement felt like a victory.

He didn't need to speak. He knew I'd come with something to say. I was the one who needed to crack first.

I stepped closer, suppressing the edge of my own nerves.

"I'm not here to threaten you," I said. "And I'm not here to make a deal."

No response.

"I just need to know if what I saw... was real."

My chest tightened, words tangling on my tongue.

I shouldn't be doing this. I hadn't told anyone what I'd found—hadn't dared to copy it. The only evidence of what I'd seen was in my memory. A flickering hologram in a sealed archive, my presence already purged from the access logs.

And now I was here, confessing it to the one man whose silence terrified the entire command chain.

"I found something," I said.

He didn't lift his head, didn't breathe differently—but I could feel the attention shift. Subtle. Focused.

"I wasn't looking for it," I continued. "Just chasing inconsistencies in a few old tags. Loose ends. I should've let them go."

Still nothing. Not even the twitch of a brow.

The suppression panels hummed with low-grade static like they were siphoning clarity straight out of the air.

"I found a report," I said. "From three years ago. A group approached the shield wall. Unregistered. Adults, children. They asked for safe passage."

My pulse was too loud in my ears. This was the line. I was either about to make a connection... or make a mistake.

"They were turned away," I said softly.

I hesitated. Then dropped the crucial piece: "The report marked them... as Sudri."

No change in expression. Nothing.

Just that low, constant hum.

But I was watching now. And I saw it—that fractional pause in his breathing. A stillness within the stillness. I pushed on. Carefully.

"That name shouldn't be in an IA report. Not unless someone

made a mistake. Or didn't know what they were looking at. It was buried under expired arrest logs. Hidden on purpose."

He still didn't look at me. But I saw the faintest tension along his jaw.

"And I think you might know why," I said. "Or what it means."

It was like talking into a storm that refused to echo back. No resistance. But no reflection either.

Not getting answers was eating away at me. I wanted something. Anything. A tiny nod, a smile. Even a lie would've been better than this endless silence.

"I think you know something about it," I pressed, voice tighter now. "Not that group, maybe. But something about the other Clans and whether they are alive."

Still nothing. But the silence wasn't passive anymore. It was deliberate.

And suddenly I wasn't sure who was interrogating who.

I glanced at him—his posture still composed, too calm. And I realized how much of a gamble this was.

Elin's voice came back to me. Her defiance on Auor, still echoing in my skull: *"Your Chairman lied. The other Clans are alive and well."*

I'd dismissed it as Resistance propaganda. But now...

Now I was the one standing on the other side of the energy barrier, holding a secret I couldn't explain. And the man in front of me—silent, impassive—might be the only person I knew who could confirm it.

And yet...

He wouldn't speak.

I stared at him, frustration coiling in my chest like a serpent.

"You're not surprised I found something," I said. "You knew someone would. Eventually."

A beat passed. Then his eyes flicked to mine.

Just once.

And in that split second—quiet, steady, unshaken—I knew.

He didn't have to confirm it.

He already had.

It should have felt like a victory. But it didn't.

Just the weight of a truth I could neither share nor prove—pressing heavier. My pulse thudded in my throat. I took a slow step back, trying to quiet the noise rising inside me.

"This is bigger than all of us. Bigger than the Resistance," I murmured. "If the Sudri still live..."

My voice trailed off. Even here, even now, the words felt too dangerous to finish.

Gabriel blinked, just once. Then looked away.

Dismissal? Resignation? Or something else? I didn't know.

And that—more than anything—infuriated me. The stillness. The restraint. The refusal to even flinch.

I leaned in slightly. My voice was low. Measured.

"Tomorrow, you'll be at Skjoldur."

No response.

"I'm sure you've heard what that place is. What they do. No one walks in and walks out the same."

Still nothing. Just the same maddening composure.

I let the quiet stretch, pressing against the weight in my chest.

A glance wasn't enough of a confirmation.

Not for a secret that could tear the Chairman's version of history apart. Not for a truth that might implicate me in something I wasn't ready to understand.

Gabriel didn't speak. He didn't confirm. But as I turned to leave, I felt his gaze follow me. Heavy. Intent. Like a whisper I couldn't shake. And somehow, that was louder than words.

I moved down the corridor with steady steps, but inside, everything was unraveling.

The report was real. The Sudri existed. The Chairman had lied. And now I was the only one—at least the only one I knew of—who'd seen it.

Gabriel hadn't given me anything I could name—except for that one brief glance. But I needed more than that. I needed *actual* proof.

Proof that wouldn't vanish with a power surge or a convenient purge command. Proof that couldn't be dismissed as a hallucination in a restricted terminal.

Someone must have lived through it. Someone who wasn't hiding in a cell. Someone still walking in the daylight. Still playing the game.

And that's when the name surfaced—slow, unwelcome.

Thorne.

The thought caught like grit behind my teeth.

He wasn't Resistance. But he'd survived things that should've ended him. Kept his rank, his house, his name. And he'd known the Gradys—intimately enough to have helped them. Maybe.

I'd never proved it.

But if anyone had seen the edges of the truth—and managed to stay above water—it was him.

The problem was... I didn't know which side of the line he stood on.

And once I opened my mouth, there'd be no way to take it back.

The sky over Falinvik was dark slate and glowing faintly at the edges as the AHV dipped lower, gliding over snow-dusted rooftops and manicured courtyards. It was just past dawn—early morning on the day of the *Leikr* finals—and the northern estate district was quiet, its silence edged with power. Here, no patrols swept the streets. No loudspeakers. Just soft whirs of automated gates and the subtle pulse of shielded defenses that shimmered faintly in the air like static.

I kept my eyes on the destination ahead: a massive home perched at the end of a perfectly cleared street. Its high-tech security shone pale blue against the snow. Metal shutters sealed the upper windows. A Valkyrie statue stood in the garden like a sentinel.

Commander Jorik Thorne's residence.

I stepped out of the vehicle, boots crunching softly against the heated walkway. The house loomed above me—clean lines, old wood, brutal elegance. The home of a man who still remembered the old Clans... and knew how to survive the new one.

This was a bad idea. But I was out of options.

I rang the signal plate.

It took nearly a minute before the door opened. Thorne stood just inside, already dressed in a black tunic cut in the sleek, angular style favored by high-ranking Clan members—futuristic in its tailoring, but unmistakably Nordic in its roots. The fabric caught the light like polished armor, subtle but imposing. A Clan Hunter medallion rested squarely against his chest, its etched sigils gleaming silver.

The sight of it landed like a punch. I used to wear one like it.

His pale blue eyes swept over me, cold and calculating as ever, already dissecting my purpose. He didn't look surprised—only mildly inconvenienced.

"Tristan," he said coldly. "You have some nerve."

"I need five minutes."

He held my gaze for a long, evaluating moment. Then stepped aside.

I entered.

Inside, the scent of oiled wood and hearth smoke wrapped around me—old comfort sharpened by danger. The fire crackled low, casting shadows across the carved runes like they were alive, writhing in slow motion against the stone. Vaulted ceilings soared above us, supported by beams engraved with mythological scenes—giants, wolves, gods. The walls were lined with old banners, seaxes, and polished metal—a Clan Hunter's heritage on full display.

I remembered this room. I'd stood here about a week ago, flanked by troopers, accusing him of aiding fugitives.

And I'd been wrong. Or at least, I hadn't been able to prove I was right.

Now, we were both a little wiser. Wearier. And something unspoken hung between us like frost.

Thorne stood near the hearth, one hand resting on the edge of the mantel, the other folded loosely behind his back, every inch the commander the Chairman had so publicly reinstated.

I hadn't been invited to sit.

Thorne gave me a dry once-over. "Well, I can't decide if this is bravery or stupidity."

"I'm not here on IA business," I said.

Thorne chuckled. "That's the second time you've walked into my home claiming you're not a threat."

"I'm not here to threaten you. And back then, I was just doing my job."

"And now you're not?"

I didn't answer. Not directly.

I walked slowly to the center of the room, studying the massive wall map that loomed behind him. I remembered it from my first visit —four Clan capitals, carved into the wood grain. No names. Just positions. The kind of thing only someone with ancestral memory could decode.

Nordri. Vestri. Austri. Sudri.

My gaze lingered too long on the last one.

Thorne followed it.

"You're not here to talk about the Gradys," he said.

"No."

"And you're not here to apologize."

"No."

He folded his arms, eyes narrowing.

"So what is this, Tristan? A last-ditch play? Trying to crawl your way back up IA's ladder with some scandal no one wants touched?"

I didn't respond right away.

Because this was the edge—the point where revealing too much could get me labeled a threat. Or worse, a traitor.

Does he still serve the Chairman? Or did he ever?

I shifted my stance. Kept my tone casual. "I was in the archives."

Thorne didn't blink.

"Not the surface-level stuff," I continued. "The buried material. Files scrubbed from active logs. Tagged under expired warrants."

He said nothing. But I caught the tension in his jaw.

He knows. Or at least, he suspects where this is going.

I kept going—slow, deliberate.

"I wasn't looking for anything in particular. Just... patterns. Old arrest reports. Site activity. Routine audit, on the surface."

Still silence.

"But I found a flag. A misfiled entry. Shouldn't have been there."

I watched him.

"You know the kind I mean, Commander. The sort that gets forgotten—because someone wanted it that way."

He finally looked at me. Direct. Hard.

"What did you find?"

There. That flicker. He cares.

I took a breath.

"Three years ago. A shield wall incident. Unregistered adults and children approached Falinvik's border asking for passage."

A pause.

"They were turned away."

I studied his face. He didn't flinch.

Didn't deny. Just waited.

One more step. Do it carefully.

I let the next words come slowly. "The file... labeled them as Sudri."

There it was again. A shift behind his eyes. Fast. Controlled. But I saw it.

He recovered instantly. But still didn't speak.

"I didn't copy the file," I added quietly. "Didn't even try. Too risky. Too traceable."

The fire cracked once behind him, loud in the stillness.

"I don't need you to confirm it," I said at last. "I just need to understand what I saw."

He turned then, walking slowly to the map on the wall. His fingers brushed over the carved outline of the southern territory.

Sudri.

"When I was younger," he said, voice low, "this part of the map was a name we knew."

"I was taught it was nothing," I replied.

He gave a dry, humorless laugh.

"Better to call it nothing than admit what was buried."

He faced me again.

"You know what happens to people who talk about the Sudri or the other Clans."

"Yes."

"And you came anyway."

"I had to."

He studied me. Hard.

"Why?" he asked. "So you could be the one to expose it? IA's fallen prodigy clawing his way back into relevance by unearthing the buried Clans?"

"No," I said. "Because if it's true... then the Chairman's version of history is a lie. And maybe the whole world I was trained to protect was built on one."

He was quiet for a long time.

Then—softly—"You said once your father was Sudri."

I nodded. "He never spoke of it after the Chairman came into power."

"He wouldn't have," Thorne said. "We were told to erase that part of ourselves. For survival."

He stepped closer, the firelight catching on the edge of his expression. Not warmth. Not threat. Warning.

"If you want answers," he said, "don't look to me. Don't look to the archives. Look to your father's line. The ones who vanished when the Chairman rose."

He hesitated."There's a trail, if you know how to follow it. But you won't come back untouched."

I nodded, the weight of it already settling in my chest.

He leaned in slightly.

"Blood remembers, Tristan. Whether you want it to or not."

We stood there—neither allies nor enemies. Just two men caught in the slow burn of the same buried truth.

He finally gave a clipped nod. "That's all I can say."

"I understand."

His smile was tight, bitter. "No. You don't."

But he let me leave.

THE SUN HAD JUST CRESTED THE EASTERN RIDGE WHEN I returned to the AHV and slid into the back seat. The light stung my eyes. Too bright after the firelight. Too honest. The AHV's seat was cold against my back, the only warmth coming from the chaos churning inside me.

I used to measure success by promotions and medals. Now, I measured it by how many lies I could survive. And lately, they were piling up faster than I could outrun them.

I leaned back, the first real breath of the day hitting cold in my lungs.

Blood remembers.

His words echoed in my skull. I didn't even know where to begin.

My father's family. Forgotten names. Disconnected lines.

But I'd find them. I had to.

My communicator vibrated.

I checked the name and groaned. *Kolve.* I tapped to answer, forcing my voice to be level. "Tristan."

His tone came through taut and all business. "You're not at HQ."

"I wasn't scheduled for finals duty," I said, careful not to add *because you left me off the roster.*

"You weren't," Kolve confirmed flatly. "Nonetheless, you're needed."

I waited. He didn't elaborate.

A flicker of unease crawled up my spine.

"Needed where?" I asked.

"Chairman's Tower," he said. "Effective immediately. Priority call."

My fingers curled slightly around the communicator. "What kind of call?"

There was a pause. Subtle, but deliberate.

"Classified until arrival."

Of course, it was.

"But I was supposed to escort the Resistance member to Skjoldur today."

"Well, that can't be helped. The tactical team can handle it. I need you on this." He continued, tone even. "All other lead investigators are assigned to *Leikr* operations. You're the only available field investigator with the necessary clearance."

So I wasn't good enough for the games—but I'm good enough for this?

I kept the thought to myself. "Understood."

Kolve's voice shifted just slightly—cool professionalism giving way to something more pointed.

"This comes directly from the Chairman's office. I expect you'll represent IA appropriately."

"I always do."

A dry pause. "I'd prefer not to receive a correction on that tomorrow."

Then the line cut out. No farewell.

The inside of the vehicle was silent except for the whisper of wind through bare branches outside and snow blowing like ash against the windows. I sat in stunned silence for a beat. Then gave the AHV its new destination.

Chairman's Tower. Immediate priority.

The skies were pale gold as we lifted off. The day of the finals had begun.

TWENTY-FOUR

The Risk

AEDAN

The lights of the club had grown too bright—sharp beams slicing through the dark like knives, flashing across sweat-slicked faces and smoke. Bass thudded in my ribs, too close, too loud, every sound turned up to unbearable. The air reeked of an unpleasant mix of mead, bodies, and heat.

Or maybe I was still reeling from the conversation I hadn't meant to have. Elin's voice echoed in my head—soft, urgent, unraveling me with every word. She'd been here. She shouldn't have been, but she had. And now she was gone again, swallowed by the crowd and shadows like some half-remembered dream.

I pushed through the pulsing throng of dancers, weaving back toward the booth where my teammates were gathered, their dark uniforms and sharper edges making them easy to spot. I needed to pull myself together before someone noticed.

Too late.

A wall of gray stepped into my path.

Not a wall—him.

Chairman Arild.

He was taller than I remembered, though I wasn't sure if that was because I was standing closer than I'd ever dared. His silver hair was slicked back with clinical precision, not a strand out of place. The lines on his face were cut deep, but there was no softness in them. Only control—of his body, his voice, the people around him.

Of me.

"Aedan," he said smoothly, as if we were old friends passing in the street. His eyes scanned my face with clinical precision. "You look... flustered."

My body locked into place. Not because he'd spoken, but because of the way he was looking at me—like I was a puzzle he'd already solved.

"I'm fine," I said quickly, too quickly. I forced my expression into something neutral.

"I hope no one's upset you." He tilted his head slightly, a subtle smile tugging at the corner of his mouth. "This is meant to be a celebration. A show of unity. I'd hate for *someone* to... disturb that."

I said nothing. My throat had gone dry.

The way he said *someone* made my skin crawl. He knew. Maybe not everything—but enough. I had no idea what game he was playing, but I was suddenly sure I was in the middle of it.

"I'm grateful to be here," I lied, carefully. Measured.

The Chairman's smile thinned. "Good. I'm glad to hear that. You've performed well under pressure, Aedan. Far better than most." His voice dropped slightly. "And it's important that you know—you're protected. I've made sure of it."

I didn't know how to respond to that. My mind immediately went to the injection. To Thyra. To the invisible chains I couldn't quite name but felt wrapped around me all the same.

"Uncle," a voice cut in—smooth, firm, and perfectly timed. Thyra stepped between us with a respectful nod. "Sorry to interrupt. I need to borrow Aedan for a moment—urgent team matter."

Arild raised an eyebrow. "Of course. Always something with these *Leikr* preparations."

He didn't step aside. He studied us for a moment longer, then finally nodded, his expression unreadable.

"Carry on," he said, and disappeared into the crowd like a shadow that had never been there.

Thyra grabbed my arm, steering me toward the far side of the club without waiting for permission. We moved fast, but not too fast —just enough to look like we had somewhere to be, not like we were running from something.

My pulse was still racing from the encounter. Thyra didn't speak until we slipped into one of the club's soundproof side lounges, the thrum of music dulling behind the glass.

She let go of my arm and crossed to the far wall, double-checking the privacy lock.

I stayed near the door. Watching her.

"What was that about?" I asked.

"You tell me," she said coolly, still not looking at me. "You looked like you were about to collapse."

"He ambushed me."

"He was making conversation."

I scoffed in disbelief. "That wasn't conversation."

She turned then, studying me. "Did he say something I should know about?"

"No," I said, a beat too quickly.

Thyra didn't push. Just watched me a moment longer, then sighed. "He's good at that, you know. Making you feel like he knows more than he does. It's a trick."

"Is it?"

She didn't answer.

I crossed my arms, my voice sharper than I meant. "If you dragged me in here to lecture me about posture in front of your uncle, we're done."

Her expression didn't change, but the temperature in the room seemed to shift. She ran a hand over her braid, fingers tightening at the end. A tell. One I'd seen when she was calculating, or bracing herself. But her eyes didn't look cold tonight. They looked tired. Focused. Like she'd already decided the cost—and was about to pay it.

"No," she said. "I dragged you in here because I want to offer you something. A risk."

That threw me. "A risk?"

Thyra took a step closer, voice low and measured. "I've been loyal to the Chairman my entire life, Aedan. But that doesn't mean I'm blind. Things don't add up—not about you, not about your family, and not about the decisions he's making. If I'm going to lead you into the finals, I need to know what we're walking into."

I blinked, caught off guard by the edge of honesty in her tone. She never said more than she had to—but this felt... different.

"You want to help me find answers," I said slowly, wary.

"I want to know what game we're playing before it kills one of us."

Her words were clean, logical. But something behind them didn't add up. People didn't risk everything for strategy alone—not like this. Not against the Chairman.

"You're serious."

Thyra nodded. "He's distracted. He'll be out there for a while—working the room, smiling for the right people. It gives us a window. I have access to his office. Not everything—but enough to get us close."

"You want to break into the Chairman's office."

"I want to see his console," she said. "If there are answers—about why you're in this, why he's protecting you—they'll be there."

"And if we're caught?"

"I'll handle it," she said flatly. "But this only works if you follow orders. No improvising. No sudden heroics."

I studied her carefully. Her face was as unreadable as ever—but something behind her eyes had shifted. Not fear. Not rebellion. Just quiet, controlled resolve.

I crossed my arms. "Why are you really doing this?"

"I told you," she said. "Because I don't like walking into

something blind. And right now, you're the biggest variable in a game I was trained to win."

I didn't move. "You expect me to believe this is about strategy?"

Her jaw flexed, but her voice didn't rise. "Believe whatever you want. But if I was trying to turn you in or sabotage you, you wouldn't be standing here."

She had a point. I hated that she had a point.

And this *was* what I'd been waiting for.

The moment. The opening. The one crack in the fortress where I might actually get answers. *Why my family's DNA was missing? Why our name had been scrubbed from the system? Who we really were?*

I'd almost blown everything trying to sneak into the Chairman's office once before—made it to the outer corridor before getting caught. He didn't punish me outright, just smiled like he'd expected it and then gave me that injection that had amped up my *megin.* I hadn't tried again—not because I didn't want to, but because there hadn't been an opportunity.

And now she was offering it to me. A key to the very door I couldn't stop staring at.

But why? Why now? Why her?

Thyra was the Chairman's niece. His protégé. My handler. She was the leash, the wall, the reminder that I didn't belong here unless someone said I did. And I'd spent weeks trying to decide whether her moments of humanity were real—or just another tactic.

Was this a genuine crack in her armor?

Or a Trojan horse?

She stepped closer. "I have access. I can get us in. But if you're not in, tell me now."

I hesitated, every muscle in my body pulled taut between instinct and desire.

Everything in me screamed *don't trust her*.

But everything I needed to know whispered *this might be your only chance*—especially given what Elin had said about the rescue tomorrow.

I glanced toward the door, toward the pulse of music and people and noise beyond it. Toward safety. Toward ignorance.

Then I looked back at her.

"Fine," I said, slowly. "I'll go."

She nodded once. "Then follow me. And don't speak unless I tell you to."

And just like that, we were moving—together—toward the heart of the thing I couldn't stop thinking about.

I didn't trust her. Not completely. But right now, that wasn't the question.

The question was—what if she was the only way I'd ever find the truth?

Thyra lowered AHV's roof as we came to a stop in mid-air just above the Chairman's private AHV platform. Below, the landing zone gleamed under pale floodlights. Sleek. Empty. Lethal.

"Cameras cover everything but that corner there." Thyra pointed to a sliver of matte-gray steel, shadowed beneath a pillar. "If we land anywhere else, we'll be flagged."

I squinted down. "You want us to *jump*?"

Thyra pulled something small and familiar from her cloak.

The Chairman's medal.

The air caught in my throat. "How—?"

"I borrowed it," she said coolly. "He was distracted. It's his duplicate. He doesn't like to remove the one around his neck."

At the club. Surrounded by people. Surrounded by suspects. Clever.

"You do realize that if we miss that corner—"

"We won't."

"I'll direct the air to slow us," she said. "You steer."

"With my *face*?"

"With your telekinesis."

I stared at her. "You're insane."

"Probably. But do you want in or not?"

She hesitated then—just for a second—and turned to me.

"Hold still."

I blinked. "Why?"

Without answering, she reached over and brushed my tunic's cuff aside. She took out the small device I had seen every day since training began and placed it against the *Hepta Baugr* on my wrist. I felt the cool snap of pressure as the *Hepta Baugr* unlocked—then a whisper of heat as it deactivated. The suppression lifted like a weight.

Megin stirred beneath my skin. Fierce. Familiar.

My breath caught.

"You'll need it," she said quietly.

She stepped onto the seat, wind already curling around her boots, then glanced back at me—a silent question in her eyes.

I drew a breath, tension coiling in my chest, and gave a single nod. I climbed next to her. Thyra pulled a length of matte-black climbing rope from her belt, her fingers moving fast. She didn't speak—just wrapped it twice around my waist, then hers, and secured the carabiner with a sharp metallic click. The sound echoed louder than it should have. A silent tether.

Without a word, we turned to face the darkness below, our movements synced by instinct and urgency—timing our leap to the hovercraft's slow drift over the target.

And then we jumped.

The wind caught us instantly, cold and slicing. Thyra's hands moved with practiced control, shaping air into a force that steadied our descent. I reached out with my *megin*, gripping the edges of the platform telekinetically, yanking us into line as the blind spot rushed up to meet us.

We landed hard—but silently.

No alarms. No cameras.

I exhaled, adrenaline thundering in my ears. As I scrambled to stand, Thyra unclipped us and crossed to the far wall without hesitation, scanning the seamless panels of matte steel. Then, with practiced precision, she knelt near a narrow groove I hadn't even noticed and pressed the Chairman's medal against a specific point—just left of center, where the pillar's base met the floor.

A faint click.

A vertical seam split the wall. A hidden panel slid open with a soft hiss, revealing a polished steel elevator tucked behind the facade.

She didn't pause—just stepped inside like she'd done it a hundred times.

Of course, she knew about a secret, hidden elevator.

Because why wouldn't she?

Apparently, growing up in the Chairman's shadow came with a built-in floor plan.

I followed her in, heart still racing.

No cameras. No guards. Just the soft whir of power as the elevator lifted above the platform and opened behind a seamless section of the Chairman's office wall.

Inside, everything was pristine. Quiet. And private.

The Chairman's office looked like a shrine—glass, steel, and smooth stone, all perfectly arranged. But the feeling of power here wasn't just aesthetic. It was in the air. In the walls.

The office was quiet in a way that felt unnatural.

She didn't speak.

Neither did I.

No footsteps. No hum of surveillance. Just the soft, sterile whisper of filtered air and the weak luminescence of the holo-interface from the center of the desk.

The Chairman's console.

Thyra stepped forward, sliding the duplicate medal into the circular port embedded in the desk's surface. A strand of light pulsed outward. The desk dissolved into layered columns of flickering blue data—floating files, audio snippets, classified dossiers, all spinning in a radial pattern around us. Nothing was restricted.

Thyra didn't touch any of it. She stepped back and gestured to me.

"You first," she said.

I hesitated. It almost felt too easy. After everything—this thing I'd dreamed of forcing open, hacking into, *breaking*, and now it was right in front of me, luminous and waiting.

I raised my hands and moved them slowly through the light.

The files responded instantly, shifting and spiraling around me like constellations. I narrowed the search using instinct more than logic—keywords that had haunted me for months.

Unregistered. DNA variance. Family archive.

The system hesitated—then pulsed with results.

And I saw it. A genetic marker tag—highlighted in red.

Subject: Aedan Grady
Match located: Harald Jarnulf – ID: CLN-7142X

I froze.

A photo flickered open.

The man staring back at me was younger than I expected—broad-shouldered, sharply dressed, with the same sea-blue eyes that haunted my reflection. There was something in the jawline. In the set of the mouth.

Harald Jarnulf. The name was unfamiliar, but the genetic marker was a perfect match. I leaned in, perhaps some obscure relative—maybe a great-grandfather, someone distant.

Still, it didn't make sense. Jarnulf wasn't a name I recognized. And definitely not one I'd ever heard in connection with my family.

It certainly wasn't my father.

But it was close.

A direct ancestor.

I opened the file further, and the details spilled out in bright, blue-lined text:

STATUS: STRATEGIC ADVISOR. STÓR-MENNI CLAN COUNCIL.
BLOODLINE: REGISTERED SON — LIAM JARNULF.
REGISTERED SPOUSE: ELISE SKARN JARNULF.
REGISTERED PARENTS - STEN JARNULF AND ASTRID KALDAL JARNULF.
REGISTERED SIBLINGS - SKARDE AND ARILD JARNULF.

My breath caught.

Registered son.

His name was Liam. And that name I recognized—it had lived in my bones since birth.

My father.

He'd always used Grady as our default surname. But being fugitives, we'd had so many over the years it was hard to keep track. One thing I was sure of was that we'd never used the name Jarnulf.

My throat went dry.

Could it be a coincidence? Another Liam?

I hesitated—then, following the sparse threads in the file, I found an image. I opened it.

A photo materialized. Along with a caption that read: *Liam Jarnulf, Protective Services, Advisor to the Chairman.*

Younger. Leaner. Hair neatly trimmed, eyes colder than I remembered—but the face was unmistakable.

Liam.

My father.

Liam *Jarnulf.*

My throat closed, and for a moment, I forgot to breathe. *My father—Liam Jarnulf. Not Grady.* Not some invisible fugitive we were pretending to be. This was real. Concrete. Part of something so much bigger—and so much darker—than I'd ever imagined.

I looked again at the name tied to him. Harald Jarnulf. The genetic match. The photo. I didn't recognize the face, not from memory. But there was something familiar in the angles, in the eyes.

And then I remembered the stories.

My parents hadn't talked about him often, but when they did, they called him Harry Grady. My grandfather. A quiet man. Sharp. Watchful. Someone who'd disappeared too early for me to remember.

But now, staring at the file, I saw it clearly. *Harry was Harald. Same man. Different name.*

He was my grandfather.

I stumbled back a step, heart pounding.

My family wasn't just connected to the *Stór-menni*. We were *entrenched* in it. Deep, woven into the roots. My father hadn't simply been running from the regime.

He'd been running from his *birthright*. From the very people now trying to control me.

Beside me, Thyra was staring at the screen too. But it wasn't the same look she usually wore—the cold, unshakable focus of a commander.

She looked... shaken.

Then her gaze flicked to me. "I didn't know," she said, barely above a whisper.

I turned toward her. "Didn't know what?"

She hesitated.

Something in her face shifted. A flicker of hesitation. Fear, maybe.

"I don't often mention it," she said, her voice low but firm. "I go by Thyra Bjorndóttir in Clan society. My mother's maiden name. I didn't always want an obvious link to the Chairman. You know how people can be—"

She paused.

"But my full name is Thyra Bjorndóttir *Jarnulf*."

The world tilted.

I stared at her, not understanding—then understanding too much.

Jarnulf.

My father's surname.

Her *father's* surname.

The same.

"I—" I tried to speak, but my throat closed.

Thyra swallowed hard, pointing at the screen. "My father's name is Skarde Jarnulf. The Chairman's younger brother."

Registered Siblings - Skarde and Arild Jarnulf.

Everything inside me went still.

That meant—

I stumbled a step back, blinking, like I could undo the words.

"That means... if Harald and Skarde are brothers..." My voice cracked, a cold dread coiling through me.

The air left my lungs. "You and I—"

She didn't answer.

She didn't need to.

Cousins.

Or technically...first cousins once removed. Harald was her uncle and my grandfather.

And that meant that the Chairman wasn't just my captor—he was *my* great-uncle.

My heartbeat slowed, then pounded harder. Not fear. Not even betrayal. Just... displacement. Like the ground beneath me had changed shape without warning, and I was still pretending it was solid.

I took a staggering step back, trying to calm my hammering heart, but nothing in the sleek, pristine office felt real anymore. Just smooth stone and steel—and *secrets*. Too many of them.

I turned toward Thyra, expecting her to still be frozen—still reeling like I was.

But she wasn't.

The shock was in her eyes, yes—but she was already moving, pushing past it. The weight of what we'd just learned was real, but so was the danger, and she knew we were on borrowed time.

In the glow of the console, her hands swiped through layers of data—confident, quick, deliberate. Then she pulled a sleek, black wand-like device from her belt, its tip shimmering pale green. She angled it toward a set of files floating just beyond my reach, and a soft pulse of light scanned through them.

I narrowed my eyes. "What are you—?"

She flinched. Just barely. Her face had gone even paler than before. Eyes locked on whatever she was looking at.

I stepped forward.

Something flickered on the screen—just for a second. A list of names, or maybe a map, I couldn't tell. But whatever it was, it hit her like a punch to the chest.

Before I could see anything more, she jerked her hand, closing the file in a fluid motion.

Her hands trembled as she did. Just a flicker. Enough to notice. Enough to know she hadn't expected what she found. And it was something she didn't want me to see.

Whatever she'd seen... it hadn't been about me. Not really. The look on her face—it wasn't shock. It was recognition. Regret, maybe. Or fear for someone else.

"I—almost forgot," she muttered quickly, forcing her voice into something more casual. "There was one more thing I needed to do. Something boring. Just in case anyone checks the logs."

She pulled up a different file. One that looked... odd. I narrowed my eyes as a grainy image flickered to life—an older man with deep-set green eyes and a face like weathered parchment.

SUBJECT: BAHRAM RISAN — AGE: 68 — SUDRI.

The surname stirred something, but not enough to land. The profile looked forgettable. Purposefully so.

"Who's that?" I asked.

"No one important," Thyra replied too quickly, already tucking the file halfway beneath a set of training logs. "Just a trace file. Old archive. Good camouflage."

Maybe it was. Maybe it wasn't. But the way she looked at it—just for a second—tight, unreadable—it didn't feel random. *Whoever Bahram Risan was, he wasn't no one.*

Her gaze didn't meet mine. "Just being careful."

I wanted to press her. Ask what she'd seen and who Bahram was. But then my gaze drifted back to the open file still floating before me.

Liam Jarnulf.

And just like that, I was pulled under again.

The questions—the years of doubt, secrecy, and names that didn't belong to us—came rushing in. The Chairman. My father. The possibility that everything I'd thought about my family had been a lie.

I didn't know what Thyra had just found. But whatever it was, it had shaken her more than the realization that we might be cousins, which said a lot.

But I didn't have the bandwidth to deal with that too. My mind was already too crowded with secrets and revelations.

The room felt too small. Too quiet.

I couldn't stop sneaking glances at Thyra—this person I'd half-resented, half-trusted, never truly known. And now we were standing in the Chairman's inner sanctum, bloodlines crashing like lightning between us.

We might be cousins.

The Chairman might be my family.

A chill shot down my spine. Part of me couldn't let myself believe it—not fully—not until I spoke to my father. *I mean, Jarnulf might be a common name in the Nordri Clan, right? It didn't necessarily mean we were related to the Chairman.*

But the look in Thyra's eyes said she already knew. And the truth was there—in the DNA logs, in the personnel records, in the stolen name I'd carried my whole life. And now I couldn't unsee it.

A low chime pulsed from the holo-console—10 seconds left until automatic system lockout. Somebody must have noticed activity on the Chairman's console feeds.

Thyra's voice came sharp and clear. "Shut that down. We need to get out of here."

I turned back to the screen, hands already working even though my mind was still whirling through all the implications of the revelation.

The Chairman hadn't just been using me.

He was trying to reclaim me. His blood. His legacy. His family.

All his offhand remarks about family snapped into focus—"*after all, family should stick together,*" "*it's in your nature,*" "*curious... how much we inherit.*" I'd thought they were offhand comments at the time. But now it was clear. *He'd been playing the long game. And I'd been walking straight into it.*

The weight of it pressed against my ribs like armor I hadn't chosen. Still buzzing with the aftershock, I turned toward the hidden elevator, needing to move—needing to do something—before the walls closed in.

But Thyra caught my arm. "Not that way."

"What?" I blinked at her. "Why not? That's our exit."

She shook her head. "They already know someone has been here. The security logs will have registered the powering on of the Chairman's console. We can't let them trace how we got in—or it won't take them long to figure out that I had something to do with it."

I frowned. "So how do we—?"

"Help me cover our tracks first," she said, already moving.

From a pouch on her belt, she pulled two small oblong devices with a curved emitter at one end and tossed one to me. "Point it at anything you and I touched. Console, floor, desk, glass. It'll scrub DNA, fingerprints, thermal residue."

I caught it and stared. "You carry around print scrubbers?"

"Do you not?"

I moved quickly, swiping it over the console, the edge of the desk, the chair—everything we might have touched. It hummed softly as it worked, a pale light trailing across every surface I'd laid a hand on.

As I cleaned with the scrubber, the reality of what I'd just seen pressed in—heavy, surreal. My name. My family. Everything I thought I knew unraveling in flickers of blue light.

Jarnulf. The word didn't fit in my mouth yet, didn't belong to me —but it was mine, all the same. My father had lied to protect me. Hidden everything.

And now the Chairman wasn't just a threat—he was blood. Legacy. A claim I hadn't asked for. And as I wiped away traces of our presence, I wasn't sure if I was cleaning up evidence or erasing the last pieces of who I used to be.

Once we were done, Thyra turned toward the massive double doors.

Before I could ask what she was doing, she pulled two thin metallic clamps from her belt—sleek, angular, each no bigger than her palm. She pressed one to the seam between the doors, just above the locking mechanism, and the other near the floor. With a soft hiss and a flash of blue light, they engaged—long filament prongs extending inward like teeth. A red light blinked once, then held steady.

"Electronic sealers," she muttered. "Should buy some time. They'll have to cut through the doors now—or blow them open. Either way, it will look like someone had enough time to steal something once the alarms go off."

I raised an eyebrow. "What alarms?"

Thyra didn't answer as she was already crossing the room to the massive floor-to-ceiling windows that looked out over the city skyline.

She pulled another device from her belt. This one was small and round, about the size of her palm, with four pronged legs and a red-lit center. Without hesitation, she pressed it against the window's center pane.

"What are you—?" I started.

"Take cover," she said. "Now."

I blinked at her. "Take cover?"

"Behind the desk. Move!"

Something in her tone jolted me into action. I ducked behind the Chairman's sleek obsidian desk and dropped into a crouch.

The device on the window began to emit a rhythmic, low-frequency thump.

Then a shriek.

Then—

BOOM.

The window exploded inward in a rain of glass and compressed air.

Alarms screamed to life. Red lights strobed across the room as an automated voice blared something about a breach.

Thyra was already moving. She jumped over the desk, grabbed my arm, and yanked me toward the gaping hole in the window. Shards of glass still glittered in the air like falling stars.

"Go!" she shouted.

I skidded to a stop. "Are you *insane*? We're twenty stories up!"

"There's no time—*jump!*"

"I don't even see a—"

She shoved me.

There was no time to think. No time to react.

Just glass and air—and then *nothing*.

The floor vanished beneath my feet as I was hurled into the open sky, and for a split second, the world held its breath.

Then gravity yanked it loose—taking me with it.

Wind punched into my chest, seizing my breath as I tumbled headfirst into the dark. My stomach lurched—then dropped harder. The skyline whipped past in streaks of gold and dark blue. The shimmering surface of a distant glass building flashed like a blade before it spun away.

My arms flailed. My *megin* surged on instinct, trying to latch onto *anything*—but there was nothing. No footing. No ledge. Just endless air and the jagged sound of panic screaming in my ears.

She pushed me.

I wasn't even sure if this was part of the plan or the last betrayal. The thought ripped through me even as I fell.

Then—

The wind shifted.

A ripple of pressure curved beneath me. Not enough to stop me—but enough to slow me. The air thickened, folding like an invisible cushion under my boots, wrapping around my limbs with growing force. The free fall became a glide, then a drag, then a decelerated drop. *Thyra.*

And there—cutting through the shadows like a phantom—our AHV. Thyra must've set it to auto-track us from the second we jumped. I latched onto it like a life raft with my telekinesis.

Its roof slid open in perfect sync, the craft hovering just below me in the middle of the empty sky.

And then she was there beside me—falling fast, cloak billowing, arms out. Her hands swept through the air, commanding it like a conductor drawing music from a storm.

Her wind met my telekinesis in the space between us.

And together, we landed.

Hard. Unsteady. But alive.

I crashed into the cushioned interior of the AHV, gasping, hands clutching the seat as the rest of me caught up with what had just happened.

Thyra dropped beside me with surgical grace, one knee hitting the floor. Her braid was loose, eyes sharp as she reached up and hit the panel to seal the roof above us.

The wind vanished.

Silence slammed down like a lid.

The alarms were now far-off echoes behind glass and distance—but I could still hear my heartbeat thundering in my ears.

I rolled to my side, half-sitting, half-sprawled across the floor of the AHV. Every limb buzzed with leftover terror.

I stared at her.

"What in *Helheim* was that?"

Thyra didn't even look over. She was already in the driver's seat, calmly engaging the controls like this was just another drill.

"An exit," she said.

Like that explained everything.

But it didn't feel like we'd escaped anything.

And nothing felt certain anymore.

The AHV peeled away from the tower, vanishing into the quiet folds of the city. The ember lights twinkled around us, quiet and distant. Somewhere beyond the horizon, the sky had begun to soften —black fading toward the indigo edge of dawn.

It was the morning of the *Leikr* finals.

I sank back into the seat, my pulse still hammering in my ears, the burn of wind still in my lungs.

Whatever happened next—at the *Leikr*, with the Chairman, with Thyra—one truth remained: Nothing about who I was—or what I was part of—was what I thought.

And the sun hadn't even risen yet.

TWENTY-FIVE

The Broken Vow

ELIN

Waking up felt like resurfacing from the bottom of the sea—slow, disoriented, and somehow heavier than when I went under.

The ceiling above me was lined with soft lighting panels, the kind used in the Resistance base's medical bay. The air was tinged with antiseptic and metal—sterile but faintly electric, like the room itself was bracing for another emergency. I was clearly in the Resistance medbay.

It was quiet. Too quiet. Until I turned my head and caught the wave of activity pulsing just beyond the glass walls—voices echoing from the corridor, equipment wheeling past, the thrum of boots heading toward the loading platforms.

I blinked through the lingering fog in my head and tried to sit up.

"Elli." Nodin's voice reached me before I saw him. He was sitting beside my hovering medical bed, hands clasped tight in front of him, eyes rimmed with shadows. "You're okay."

That wasn't the whole truth. I could still feel the burn where the Chairman's psychic assault had touched me—like an echo behind my eyes. But I nodded.

The Gradys were gathered nearby—Mr. and Mrs. Grady, Claire, and Edvin, standing with Reo and Sigrid. Commander Yrsa and McHaill hovered by the door, half in, half out of the room as if ready to jump back into motion at any second.

They were all here.

And, by the looks on their faces, they all knew.

I glanced at Nodin. "You told them?"

He gave a grim nod. "They needed to understand what we were dealing with."

Claire crossed her arms. "What you did back there—when the Chairman attacked you—that was *Ljós*, wasn't it?"

I hesitated, but there was no point hiding anymore. "I think so."

Reo's expression didn't shift, but a long breath escaped him—quiet, deliberate. "Then it is as I feared. The Chairman has already seen what you carry."

Sigrid stepped forward, her brow creased. "Elin... what you did may have saved your life. But it was reckless. *Ljós* isn't like *megin*. It's not meant to be unleashed like that—not without control."

I frowned. "I didn't have a choice. He was—he was going to take over my mind."

"You did what you had to," Nodin said gently, his voice tight with something like fear. "But *Ljós* burns hot and fast. You aren't trained to use it like that. If you'd gone even a few seconds longer..."

He didn't finish.

"It could've consumed you," Sigrid said, softer now. "You wouldn't have survived."

My pulse kicked. "But I didn't even know how I was doing it."

"That's exactly the problem," Nodin said. "You need to learn to control it—how to call it, how to stop it. Or next time..." His jaw tightened. "Next time, there might not be one."

The words settled like ice in my chest. I sat there for a beat, the magnitude of it pressing down, sharper than any pain in my body. But underneath the fear was something else.

A quiet, gathering resolve.

I looked at Nodin, my voice steady. "We're still going after Aedan, right?"

Before Nodin could answer, Mrs. Grady stepped forward, her voice steady but strained. "Of course. As soon as Gabriel's team is airborne."

I swung my legs off the hovering bed, ignoring the rush of blood to my head and the pinch of pain that sparked behind my temples. My bare feet hit the cold floor with a soft slap.

"Then I'm coming," I said, lifting my chin.

Nodin stood so fast his chair scraped the floor. "No. You're not."

I blinked, startled by the sharpness in his tone. "What?"

"You need to stay here."

How he said it—quiet but immovable—lit a fire in my chest. I stepped toward him, fists curling at my sides. "No, I don't. This is a team plan. You need me."

His fingers raked through his hair, tousling it into further disarray. He wasn't just stressed—he was unraveling, holding something back with both hands and losing grip by the second.

"You don't understand," he said, not looking at me.

I planted myself in front of him, forcing his eyes to meet mine. "You're right. I don't understand. So what are you not telling me?"

His breath caught, and for a second, he looked like he might turn away again. But he didn't. He stood there—rigid, jaw clenched, shoulders drawn tight like a bow about to snap. His gaze flicked to the others in the room—Mr. and Mrs. Grady, Claire and Edvin, Reo, Sigrid—then back to me.

The air in the room shifted. Everyone felt it.

"I wasn't supposed to tell you any of this," he said at last, voice low, raw. "But you deserve the truth now. You need it—for your safety. For all of ours."

Something in the way he said it made the entire room still. Claire stopped fidgeting with the strap of her utility belt. Edvin's cocky expression faded, arms folding tight across his chest. Reo's posture straightened slightly, brows furrowed in thought. Even Sigrid leaned forward, bracing her hands on her hips, as if preparing for impact.

"My journey to Falinvik wasn't some diplomatic visit or a last-minute strategy meeting with Sigrid. That was just the cover. The real reason I came here was because my clan elders sent me—to find out what the Chairman's doing to Dormants. Something's been escalating. Quietly. And dangerously."

He looked down, flexing his fingers, as if bracing himself.

"The Vestri Clan has more Dormants than any other Clan. It's in our bloodlines—how we've always lived closer to the human world than the others. We've always protected our own. But lately... some of ours have vanished. Taken without warning. Without trace. Including the Clan Chief's own daughter."

A strange tension flickered across Nodin's face—gone in an instant, but I felt it. Not just heard it, felt it—like a ripple in the air, the slightest pull at the edge of my awareness, the way my visions sometimes brushed up against the present before breaking free. He'd spoken the words with gravity, yes—but there was something else buried underneath. Something personal. His voice didn't just carry concern for a mission. It carried loss. Guilt. A name he wasn't saying.

I studied him more closely, but he didn't meet my eyes. His shoulders had stiffened again, like they were holding something too fragile to release.

"I was sent to uncover the truth. But on the way in, the *Stórmenni's* defensive system locked onto my HTV. Shot me out of the sky just outside the Shield Wall. I crash-landed in the woods but didn't have the technical skills to repair the hover vehicle. And the only person I knew who might help—who might still be free—was Sigrid. So I made my way to her. That's how I ended up here. That's how I met all of you."

His eyes found mine for a heartbeat—then dropped, like they couldn't hold the burden of what he'd just said.

"Disappearances without explanation..." Reo said softly, almost to himself. "It is a warning written in silence. And silence, left unchallenged, becomes complicity."

He stepped forward, folding his hands neatly behind his back. There was no accusation in his voice—only gravity.

"Your coming here, Nodin-kun, was not just brave. It was necessary. Too many wait until the pattern is complete before calling it a threat. Your Clan chose to see the first strokes."

Claire's voice followed, quieter now. "The Chief's daughter was really taken?"

"By the Clan Hunters, we suspect. My Clan Chief fears the Chairman is experimenting—using Dormants for something. That's what I've been trying to find out."

"And you did," Sigrid said quietly.

Nodin's voice dropped, the words tight and deliberate. "Last night, when Aedan said the Chairman injected him with something that amplified his *megin*... everything finally clicked."

He took a step back from the group as if needing space from the truth he was about to lay bare.

"My Clan has spent months collecting fragments—rumors, encrypted reports, silenced witnesses. We knew the Chairman was after Dormants, and suspected that he wanted their *Ljós* for something. But it never made sense. *Ljós* can't be stolen. It can only be given—willingly—and only to another Dormant. That's the law of our nature. The boundary no one's ever been able to cross."

He looked up, his eyes catching mine—and then sweeping across the rest of the room.

"But it looks like the Chairman has figured out a way to extract it anyway. Not just extract it—weaponize it. Inject it into others. Infuse it into himself."

A silence fell, heavy and stunned.

"That's how he's grown so powerful these last few years," Nodin said, his voice barely above a whisper now. "He's been feeding on what was never meant to be taken."

"Oh gods," Mrs. Grady whispered.

Nodin looked at each of us. “That’s why he’s hunting them. That’s why he wanted Elin.”

My body stilled. “He’s using Dormants like fuel?”

“I don’t know the full extent of it,” Nodin admitted. “But it’s clear now—this power surge, this control over the Nordri clan members, even his psychic assault—it all traces back to what he’s stealing from Dormants.”

“But why?” Edvin asked. “What’s he trying to do with all that power?”

“That’s what we still don’t know.” Nodin’s voice hardened. “But it’s why I had to tell you. You need to know what we are up against. You need to know what he is.”

For a moment, no one said anything. The weight of it hung in the air like a wet mop.

Reo’s voice cut through the stillness—quiet, but steady. “If what you say is true, then the storm has already begun. We must be ready—not only to weather it but to confront its maker.”

A murmur of assent moved through the room—not loud, but unanimous. Commander Yrsa gave a sharp nod, Sigrid’s jaw tightened with purpose, and even Edvin, uncharacteristically serious, squared his shoulders in silent agreement. Whatever doubts had lingered before, Reo’s words had gathered them into a single current of resolve.

As the moment settled, Claire stepped closer to Nodin, her eyes narrowing with concern. “You’re bleeding,” she said gently.

Nodin instinctively tried to pull his hand back, but she was quicker. Her fingers caught his wrist, turning it palm-up before he could stop her.

A sharp gasp slipped from her lips.

The skin across his palm was mottled and angry—red, blistered, oozing blood, curling at the edges like a burn that didn’t come from heat.

“Nodin...” she breathed, her voice caught between concern and realization.

I took a step forward, heart lurching. "What happened?" I asked, my voice tighter than I meant it to be.

He didn't look at me. His jaw locked, chest rising and falling with short, shallow breaths.

Claire glanced at me, then back at him. Her expression softened with something almost like sympathy."You broke a Solemn Vow, didn't you?"

Nodin hesitated, then gave a small, reluctant nod. "Just now. To my Clan Chief."

My stomach dropped. I closed the distance between us, my voice barely a whisper. "What's a 'Solemn Vow'?"

Claire met my gaze with a grim kind of gentleness. "It's a sacred promise bound with *megin*—one that binds your wellbeing to your word. If you break it, you have only a few days to receive absolution from the person you swore it to. Otherwise..."

I swallowed. "Otherwise, what?"

"It starts with a burn, a rash," Claire said quietly. "Then fever. Then worse."

My eyes flicked to Nodin's hand, to the damage already spreading across his skin. I reached out and touched his wrist, gently, grounding him. "That's why you didn't tell anyone before now."

He finally looked at me, and there was no mask left—just exhaustion, and something raw beneath it.

"I couldn't," he murmured. "But now... I didn't have a choice. I couldn't put you—all of you— in danger not knowing the truth."

Before I could say anything else, McHaill's comm crackled to life.

"Commander," came a voice, clipped and urgent. "Ops needs you in Launch Bay Two. Both missions are finalizing prep now."

McHaill's gaze slid to Sigrid, then back to Nodin. A glint sharpened behind his otherwise unreadable expression.

"Time's up," he said. He turned to the door, then added, almost offhand, "Nodin, you and I will need a longer conversation. Later."

McHaill's words lingered as he left, and for a heartbeat, no one moved. Nodin's gaze remained on the door. I could see the tremor in his jaw, the conflict still clinging to him like mist. I wanted to reach for him again, say something more—but the room stirred into motion.

The Gradys moved first, gathering their gear with quiet efficiency. Reo murmured something to Yrsa before vanishing into the corridor. Claire gave Nodin's hand a quick, silent squeeze before slipping after them. Sigrid paused at the threshold and gave me a look —half warning, half reassurance, and all gravity.

I touched Nodin's arm. "You broke your vow for me...for all of us."

"I'd do it again," he said, without hesitation.

But the way he looked at me—like the cost of that choice hadn't quite been tallied—told me it wasn't over yet.

He started to turn, ready to follow the others—but I caught his wrist, gently but firmly, holding him in place. His skin was too warm. I could feel the strain thrumming beneath it, the burn creeping higher past the band of dried blood. I didn't let go.

Instead, I tugged him gently toward one of the empty medbay benches just behind us. "Sit," I said, quieter this time. "Let me see it."

"Elli—"

"I'm not asking."

He hesitated—just for a second—then sat. Slowly. Warily. I crouched beside him and pulled the medkit from the nearby cart. His injured hand rested in his lap, palm up, the mottled skin blistered and peeling along the edges of the megin-wound. I opened a sterile wipe and began cleaning around it, careful not to touch the worst of the burn.

His breath hitched.

"I know this hurts," I said, not looking up. "You don't have to pretend you're fine. Not with me."

He gave a short, quiet laugh that held no humor. "That's supposed to be my line."

I looked up at him then—and found his gaze already on me. Unshielded. Wounded in ways even *Ljós* couldn't illuminate.

"You don't have to carry it alone," I said softly.

He didn't answer. But he didn't look away, either.

I wrapped the clean bandage carefully around his palm, my fingers brushing his in the process—just barely, but enough to spark something warm beneath the chaos. A moment that didn't belong to the mission or the plan or the danger pressing in from every direction.

Just us. Just this.

When I tied the final knot, I let my hand rest over his—briefly, firmly. A silent promise that didn't need words.

"You're not invincible, Nodin," I said softly, still focused on his hand. "Whatever vow you broke—it won't mean anything if it kills you."

His jaw tightened. "That's not the plan."

I looked up, met his eyes. "No. The plan is getting everyone through this alive."

He paused, glancing down at my hand, then back up at me, weariness tugging at the corners of his expression. "Elli—"

"I'm not staying behind." My voice was steady. I looked past him, toward the corridor where the rest of the team was disappearing down the hall. "We both know this plan hinges on trust and timing. And you don't have either without me."

"You need rest," he said, but there was no real force behind it. "Didn't everything I just told you make that clear? You're in danger. Yesterday, you almost—"

"Died?" I cut in. "Maybe. But I didn't. I pushed him out. I held him off. And if you think I can't do it again to protect everyone, then you're wrong." I paused, letting the weight of that settle before adding, more quietly, "Besides—you're a Dormant too, Nodin. That means you're just as much a target as I am."

Nodin's jaw twitched.

"You think the plan's going to work without all of us?" I said, taking a step toward him. My voice was steady, but my heart was already racing. "It includes my visions. You need them. It could be the only thing that gets us through that stadium alive."

I kept my eyes on Nodin, watching the way his shoulders tensed, the slight shift in his stance like he was bracing for something he didn't want to hear—but couldn't ignore. He wouldn't meet my gaze at first, but when he finally did, there was a flicker of conflict behind his eyes.

"And I'm not just saying this because I want to fight," I added, quieter now, but somehow more certain. "I'm saying it because I can't let you walk into that place alone."

The silence that followed wasn't tense—it was charged, something unspoken passing between us that made my chest ache. I swallowed hard.

"I know you're scared for me. But I'm scared for you, too. So if you think I'm going to stay behind while the people I care about put their lives on the line... then you really don't know me at all."

Nodin's lips parted, but I kept going.

"I've confronted the Chairman and lived to tell the tale. And more importantly, I know Aedan. I know how to reach him—when he's spiraling or shutting down. We're not getting him out unless we bring every advantage we have."

Footsteps echoed back down the hall. The Gradys had paused just beyond the corridor junction, clearly listening. Reo stood with his arms crossed, while Claire and Edvin traded glances.

I raised my voice. "You all know I'm right. We've gotten this far because we stuck together. We fought as a team. If you leave me behind now, you're gambling on luck instead of strategy."

Silence. A long beat of it.

Then Mr. Grady cleared his throat and stepped into view. "She's right."

Mrs. Grady looked at him, surprised.

He met my eyes. "If we're going to do this... if we're going to get our son back, then we don't leave anyone behind. Especially not the person who stood up to that monster and walked away."

Claire grinned. "Told you she was tougher than she looks."

Edvin gave me a wink. "Didn't want to say it, but yeah, you're basically terrifying."

Reo just nodded, solemn. "We'll need you inside."

Nodin exhaled slowly. He didn't argue. He just looked at me the way he did back when we first arrived at the base—like he'd already calculated the odds and knew better than to stand in my way.

"You're not bluffing, are you?" he asked.

"No," I said. "So you can take me as part of the team... or I'll see you at the stadium."

He shook his head, defeated—but something like admiration flickered in his eyes. "Fine. But you stay close to me. No hero moves unless I'm right behind you."

"Deal."

And just like that, it was settled.

The team turned back down the hall, this time with me in step beside them.

By the time we reached the launch bay, the energy had changed. The frantic urgency of the medbay and planning rooms was gone—replaced by something tighter, more controlled. Here, everything was pared down to function: gears aligned, breaths measured, voices low and precise. Several AHVs and HTVs lined the launch bay, their hulls gleaming under the overhead lights as engineers wove between them—tightening panels, recalibrating instruments, and barking updates over comms.

The air vibrated with the deep-throated growl of turbines cycling in standby. Steam hissed from floor grates, curling through the dim light as small assistant drones raced across the bay, chirping and beeping in bursts of synthetic urgency as they carried out their tasks. The lighting was colder now, stark and unfeeling, as if even the walls understood the gravity of what we were about to attempt.

Just ahead of us, an HTV powered up near the launch doors—stealth-gray, narrow, built for speed. Bae and Mr. Tibadeau were already heading up its boarding ramp when I crossed to them.

"I checked again—just now," I said quietly. "Tristan's still headed toward the Chairman's tower. Not the detention center."

It had become a rhythm over the last couple of days—brief flashes of temporal sight, just enough to confirm Tristan's location. After McHaill's warning and Yrsa's request, it was the least I could do to give the Gabriel team a chance.

Bae gave me a sharp nod, then softened it with the faintest grin. "Good. Then we stick with the plan."

"Come back in one piece, alright?" I said.

"Always. And you watch yourself, Elin." Her tone carried both lightness and weight, the way only Bae could manage.

Mr. Tibadeau touched two fingers to his temple in acknowledgment, then followed Bae up the ramp without another word. The hatch sealed behind them with a soft hiss.

I stepped back as their HTV lifted off, wind from the turbines tugging at the edges of my cloak.

Please work. Please let it be enough.

The craft vanished into the morning sky—one mission already in motion, another about to begin. I watched it disappear until the bay lights swallowed the last glint of metal, the tight knot in my chest barely loosening. Hope and dread curled together there like twin shadows.

Near the far wall, our team's assigned HTV crouched on its landing struts, sleek and slate-gray. From a distance, it looked indistinguishable from the dozens of others that buzzed through Falinvik skies. Up close, I could just make out the pale *Stór-menni* insignia stamped along its hull—weathered enough to pass for official, clean enough to avoid suspicion.

We were dressed in tunics, armor reinforced at the shoulders and sides, matching combat boots, and Clan cloaks that signaled our supposed *Leikr* affiliations. Half of us wore the Chairman's team's colors: slate-gray over steel. The others—like Claire, Edvin, and Reo—were cloaked in black threaded with crimson, mimicking the elite rivals from the opposing faction. We'd blend in easily among the players, spectators, and officials funneling through the outer levels of the stadium.

As I was about to learn, our disguises ran deeper than fabric. Claire tossed each of us a thin case as we lined up near our HTV. I turned the case over in my hands, small and unmarked. Lightweight. Some kind of tech, but I couldn't place it.

"Facial-shifters," Claire said, already peeling hers open. "Just in case Tristan or any of his trackers flagged us after the alley debacle."

I popped mine open. The tech looked unimpressive—just a translucent patch about the size of my thumb. But once I pressed it to the side of my neck, a gentle pulse spread across my face. Cool. Electric.

A shimmer distorted my reflection in a polished panel nearby. My features reformed—shorter hair, a broader chin, slightly crooked nose. Still me beneath, but if someone tried to match me to surveillance footage, they'd come up empty.

Claire activated hers and blinked at her reflection. "Ugh. Why do I look like someone who manages spreadsheets and judges everyone's lunch choices?"

"Alright," Edvin muttered, turning a small brass disc between his fingers. "Moment of truth."

He pressed the center.

A wave of light shimmered up from his collar, spreading across his features like liquid mercury. A second later, he no longer looked like himself. His grin widened on a face that now had a crooked nose and a thin scar across one cheek.

"Whoa," Claire said, adjusting her device behind her ear. "You look like our high school gym teacher."

"Don't insult me," Edvin said in a voice two octaves deeper, "or I'll make you run laps."

I looked at my reflection in a polished panel again—the face that stared back was of someone I wasn't used to seeing. "This doesn't feel like me," I muttered.

Nodin glanced over, his own altered face unreadable. His

disguise had given him a sharp jawline and closely cropped hair, with a faint scar at his temple. He looked older. Harsher.

"I think that's the point," he said with a small grin. "But it's still you where it counts."

I arched a brow. "That easy to tell?"

Nodin, adjusting the edge of his cloak, didn't even look up when he said, "For me? Yeah. Always."

The words were automatic—barely a breath between thoughts, like he was already on to the next tactical detail.

I turned toward him, caught off guard. He didn't notice. Just tightened the strap on his gauntlet, gaze fixed on the HTV.

"Right," I said softly, more to myself than to him. "Let's just hope no one else does."

Reo passed behind us, tugging at the hood of his cloak with elegant precision. "Forgettable faces. A tactical virtue... though not one I'm often afforded." His facial-shifter had softened the angles of his face, dulled the depth of his eyes, and added a soft sallow undertone to his skin—less commanding, more unremarkable. He looked like someone you'd forget in a crowd.

It was strange, hearing familiar voices behind unfamiliar faces—like we'd been peeled back and re-layered into ghosts of ourselves.

The Facial-shifters were essential—we planned to walk in through the main gates, cloaked and ticketed, just another cluster of Clan spectators. Once inside, we'd split—Claire, Edvin, Nodin, and I heading for the lower levels near the competitor platform, while Sigrid, Reo, Mr. Grady, and Mrs. Grady made their way to the upper decks. From their position, Mr. Grady would set the illusion in motion—whatever he had planned, it was big enough to give us the opening we needed. Just long enough to move. Just long enough to reach Aedan.

Claire and Edvin would handle the extraction—getting Aedan off the competitor platform and to the fallback corridor. My role was to help guide them in using my visions, reading the stadium's patterns, and finding blind spots in patrols. Nodin was my shadow, watching my back while I focused ahead.

We'd walked the plan three times in the old storage deck below the Resistance base. Still, it didn't feel like enough.

"What if Aedan's not in position when we reach the platform?" Claire asked, voice low but steady.

"He will be," I said, reaching for the inner pocket of my jacket. "I've been thinking about it and have a way to make sure."

I pulled out Aedan's iPod—the same one I took from his room back on Auor Island. The casing was worn and scratched, but it still worked. I'd kept it charged with my old iPhone adapter from Auor. Just in case.

The moment I held it up, a few curious looks flicked my way.

To most Nordri Clan members, the device was obsolete tech from a world long buried. Decades of cultural lockdown under the Chairman's mandates had severed them from the human world—no music, no films, no internet. Pop culture was treated like a contaminant, and any remnants of it had quietly disappeared behind locked doors and firewalls. Most of them wouldn't recognize the music stored inside this thing.

But Aedan would.

Edvin blinked. "Wait, we're going to *DJ* the signal?"

"It's not just music," I said, scrolling through the ancient playlist. "It's *his* music. He'll recognize it instantly—and no one else in the stadium will know what the heck they're hearing."

I stopped on the track. *Back in Black.* Heavy, defiant, unrelenting. It wasn't subtle. But it didn't need to be.

"It'll blast through the comm system when Mr. Grady's illusion starts," I explained. "It'll match the chaos, and Aedan will know it's time to move."

Claire smirked. "Dramatic."

"Appropriate," Reo murmured, adjusting the edge of his cloak. "He'll recognize the spirit behind it—even if the rest won't."

"You two trigger the track when I give the signal," I said, handing the device to Edvin.

He took it, tucking it into a lined pouch on his belt.

Claire exhaled. "Let's just hope he still likes vintage rebellion."

"Oh, he does," I said, smiling faintly. "He told me once that this song makes him feel like a one-man army."

The hatch to the HTV cycled open with a soft hiss. Reo turned toward it, then cast a calm glance across the team.

"Go with resolve," he said quietly. "Let hesitation be someone else's flaw today."

Nodin's hand brushed mine briefly—a quiet promise—as we moved up the ramp together.

"You good?" he asked, voice low.

I nodded, not breaking eye contact. "You?"

He hesitated, then nodded too. "Just don't do anything reckless."

"No hero moves unless you're right behind me," I said, echoing his words from earlier.

He gave a subtle smile. "Deal."

Inside, the cabin was dim and metallic, humming with stored power and silent tension. Seats lined the sides, harnesses clipped and waiting. We took our places, pulling the straps tight.

The doors slid shut, sealing us into the moment between the last planning and execution. Whatever came next, we were going in cloaked, masked, and armed with the one thing the Chairman never counted on. Each other.

The crowd swallowed us the moment we stepped off the aerial transit shuttle—a streamlined skimmer that raced down from the hover vehicle platforms, silent on its magnetic runners. Frost still clung to the edge of its doors, and the instant they folded shut behind us, a blast of wintry air sliced through the noise, stealing the last moment of stillness before we dropped into the chaos of the stadium's concourse.

It was like entering another world. Flags of the remaining two teams snapped overhead in the stadium—gray and crimson and black—whipping sharply in the frigid wind. Snow crusted the edges of the wide plaza, shoveled into frozen ridges along the walkways where vendors called out prices for roasted meat skewers and steaming, mead-infused drinks. The smell of spice and smoke hung heavy in the air, fighting the bitter cold. Spectators surged around us in clusters, wrapped in wool cloaks and thick gloves, laughing and shouting to be heard over the distant thunder of drums. It felt like any championship back in the human world. If you didn't know what the *Leikr* was, you'd almost believe this was just sport.

Almost.

Beneath the noise, tension curled in my gut. The checkpoint loomed ahead—five lanes, heavily fortified. Drones drifted like slow wasps overhead, their red optics flickering through the flurries. Behind the medal scanners, *Stór-menni* guards stood with shoulders hunched against the cold—armed, alert, scanning faces beneath the brims of their frost-dusted helmets.

Nodin leaned in. His voice was barely audible beneath the stadium din. "Left lane. That guard's already waved two spectators through without flagging them."

I nodded, shifting my hood to cover more of my altered features as another gust of icy wind slid down my collar.

Ahead of us, Claire and Edvin were already moving. She strode confidently, her cloak billowing in the icy wind, face passive but her posture slightly haughty—just enough to suggest an elite Clan member. Edvin followed a few paces behind, hands in his pockets, bored like a technician dragged into duty. They didn't acknowledge each other. Didn't look back.

Just two strangers heading into the finals.

Our turn came quickly.

The guard held up a scanner and motioned me forward. My

breath hitched, but I forced my steps to stay smooth. The Facial-shifter hummed softly against my skin as the beam passed over me. For a second—just one—I thought the red light would hold, that something in my heartbeat or my energy signature would give me away.

Then: green.

The guard nodded once and jerked his head toward the entry gate.

I stepped through.

Nodin came next. The scanner paused on him longer. One beat. Two.

The guard frowned, taking a closer look at Nodin's fake Clan medal.

My pulse spiked. I shifted just slightly, hand drifting toward my belt—not to reach for anything, just to be ready.

Then the scanner chirped. Green.

Nodin gave a shallow nod and moved forward, catching up beside me like nothing had happened.

Behind us, someone else in the crowd was stopped—an older man with a limp and a tattered cloak. Guards were already moving toward him. We didn't look back.

Once inside, we didn't regroup. We couldn't afford to.

The plan was already in motion.

Claire and Edvin peeled off with the next cluster of spectators, disappearing into the lower concourse that would eventually loop behind the competitor platform. Reo slipped along a different corridor, timing his approach to the upper decks.

Sigrid, Mr. Grady, and Mrs. Grady had already broken off, vanishing into the pulse of bodies flooding the stairwells.

The Chairman's speech would begin in minutes.

"Northeast tunnel," Nodin said, motioning toward the far edge of the concourse. "That's our entry point."

We moved quickly, weaving through food stalls, families, and loud groups in team cloaks. The tension pressed in at every step, but the crowd was buoyant, festive. They were here for glory. For tradition. For spectacle.

They had no idea what was coming.

I kept my eyes forward. We weren't here to cheer.

We were here to rescue Aedan. And the clock was ticking.

My thoughts flickered—unbidden—to Gabriel's team.

They'd launched not long before us, heading for the detention center buried in the cliffs beyond the eastern perimeter. Their job was harder in every way: no disguises, no crowd to hide in. Just brute force, stealth, and a narrow window carved out by the Chairman's own vanity.

I glanced up, past the banners and stone arches, toward the looming balcony above the field.

That speech—his moment of glory, when he would command the arena's full attention—was everything. It would force every Clan guard in the stadium to stand at attention and salute, even those monitoring the detention perimeter. Thirty seconds. That was all Gabriel's team had to bypass the final checkpoint. I just hoped Bae, Mr. Tibadeau, and the rest of the team could hold the line long enough—and get Gabriel out before the window slammed shut.

We cut across a small plaza flanked by food vendors and souvenir booths—smells of roasted meat and fried root vegetables clashed with the sharp scent of ozone from charging cables and security drones. Spectators clustered in front of floating holo-screens suspended between archways, the broadcasts flickering with crowd shots, sponsor banners, and pre-match commentary.

Then the feed changed.

The camera swept across the arena interior—tight shots of the elevated platforms where the *Leikr* finalists waited in formation.

I stopped cold.

There he was.

Aedan.

He stood near the edge of the Gray's team platform, shoulders squared, eyes forward. The cloak draped over his frame was a deeper gray than I remembered, and his hair had been slicked back in a way that made him look sharper, older. His expression was calm. Too calm.

But I knew that look.

I'd seen it when he shut down before a fight—when the chaos outside forced him to go still inside. His hands were clasped behind his back, but the way his fingers flexed gave him away. He was listening. Waiting.

Waiting for us.

Nodin stepped close beside me, his eyes following mine to the screen. He didn't speak, just let the moment land.

"He's ready," I said quietly.

"Good," Nodin replied. "Because everything's about to move."

The feed shifted again, cutting to a live shot of the Chairman's balcony. A countdown ticked in the corner. Five minutes.

I pulled my hood lower and turned toward the northeast tunnel.

No more room for doubt. Aedan was in place. Now it was our turn.

The noise of the crowd thinned as we passed beneath the northeast archway, replaced by the sterile hum of service lighting and the faint hiss of pressurized doors. Here, the air felt different—closer, colder. The corridor ahead stretched long and silent, curving gradually with the stadium's inner wall.

We were officially in restricted territory.

A large sign scrolled a warning across the far wall: AUTHORIZED PERSONNEL ONLY. TRESPASSERS WILL BE DETAINED.

At the threshold, a slim security panel pulsed red beside the sealed access door. I reached into the lining of my cloak and pulled out the clearance key—a low-frequency decryptor McHaill had rigged from salvaged *Stór-menni* tech. Barely larger than a coin, but dense with illicit code. I pressed it to the panel.

A beat passed. Then another.

The light flickered from red... to orange...

...and finally to green.

The door hissed open with a soft hydraulic click.

Nodin allowed himself the ghost of a smile.. "Nice. Remind me to thank McHaill if we make it out alive."

We slipped through, the door sealing quietly behind us—muting the roar of the stadium and sweeping us into the quiet of enemy territory.

Nodin and I didn't speak—we didn't have to. Every footstep we took was calculated, every breath measured. The sound of my boots against the polished concrete felt too loud, even though I was moving lightly.

A fork in the corridor approached.

I stopped and closed my eyes for just a second, drawing on the smallest thread of *megin*. The vision came in a flash—disconnected images, sharp and quick:

A guard turning the corner up ahead, shifting his grip on his shock staff.

Nodin's cloak catching on a protruding bolt.

My foot pressing down on a pressure plate near the junction.

I inhaled sharply, blinking it away.

"Wait," I whispered, reaching for Nodin's arm.

He paused immediately, shifting his weight so silently it almost startled me. He leaned in, and I murmured, "One guard incoming. Right corridor. We go left, but there's a pressure plate."

Without asking questions, he tilted his fingers subtly. A tiny current of wind whipped beneath the edges of our cloaks, stirring dust as it moved ahead of us—soft enough to be soundless, focused enough to test for other traps.

Nothing triggered.

We stepped around the junction, my foot skimming just beside the plate I'd seen in the vision. A few yards later, we ducked behind a half-shielded maintenance unit as the sound of the approaching guard reached our ears—boots, static chatter, a yawn. He passed right by us, never looking down.

When it was safe, Nodin tapped twice against my shoulder.

We moved again.

Twice more we stopped—once to slip into a service conduit when a team of *Stór-menni* guards marched through, and again when I heard the buzz of a security drone above the archway. Nodin raised one hand, his fingers slicing the air in a crescent. A whisper of wind rose, nudging the drone's flight pattern just enough to trigger a false echo in the opposite direction.

I noticed it then—just a tremor in his fingertips like the effort cost more than it should have. The burn on his palm from the broken vow glowed an angry red. It had spread further up his hand. He was holding it together by sheer will.

I looked at him, concerned. Just a flick of my gaze to his hand.

He caught it, and for a heartbeat, our eyes met.

Then he shook his head once—barely perceptible, more breath than movement—and closed his fist, tucking it back into his cloak as if to say *not now*.

The drone veered off, chasing the wrong sound.

My skin prickled. Every use of power—even that small—was a risk. We were betting everything on the crowd—on the noise and energy and layered *megin* signatures masking us from the Chairman's reach. But every time I reached inward, even for the shortest vision, I wondered if I could feel him stirring in the distance.

We turned one final corner—and there it was.

The alcove.

A narrow, half-recessed service niche tucked behind the structural supports beneath the stadium's northern seating. From here, we had a partial view of the arena floor—just enough to see the edge of the competitor dais and the sleek silver rise of the Gray team's platform.

We had made it.

I pressed back against the wall, adrenaline still sharp in my chest, my eyes drifting to Aedan's platform in the distance.

He'd looked calm up there. Steady. Like the chaos hadn't touched him. Like that night at the club hadn't happened at all.

The thought caught me off guard—cut deeper than I expected. I tried to shove it down, to focus on the mission, on the timings and the turns and the exact window we'd trained to hit. But the memory surfaced anyway. That quiet moment, tucked in the corner of the club, when he'd pulled me into the alcove and grabbed my wrist like it was the only thing tethering him to reality. The crack in his voice when I told him his family was safe. The way his hand hovered near my cheek—uncertain, trembling, like he wanted to reach me and didn't know how.

And still… he hadn't kissed me.

Not then. Not even when the moment all but begged for it.

Was it fear? Restraint? Or something else I hadn't wanted to see?

Or maybe—maybe he'd held back because I hadn't leaned in either. Because part of me, in that fractured heartbeat, wasn't sure I wanted him to.

My fingers twitched against my thigh.

What if he was pulling away? What if Thyra's closeness meant more than strategy? What if I misread everything?

It was stupid. We were here to rescue him, not sort through half-spoken feelings and second-guess our hearts. But in the hush of this alcove, beneath the buzz of the overhead conduits and the muffled roar of a crowd that had no idea what was coming, doubt wormed its way in.

I shut my eyes for a beat. *Steady. Focus.*

There would be time—if we made it out—to ask the hard questions. To hear the answers I wasn't sure I wanted.

But right now, I had a job to do.

And nothing—not even him—could be allowed to break that focus.

A burst of static flared across a nearby holo-screen, drawing my eyes up just in time to see the image flicker—first the arena, then the Chairman's crest, then black.

Somewhere above us, a trumpet call rang out—short, clipped, ceremonial. The kind of sound that told a thousand people to hold their breath.

It was almost time.

Nodin stood close beside me, cloak drawing around him like mist. His chest rose and fell steadily, but his fingers were clenched at his sides.

I followed his gaze.

Two alcoves down, just beyond a pillar covered in exposed conduit, I spotted Claire and Edvin. They were hidden in a similar recess, still as shadows, eyes fixed on the platform above.

Claire met my gaze across the distance.

Just once, she nodded.

We were all in place.

Now all we had to do—

—was wait for chaos.

TWENTY-SIX

The Stadium

ELIN

The final word of the Clan alliance oath rang out like a bell—sharp, rehearsed, hollow with centuries of history.

The Chairman lowered his arms with theatrical solemnity, his expression one of serene command. The crowd erupted into applause, a sea of cloaks and insignias clapping in perfect sync. A thousand Clan voices, unified. On the surface, anyway.

But the surface was a lie.

He stepped forward to the edge of the balcony, ready to begin the second half of his speech—and that's when the sky inside the stadium began to darken.

A collective hush fell.

It was impossible, what we were seeing. Storm clouds gathered above the arena—not just projected, not filtered, but real. The kind that churned with layered shadow and streaks of silver light, unfathomably contained beneath the stadium's dome. Wind rippled down from nowhere, tugging at flags and cloaks. Shadows thickened, turning the arena floor a gunmetal gray.

Then came the sound.

One beat. A second.

The opening riff of *Back in Black* dropped like a war drum into the silence.

Gasps flared across the stands. Heads turned. The Chairman froze mid-sentence.

Aedan's song was playing.

My heart spiked. I scanned the arena and saw them—Claire and Edvin—breaking into a sprint across the competitor platform, cloaks streaming behind them like war banners.

And then the sky cracked open.

A thunderclap rolled overhead as a figure dropped from the clouds, standing atop a floating metallic disc that gleamed like forged lightning. Mist coiled around his boots, and arcs of static danced in the air behind him, trailing sparks across the sky.

For a heartbeat, the crowd froze—caught between awe and confusion. The figure hovered in silhouette, cloaked in swirling vapor, his face obscured by shadow.

And then—he stepped into the light.

My breath caught.

It was Mr. Grady.

But not Mr. Grady as I knew him.

He wore a black asymmetric tunic lined with futuristic threads of polished silver, his shoulders squared beneath a billowing cloak that bore the Chairman's Valknut insignia. The uniform of a high *Stórmenni* commander. Power radiated off him in waves.

Gasps echoed through the stadium. Even the guards faltered, unsure whether to salute or run.

Then, before our eyes, the illusion shifted. The uniform darkened, blurred—and peeled away. In its place stood a man in simple Clan clothing. Unarmed. Unassuming. Ordinary.

It was the truth made flesh: one of their own, hidden in plain sight.

"I was like you once," his voice boomed across the stadium. "I believed what he told me. That the other Clans were gone. That obedience meant survival. That fear kept us safe."

A hush fell again—not imposed, but stunned. The audience leaned in. For the first time, they were listening.

"And then I saw what lies beneath his promises," Mr. Grady continued. "What he takes from us. Our minds. Our memories. Our power. But the truth survived him. The Clans—survived him."

But before Mr. Grady could say anything more, the crowd fractured.

It began with a flutter—an almost imperceptible tremor, like a wire pulled too tight.

Then came the sound. Not a shout or a cheer, but something far stranger. A low murmur rippling across the lower rows, rising in volume until it became a chorus of dissonance: gasps, moans, the crackle of someone's breath snagging in their throat. A metallic clang echoed where someone dropped their drink. A child whimpered. A woman cried out.

Hands jerked upward—first a few, then dozens. Covering ears. Pressing hard, as if to block out something no one else could hear.

Then came the shiver.

Not from the cold, but something deeper—an invisible current humming through the crowd, threading through every mind like a needle pulling taut.

And then—unthinkably—movement.

Hands lifted in eerie synchronization. Thousands of them. Covering ears. Not to block out sound, but as if obeying a silent command.

As if the very will to resist had been severed.

I went still. The hairs on my arms rose.

"That's not right," I whispered, dread curling in my chest like smoke.

Beside me, Nodin leaned forward, alarm blooming across his face. "It's not the illusion—"

"It's him. The Chairman. He's doing it. He's overriding them."

Nodin's eyes widened. "All of them? At once?"

We both looked out at the crowd—thousands of Clan members

moving in unnatural unison. Not a single scream. Not a single question.

Just silence. And pressure.

"The power it would take..." Nodin murmured. "This isn't just psychic control. It's domination."

"Why isn't it affecting us?" I whispered. The words barely stirred the air, but the question coiled in my stomach like fire. Whatever was sweeping through the crowd had curved around us—deliberate, precise. As if it saw us... and chose to wait.

Then, across the arena—

Movement.

A flash of gray and crimson between the risers.

Claire, Edvin, and Aedan burst from behind the competitor platform, sprinting hard for the corridor's edge. Aedan's cloak whipped behind him, his eyes fixed forward, jaw set. Claire led the way, Edvin close on his heels.

I turned to Nodin, pulse thundering. "That's our cue."

He didn't hesitate. We pulled up our hoods and moved.

Aedan reached us first.

His hood had fallen back, revealing windblown hair and a face slick with sweat, but his eyes—those sea-blue, stormy eyes—were focused on me like nothing else existed.

"Elin," he breathed.

I didn't hesitate. Just threw my arms around him.

It wasn't a long embrace—there was no time—but it was enough. Enough to feel that he was alive, solid, still himself. His arms locked around me for a second too long, just enough to whisper everything he couldn't say aloud before we pulled apart.

"You came," he said quietly. His voice cracked on the second word, low and disbelieving. I could still feel the tremor in his hands when we let go.

"Of course we did," I replied, brushing a strand of hair from his face. "But we need to move. Now."

Claire glanced over her shoulder. "The corridor—this way!"

We plunged into the passage together, five sets of footsteps echoing off the polished floor. The moment the heavy door hissed shut behind us, the noise from the arena cut off like a severed wire.

The air inside the hall was still, the lights twinkling in rhythmic patterns above.

I reached out, letting a thread of *megin* spin from my chest and settle behind my eyes. The passageway stretched ahead—no guards. Not yet. No footsteps, no droids. Just silence. Unnatural silence.

"Something's wrong," I muttered.

"Define wrong," Edvin said tensely.

"No guards," I answered. "None. There should be patrols. Or at least someone."

"We'll take the gift," Nodin said behind me, though his voice was tight. He didn't trust it either.

We kept going. I warned them when to duck to avoid a wall sensor, where to step around a pressure plate disguised beneath the tile grout. It was too easy. Too smooth.

By the time we reached the stadium's main hall—a wide corridor lined with food stalls and glinting signage—we'd slipped through without a single direct threat.

Claire whispered, "We made it. I can't believe it."

That's when it changed.

A slight rustling sound, like paper stirring in a breeze, crept along the edges of my awareness. I turned just in time to see a group freeze—three adults, two children, an elderly man. All of them turned in eerie, puppet-like unison—as if triggered by a single, silent command.

Then another cluster. And another.

Across the hall, more and more people stilled mid-step. Drinks dropped from slack hands. Holo-banners quivered as if responding to static. Heads turned toward us with vacant stares.

"Oh no," I whispered.

"What is it?" Claire said, her voice going sharp.

I didn't answer right away. I couldn't. My *megin* stretched out instinctively and hit a wall of pressure. Not a physical one. A mental one.

"He's doing it again," I said. "The Chairman. He's... in them."

"Through all these people?" Edvin said, stunned. "That's not possible—"

"It is," Nodin cut in, voice low with horror. "But the power it would take—"

He didn't finish the thought.

Because the crowd moved.

Not chaotically. Not with fear. With precision.

Step by step, they converged, closing off the main hallway ahead. Behind us, another group began to form—corralling, not attacking. Herding us.

"Back," I said. "We have to—"

But the path we came through was already blocked by a wall of people. Not hostile. Just... standing. Waiting.

The lights above us dimmed. Then fluttered. Once. Twice.

"This wasn't part of the plan," Claire hissed.

"No," I said, pulling Aedan to my side. "But if he's trying to force us somewhere—"

"Then he has something waiting," Nodin finished grimly.

We were being redirected.

And whatever was at the end of this corridor—it wasn't freedom.

We moved fast, forced down the unfamiliar corridor by a tide of glassy-eyed civilians whose footsteps echoed in perfect rhythm. The air was close here—stale with disuse and faintly metallic. We barely had time to glance at the signage before the next turn loomed, and more bodies appeared behind us, blocking any hope of retreat.

"This way isn't part of the plan," Claire muttered, her voice tight as she kept pace beside Edvin and Aedan.

"No guards. Just... them," Edvin said, eyes flicking toward the eerily silent crowd.

"They're pushing us," I said, glancing back. "Steering us. Like a current."

"Toward the Chairman's balcony," Nodin added grimly. He stumbled for half a step, catching himself against the wall.

"You good?" Edvin asked, frowning.

Nodin gave a tight nod, but I saw the sheen of sweat on his brow, the way his left hand curled protectively around his right.

"It's the vow," he muttered, more to himself than anyone else. "I'm holding together—for now."

But his breath came shorter with each stride.

Aedan's voice caught in his throat. "This is my fault."

"Don't," Claire snapped, not unkindly. "Don't even start."

"If you hadn't come for me—"

"You didn't start this or bring this on us. The Chairman did," Edvin said.

"And we would always come for you, Aedan," Claire said, glancing at him. "You're our brother. And he doesn't get to keep you."

Aedan didn't respond, but his eyes dropped, jaw tightening. He kept moving, silent but not alone.

Ahead, the corridor bent sharply left, and the hallway widened into a loading junction. At first, we froze—half-expecting more civilians or worse.

Then a shape moved in the shadows.

Nodin stepped forward instinctively, hands raised.

"Stay back," I whispered, trying to reach for a vision but stopping short. Too many people nearby. Too many minds already twisted by control.

The figures approached fast.

Claire drew a blade. Edvin shifted closer to Aedan.

Then—

"Elin?"

It was Sigrid's voice.

My breath whooshed out, relief crashing into me. "Wait—it's them!"

Reo was next, stepping into the light. His face had resumed its original form, and his eyes immediately scanned us with calm focus.

Behind him, Mr. and Mrs. Grady followed, cloaks drawn tight, eyes searching—

"Aedan?" Mrs. Grady gasped.

Aedan blinked. "Mom?"

She didn't wait. She threw her arms around him, pulling him in tight.

Mr. Grady was close behind, hand gripping Aedan's shoulder with fierce, silent joy. "You're safe."

"I—yeah," Aedan stammered. "I'm here. I didn't think—"

"We came," Mrs. Grady said firmly. "Of course we did."

I looked to Sigrid, expecting her usual alertness—but her posture sagged ever so slightly, her hand gripping the wall as if for balance. Her skin was pale, almost gray beneath the overhead lights.

"Are you okay?" I asked, voice low.

She nodded once, but there was strain in it. "Helping Liam... that illusion took more out of me than I expected. I took a page from the Chairman and used my *Ljós* to bolster him, but it doesn't come for free."

Mr. Grady gave her a quick glance, concern flashing behind his eyes.

She waved it off. "I'll manage. Just don't ask me to do it again today."

A brief silence followed, thick with unspoken relief and exhaustion.

Then Aedan's gaze shifted—and froze.

His eyes widened. "Reo?"

He took a step forward, almost disbelieving. "You're here too? How?"

Reo offered the faintest smile. "Unexpected journeys, Aedan-kun. But sometimes, the path chooses us."

Aedan shook his head, speechless, and pulled him into a brief, surprised hug.

"We're not clear yet," Sigrid warned, already turning back toward the junction. "The Chairman is still moving pieces."

Aedan blinked, as if seeing her clearly for the first time through the adrenaline haze. "Sigrid," he said, his voice threaded with surprise and relief. "I didn't think I'd see you ever again." A small smile tugged at the corner of his mouth. "Glad you're still standing."

She gave him a dry look, but there was warmth behind it. "Barely."

The moment hung for a heartbeat—then the urgency snapped back into place.

"And he knows we're together now," I added.

Mr. Grady gave a small nod. "Then we try to stay ahead of him."

We didn't need another signal.

Together now—truly together—we turned down the corridor and ran.

We hadn't gone far before the corridor spilled into a vast, cathedral-like hall—its arched ceilings ribbed with polished alloy, the upper beams laced with skylights that filtered the glare of the stadium's spotlights. The light slanted through in ghostly shafts, fractured and restless.

I recognized the space from the holo-map—the grand hall beneath the Chairman's balcony. But the scale of it landed differently in person. Too wide. Too quiet.

As we moved, my gaze slid along the walls—sleek metal broken at intervals by barely-there seams. Each was marked by a faintly glowing panel in the wall. I hadn't noticed them on the projection. Emergency systems, most likely a barrier of some kind. Fire. Flood. Security breach. Whatever brand of catastrophe this place was built to survive.

Naturally, they only lined the Chairman's Hall.

Suddenly, a prickle ran up my spine. I didn't need a vision to sense the shift—like the air itself had braced for impact.

We froze.

At the far end of the corridor, the crowd parted—

And there he was.

The Chairman.

He walked with careful, measured steps, his cloak trailing like liquid shadow. And he wasn't alone.

At his side was a girl, no older than us. Her fingers were laced through his as if she belonged there. But her expression... *her gaze was vacant*. Not afraid. Not aware. Her steps were perfectly in time with his. Too perfect.

She wore a deep gray cloak similar to the Chairman's, but hers shimmered hazily under the corridor's lighting—every seam traced with gold piping. Her long, dark hair flowed loose down her back, partially braided in the style of ceremonial Clan nobility. Her skin was warm-toned, her features high-cheekboned and elegant, with eyes that might once have been sharp with curiosity or fire—but now stared ahead, glassy and dulled. Vestri roots, if I had to guess. But it was the emptiness behind her expression that chilled me most.

She wasn't walking beside him.

She was being led.

Nodin inhaled sharply beside me but said nothing. His entire body had gone rigid like he'd been hit by a different kind of impact.

Several paces behind the Chairman, Thyra emerged, flanked by a full squad of armed *Stór-menni* guards. Her stride was smooth, controlled—but not as crisp as usual. There was a tension in her frame, like a violin string drawn too tight.

She didn't look at us. Didn't look at Aedan. But I felt it—something held just behind her eyes, just beneath the armor.

The Chairman and the girl passed the final recessed panel ahead of her. The guards moved to follow.

But Thyra—

She faltered. And the guards stopped behind her.

It was precise. Timed. A pause that could be written off as a tactical scan, a hesitation in formation.

But it was just long enough.

Just long enough for Aedan to move.

With one smooth motion, he snatched a dagger from Claire's belt.

And with his telekinesis guided the blade like a whisper. He didn't even pause to think.

The dagger spun across the hall, slicing into the recessed panel by the last seam.

With a hydraulic hiss, the translucent security shield dropped into place behind the Chairman and the girl—trapping Thyra and the guards on the other side of the corridor.

Before anyone could react, Aedan whirled and hurled the same dagger in the opposite direction—toward the control panel at the far end.

The second barrier slammed down behind us.

The horde of civilians that had been marching toward us stopped, pressing up against the barrier's shimmering field like moths to a wall of fire. Trapped. Unmoving. Mind-controlled.

And for a moment—we were alone with the Chairman. In the eye of the storm.

The Chairman stopped mid-step, his head turning slightly as if to savor the gravity of the moment. He looked toward Aedan, not with anger.

But with pride.

A slow smile spread across his face, unsettling in its warmth.

"Well done, my boy," he said, his voice deep and confident, almost fatherly. "Quick. Clean. Precise."

Aedan's breathing was sharp, his eyes locked on the Chairman like a blade pulled tight against a whetstone.

The Chairman tilted his head. "But do you really think that will stop the inevitable?"

His hand curled more tightly around the girl's. She didn't blink.

No one moved. Not yet.

But we would. Because this corridor had just become the battlefield.

"So it's true," the Chairman said softly, almost to himself. Then, louder: "You always were clever, Liam."

His voice oozed through the corridor, smooth and cold.

"Commander Jarnulf, risen from the ashes. You vanished so completely, for so long, I almost believed you *were* dead."

Mr. Grady said nothing.

"Almost," the Chairman continued, taking a slow step forward. "But then I saw it—his DNA. I knew the bloodline couldn't lie. And today... you confirmed it."

He smiled—not with joy, but with something darker. "Quite the performance. A bit dramatic, perhaps, but effective. You always did enjoy spectacle when it served your purpose."

"And to think," he added, voice curling with pride, "all I had to do was put the boy in the *Leikr*. I knew you wouldn't stay hidden if your son was out there—vulnerable, in plain sight. The only thing I misjudged," he chuckled, "was the timing. I thought you'd come sooner... not let him fight his way through half the tournament before you finally showed your face."

The words hit like a slap.

I felt the breath catch in my throat.

It was a trap.

The *Leikr*—every round, every risk—Aedan hadn't just been playing for his freedom. He'd been bait. The Chairman had used him like a lure, strung out the tournament like a line cast into dark water, waiting for Mr. Grady to surface. And we'd walked right into it.

Not by mistake.

By design.

Mr. Grady met his gaze, steady and silent.

A chuckle—low, amused, disturbingly warm. "Don't pretend you haven't missed this, nephew."

The word hit like a strike. Nephew.

Claire's head whipped toward him. Edvin froze, mouth half open.

But Aedan—he didn't look confused. He looked like he'd already put the pieces together.

The Chairman's voice dipped, warmer now. "You could've come back any time, you know. You still can. This doesn't have to end in fire and resistance. You and your family—you don't have to run anymore. You can live like true Clan members. No more shadows. No more lies. Just home. Unity. Power. Together."

His eyes drifted toward Mrs. Grady, then Claire and Edvin. "They're strong. Loyal. I'd welcome them with open arms. Even your wife. She has courage—she raised three remarkable children. All I ask is your return."

Mr. Grady's voice was calm, but iron-hard. "We're not coming back."

"Why not?" the Chairman asked, feigning confusion. "What are you protecting them from, Liam? Comfort? Legacy? They'll be safe. Trained. Honored. It's what every Clan family dreams of—"

"Not mine." Mr. Grady took a step forward. "I left because I saw what you were becoming. Before the rest did. Before you drowned this world in your fear. You turned truth into a weapon. Loyalty into surveillance. And trapped the Clan in a cage."

The Chairman's smile tightened. "I gave them structure. I gave them order."

"You gave them silence."

Mr. Grady's eyes burned. "And now you stand there draining light from a girl barely old enough to understand what's happening to her, and you still have the gall to speak of unity?"

The Chairman glanced at the girl, still glowing at his side, limp and vacant. "Sacrifice is part of survival."

"You don't survive by hollowing people out," Mr. Grady said. "You survive by protecting them. By letting them be *whole*."

The Chairman tilted his head. "And what happens when the whole resists? When it refuses to obey?"

"Then it was never yours to command," Mr. Grady said.

The silence crackled.

"Don't be a fool, Liam," the Chairman said at last, quieter now, but no less dangerous. "You know what I can do. You know what I've already done. Walk through that door, and your family lives. Stay on this path..."

He let the sentence hang, unfinished.

Mr. Grady didn't flinch. "They are not bargaining chips. And I will not raise my children in your shadow."

The Chairman's smile returned, slow and cold.

"Then I'll take them all," the Chairman said, and smiled. "One by one—or all at once."

He raised his hand.

Pain detonated through my skull like shrapnel.

A white-hot spike behind my eyes. I screamed, staggering. The world lurched sideways. Around me, the others fell like dominoes—Claire clutching her head, Edvin writhing on the ground, Aedan collapsing to one knee with a gasp. Reo leaned against the wall, eyes clenched. Sigrid and Mrs. Grady dropped back against each other. Mr. Grady gritted his teeth, trembling with the effort to stay upright. Even Nodin crumpled beside me, hands pressed hard against his temple.

The Chairman hadn't taken a step.

But he was inside us.

Burrowing. Peeling. Commanding. His strength was undeniable. And his presence wasn't just inside my head—it was everywhere. Flooding the space around us like a pressure system, probing for cracks, filling lungs that weren't his. His psychic tendrils didn't knock like before—they *tore.*

Mr. Grady gritted his teeth and forced himself upright. "Remember—" he shouted through clenched jaws. "Remember what I taught you. Root yourself. Anchor in memory, music, books. Visualize the boundary. Push back!"

I clawed through the chaos for something—anything.

The cliffs in Auor. My mother's hands, rough with salt and warmth. Aedan's smile when we were on Tower Island, the wind in our hair, sun bouncing off the sea. Nodin's hand brushing mine in the herbarium, his voice low as he named the flower that steadied my pulse. Music—loud, defiant, impossible to ignore. The taste of wind and freedom and fear.

The pressure lifted—just slightly.

And then I saw it.

The girl. Her fingers clenched, then loosened. Her head tipped, the braid shifting slightly as if she were trying to pull away. Her lips trembled. Not much—but enough. The shine between their joined hands wasn't metaphorical anymore. It was *real. Ljós—her Ljós*—was flowing like molten gold from her body into the Chairman's veins, fueling the assault he was laying down upon us.

The truth struck like a spark in the dark.

She wasn't just a conduit. She was the *source.*

Her light—radiant and wrong— was being *siphoned.* Her skin was too bright, veins illuminated gold. Her knees buckled, but his grip held firm.

She was being *drained.* And she was dying.

Beside me, Nodin's head jerked up. His gaze locked on her, and something in him cracked.

"Aylen!" he choked out, voice thick with horror.

A jolt ran through me. He knew her. That name... it meant something to him. Something deep, buried, and sacred. Something he never told me. I didn't know who Aylen was to him. But I saw the crack it left.

She didn't respond. Her eyes fluttered, unfocused, mouth slack. But her body twitched in protest. She was trying. Failing.

The Chairman didn't even glance at her. His expression was rapture—pure, terrible bliss as the *Ljós* poured into him.

And suddenly, I knew.

We were going to lose.

One by one, we were all falling—Claire had collapsed beside Edvin, who was barely conscious, curled around her like a shield. Mr. Grady now on one knee, shaking violently. Sigrid hadn't moved since she dropped to a crouch. Her eyes were wide but unfocused, and the pale *Ljós* around her had already gone dull. Spent.

Mrs. Grady was on her knees beside her, but her hands were wrapped around her own head. Aedan was hunched over, hands to his temples, teeth clenched in silent fury. Reo's eyes were closed, sweat rolling down his brow as he silently mouthed some ancient prayer. And Nodin—he wasn't just weakened. He was breaking. His vow-burned palm trembled violently, the skin split and bleeding, his breath shallow as if each inhale came through glass.

On the other side of the barrier, the *Stór-menni* squad clustered in confusion—rifles raised, barking orders, trying in vain to override the control panel.

But Thyra... Thyra didn't move.

She stood motionless in the dim light, one hand braced against the barrier's edge, palm splayed flat on the translucent surface as if she could will it to dissolve.

Her eyes were fixed on us. No—on *him*.

On the Chairman.

And as she watched what he was doing—the way he gripped the girl's hand, the way her light pulsed and flared and poured into him—something changed in her posture.

She leaned in, lips parting just enough for a whisper I couldn't hear, though I thought I saw the shape of the word: *Stop*.

The sight of what he was doing knocked something out of her.

Her jaw tightened. Her fingers curled into a fist against the glass.

And then—she moved.

She spun toward two guards, her mouth forming a sharp, unmistakable *"Go."*

Her gestures followed fast and clipped—pointing down a side corridor, then back at the barrier. I couldn't hear her words, but I could read the urgency in them: *Find another way in. Now.*

One of the guards hesitated, giving a short reply I couldn't catch. Thyra stepped forward, her expression darkening, and repeated the command with even more force. The second time, they didn't argue.

The two guards sprinted down the side hall, rifles ready, comms blinking.

But Thyra didn't follow.

She turned back toward the barrier, eyes scanning Aedan's side of the corridor—lingering for half a second too long on him, on Mrs. Grady, on the girl now glowing too brightly in the Chairman's grasp.

Her face was unreadable. Trained. Controlled. But something in her posture betrayed her.

She didn't want this.

And in that moment, as she pressed her palm once more to the barrier's edge, I felt it—*not certainty*, but doubt. Not loyalty. Something else.

A fracture beneath the surface. A silent war behind her eyes.

But there was no time to understand it.

Because we were falling—losing this battle.

I could feel it—the way the Chairman was spreading through us like smoke, like rot. His mind inside ours. Tearing through everything.

I dropped to my knees.

My hands trembled.

Fear and rage collided in my chest—but fear didn't matter anymore.

Not when the people I loved were being crushed under the arrogance of a man who called them nothing.

Not when the Chairman stood there, feeding on stolen light, drunk on his own delusion, while my friends writhed in agony on the floor.

He'd lied to us all.

Lied to the Nordri Clan. Lied to the world. Lied as he carved away at truth and memory and trust until there was nothing left but obedience and fear.

He hunted Dormants like predators hunt prey—not because we were dangerous, but because we *meant something*. Because we were the one thing he couldn't fully control.

He put my parents in danger without them ever knowing why.

My mom, who still hummed while folding laundry. My dad, who thought the world could be fixed with books and kindness. They didn't even know his name. They didn't know what I was. But that wouldn't stop him from using them—just because they matter to me.

He turned my life into a lie. He turned *me* into a target. All in the name of greatness.

And now he wanted more.

Now he wanted *everything*.

He dared to put Aedan, Claire, Edvin—*all of us*—in chains made of silence and mind control, and then had the audacity to smile while doing it.

How many had he erased already? How many Dormants ripped open like vessels just to make him stronger?

I didn't know the number. But I felt the weight of every one of them.

Every lie. Every life. Every drop of light he'd stolen.

And now—he was going to kill the people I loved.

Right in front of me.

No. No more.

Something cracked open inside me.

Not gently. Not like a door easing ajar. It split—violently, viscerally—like bone under pressure, like a dam tearing loose from its moorings.

It didn't roar. It didn't tremble. It blazed.

Ljós erupted from my core—wild, ancient, alive. It tore through me like a white-hot star uncaged, a storm of radiance uncoiling from the place no shadow could reach.

I didn't aim. I didn't brace. I just let it take me.

My body arched as the power surged upward, ripping through every nerve ending, igniting along my veins with a heat that bordered on agony. The air warped around me, bending inward as if the universe itself held its breath.

Then—with a soundless, throat-ripping cry—I let it go.

A beam of blinding white-gold light exploded from my chest. Not shaped. Not controlled. Unrelenting. It speared forward like judgment itself—pure, sacred fire aimed straight at the Chairman.

The impact was immediate.

He was lifted off his feet—no resistance, no defense—flung backward with the weight of my soul behind it. The girl's hand wrenched free just as he hit the barrier behind him, hard enough to shake the corridor.

Smoke curled from his skin as his cloak disintegrated in midair, revealing gleaming gold chainmail beneath—filigreed and ancient, energy dancing across it in furious bursts. It shimmered in the aftermath, absorbing what would have vaporized anyone else.

But he wasn't moving.

He was unconscious.

The pressure snapped like a tether.

All around me, groans rose—Claire, Edvin, Mr. Grady—stirring, crawling, gasping for air that now felt real again.

They were alive.

I smiled. Just once.

And then my body began to unravel.

The heat didn't recede—it deepened, turning inward. My vision blurred, edges curling black like burning paper. My knees gave, but I barely felt the impact. My skin throbbed with raw energy, too much for this vessel.

It wasn't just exhaustion. It was evacuation. Like the light had taken everything with it—blood, spirit, memory. My heartbeat staggered, uneven, then slowed.

My thoughts flickered.

Aedan's arms around me. Rain against the window pane. Nodin's voice in the herbarium. Sunshine on autumn leaves. Anders teasing me in the mornings. My mom's laughter across wind-polished cliffs. My dad reading to me. A flower blooming in a storm.

I think I was still smiling.

Then the dark rose to meet me.

And I let it.

TWENTY-SEVEN

The Reckoning

TRISTAN

The Chairman's tower loomed ahead, all glass, steel, and silent menace. I couldn't shake the feeling that I was walking into a trap.

Each step through the front atrium echoed louder than it should've. I tried to ignore the sleek silver AHVs docking above and the crisp, angular sculpture of the *Stór-menni* sigil stretching toward the ceiling. Eyes tracked me from every corner—security lenses, retina scanners, biometric probes disguised as lights. I'd been in this building a hundred times before, but today, it felt like it was watching me back.

I approached the high-speed express elevators—glass-paneled capsules clinging to the outer edge of the Tower like vertical passenger-train cars. They ran on magnetic rails beside the AHV landing platforms, offering a full, dizzying view of the city below. One slid open with a soft hiss, and I stepped inside. Other passengers were already aboard, sitting in silence as the car tilted vertically and began its steep climb. I ignored them as they peeled off floor by floor.

On the 24th, two guards entered—stoic, black-clad men bearing the Valknut emblem in golden thread on their cloaks. Security check. My stomach twisted.

I presented my IA medallion and the glowing red banner on my SRT indicating my authorization to enter the Chairman's floors above. They scanned the screen in silence. One nodded. "Proceed."

No smug Thyra this time. No interference. Just the faded hum as the elevator tilted and resumed its vertical climb. One final breath before the doors opened onto the 26th floor.

I clenched my jaw. Either Kolve was telling the truth, and I was here for a legitimate investigation... or this was a beautifully staged ambush. A fitting end for a man who'd been digging where he shouldn't.

The decor of the Chairman's lobby hit me like it always did.

Vaulted ceilings stretched high above, carved dragons glaring from the beams, jeweled eyes seeming to track my every move. The circular hearth at the center blazed defiantly as if the fire itself guarded the secrets held here. Banners, seaxes, ancient shields—intimidation disguised as heritage.

But today, the air smelled not just of aged wood and smoke—but ozone and antiseptic.

"Ah, Investigator Rees," came a clipped voice. A young IA officer emerged from the side hallway, her uniform crisp, her tone efficient. "This way."

No handcuffs. No accusations. Just professionalism. Too professional.

I gave a brief nod and followed her past the hearth, where the flames snapped inside the ornate pit like they didn't know something was wrong. Every step closer to the double doors felt like a countdown—one I wasn't sure I wanted to reach zero.

If this was a trap, it was a polished one. Smooth floors, protocol language, no sudden moves. My every instinct screamed *controlled environment.* Too quiet. Too clean. I'd prepared myself to face the Chairman. Prepared to be cornered. Exposed.

But I wasn't prepared for what waited behind those doors.

The doors loomed ahead, pristine at first glance, but as we approached, I caught a faint scorched scent—metal and ozone—like someone had run a torch too close and tried to polish it clean.

They parted without a sound, but inside—chaos.

Not theatrical chaos—but *investigative* chaos.

An army of IA personnel filled the Chairman's office, moving with precision—scanning surfaces with finger-length emitters, speaking in clipped technical phrases. Droids hovered near the jagged edge of the panoramic window, projecting shimmering hard-light reconstructions of the room seconds before impact.

And that window—*shattered.* What had once framed the skyline of Falinvik was now a sawtoothed hole, sealed off with a translucent shield barrier that hummed softly, keeping the icy wind at bay.

My mind blanked for a moment.

This wasn't an ambush. The Chairman's office had been breached.

Breached.

The one place in the entire capital that was supposed to be untouchable. This wasn't just unexpected. It was unthinkable.

My mind reeled as it tried to catch up to what my eyes were seeing.

I kept my face neutral. *Let none of it show.*

My guide gestured me in. "Lead forensics officer is on-site. They've been waiting on you to take point. You've been cleared for Top-level access. It's your scene, sir."

I gave a curt nod, though my pulse hammered in my ears.

I knew what Kolve had said. Knew this was the assignment.

But nothing prepared me for this.

This wasn't just a break-in. This was a message. Whoever had done this hadn't just broken into the most secure office in the nation—they wanted us to *see* it.

My guide turned and left before I could ask anything else.

I stepped into the room, keeping my posture straight, my expression unreadable.

Inside, I was still spinning. Recalculating.

Because if this was real—and it clearly *was*—then something in the heart of the *Stór-menni* was cracking. And I had just been handed the front-row seat.

"Someone went out through that window," a technician muttered, scanning the frame. "Or in. Or both. Still working on the trajectory matrix."

I nodded absently, already tuning him out. My eyes had drifted to the cluster of holo-screens hovering above the Chairman's desk—still glowing, still active.

Whoever broke in hadn't shut them down.

Or maybe the Chairman had left them running.

One display on the far wall flickered with motion—quiet, but unmistakably live. A broadcast.

The *Leikr* finals.

Someone had tuned it in. The sound was muted, but I didn't need audio to feel the weight of the moment playing out onscreen. The glossy stadium camera feeds panned across roaring crowds and blazing torchlight. A familiar orchestration boomed, the showy anthem of Clan pride. I was about to turn away—

When the storm clouds rolled in.

Inside the stadium dome.

The skies above the arena floor blackened with a cinematic flourish, and even with the muted audio, a bass-heavy pulse vibrated the speakers.

What the—

The camera shakily zoomed in on the center platform. A figure descended through the storm like something out of a myth—dripping in *Stór-menni* regalia, backlit by lightning. And then, a dramatic reveal.

Liam Jarnulf.

My eyes narrowed. Not dead, then. Not banished. *Staging a resurrection in the middle of the Leikr finals.*

As his clothing changed to normal Clan attire, he was saying something that clearly shocked the spectators at the stadium.

Suddenly, the crowd froze—not in awe, but in eerie synchronicity. All the civilians covered their ears at once, their mouths slack. Like a childhood game of not listening. But it wasn't a game.

It was coordinated control.

And there was only one answer. Only one who could have that much power. The Chairman.

My heart stuttered. Whatever Jarnulf was saying, it wasn't just a Resistance stunt—it was a move. A big one. And it made the Chairman nervous enough to flex his power.

I stepped closer to the screen.

Before I could process more, the feed abruptly cut out. The screen turned black.

Then the *Leikr* logo appeared in its place—gleaming white on red. Official. Sanitized. Controlled. They were trying to smother whatever had just happened.

I swallowed hard and glanced around the room.

The other IA agents hadn't seemed to notice. They were still focused on finishing the window scans and energy diagnostics. I turned away from the screen, a new urgency rising in my chest.

The stunt at the stadium. Jarnulf's return. The break-in at the Chairman's office.

Was it connected? Or just a disruption overlapping by chance?

I didn't know. But I needed to.

I crossed to the console and brought up the last accessed files. Redacted documents, high-clearance archives... most of it nonsense at first glance, but I knew the pattern. I'd seen it before. The layering of permissions, the misdirection. There was something buried beneath it all.

I lost myself in it—dragging open one access log, cross-referencing timestamps, overriding minor security flags, and peeling away layer after layer of misdirection. Minutes stretched. Outside the window, the city gleamed under the outer shield wall's soft flicker.

The forensic team began wrapping up. One by one, the droids powered down or zipped toward the corridor with samples. Analysts called out updates before vanishing into the hall. Within minutes, I was alone in the Chairman's office.

Just me... and the truth.

I sank into the high-backed chair and cracked my knuckles, scanning the chaos of the room and the Chairman's holo-screens. Whoever had broken in hadn't exactly been subtle—they'd blasted out the window and left the console glowing with a mess of half-open files.

Access history. A map of the city grid. I clicked through, hunting for traces of what they were after. A digital footprint. A clue.

The training logs were the only files I hadn't touched—standard mentorship reports, usually boilerplate. The kind of data no one would risk a breach of the Chairman's office to retrieve. So I'd ignored them.

But then one tab caught my eye.

It sat dead center in the window stack, partially buried beneath the logs, pinned open like someone had forgotten to close it.

My fingers hovered over it, expecting more standard trainee reports. With a flick of my wrist, I expanded it.

A name blinked across the top of the file.

Subject: Bahram Risan
Age: 68
Clan Designation: Sudri
Status: External Threat — Detain on Contact

I stared at the name for a full three seconds before my mind accepted what my eyes were seeing.

Bahram.

My grandfather.

My heart pounded in my chest.

My father had reshaped our name after the Chairman's rise, softening Risan into Rees to sound more Nordri. Safer. Less *Sudri.*

Just a practical decision, given the times. But the name on this file hadn't changed.

The screen seemed to blur at the edges, the cold in the room suddenly too sharp, too invasive. I blinked hard and scrolled down.

"Subject has attempted unauthorized entry into Falinvik every year since the city was sealed. Motivations unclear. Claims he seeks to ascertain the safety and whereabouts of his son and grandson. Recommend continued border denial. Should the subject breach the entry perimeter, detain immediately and transfer for interrogation."

I couldn't breathe.

I read it again. And again. The words were clinical, mechanical. A man—a *family*—reduced to bullet points and warnings. They'd branded him a threat. A man whose only crime was wanting to see his son and grandson. To see *me.*

A green icon blinked in the corner of the file:

[**SECURITY FOOTAGE:** BORDER INCIDENT — RECORD NUMBER: 14.2.41 A.C.]

I tapped it.

The holo flickered. A border checkpoint loaded—a towering gate flanked by armored guards. The snowy ground was scuffed with boot prints. Then I saw him. Frailer than I remembered, but still proud. A thick scarf wrapped around his neck, shoulders squared despite the wind. His voice was muffled, but the words were clear:

"He is my blood. My family. You cannot keep me from them."

A guard shoved him backward. Hard. My breath hitched.

He fell—no, was thrown—into the snow. Another guard raised his stun baton.

But then, figures emerged from the shadows. Two others—Sudri by the look of them—rushed forward, intercepting the strike. Voices rose in protest. One shouted in ancient Egyptian.

The clip ended abruptly.

I sat there, the afterimage of my grandfather sprawled in the snow burned into my vision.

He was alive.

He was alive.

The name in the file wasn't a historical record. This wasn't some decades-old report buried in the archives. It was a living record. A warning. An *active* flag.

Bahram had come to the gates. Falinvik's gates. Risked everything, again and again, just to find us.

Not once. *Every year.*

Through snow, through checkpoints, through armed guards. And they had labeled him a threat. Beaten him for trying.

But still, he came.

He wasn't a ghost. Not just some faded memory of a man laughing through mouthfuls of honeyed dates, rocking me to sleep with songs in a language I'd nearly forgotten.

He was real.

Still out there. Still searching.

I clenched my fists so tightly that the skin stretched white over the bone.

I didn't have many memories of my childhood before the mentorship program, but the few I did have had him in them. His visits had brought noise and warmth to our house, his voice rippling through the air like a stream—fluid, lyrical, alive. I used to speak Egyptian as a toddler, my mother had told me, because I loved how he smiled when I did.

That all vanished when the visits stopped. When the Chairman ascended.

And now I knew why.

He hadn't left us. He'd been *locked out.*

I slammed my palm against the console. The holo-image

quivered.

I wanted to scream. To rip this place apart. To break every lens that had watched me grow into a tool they could wield. Every silent corridor, every false medal they pinned to my chest. All of it.

I'd learned that the Chairman had lied. I'd seen it in data, in patterns, in whispers buried in reports. But this—*this* was personal. This was betrayal carved into the bones of my past.

He hadn't just kept the truth from everyone.

He'd kept *me* from my grandfather. The one good memory I had clung to all my life.

Erased my entire family like they were a threat to control or a distraction to eliminate. Either through his lies or the *Stór-menni* mentorship program. My grandfather, my mother, my father—

Thorne had tried to tell me. *Blood remembers.* His careful half-answer. It hadn't made sense to me. But now—now I understood.

Before I could fully process it, a red alert flared across the main interface, and an urgent, incessant beeping filled the room.

AUTHORIZATION REQUIRED – CITYWIDE DEFENSE SYSTEM INITIATION

Deploy Inner Shield Wall?

Confirm Authorization: **Y/N**

10 Seconds Until Auto-Deployment.

My heart thudded. It wasn't a flag on my access. This was an emergency protocol.

Unprompted, a live drone feed flickered to life on the holo-screen—internal surveillance, not part of the public broadcast. It showed the stadium's western wall erupting in a burst of fire and debris. Smoke poured into the air as figures in cloaks scrambled through the chaos.

One of them—

Looked like Elin.

She was unconscious, slumped in the arms of a tall figure moving fast through the smoke. Something about his stance, the shape of his build, tugged at my memory. Then it clicked.

Edvin. From the alley fight.

There was no mistaking her now. It was Elin. Her auburn hair spilled over his arms, catching the light as he shifted her weight for a better grip.

The alert blared again.

8 seconds remaining.

It wasn't a hypothetical now. The system wasn't asking whether to authorize a lockdown *in theory*.

It was asking whether to trap her.

Trap *them*.

I didn't move.

I had chased her for so long—through shadows, through the ruins she left in her wake. She had evaded me, exposed fractures I hadn't wanted to see, dragged me into questions I never meant to ask.

And now I was watching her escape.

Part of me still resented her for it. For setting this unraveling in motion. For forcing me to see the cracks in the world I'd sworn to uphold. Maybe even for being right.

The system pulsed again—louder this time, insistent.

Behind the alert, the holo-screen still showed the document I'd pulled up on my grandfather—Bahram Risan, branded an external threat by the man I had served without question.

The report didn't lie. The footage didn't lie.

This was the Chairman's console. His words. His orders.

And I had believed him—in all of it. Swallowed it. Repeated it. Enforced it.

I'd spent years becoming the perfect soldier in a broken system, blind to the fractures because I thought loyalty meant strength. Order. Control. But order built on silence and exile and the erasure of everything I once loved… that wasn't order. It was rot disguised as discipline.

Bahram had never abandoned us. He'd come back, year after

year, just to see if I was still alive. And each time, they'd turned him away. Beaten him. Covered it up.

Thorne had hinted at the truth. So had the files buried deep in the archives. And now I had seen it for myself.

The Chairman had not just lied to the world—he had stolen *my family*.

The red alert flared again, more urgent now.

AUTHORIZATION REQUIRED — CITYWIDE DEFENSE SYSTEM INITIATION

Deploy Inner Shield Wall?

Confirm Authorization: **Y/N**

5 Seconds Until Auto-Deployment.

If I tapped "yes," the inner shield wall would activate—an impenetrable perimeter sealing Falinvik from within. No one in. No one out.

I'd trap them. Elin. The Resistance.

And *myself*.

Tapping *yes* would restore everything I'd worked for, giving me my old life back and the promotion I had always hoped for. I'd be the one who saved the capital and captured the interlopers. The *Stórmenni* would laud me as a rising star. Loyal. Trusted. Reforged in fire. It was what I'd spent so many of my days, nights, blood, and sweat working toward.

But at what cost?

The lies wouldn't stop. The truth would stay buried. My grandfather's name would remain stamped with red ink, his memory distorted in the records—his love for us rewritten as a threat.

And my connection to him? To my past? That had already been severed. Hidden beneath secrets and lies. A mentorship program. A demand for absolute loyalty.

Tapping *no*... that was something else entirely.

It would make me an instant outlaw, and I would be lucky to

escape with my life. I'd be a traitor. I would lose everything I'd built—every rank, every alliance, every carefully measured step of my career. But maybe it would give me a chance to rebuild something real. And it would certainly be a small but very satisfying act of retribution.

And if I could get out of this city before anyone discovered what I'd done. Maybe steal one of the Chairman's AHVs from the private landing pad just outside. With its advanced tech and built-in authority clearance, I could go anywhere.

And I could find him. *Bahram*. My grandfather.

If I let this moment slip past me—if I answered *yes*—I'd never escape. The inner shield would come down, and I'd be trapped.

And I'd never know the full truth. Or see my grandfather.

The screen pulsed again. *Four seconds.*

I stared at the prompt.

This wasn't about Elin anymore.

This was about *me.*

About everything that had been taken from me and everything I still had left to reclaim.

The countdown ticked to *three*.

My fingers hovered.

I thought of the oaths I'd taken. The evaluations. The years of silence drills, edict learning, and loyalty conditioning that taught us to obey without question. My fingers twitched—not from hesitation, but from the ghost of who I used to be.

Then, for the first time in my life, I didn't reach for what was expected of me.

I reached for what was mine—and I pressed *No.* For my grandfather. For me. For the truth they never wanted me to see.

TWENTY-EIGHT

The Burn

AEDAN

I woke to pain—and the acrid sting of scorched air. For a moment, I didn't know where I was. Then it crashed back: the corridor, the battle... *Elin.*

The corridor spun above me as I blinked through the haze. My head throbbed, and I couldn't tell if the fluttering light on the walls was real—or just seared into my vision. Then I heard the sound—the faintest thud. A body hitting the floor.

I turned just in time to see Elin collapse to her knees.

"Elin!"

I scrambled forward as she crumpled completely, hitting the scorched floor hard. I reached for her—

And recoiled with a curse. She was blazing hot. My fingers barely brushed her skin before a searing jolt ran up my arm.

I looked up, desperate. "She's burning. I can't—I can't touch her!"

My heart pounded as I scanned the corridor for something—someone—anything that could help. Around me, the others were beginning to stir. Claire groaned somewhere behind me, Edvin coughed and muttered something incoherent. Reo leaned against the wall, shaking his head like he was trying to shake loose a memory.

That's when I saw him.

The Chairman lay in a heap near the far wall, golden chainmail gleaming dully in the aftermath. His cloak was gone, his body twisted at an unnatural angle. He wasn't moving.

What in Helheim had happened?

I turned back to Elin.

Her breathing was shallow, her skin glowing softly like the heat was coming from somewhere inside her. Whatever she had done—whatever she had unleashed—it hadn't left her untouched.

"Sigrid, help!" I shouted, turning to find her. "She's burning up. We need to cool her—fast."

Sigrid, still dazed but rising to her feet, stumbled over to me, her expression shifting from exhaustion to sharp focus the second she laid eyes on Elin.

"Don't touch her skin," Sigrid warned, kneeling beside me. "Not with bare hands. She's in *Ljós* overdrive. "

I blinked at her. "Her what is in overdrive?"

"*Ljós*," she said quickly, already scanning Elin's condition. "I don't have time to explain it right now. We need to cool her down immediately."

Ljós. The word caught in my mind like a splinter. I'd never heard it before. But Sigrid said it like it explained everything. And somehow, in that moment, it did.

Sigrid paused, thinking fast. "The snow. We need to get her outside. Into the snow."

"She collapsed," I said, my voice cracking. "I think she... she knocked the Chairman out with it. Whatever *it* is."

My eyes flicked to the heap of gold armor nearby. The Chairman —no longer the terrifying force he had been moments ago.

Sigrid reached into her cloak and pulled free a wrapped cloth, laying it gently against Elin's cheek, testing. Then she turned, her voice softer now. "Wrap her in something thick. We'll carry her that way."

Across the corridor, another cry shattered the stillness.

"*Aylen*!"

I turned to see Nodin pushing himself upright. He staggered toward the girl who had been standing beside the Chairman—the girl he'd called by name. Her body was limp now, her skin far too pale against the dark floor. Her eyes were half open, glassy.

Nodin dropped beside her, breath hitching like a snapped wire.

"No—no, Aylen, please—"

His hands hovered over her, shaking, as if afraid she might shatter beneath them.

"She's cold," he said, his voice cracking. "She's not breathing."

Sigrid moved to him next, placing two fingers gently on Aylen's neck, then her forehead. I watched her expression shift the second her fingers brushed Aylen's neck.

A beat of silence.

Then came the quiet tilt of her head, heavy with meaning. "I'm so... so sorry, Nodin. I don't think... there's much I can do."

My mother turned away, one hand clamping over her mouth. My father swore softly under his breath and looked down.

"She tried," my mother said hoarsely. "We all saw her. She was trying to fight it."

Sigrid placed her hand on Nodin's shoulder as he clutched Aylen to his chest. He didn't move. He just stared at Aylen's face like he could will her back to life.

The air in the corridor shifted—heavier now. Grief hung between us like smoke, thick and silent.

But then Elin let out a shallow gasp—barely audible, barely there.

My attention snapped back to her.

She was still incandescent, still searing from within.

My mother stepped beside me without a word, her face pale and tight with concern. She unfastened her cloak with steady hands and offered it to me.

"Use this," she said.

I wrapped it around Elin's shoulders, careful not to let my skin touch hers. Her body was too hot, too wrong. Whatever this was, it wasn't just exhaustion—it was like the light she'd unleashed had never stopped burning. She didn't stir at my efforts. My chest tightened. It was like holding a star that had scorched itself hollow.

Behind us, Claire had pulled herself to her feet, leaning heavily against the wall. Edvin groaned and sat up.

"Are we... alive?" he muttered.

"Barely," Claire said. "And we're still trapped."

She was right. The barriers were still up—both ends of the corridor sealed. Through the far shield, I saw Thyra and the guards watching, motionless. She hadn't moved since the moment the shields came down. Her eyes were locked on us—on me.

For a heartbeat, I saw the same fierce focus she'd had the night we broke into the Chairman's office. The same unspoken understanding. Whatever side she stood on, she knew what was happening here. And maybe, just maybe, she was hoping we'd make it out.

She gave a subtle nod—quiet but deliberate. I met it with one of my own. It was all we had, and it was enough.

"We've got to move. The corridor won't stay quiet for long," my father said, glancing around for any possible solution.

Reo, still kneeling with one hand against the wall, reached into a pocket hidden inside his cloak.

He pulled out a small circular disc.

"For emergencies," he said as if announcing a cup of tea.

Edvin, who had been eyeing the wall like he was calculating whether to hurl himself against it, blinked.

"You absolute legend," he said, eyes wide. "How did you even get an explosive disc in here? I was this close to ramming myself at that outside wall like a heroic meat shield. But now..." He placed a hand over his chest. "I think I love you."

Reo arched a brow. "That's sudden."

Edvin clutched his chest dramatically. "You rescued me from a very poor life choice."

Claire groaned. "Can we blow the wall now, *please*?"

Reo nodded once. "Take cover, everyone. And brace yourselves."

The others gathered close, supporting one another. Nodin stood last, cradling Aylen's body in his arms, his expression unreadable.

Reo pressed the disc to the base of the wall. A low whine built in the air, barely audible.

The world snapped white—then *roared.*

The wall exploded outward with a muffled *boom*, unleashing a rush of cold wind and swirling snow. Relief and icy dread hit me at once. *At least we were out.*

I didn't stop to think. I carried Elin into the snow, letting it rush around her like water. The instant the chill hit her skin, her glow began to dim—just slightly, but enough. She was still alive. Still blistering. But she was alive.

I dropped to my knees beside her, my breath fogging the air, and whispered the only thing I could.

"Please stay with us, Elin. *Please.*"

Her heat still radiated through the fabric of the cloak, but she was cooling—slowly—the rise and fall of her chest barely there.

That's when I heard it.

A distinct, high-pitched whine. Shrill, too smooth for wind and too sharp for engines.

My heart stuttered.

"SASUs," Claire breathed. "Incoming!"

Security Aerial Surveillance Units. I'd seen them once before during my capture in Auor—swift, vicious things with red optics and offensive capabilities. They moved like insects in the air. Each operated like an extension of a hive—calculating, merciless, and precise. Not meant to warn. Only to observe, track, subdue, or kill.

"They'll box us in!" Sigrid snapped, scanning the sky. "We need cover!"

That's when I remembered.

I fumbled at my belt, fingers shaking as I tore open the pouch I'd nearly forgotten. "Shields," I said. "I grabbed them off the team platform."

Six compact loops—cold, familiar metal against my palm. I hadn't grabbed them for nostalgia. I'd grabbed the shields because I knew exactly how fast things could go wrong.

I tossed one each to my parents, Reo, Claire, and Sigrid. "Push the seal with your palm—loop to the thumb!"

Claire caught hers mid-air. "You beautiful, overprepared nerd."

They put them on immediately, practiced hands snapping the devices into place. As the shields flared to life, I felt something sharp and familiar rise inside me—not panic, but purpose. The *Leikr* had taught me how to survive chaos. This... this was just another trial. Except this time, the score didn't matter. Only getting out did.

The first SASU shrieked past overhead, a red-targeting light sweeping the snowbank just behind us.

Edvin looked up. "We're sitting ducks if we don't move!"

"I've got Elin," he said before I could argue, lifting her again into his arms like she weighed nothing.

Nodin hadn't spoken. He still carried Aylen, his arms locked around her, ignoring the pain written all over his face and his blistered hand. He wouldn't let her go.

The others took point—my parents, Reo, Claire. Their shields locked into a rough front line, intercepting the first barrage of fire as the SASUs swarmed from above, a half dozen glinting drones weaving together like a net.

None of them reached for their *megin*—not my parents, Sigrid, or Reo. It wasn't hesitation. It was depletion. The illusion at the stadium, the mental onslaught from the Chairman—it had drained them. Whatever strength they had left, they were saving for survival.

Sigrid pressed beside me, shield raised, her jaw tight. "We have to punch through. Head west—toward the fjord and AHV platforms!"

We ran, the wind lashing against our faces, the slope shallow but treacherous under the churn of snow and fire. I reached for my *megin* —half expecting it to be gone, burned out like the others'. But it surged.

Still there. Still potent.

Whatever the Chairman had injected into me—whatever twisted

boost he'd buried in my veins—it hadn't faded yet. Maybe it should've terrified me. But right now, it was the only reason we might survive.

I flung debris into the air—shards of metal, shattered stones, even a half-buried holo banner—sending them spinning skyward like shrapnel. One struck a SASU head-on. It spiraled and exploded in a blossom of flame.

Another hissed downward. Reo's shield flared as it took the hit and held.

But there were too many of them. We weren't going to make it. Not in time.

Then something slammed into the sky like a thunderclap.

I looked up—and for a heartbeat, I thought we were done. A shadow dropped fast—an HTV, black and unmarked, engines flaring hot. It didn't hesitate.

It opened fire—

Straight into the SASUs.

Not at us.

Blue flashes lit the sky as rounds tore through the SASUs. One exploded mid-dive. The rest scattered, recalibrating.

The HTV angled lower—and the rear hatch dropped open.

Two figures leapt out. I didn't recognize them. But the others did.

"Gabriel!" Claire shouted. "And Bae—*oh, thank gods*!"

I stared at them, confused—but no one else hesitated. The relief on my parents' faces said everything.

"They did it," Reo murmured. "They got Gabriel out."

The HTV hovered above us, continuing to lay down cover fire.

Gabriel sprinted forward, cutting across the field between us and the HTV, his cloak flaring behind him. Bae skidded to a stop behind him, planting her feet in the snow. With one swift motion, she opened a portal. A shimmer ignited in the air—oval, gold-rimmed, pulsing with warm light.

On the other side lay a garage. A way out.

"Move!" she shouted. "Through the portal—go!"

My parents were the first to reach it, shouting back at us but moving fast. Reo was close behind them, helping Claire, who had started limping.

The front group disappeared into the light, swallowed by safety.

But we were still too far behind.

Gabriel reached us, his arm slinging under Nodin's to help with Aylen. "*Presque là*!" Gabriel shouted in his native French, encouraging us that we were almost there. "Come on, *vite*—move!"

A shot cracked the air—sharp, final.

Bae screamed, stumbling as red bloomed across her shoulder like spilled fire.

Gabriel surged toward her—

"No!"

She staggered toward the portal, but her knees buckled—

Mr. Grady's hand shot out from the other side and yanked her in just before she fell.

Gabriel's voice was raw. "*Bae*!"

But it was too late. The portal closed with a *crack* like a slammed door, leaving only swirling snow and no answer.

At the same moment, the HTV above us rocked sideways. A blast hit its undercarriage from a second aircraft—the telltale black profile of an approaching *Stór-menni* HTV.

Our ride peeled away, fire trailing from its rear engine.

Gone.

We stood in the open. Snow swirling. SASUs regrouping.

No portal. No HTV.

Just five of us—and two unconscious bodies in our arms.

Edvin swore. A cluster of approaching guards was now advancing through the smoke and snow.

My hands trembled.

Then Nodin looked up, his voice raw. "My HTV."

We all turned to him.

"I crashed it in the woods. Just on the other side of the fjord here. If Gabriel can fix it... we might have a chance."

Gabriel's eyes narrowed. "*Quels dégâts?* What kind of damage are we talking about?"

"Electrical, I think. But not irrecoverable. It's the old Vestri model —manual override still works."

Sigrid's expression tightened. "We have no choice. If it flies, we take it."

"There's an old pier," Nodin said, winded. "Just a little farther down the coast. It used to be a shipping entry point—one of the only ones near the shield wall. Before I came, I studied every possible entry and exit. If we can cross the frozen water, we'll be close to the crash site. As long as the Inner Shield Wall hasn't come down... it might be our only shot."

"Inner Shield Wall?" Edvin asked.

"It is the emergency shield wall to protect the city when attacked. It lets nothing in or out. And I'm sure the *Stór-menni* are trying to deploy it as we speak, given that their Chairman is lying unconscious in a hallway at the stadium," Sigrid explained.

"And if it's down?" I asked.

"Then we die on a frozen dock," Nodin answered.

I looked at the people around me—wounded, freezing, burdened by the weight of two unconscious bodies.

We had no choice.

"Then let's run."

And we ran.

The old pier jutted out like a frozen finger from the coastline, slick with ice and weather-beaten from disuse. The wind knifed off the fjord, stinging my face and stealing what little air I had left. Snow lashed our hoods, turning every blink into grit.

Sigrid was the first to slow, throwing an arm out to stop the rest of us. "Wait—don't step out yet."

We all hesitated near the edge of the wooden dock, the frozen surface of the fjord stretching before us in pale, moonlit silence.

"The Inner Shield Wall," Nodin reminded us, his breath white in the air. "We don't know if it's up or not."

Gabriel scanned the sky. "And we don't want to find out the hard way."

Sigrid stepped forward and picked up a jagged shard of drone casing from the snow. Without a word, she hurled it off the edge of the pier.

We all watched as it sailed outward—clearing the lip of the dock—and didn't bounce back. No sparks. No resistance.

It landed on the frozen fjord with a sharp *crack*, skidding a few feet before coming to rest.

We stared.

"No repulsion field," Sigrid said slowly. "The Inner Shield Wall hasn't been deployed yet."

Gabriel exhaled. "*Là—regardez.*" He pointed toward the edge of the pier, where the ice shimmered faintly against the open air. "A structural gap in the Outer Shield Wall. Old freight access, I think. It's low, *étroit*—but it's open."

Nodin gave a short nod, unsurprised. "That's the one. Figured it might still be operational. Normally, there's a guard posted—but I gambled they'd be pulled for the *Leikr* finals."

"It's barely above the waterline," Edvin noted.

"So we go *under* the outer wall," I said, my chest tightening. "On the ice."

Sigrid gave a tight nod. "We'll have to move quickly—before anyone realizes there's a gap."

Edvin shifted Elin's weight in his arms with a grimace. "Great. Ice-walking under enemy fire. This just keeps getting better."

"The current runs strong here," Sigrid said grimly. "River meets the fjord just beneath this stretch. Ice never settles right."

That explained it. The frost shimmered differently here—thinner, almost translucent in places, like a cracked mirror stretched over black water. And the snow... it wasn't as deep as it should've been.

Nodin followed my gaze. "Shield field causes it," he murmured. "Outer Shield deflects anything light. Snow hits it and bounces back a few feet—then the wind takes over. Most of it piles into uneven drifts a few yards off."

"Leaves this halo zone," Sigrid added. "Light cover only. Easier to spot cracks. Easier to slip, too."

"Stay low. Distribute your weight," Nodin said, his voice shaking slightly. "We cross fast, or not at all."

We stepped onto the ice, but within minutes I saw it—the hairline splinters webbing under Edvin's boots.

"Too heavy," Sigrid snapped. "You need to shift weight. *Now.*"

Gabriel knelt in the snow, yanked off his cloak, and spread it over the ice. "On the cloaks—drag them. Better than cracking the ice, *non*?"

Nodin followed, unfastening his own and doing the same for Aylen. "Keep them moving. Gently. No hard footfalls."

Together, Edvin and Gabriel dragged Elin forward. I stepped next to Nodin to help him with Aylen. He refused to let her go—but allowed my help. He moved slower, steadier, his face twisted in silent pain.

The SASUs hissed in the air behind us, circling. But as we moved deeper onto the ice, their fire couldn't reach us. The outer shield wall—though invisible—blocked their fire. They tracked us, but couldn't shoot.

It bought us time.

We didn't speak. Just moved—slow, silent, lungs tight with cold. The frost clawed through every layer, numbing fingers and faces alike. Beneath us, the ice moaned with long, echoing groans, splintering in places like it might give way at any step. Even the snow felt brittle, crackling underfoot like glass.

Then—relief. Sudden, jarring.

Our feet struck solid ground.

We stumbled, almost disbelieving, onto the other side—scrambling over jagged snowbanks and into the tangle of woods beyond. Branches scraped our arms, and the ground sloped sharply, but no one stopped—not until we saw it.

Nodin's HTV.

It loomed out of the snowbank like a buried beast—tilted, scorched, and half-swallowed by the forest. The hull dented but intact.

"There!" Nodin called out, his voice hoarse. "That's it!"

We clambered to it, Gabriel already darting forward to the sealed side panel. He slapped his palm against it—nothing happened.

"*Allez, mon vieux*," Gabriel muttered to the machine, coaxing it to talk to him. "*Parle-moi...*"

"What's he doing?" I asked, blinking snow from my eyes.

"Technopath," Sigrid said. "Just give him space."

Gabriel's fingers traced the panel—tapping, adjusting, reading the *megin* nodes hidden beneath the plating. Sparks flickered around his knuckles. His brow furrowed.

Behind us, the hum of engines grew louder.

"*Stór-menni* HTV incoming," Claire shouted. "We need cover now!"

"We don't have cover!" Edvin shouted back. "We have a pile of snow and hope!"

"*C'est tout qu'il faut*—all you ever need," Gabriel growled—and the hatch hissed open.

We surged inside.

The interior lights flickered, systems glitching from cold and disrepair. Gabriel threw himself into the pilot's seat, ripped open the diagnostics panel, and plunged his fingers into the conduit.

Energy sparked. The engines coughed.

"Gabriel?" Sigrid said sharply.

"*Ne parle pas*," he gritted out. "She needs some... encouragement."

Reo leaned over him. "Can I assist?"

"Only if you speak fluent *stubborn Vestri diagnostics*."

The ship sputtered. Then lurched.

"*Ça y est*! We've got power!" Gabriel yelled. "Strap in, *maintenant*!"

Sigrid and I moved fast, carrying Elin into the HTV's small medbay. She was still burning beneath the cloak, her skin pale and too still. We eased her into one of the emergency stabilizers—one of the compact meditech pods with biofeedback controls—and I held her steady while Sigrid snapped the clamps into place.

"Hold her head—gently," Sigrid instructed. I obeyed without question, fingers trembling as I brushed sweat-damp hair from her forehead. Her breathing was shallow, but there.

Across from us, Nodin was already strapping Aylen onto the second cot. He didn't speak. Just moved in silence, his hands steady but slow, as if every buckle was a prayer.

Sigrid turned back to the panel and barked commands into the pod's interface, calibrating Elin's vitals as the engines roared louder overhead.

"Will she make it?" I asked, my voice barely audible over the engines.

Sigrid didn't answer right away. Her eyes stayed on the stabilizer screen, tracking Elin's vitals, her jaw tight.

"I don't know," she said finally. "She needs Brigitta. If we're lucky, Brigitta is already in Auor—left a few days ago with Mia and Joel to deliver a Bubble Shield Wall to the Resistance there."

The ground shook. A *Stór-menni* blast clipped the edge of the HTV, rocking us sideways.

"GABRIEL!" Edvin yelled from the co-pilot seat.

The engines screamed—and lifted.

Snow exploded outward. The HTV groaned, then surged into the air, climbing in a zigzag as the trees fell away beneath us.

"YES!" Edvin whooped, throwing one fist skyward even as the cabin rattled violently.

I glanced back through the rear viewport—nothing but swirling smoke and distant treetops. The *Stór-menni* HTVs had peeled away, banking hard toward Falinvik. They wouldn't follow us into *Mannlegur* airspace. Couldn't. Not without revealing their existence—something their own edicts forbade.

The fjord fell away in a blur of white and shadow, the jagged coastline vanishing beneath us. Falinvik was already lost behind the shimmer of the Outer Shield Wall, its towering curve cloaking the city like a mirage. All that remained in view were the snow-drenched peaks of the surrounding mountains—vast, silent, and ancient—rising like frozen sentinels above the icy expanse below.

I gripped the edge of the seat, heart still pounding, lungs aching—but for the first time in months, I wasn't trapped.

Not behind an energy barrier. Not on a broadcast. Not inside Ginnungagap.

No *Hepta Baugr*. No arena. No crowd. No *Leikr*.

Just the open sky and the roar of an engine that I chose to be inside. Whatever else waited beyond these mountains—this moment was *mine*.

We didn't stop climbing—not until the radar showed we were way beyond the city's reach, and the dark sky finally opened wide in front of us.

Only then did anyone exhale. We were clear. And for now, Falinvik was behind us.

But even with freedom stretched out before us—all I could see was Elin's face, pale against the dark. And that light beneath her skin... still burning.

TWENTY-NINE

The Return

ELIN

Warmth. That was the first thing I felt.

It curled around me like a soft blanket, anchoring me to the moment—real and safe in a way I hadn't felt in days. My eyelids fluttered open to golden light, flickering against rough-hewn wooden walls. The air smelled of woodsmoke, sea salt, and something herbal—crushed lavender, maybe, or thyme. A slow grinding sound scraped softly nearby, rhythmic and soothing.

I turned my head toward it.

Brigitta sat beside a stone hearth, hunched over a wide clay bowl as she ground herbs in slow, practiced circles. Her blue woolen dress brushed the floor, and the white apron tied around her waist was smudged with leaves and powdery petals. Her braid—light brown with threads of silver—curved down her back like a ribbon. When she noticed me stir, her head jerked up, and her face lit with a quiet, radiant joy.

"Oh, thank Freyja," she whispered, voice thick. She set down the pestle and crossed to me in two quick steps. "You're awake."

My throat felt like it had been lined with ash. I opened my mouth, but no sound came—only the brittle rasp of breath.

Brigitta knelt beside me and lifted a mug to my lips. Steam curled into the air. The tea was warm and earthy, with a hint of honey and something dark beneath—bitter but grounding. I drank, and it filled me slowly, a tether pulling me fully back into my body.

"You've been out for nearly two days," she said softly, brushing a strand of hair from my forehead. "We were starting to worry."

My eyes wandered across the room—wooden beams, the flicker of firelight, the worn wool blankets tucked around me. Outside the window, I thought I caught the glint of ocean light and the faint rush of wind through evergreens.

"Where... am I?" I whispered.

Brigitta smiled, her voice like sea glass worn smooth. "Back on Auor," she said. "A Resistance safehouse in the northern part near Lighthouse Park."

Auor. The word alone carried weight—cool wind, soft earth, safety.

My lungs shook with a breath I hadn't known I was holding. We'd made it. Somehow, through fire and frost and darkness—we were home.

But even as the word settled over me, the memory of running through darkened woods with Clan Hunters on our heels stirred beneath it like a warning.

"Is it... safe?" I asked, my voice thin. "Last time I was here, we barely got out alive. And you—Brigitta, what are you doing here?"

She gave a small, knowing smile. "I came to deliver a Bubble Shield Wall," she said. "The Resistance has already installed it across half the island. You're safe now."

The words sank into me like warmth through frost. *Safe*. And for the first time in what felt like forever, the word didn't feel like a lie.

But the quiet didn't hold.

Just beneath it, something cracked—softly at first, then all at once—as another memory rose to the surface, uninvited and unrelenting.

Aylen's glow, burning and fading. The Chairman's voice—a blade in my mind. The flood of light tearing through me, more than I could hold—*Ljós* spilling out of me like fire. My vision tilting, falling, the world white-hot and gone.

I grabbed Brigitta's wrist, my voice raw. "The others... are they...?"

"They're fine," she said quickly, her hand tightening over mine. "They made it out. You saved them, Elin."

Relief hit me like a wave, knocking the air from my lungs.

Then—his voice.

"Elin?"

I looked up just as Aedan stepped into the room, his wavy hair disheveled, his sea-blue eyes wide and rimmed with exhaustion. He crossed the space to me in three strides, dropping to his knees beside the bed.

"You're okay," he breathed, like he didn't believe it until he saw it for himself. "You're actually okay."

My chest tightened at the rawness in his voice. I swallowed, the words catching at first before they made it out—quiet, but steady. "I'm here."

His eyes closed for a moment, just long enough for me to see the weight he'd been carrying. When they opened again, they were softer, but no less intense.

He reached for my hand and held it gently, like he thought I might shatter.

His touch was warm, familiar. Steady in a way that made my chest ache. I'd imagined this moment—hoped for it in the back of my mind when everything else had gone quiet. But seeing the pain etched into his face now, the worry still lingering in his eyes—it struck me harder than I expected.

"You don't know what it was like... seeing you go down like that."

His voice cracked at the edges, and something twisted in my chest. I wanted to say something—anything—to take that pain from him. To let him know that I was still here, that I'd fought to come back. But all I could do was squeeze his hand and hope he could feel it through my silence.

A voice called from down the hall. “Aedan! The med officer needs you. It’s about the injection readings—we can’t decrypt them without you.”

He didn’t move right away. His grip tightened.

“I’ll go tell the others you’re awake,” he said, his voice low, reluctant. “And I’ll deal with whatever this is. But I’ll be back. I promise.”

His eyes lingered on mine—longer than they should have if he meant to move quickly—and in that pause, something passed between us. Something that had been building since the day we met. There was still so much unsaid between us. Still so much I didn’t understand. But I felt the gravity of him in that moment, quiet and real and undeniable.

Then, gently, he leaned down and pressed a soft kiss to my forehead.

It was nothing and everything all at once. The kind of touch that said *I’m here—I almost lost you*—in the same breath.

It was so simple, and yet my heart stuttered.

When he pulled back, I could still feel it—his warmth, the tremor beneath it, the echo of something neither of us was ready to name.

When he stood, his voice carried toward the door. “She’s awake! Claire, Mia, Joel—get in here!”

And then he turned and strode out of the room as the others rushed in.

They poured in like a tide returning to shore—Claire, Mrs. Grady, Mr. Grady—and then came Mia and Joel.

The moment I saw them, something inside me cracked open.

Mia’s long, dark hair and familiar intelligent eyes, Joel’s crooked grin even as his scarf hung halfway off—just the sight of them brought a rush of warmth so sudden it felt like sunlight breaking through a storm.

Home. They were home. Or maybe *they* were what home had always meant.

Tears welled in my eyes before I could stop them. I hadn’t

realized how much I'd missed them until now—how much I needed their presence to tether me back to who I was before Falinvik, before the Chairman, before everything had changed.

Claire reached me first, crouching at the bedside, her eyes brimming but dry. "Hey," she said softly. "You scared the hell out of us."

Mrs. Grady folded me into a warm, gentle hug that smelled like cedar and cloves. "Oh, sweet girl," she whispered. "We thought... we thought we'd lost you."

Mr. Grady stood behind her, steady and silent. His nod said everything.

Then Mia flung herself onto the edge of the bed, half-laughing, half-crying. "You ridiculous, self-sacrificing, beautiful lunatic," she said, pulling me into a fierce hug. "Don't ever do that again."

"Seconded," Joel chimed in, plopping dramatically into the chair beside me. "Once we heard what you did, I almost made a shrine. Mia vetoed it, which I still think was a mistake."

I gave a rough laugh. "A shrine?"

"With candles," he said solemnly. "And a picture of you mid-glow. I was gonna write poetry."

"You write poetry now?"

"Tragedy unlocks my creative side."

Laughter rolled around the room, and for a moment, I let it hold me. Their voices, their faces—safe. Alive. It was everything.

Just as Joel launched into an exaggerated retelling of how he almost built the shrine, the door creaked open again.

I looked up just as McHaill stepped into the room, his coat dusted with snow and his expression as unreadable as ever.

"Hope I'm not interrupting," he said, eyes sweeping across the group before landing on me.

"Not at all," Mrs. Grady said, stepping aside to give him room.

"You're a hard one to keep down," McHaill said to me, his tone gruff but not unkind. "Good to see you up."

"I feel like I was hit by a hovercraft," I admitted.

He gave a dry chuckle. "You kind of were."

Something in his expression shifted, and before I could ask, he added, "I figured you should know—we got Gabriel."

The words landed like a breath I didn't know I was holding.

Gabriel. Safe.

Relief surged through me, swift and overwhelming. After everything—the chaos at the stadium, the blur of waking to a world I didn't recognize—it was the first clean, bright piece of news.

They'd done it. They'd brought him home.

I let out a breath I hadn't realized I was holding, my chest loosening for the first time since I woke up. "Seriously? That's amazing."

My eyes widened. "Wait—how did it go? Everyone safe?"

"His rescue was cleaner than your mission," McHaill said. "Gabriel helped make it a *lot* easier. By the time the team got in, he'd already started escaping on his own."

I blinked. "He—how?"

"They didn't know he was a Technopath," McHaill said, glancing toward the others. "They stuck him in a cell with an old electrical panel for the toilet system. Idiots didn't realize he could talk to it."

Joel made a low whistling sound. "So he hacked the detention center from the inside?"

McHaill nodded. "Accessed the entire layout. Used the infrastructure he mapped out during that Holo-lounge incident to tap into their systems. By the time we reached him, he'd already opened half the corridors and jammed their internal comms."

"And the guards?" I asked, breath catching.

"Completely outplayed," McHaill said. "Still don't know what hit them."

"And Bae?" I asked suddenly, heart rising. "Wasn't she with him?"

A small silence followed.

"She was," McHaill said, quieter now.

I sat up a little straighter. "What happened to her?"

Mr. Grady stepped closer to the bed and rested a hand gently on the frame. "She's all right," he assured quickly. "She's here in the safehouse. A few rooms down, resting."

I exhaled hard, the knot in my chest loosening just a little.

"She got shot," he continued, voice thickening slightly. "During the escape at the stadium."

My breath caught. "What?"

Mr. Grady nodded slowly. "After they heard we weren't back yet, she and Gabriel flew in on a Resistance HTV. They came to help us. Bae got her portal open and held it while the first wave of us went through—me, Dara, Reo, Claire."

He paused, eyes distant for a moment. "There were drones everywhere. SASUs. And a sniper. She took a hit to the shoulder while holding the portal steady. Would've gone down right there, but I—" he gave a rough exhale, "I was still close enough to reach back through and drag her in just before she collapsed. Got her through just in time."

My chest ached. "And after that?"

"The portal closed," he said quietly. "There was no going back."

"But she's going to be okay?"

"She will be," he said. "They said it missed anything vital. She was lucid by the time the medics got to her. Stubborn, too. Kept apologizing for not holding it longer."

I nodded slowly, throat tight. "I want to see her."

"You will," he said. "But let her rest a little longer. She's earned it."

A hush settled, warm and weighted. Then, as if cued by some unspoken rhythm, the others began to fill in the gaps—taking turns, as they pieced together the rest of the story for me—how we'd made it out of the stadium, out of Falinvik, while I lay unconscious, oblivious to it all. A battle with SASUs under a sky thick with smoke. A desperate sprint across a frozen river, the ice groaning beneath their boots. All of it leading to Nodin's broken HTV, half-buried in snow, their only hope of escape.

I listened, stunned, as the details unfolded like fragments of a dream I never lived but somehow carried in my chest. My mind reeled, trying to stitch it all together—but above everything, one feeling pulsed through me like a quiet current.

Gratitude.

For every soul in that room who had fought to get me home. And yet, even in their presence, one absence pulled at me like a missing note in a familiar song.

My eyes drifted to the doorway.

Nodin hadn't come yet.

Claire shifted beside me. "You're looking for him," she said gently.

I met her eyes. "Where is he?"

She hesitated, then moved closer, speaking just loud enough for only me to hear. The others were caught in Joel's latest performance, their laughter a soft veil.

"He waited as long as he could," she said quietly. "He wouldn't leave until he was sure you were safe. But Nodin... he has to go today."

I straightened slightly. "Go? Why?"

"He's running out of time," she said. "He has to return to the Vestri. The Solemn Vow he broke—it's growing worse. Brigitta has helped stabilize him so far, but if he stays any longer..."

Her voice faltered, then softened even more. "He's also bringing Aylen's body home. What happened to her... he took it hard."

I blinked, still catching up. "She didn't make it?"

Claire shook her head. "They tried everything, but the Chairman had drained her too much. There was nothing anyone could do."

She hesitated, her eyes flicking toward the others. They'd drifted into a low hum of conversation across the room—talk of transport schedules and missing supplies, the kind of planning that filled silence when no one wanted to feel it.

Then her gaze returned to me. "Aylen was the Vestri Chief's daughter. And..."

I felt the breath catch in my chest.

Claire met my eyes, steady and gentle. "She was his promised one."

The words hit like a cold wind.

"What?" My voice barely left my lips.

"They were betrothed," she said gently. "Since childhood. "

He never told me.

Not when we escaped through the metro tunnels. Not during my forging. Not in the moments between the chaos, when something fragile and unspoken passed between us like breath.

The ache that bloomed in my chest wasn't jealousy. It was sorrow. For what he had carried. For what he had lost. For what I hadn't seen until now.

"Is he still here?" I asked, barely holding my voice steady.

Claire nodded. "I think so. "

I pressed my hand to my chest. It was like I could still feel it—the echo of his *Ljós* brushing against mine.

Brigitta had been watching quietly from her chair, not intruding but ever-present. Now she stood, smoothing her apron. "If you're strong enough, a short walk would be good for you. I can walk you out." Then she added softly, "he's down by the small meadow."

I swung my legs over the edge of the bed. My body protested, muscles aching, but I pushed through it.

I had to see him. Before the chance slipped away. Before he was gone.

THE COLD MET ME LIKE AN OLD MEMORY—SHARP AND immediate as I stepped out into the midday light. My legs ached with every step, the lingering fatigue from the battle with the Chairman still clinging to my bones like frost. Two days of rest hadn't been nearly enough.

The sky was overcast, as it often was this time of year, painting the snow-draped landscape in a muted palette of gray and silver. The evergreens surrounding the meadow were heavy with frost, their branches bowed under the weight of the season. Wind whispered low through them, stirring flurries of powder into the air.

As I walked, breath fogging in the chill, I took in the full shape of the place. The Resistance safehouse was more than just the main farmhouse behind me—it was an old Nordic farmstead spread across the land like a memory rooted deep in the snow. Outbuildings and storage barns dotted the slope, their timbered walls bowed with age and snow, but smoke curled from some of their chimneys, and movement flickered behind frost-glazed windows. I spotted a pair of Resistance members emerging from one shed with crates in hand, while others crossed between buildings with tools or gear, their heads ducked against the cold. The farm might have been centuries old, but it was far from abandoned. It was alive with quiet purpose.

The trek across the snow-covered meadow was winding me, my breath coming in shallow puffs. Every muscle in my body protested, but I kept walking.

In the clearing ahead, I saw the dark silhouette of his HTV.

Nodin stood beside it, hunched slightly as he secured a large pack to the rear storage rails. The hover transport sat low in the snow, its undercarriage glowing dimly from the residual heat of preflight. A few other Resistance hover vehicles were scattered nearby—some being loaded, others being repaired. There was movement everywhere, quiet and focused. The Resistance was stirring again, regrouping. Noticeably bolder now with the BSW in place. Preparing for whatever came next.

He didn't see me at first.

I stopped just shy of the transport, hugging the cloak tighter around my shoulders. The cold was seeping in, deeper now. My vision swam a little at the edges, but I forced myself to stay upright.

Then he turned.

The moment his eyes landed on me, Nodin froze. His entire body stilled. For a breathless second, neither of us moved.

His expression shifted all at once—grief and fatigue crashing into something that looked almost like wonder. Or maybe relief. His shoulders sagged with it.

"Elli."

Just my name, carried like a breath across the snow.

I managed a step closer. Then another.

He crossed the remaining distance in two strides, reaching me just as my knees buckled slightly. His arms caught me instinctively, one hand gripping my elbow, the other steadying my back.

"You're freezing," he said, his voice rough with something more than concern. He guided me gently toward a pair of low, snow-dusted Resistance crates near the HTV and out of the wind. "Sit. Please."

I didn't argue.

The metal was cold beneath me, but the relief of sitting was immediate. I drew in a shaky breath as Nodin crouched beside me, studying my face like he still couldn't quite believe I was real.

"I didn't think..." He broke off, shaking his head. "You're awake. You're okay."

"I'm okay," I murmured, with a faint half-smile. "I walked here, didn't I? Well, mostly."

Nodin let out a quiet, choked laugh—but it carried more than words. He reached out and gently tucked a loose strand of hair behind my ear, his blistered fingers trembling. The skin along his neck looked worse up close, raw and inflamed. The Solemn Vow was eating him alive, and still, all I saw in his eyes was light.

"I told you I could push him out again...the Chairman," I said gently. "That I'd be okay... that I could do this."

Nodin didn't answer. Just nodded, jaw clenched, his gaze dropping for a moment like he couldn't hold mine without unraveling. Then, without a word, he pushed to his feet, the weight of the moment settling into his shoulders. His back was to me now, his posture sharp with purpose.

"You're really leaving."

His voice was quiet when it came. "I have to bring her home."

His voice cracked just slightly on the last word. He stepped to the rear of the HTV to adjust the final straps on a sealed crate. The Resistance's insignia marked it in white: *Bubble Shield Wall Technology – Classified Cargo.*

"They're giving you part of the shield?" I asked.

"For the Vestri," he said. "Half of what Brigitta brought. The Chairman won't give up on coming after our Dormants. And we can't have more of them disappear... just like Aylen. My people need protection. Now more than ever."

Silence stretched between us.

"And you?" I asked quietly. "What do you need?"

He looked down at his burned hands, flexing his fingers slowly, painfully. "A healer would be a good start."

I almost smiled. Almost.

"I know," I said, after a long moment. "About Aylen. Why didn't you tell me?"

His answer came slowly, like it had been waiting in the back of his throat for too long. "Because if I told you about her... I'd have to tell you everything. And I couldn't risk that. Not then. Breaking the Vow too early—" He didn't finish. Just looked down at his hands again.

I took a step closer. "So you let me think you were..."

"Unburdened?" He gave a quiet, broken laugh. "I wanted to be. Maybe too much."

I didn't know what to say to that.

He closed his eyes for a moment. Snow collected in his lashes. When he opened them again, they were steady. Clear.

"She was important to me," he said. "But our bond was arranged by our parents before we were old enough to speak. We grew up together. She was my best friend. And maybe... maybe we would've found something deeper, eventually. But it hadn't happened yet. And we didn't know if it would."

He looked at me, and something raw edged into his voice. "What I did know was that I couldn't be bound to her and open with you—

not at the same time. I had to find her first. There were things I needed to say... things she deserved to hear."

The silence that followed didn't feel empty. It felt full—of everything unspoken, everything too complicated to name.

I nodded, barely, as the wind stirred the snow-laced branches overhead.

"She deserved better than what happened to her," I whispered.

"She did," he said quietly. "And I'll make sure my Clan remembers her for who she was... not just how she died."

He hesitated, then added, "But you weren't exactly unburdened either."

I glanced at him, unsure what he meant.

"You came to Falinvik to rescue your boyfriend," he said, and though his voice was even, there was a flicker of something deeper behind the words—hurt, maybe. Or hope.

I shook my head. "Aedan's not... I mean, I don't know what we are."

My voice faltered. "It's complicated."

His gaze held mine for a heartbeat too long, the snow still drifting around us in lazy spirals.

"Yeah," he said, so softly it was almost lost to the wind. "It is."

I looked down, not trusting my voice.

Then, softly, he added, "You should come. Once you're stronger."

I blinked up at him. "Come where?"

"To the Vestri." His smile was weak, but real. "We have people who understand *Ljós*. Who can help you learn to use it... without turning yourself into a fireball."

Despite everything, I laughed—a small sound, but honest.

He shrugged. "You know. If staying alive is a skill you'd like to pick up."

"Sounds useful," I murmured.

His gaze lingered on mine, steady and warm. "When you're ready," he said quietly, "just send word. I'll come get you."

A pause. Then softer, almost as an afterthought—but not really: "For that. Or... anything else."

The words hung there, delicate and open-ended.

His eyes searched mine then, and something passed between us. A thread that hadn't broken, even after all that had happened.

"I should go," he said. "Before this thing decides it won't fly after all."

I didn't move. "Be careful."

"I always am."

"That's a lie," I said quietly.

His smile flickered again. "Yeah. But it sounded good."

He stepped back toward the HTV and placed one gloved hand against the hull. Then he paused—just for a heartbeat—and turned to look at me one last time.

"Take care of yourself, Elli."

I nodded, but before he could turn away again, I stepped forward and wrapped my arms around him.

He froze, just for a moment—then returned the embrace, pulling me close. His coat was cold, his breath warm against my temple, and beneath it all, I could feel the trembling effort it took for him to hold himself together.

His chin dipped, just barely brushing my hair. "You have no idea how glad I am that you woke up," he murmured.

I wanted to say something. Anything. But the words caught in my throat, tangled in the ache behind my ribs. There was too much I didn't know how to say—too much I was only just beginning to understand. So I held him tighter, hoping he'd feel what I couldn't find the breath to speak.

When we finally pulled apart, there was something in his eyes—tender, aching, and threaded with everything unspoken. He gave me a small, pained smile, then turned and climbed into the HTV.

The engine hummed to life, low and steady, as the hover transport lifted into the pale sky. Snow swept in spirals behind it, trailing like a whispered goodbye.

I stood there until the speck of it disappeared into the clouds.

And still, I felt it—his *Ljós*, distant but tethered, brushing against mine like a promise left unfinished.

The sound of crunching boots in the snow made me turn.

Mia was walking toward me through the meadow, her coat bundled tight, her long dark hair dusted with frost. She didn't say anything at first—just slipped into step beside me and followed my gaze to the sky where Nodin's HTV had vanished moments ago.

For a long moment, we stood like that, shoulder to shoulder, surrounded by evergreens bowed under the weight of snow, the pale gray light of midday soft against the treetops. Around us, the Resistance base hummed with quiet motion, but this pocket of the world felt still.

Mia looked over at me. "You okay?"

I didn't answer right away.

I wasn't okay yet. Not fully. But I was here. And that was a start.

I nodded, the cold catching at the edge of my breath. "I will be."

She didn't press. Just gave my gloved hand a brief squeeze before we turned back toward the safehouse.

Epilogue

ELIN

Snow blanketed the hills in thick, glittering silence. Warm light glowed from the windows of our house, soft and golden against the hush of early winter twilight. Evergreen boughs lined the porch railing, woven with tiny lights and red ribbon. Paper stars hung in each window, gently spinning in the draft. A straw julbock sat by the front door, its red ribbon tail wagging slightly each time the wind shifted. It was the kind of evening that made you believe in peace, even if it had to be borrowed.

Inside, the house smelled of cinnamon, cloves, and something roasting in the oven. My mother moved through the kitchen with purpose, handing out steaming cups of *glögg*—deep red and fragrant—pressed into hands whether people wanted it or not.

"Drink it while it's warm!" she insisted cheerfully, passing one to Mr. Grady, who accepted it with a chuckle and a wink.

Mia and Joel sat by the fireplace, bundled in borrowed wool socks and flannel-lined slippers, helping Maria string garlands of dried orange slices and cranberries. Anders stood by the front closet, dramatically zipping up his winter coat like he was preparing for a military campaign.

"Alright, troops," he declared. "Tree-cutting expedition departs in five minutes. Last call for thermal socks."

I stood in the middle of it all—wrapped in the scent of pine and twinkle lights, surrounded by the buzz of my family's voices—and still felt the echo of everything that had happened in Falinvik.

But I was here. I'd made it back.

After Nodin left, I stayed one more night in the safehouse with Mia, Joel, and Aedan. None of us wanted to admit how much we needed that quiet. And the chance to catch up on everything that had happened to each of us. The next morning, Anders came barreling through the doors, arms open and voice too loud, his protectiveness turned all the way up.

He hadn't let go of me for a full minute. And I hadn't stopped him.

Since then, he'd been exactly what I needed him to be—steady, loud, completely Anders. But in quieter moments, I'd noticed little things. The way he sometimes rubbed at his temples or blinked too long at the overhead lights. Anders never got migraines. Not before.

He joked it was the stress of having me back or the dry winter air, but something about it stuck with me—just enough to tuck it away.

We'd kept the Paris story intact—one last nod to Monsieur Tibadeau's fictional itinerary. According to the version my parents believed, we'd spent the past couple of weeks roaming the Louvre, eating too many croissants, and learning about *haute couture* from actual Parisians. My mom cried when I walked in the door. My dad made me a cup of chamomile tea. Maria, home from university with flushed cheeks and tangled earbuds, wrapped me in a blanket before demanding every detail I couldn't tell her.

We knew we couldn't keep the truth from them forever. The war with the Chairman was only beginning—not ending—and the Bubble Shield Wall couldn't stretch everywhere and probably wouldn't hold forever. Not against what was coming. My parents deserved to know what we were facing... and what it meant for them. For Maria. For Anders.

But just for tonight, I wanted one last quiet Christmas. One more moment wrapped in light and laughter, before we turned their world upside down.

The Gradys were here—a part of the family now, as far as my parents were concerned. Ever since last fall, when Mr. Grady's "autoimmune condition" had become the official reason for Aedan not being around and the family going off-grid, my parents had treated them with a kind of quiet reverence. Now that Mr. Grady was "in recovery" and able to socialize again, they'd decided he needed spoiling—extra dessert, zero questions. My mom had fussed over Mrs. Grady's spiced pear preserves, complimented her cookie recipe, and tried (twice) to give Aedan a pair of Anders' wool mittens. Joel had been roped into helping carry the tree. Mia had been declared "a natural" at decorating.

And I... I was still stitching myself back together. Quietly. Carefully. But tonight, I let it go just a little.

I held my glögg in both hands as we stepped outside into the snow, our breath clouding the air, our boots crunching over the frozen path that led toward the grove. Laughter echoed ahead—Maria's high and delighted, Joel's unmistakable—and behind me, my mom whispered to my dad about forgetting to charge the electric clippers.

Aedan walked beside me in silence, our shoulders brushing once, then again, as the wind picked up.

He'd told me everything that night at the safehouse—about the files, the names, the bloodline he never asked for. That his father had once served the Chairman. That his grandfather had been Harald Jarnulf himself. For so long, the Gradys had felt like a mystery just out of reach. Now, they were something far more complicated—threads running straight through the heart of the world we were trying to unravel. And Aedan... he was carrying all of it.

But he was with his family again. With me. And for the first time, it felt like maybe he didn't have to shoulder it all on his own. And now, with his parents beside him, the answers he'd been searching for weren't so far away.

Up ahead, Mia turned back toward us, waving one mittened hand over her head.

"Hurry up, slowpokes!" she called. "Joel's about to name every tree in the grove after one of the reindeer."

"I'm not!" Joel shouted from somewhere in the trees. "But if I were, this one is definitely a Blitzen."

Aedan gave a quiet laugh beside me—soft and real.

I smiled too, letting their voices draw me back to the moment. Snow crunched beneath our boots, and the scent of pine sharpened as we crested the slope.

Ahead, the forest waited, quiet and ancient. Somewhere among the pines stood the perfect tree, waiting for us to bring it home.

And yet, beneath the snow and silence, I could feel it—the world holding its breath. As if something unseen was stirring just beneath the surface.

Still, just for this one moment, I let myself feel it—joy. Pure and unsplintered.

Extras

Translation Dictionary

Old Norse Words

Austri: one in the East
Hvíla: sleep, rest, lie
Láta: declare, command
Leikr: game, competition
Leynask: hide oneself, be concealed
Mannlegur: human
Megin: ability, might, power; strength; supernatural strength
Naglar: nails
Nordri (also Norðri): one in the North
Smá-menn: insignificant men, men of little power
Stór-menni: big men, men of rank
Sudri (also Suðri): one in the South
Vestri: one in the West

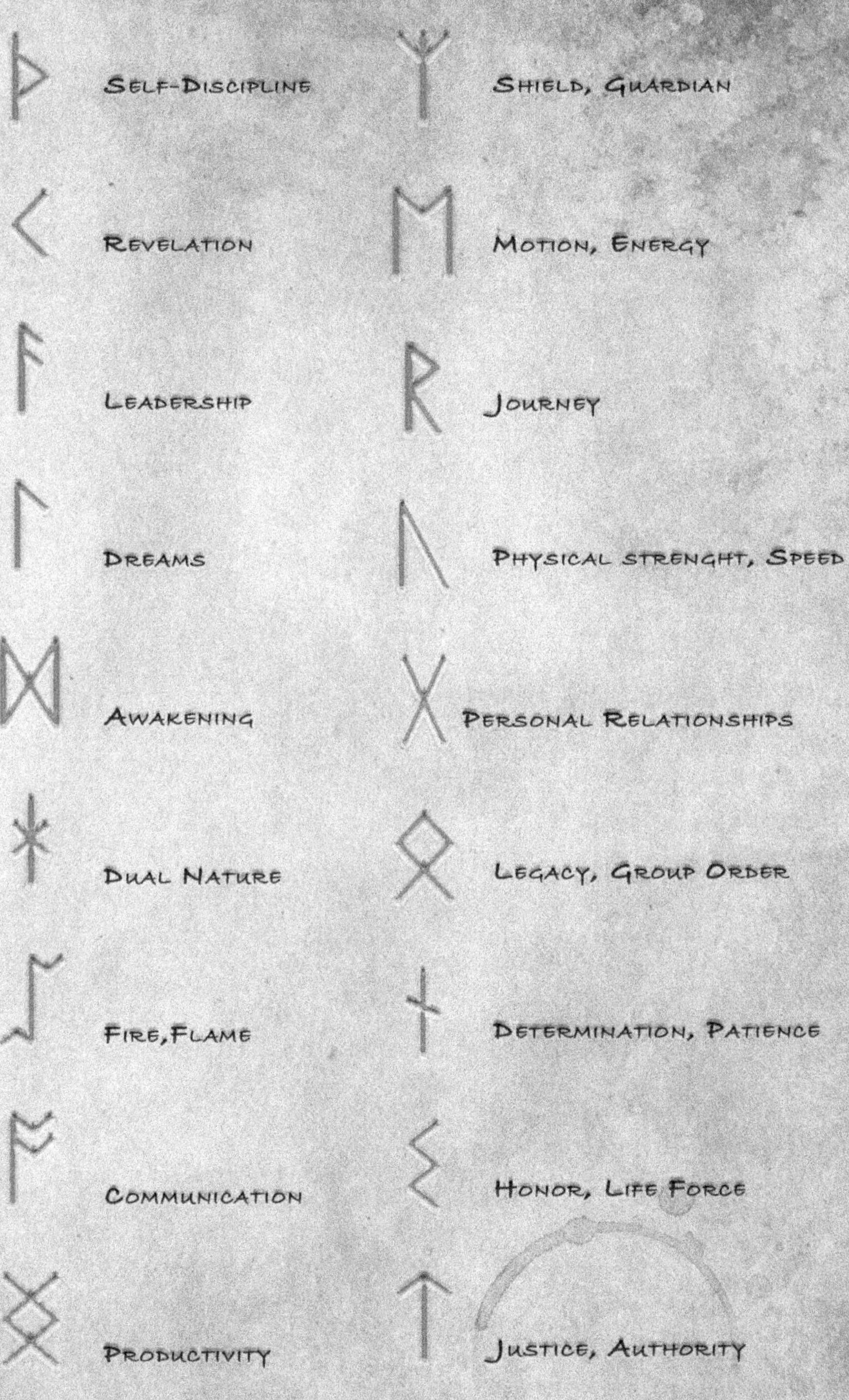
Self-Discipline
Shield, Guardian
Revelation
Motion, Energy
Leadership
Journey
Dreams
Physical strenght, Speed
Awakening
Personal Relationships
Dual Nature
Legacy, Group Order
Fire,Flame
Determination, Patience
Communication
Honor, Life Force
Productivity
Justice, Authority

Thanks for reading!

PLEASE LEAVE A REVIEW

I hope you enjoyed *The Leikr Trials*! If you'd like to support the continuation of the Nordri Series, the best way is to help other readers discover the book.

Share your enjoyment of the book with your friends and family, and please leave a review on **Amazon, Goodreads,** and **Bookbub**.

To hear news and updates on my books, please sign up for my author newsletter at: www.jovisuri.com/newsletter

Or follow me on:
TikTok @author.jo.visuri | Facebook auorauthor

NORDRI SERIES BOOK 4

COMING SOON

Sign up for Jo's newsletter to be the first to hear when BOOK 4 is available.

Also, get exclusive deals and sneak previews before anyone else!

www.jovisuri.com/signup

CATCH UP ON THE NORDRI SERIES

Book #2

Continue the extraordinary journey in the frozen fjord!

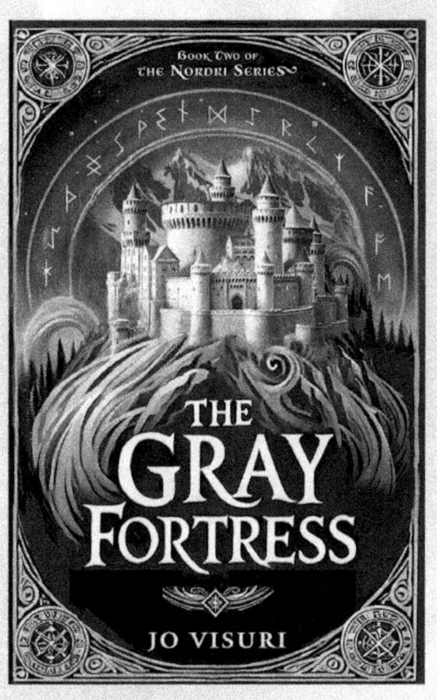

Book #1

Start the adventure on mystical Auor Island!

Learn more at www.jovisuri.com

Acknowledgments

Writing *The Leikr Trials* has been both a challenge and a joy, one fueled by persistence, passion, and the unwavering support of those around me.

To my family and friends — thank you for your patience, encouragement, and understanding as I once again disappeared into weekends, late nights, and countless cups of tea to bring this story to life. Your belief in me, even during the most chaotic of writing sprints, has meant more than I can express.

To my amazing Beta Readers: your thoughtful feedback, sharp eyes, and boundless enthusiasm helped shape this book in ways both subtle and profound. Your early support is the spark that keeps the flame burning.

To my incredible ARC readers—thank you for diving in early in *The Nordri Series*, for your encouragement, and for sharing your reviews with such generosity. Your words help light the way for new readers, and your support has a ripple effect that means more than you know.

And finally, to every reader who has joined me on this journey through the Nordri Series—thank you. Your messages, reviews, and recommendations are what allow these stories to keep growing. You are the true heartbeat behind these pages.

About the Author

Jo Visuri was born and raised on an island in Finland's famous archipelago, where she found her one and only Viking coin at the age of six. After spending a few formative years living by a Norwegian fjord, Jo's family uprooted to the sunny beaches of Los Angeles, CA.

A graduate of Brown University, Jo has been privately writing stories since she could read one. She concocts myth-inspired fantasy tales appropriate for all ages that take the reader on adventures in the real world with magic, hidden worlds, secret societies, and tales of family and friendships.

She now lives and writes in San Diego, CA, when she isn't distracted by her cuddly and demanding pup.

Subscribe to Jo's Newsletter for exclusive content and to be automatically notified when she releases her next book: https://www.jovisuri.com/newsletter

facebook.com/auorauthor

tiktok.com/@author.jo.visuri

instagram.com/auorauthor

bookbub.com/authors/jo-visuri

amazon.com/author/jovisuri